red skies and golden lies

WENDELL BEACH
BOOK TWO

REBECCA V. ARCHER

GOLDEN ALE PRESS LLC

Developmental Edits by Tere Michaels

Edits by Julia Ganis, JuliaEdits.com

Proofread by Laura Helseth of Read Head Editing

Cover art by Qamber Designs

Interior art by Taryn Siegle

For Jessika
You've been with me since the beginning

content note

Cheating (secondary character, in the past), mentions of Covid and the 2020 pandemic, kitchen injury involving a knife

This book is high heat with multiple explicit scenes.

This list may not be exhaustive. Please contact the author if you have any questions or concerns. Any updates will be posted to:

https://rebeccavarcher.com/red-skies-content-notes

ONE

RANSOM

NOVEMBER

A WEEK AGO, IF SOMEONE HAD TOLD ME I'D BE ORDERING A SCOTCH
at four a.m. while stowing my own bag and preparing to work on
a flight to the Maldives, I would have asked why I was flying
commercial.

The answer to that question is simple enough. I had expected
to fly private with my friends the day before. But I got wrapped
up in what someone else thought was a catastrophe, and my
Maldives trip was delayed. On the last-minute flights, first class
was booked so I was relegated to business. The flight from
London to Dubai had been miserable. I'm a terrible sleeper in the
best of times and planes are impossible. Even the lie-flat seat and
premium toiletries didn't help.

I'm exhausted and want a shower. Nothing can brighten my
mood. Having an aisle seat in the center section is the only thing
I'm thankful for. I'm about to sit when I catch the eye of the
passenger in the middle seat next to me. I blink, my brain taking
a minute to register what I'm seeing, and she looks away, turning
to say something to the dark-haired woman on her other side.

"

Fuck, being exhausted must also make me horny. I cannot be thinking about a stranger's knickers.

The partition between our seats is lowered for boarding, and I pray to whichever god of travel will have me that she leaves it down for the flight.

She looks to be in her early thirties with chestnut brown hair pulled up messily on the top of her head. She wears a pink-and-white floral print dress with thin straps. She's clearly not wearing a bra and the V neckline highlights the curve of her small breasts. She looks comfortable and cozy and beautiful. She's a spark of warmth in this ocean of beige, after I've spent the last month in gray, dreary London.

I see beautiful women all the time. It doesn't take me any effort to get attention from them. My ex-girlfriend, Lena, is waiting on the private island her father booked for our group. I'd only have to beckon her with one finger and she'd be in my bed.

I down my scotch as my seatmate finishes her champagne and the cabin crew prepares for departure. I'm aware of everything she does in my periphery. Her partner puts on headphones, leaving me to notice when she gets pale as we barrel down the runway before takeoff.

"Are you going to be sick?" I ask, reaching for anything to help her. Did she have more to drink than the champagne, or is this how she reacts to flying?

She shakes her head, gripping the armrests. "No. I'm fine. I just need this part to be over." She's American, as I had guessed, with a soft voice.

She squeezes her eyes shut as the plane becomes airborne. I watch her, waiting for any sign this will escalate. But it also allows me to take in her features.

She exhales slowly as we level off and I lean back into my seat. I wouldn't want her to catch me staring even if it was primarily out of concern.

I should retrieve my laptop as soon as I can and work since

it'll be confiscated by Lena as soon as I arrive. We work together and her father is our boss. They've given me their permission to take a break and enjoy a tropical paradise with eight of my closest friends. But I can't rest when I've just gotten to where I am in my career. I have more to gain and my hold on what I have is tenuous at best.

Lena doesn't have to live up to the same standards. It's impossible for her to fall from grace. Even if she did, she has generations of wealth to fall back on. I can't risk being complacent for one moment. I haven't decompressed fully since I was a teenager. Certainly, a beach trip won't do it. I've worked hard to earn these friendships. I enjoy the time I spend with them. But I can't get excited about the prospect of day drinking for a week and racing jet skis.

The pilot makes an announcement about our altitude, and I check on the woman next to me. She appears to have relaxed, and color is returning to her face. She is already tan, like she's on her way home from a holiday instead of heading to it. She doesn't move to raise the partition, even as they have gone up around us. Couples in matching shirts who must be on their honeymoons are blocking each other. While she has left the barrier down, she doesn't give any indication she wants to talk. Resigned, I open my laptop.

"Can you post that picture as soon as you have Wi-Fi?" The other woman leans over, her headphones around her neck. She's pretty too, but she's not moving me. They're likely a couple, so I should stop this line of thought anyway.

"I thought we weren't posting until after we get back?" the brunette says.

"Just the one. I want him to know I'm having the best time without him."

"Sienna, we talked about this. Because (a) you blocked him. And (b) you said the best revenge is having a good time and forgetting him. He knows he isn't getting you back. You said you didn't want him to ruin this trip for you. Girls' trip rules: no more discussions of men."

I have so many questions.

Sienna groans. "Fine." She sits back and puts her headphones on.

The woman next to me turns in her seat and sees me eavesdropping. Someone with shame might have looked away or tried to deny it. But I won't.

She shakes her head and smiles. Have I really been so deprived of the sun at home that all it takes is a smile and honey brown eyes to awaken something in me?

"It's not my story to tell," she says.

I raise my hands in surrender. "I wasn't going to ask."

We have this awkward moment where we realize we're two strangers forced to share a space for a few hours. There is intimacy, but we want to deny it. I want the story. I want to know what happened to her friend. I don't want to look away.

I must be exhausted because I don't want to do any work.

She breaks first, tapping her seat back screen, and curling her feet under her. She's petite and so she has plenty of room in the seat. And with the way she's leaning, the strap on her right shoulder has enough give that it's threatening to slide down her arm. I could stare at that space of skin forever. I return to my spreadsheets, instead, compromising by observing out of the corner of my eye as she plays a live-action princess movie. I watched the original with my younger sister often when we were kids, but I haven't seen this version. It's beautiful and I find myself paying more attention to her screen than my own and watching her reactions and the subtle way she smiles through the sweet parts. Do these spreadsheets really need adjusting? The tables can pivot themselves.

Fuck. She blushes a little when they kiss.

I want to blame my sister for my feelings. That remembering the games we played in our garden has shifted my brain chemistry, leading me to forget my priorities. This is Merit's fault.

The flight attendant comes around and we both order drinks. She's addressed as "Ms. Stewart" and I want the first name that goes with her order of champagne and an espresso. Her friend has fallen asleep and is left alone.

I get little peeks of who she is as the flight continues. When she returns from the loo, her eyes are bright and her mouth is slightly rosier. She was beautiful before, but I selfishly want her to have adjusted her makeup for me. I think about pulling the strap of her dress down her arm with my teeth. It hasn't even been that long since I got laid, but it's all I can think about now. I both love and hate not being in first class. There I'd have a private room where we could hide. But then I wouldn't be in this row with her.

When it's time for breakfast, I request the spinach and egg frittata, and she gets the local option, but not before asking about a dozen questions. She doesn't seem picky, just curious.

She notices me watching her again.

"I'm a chef," she explains.

"I see," I answer. "You didn't examine the menu in advance?"

"Normally I would, but this was a last-minute trip," she says.

"Really?" Maybe this is how I get the details I'm desperate for.

She can see right through me. That I overheard a hint of something and I'm dying to know the rest. She looks at her friend who is still sleeping and then leans in close to me. "This was supposed to be her honeymoon. It fell apart at the last minute. Now it's her revenge-moon."

"That works out in your favor," I say.

She seems unsure. "Maybe. I introduced them and was supposed to be maid of honor. It feels like it was my fault."

"Well, Ms. Stewart," I say.

"Haley," she says.

"Haley." I smile, loving the small victory of getting her name, and knowing women in the past have found my smile irresistible. "I wouldn't put much stock in your past mistakes. It landed you here, didn't it? I wasn't supposed to be on this flight either."

She has a soft smile and looks to her friend a little guiltily. As if Haley being happy about where she's ended up is disloyal. But she turns back to me, and I feel like she's giving in a little. She's letting herself have this small flirtation we know will only last the duration of the flight.

She picks up her glass of champagne and offers me a toast. "Well, Mr.—"

"West. Ransom West."

"Ransom. Here's to the unlikely chance that both of us are on this flight."

We clink our glasses. This flight could go for days, and I'd never get bored of staring into her eyes.

* * *

WHEN WE DEPLANE HOURS LATER, my assessment remains: I could have listened to her talk for days. Her favorite topics are food and her hometown of Wendell Beach, Florida. I learned nothing beats a fresh Florida blueberry, and while she hadn't planned on going on this trip, she helped the bride pick the resort with the best restaurants in the Indian Ocean.

I wish one thing made me as excited as so many things excite her.

We don't get the chance to say goodbye. We're lost in the shuffle of overhead bins and her bags being on the other aisle. She's off before me, and when I get into the terminal she's nowhere to be found in the lines of customs and representatives from the various resorts picking up their guests.

I give in to letting her go as I allow the staff of the private island to whisk me through the throngs of tourists to the seaplane for the final leg of my journey.

* * *

THE NEXT DAYS pass as I expected them to. I can't enjoy the beach. I used to think this was all I wanted—friends who accept me as their own enough to invite me on holiday. I've traveled to places I dreamed of as a child. But I've never been able to relax into this lifestyle. I've worked hard to get to where I am. I'm aware how much my position is dependent on the patronage of others.

When I arrived, Lena told me I couldn't use my laptop, but I managed to convince her I was using my iPad for leisure and not work. It's not a lie. I am using my art app to draw the overwater villas and replicate the exact color of the water and the changes in the shades of turquoise.

Somehow I keep adding in pops of pink.

It's not unexpected really. There are plumeria trees with pink flowers everywhere. It's not that I'm thinking of Haley and her bright dress.

Everything here is so vivid, but it still feels dull and I want to add some color.

It becomes a challenge to remedy this: I'm on a private island; Haley is at a resort miles of ocean away with no reason to leave. How do I get to see her again?

I'm chasing a thrill and nothing else. An obstacle is in my path, and I seek a way around it. I do this every day and have for years. If anyone asks me, I'm not thinking about her already tan skin and what she was hiding underneath her dress. But it wasn't difficult to work with the staff of both resorts to organize a day trip. The only snag is convincing my friends it is worth the effort.

"The restaurant is amazing, I promise," I tell them. "I arranged for an exclusive menu."

Lena raises an eyebrow at me. "Since when do you care about food?"

Since I met a chef, and I want to lick her toes.

"It's forty minutes on the speedboat. We'll have a section of the beach to ourselves, and for dinner we'll have their underwater restaurant completely reserved for us," I explain. "If you all hate it, we can always come back here."

Her sister, Georgina, is on my side, scrolling on her phone. "You should see the pictures of this place. Our island might be more exclusive, but this one is gorgeous. I say we go."

Lena looks between her sister, her brother-in-law, and me. The rest of the group is already gathering their bags. "Okay, if everyone wants to go. We didn't have anything else planned, did we?"

"No, just snorkeling, which we can do there. I have it on good authority their reef is better than this one," I say. Sienna, Haley's friend, had eventually woken up and explained the high levels of biodiversity in the waters.

"Sounds brilliant," Lena says, watching me. When Georgina dashes off to get her bag, I'm not surprised she addresses me again. "What's really going on, Ransom?"

"Nothing." I dig through my tote to make sure I have everything. There's a chance this doesn't work and I'll have free time on my hands, sitting on a slightly different beach. I pack my iPad. I want to sketch Haley, but I haven't drawn people in years.

"I don't believe you. You barely cared about this trip. You were a day late because of some work emergency even though I told you it could wait until we got back. There's a woman, isn't there?"

I look up at her, annoyed she knows me this well. "Is that a problem?" I keep coming back to the accident of it. I shouldn't have been on that plane. I should have flown private with the rest of them. Nothing significant is going to come of this—it'll be a one-time thing. But it feels more interesting to me than anything else happening. I just want to get in front of her and make my case that we should spend time together.

She breathes out quickly. "No. It's fine. I just wasn't aware there was anyone. Is it serious?"

"I met her on the plane. No." I place my hands on Lena's shoulders. "It's nothing, darling. You'll have a great day. Everyone will. You won't miss me."

She doesn't look convinced, but this is our deal. We broke up when I started working for her father. She thought it was a bad idea for us to date as colleagues. She might reach out occasionally for a hookup, which I've always turned down, but that's all she sees me as. One of her other playthings will be next to her all day. She can hook up with him just as easily as she can hook up with me. It's all the same to her.

We arrive at the dock of the other resort where staff greet us and serve us flutes of champagne and jasmine-scented hand towels. They lead us to our reserved section of the beach, explaining that everything is available to us—all we need to do is ask. Once everyone is planted, I make my move.

I take a rare selfie that makes it clear where I am and send it to Haley. We exchanged social media information. We said we'd be in touch over the week. And since I'm already here when I send it, it's casual. Almost an afterthought. It's a gamble on my end. She could be off swimming with whale sharks or deep-sea fishing.

But if she's here and available, then I have plans for her. For us.

She responds almost at once.

COOKING_WITH_HALEY

How are you here?

ME

Where are you? I'll tell you over a drink.

COOKING_WITH_HALEY

I'm at the infinity pool.

"I have a spa appointment," I tell the group. "I'll be back before dinner."

"Of course you do," Myles jokes. "It takes a lot of work to keep you that pretty."

I ignore him. He's never worked for anything in his life.

"You spent all morning telling us about the reef and why we needed to check it out, and now you leave for the spa?" Estella, Lena's best friend, says.

"It is the best in the Maldives," I respond.

"It's a woman," Lena says. "Leave him be."

The guys holler their encouragement.

"Would you rather I be working? You'll have my undivided attention the rest of the trip," I say.

"I doubt it, but whatever. Get her out of your system." Lena takes a long drink from her cocktail.

two

HALEY

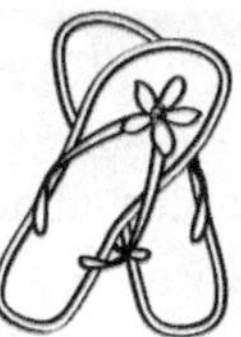

I'M NOT SURE HOW I FEEL ABOUT THE HOT GUY FROM THE PLANE suddenly showing up at our resort. Yes, I flirted, and I'm definitely attracted to him. But it was a relationship contained to the metal tube in the sky—nothing more.

This is a girls' trip. A "Sienna needs to get over Beckett" trip. There are rules. Rule number one is Haley does not indulge in any attention from men. It's basic friend math. I can't get laid until my friend, who found out her fiancé was cheating a week before the wedding, gets laid.

Not that I'm particularly looking to get laid. I've never had sex outside of a relationship. That won't change on this trip.

But he did have an amazing English accent and dimples...

My body aches. Sienna and I spent the last few days completely on the go. She's following the guidance of sharks: if she stays in motion, then nothing bad will catch her. It's been days of snorkeling and jet skiing and trying to figure out the exact ratio of seawater on the outside and alcohol on the inside we can tolerate. I begged her for one day to relax. My sleep schedule is unusual anyway since I prefer to work late into the night, and the twelve-hour difference is messing with me. And I never sleep well in a strange place. Tomorrow is our biggest excursion—swimming with whale sharks. We need to be well rested.

To prepare, I'm sitting on a lounge chair in the shallow end of the infinity pool. Yes, I have a drink in my hand, but my body is still. Sienna is at the bar flirting with a couple on their honeymoon. I doubt my celibacy for the sake of hers will be required for much longer. There are just the thousand other reasons.

But the green light for their downfall is walking toward me.

He's wearing cream linen pants and a light blue Oxford shirt with the sleeves rolled up to his elbows. I didn't get to appreciate how tall he is on the plane. I use a step stool to get things on the top shelf of the kitchen all the time. He'd be able to grab them for me. But I can't imagine this man ever stepping foot in my apartment's tiny kitchen. He has a narrow frame, with his biceps defined underneath his shirt. I'd bet money if I undid his buttons, I'd find at least a few ab muscles visible.

I grab my cover-up and pull it on. I should have done it as soon as I saw the message from him, but I didn't believe he was really here. It's too perfect. I shouldn't have seen his message anyway since I turned notifications off. But I was in the app sending a picture to my family.

It doesn't take him long to spot me. The resort is fully booked, but there's so much space over the island and so many things to do that no one area is crowded. It feels empty, especially considering the flocks of people I'm used to in Wendell Beach.

He sits on the chair next to me, our feet cool in the water.

"Hi there. I'm definitely surprised to see you," I say.

"Who doesn't love a good surprise?" His dimple is working overtime and the hair that looked completely normal brown on the plane is now bronze in the sun. He leans toward me, his forearms resting on the tops of his thighs. I stared at those forearms on the plane—anyone would have. His expensive watch is gone, but his corded muscles remain. He's tanned a little in the few days since I've seen him, despite the fact that I can smell his sunscreen.

I bite the inside of my lip to keep myself from smiling too hard, but I'm grinning like an idiot anyway. It doesn't matter if I have to turn him down for the drink in one minute. He still sought me out. It's been ages since anyone has done that. "I thought you were meeting up with friends at a different resort. Did that not work out?"

"No, they're over at the beach. We're visiting this island for the day."

I nod. "Because this beach is better than the beach you were at." He told me they had an entire private island to themselves. Their own dedicated staff. I thought about looking it up but avoided the temptation. I want to appreciate what I have and not get jealous over the one percent I'm missing.

"We have a lovely beach. But your reef has had more shark sightings, and they wanted to see sharks."

"You're going snorkeling?" Maybe he'll ask us to join. Sienna could get excited about that. She's a marine biologist getting a graduate degree in Boston. She'll talk about fish for days. It's probably what she's talking about with the couple. She'll explain how the shape of the island changes the currents, which affects the fish that come close to the reef.

"They might. They might also drink on the beach all afternoon. I'm headed to the spa. Did you know this spa has the only Balinese massage therapists on this atoll?"

"I didn't. But I thought the spa was for resort guests only." This is more than just taking a boat ride over here. He's put in substantial effort to be here. His sunglasses cover his eyes, so I can't get any more hints from them. But he can't mean what I think he's going to suggest. It's one thing to run into me after his massage. But to seek me out before it...

"I have my ways. But the problem is the specific treatment I want is only available in couples packages. I was going to attend alone…but since you're here, would you like to join me?"

He's lying about this setup. But I don't care. I'm not accepting, but not because of anything about him. I can't leave Sienna. I turn to where she is at the bar. "I appreciate the offer." It was a fun fantasy for a moment.

She must have noticed that I wasn't alone, and she walks over, her Tiger beer in one hand. "What's going on? Do you want to head back to the room?"

"No, it's fine," I say, realizing she might not recognize him. "This is Ransom. He sat next to me on the plane."

Sienna narrows her eyes at him from underneath her floppy hat. "Right." She doesn't sound impressed.

"He's invited me to the spa with him. He has a couples package scheduled."

Sienna grabs me by the arm. "We'll be right back." We stumble over to the other side of the pool, our feet splashing. "Are you into him? Do you want this?"

"It doesn't matter what I want. I'm not leaving you," I say.

"Come on, Haley. I'm about to have a threesome in one of the extra-fancy villas. You need this just as bad as I do."

"I'm fine."

"Really? Tell me about the last penis you saw. Oh wait. It was my fiancé's, so I know all about it."

"Ex-fiancé."

"Not at the time he wasn't. And it definitely wasn't one you wanted to see. At the very least, get the massage. You were just complaining about how sore you are. You don't have to sleep with him."

I kind of do want to sleep with him. These last few weeks have been so incredibly stressful with the wedding planning falling apart, immediately followed by a tropical storm, and I learned our other friend had been secretly dating her neighbor for months. All the relationships around me are changing. Don't I deserve something nice for myself?

It won't be anything serious. I'm not expecting a happily ever after. Just a romantic date with someone who is putting in effort. I'm not against one-night stands. I just want someone to try a little. Ransom is doing that.

Are my standards that low that a guy shows an ounce of work and I'm ready to lift my skirts for him?

Granted, he is obscenely attractive. And this isn't just an "open the car door" level of effort. This is "rearranging travel plans" effort. This is a thousand dollars of spa treatments.

"Okay. I'll go to the spa with him. But you'll text me if you want me to leave? Or call?" The staff would interrupt my service if requested.

"Don't worry about me. Just let me know if you go back to the villa with him."

"Sure. I'll put a sock on the door," I say.

We hug and she heads to the bar, and I go back to Ransom.

"Wait, did you even pack socks?" Sienna calls back.

"I'll let you know!" I reply, feeling my cheeks getting hot. I smile at Ransom and gather my things into my tote bag. "Couples massage sounds great."

"Wonderful. It'll be worth it. I promise."

We walk to the other end of the island and the spa. The resort itself takes up the whole narrow island. It's only a few minutes to walk from end to end. The spa is in a complex of overwater bungalows just past the northern tip. I'm content to let the walk pass in silence.

"Is 'socks' code for something?" he asks after a few moments.

I look up at him. He must be at least six feet. I only come up to his shoulder. I wonder if he's asking because he understands the code and wants me to admit it, or if it's an American thing. "Not exactly, no. It's an old joke from college," I say. I haven't agreed to anything more than a massage yet. I don't want to get ahead of myself.

"Is that how long you've known each other?" he asks.

He was like this on the plane—asking questions about me. Having good follow-up questions. He seemed to really pay attention to what I was saying. The last guy I dated could only be bothered to listen if I wasn't wearing a low-cut dress. "Yes, we met as first-year students in the dorms. Been friends ever since."

"How's she doing with the whole 'supposed to be on her honeymoon' thing?"

"She's okay." It feels like the truth. She's trying extremely hard, but I think overall she's handling it better than I would. "She keeps telling me I deserve this as much as she does, since I'm the one who discovered him."

"You caught him cheating?"

"Yes. The best man and me. With the best man's girlfriend."

"She should shag the best man for revenge," he suggests.

"She's probably considered it." I try to imagine if Sienna would sleep with Alex. I've been friends with him for so long, he's practically my brother. But the two of them didn't meet until she visited me during breaks in college.

"Has the food lived up to your standards?" he asks.

"It's been great. Each meal better than the last. But I'm not particularly hard to please. I mostly focus on home cooking and casual restaurants." I'm not a food snob. As long as there are fresh ingredients, I'm usually happy.

"I bet everyone likes being your friend," he says. "Always bringing something good to eat to a party."

"Yep!" That's definitely a plus for everyone around me, but just once I'd like someone to take care of me. I change the subject. "It's lucky you came today. We have excursions planned for every other day we're here."

"Have you swum with whale sharks yet?" he asks, remembering I'd been excited about it.

"That's tomorrow." We break through the trees and step onto the beach where the Indian Ocean reaches out to the horizon. To our left is the spa, and when we walk in, a young South Asian woman greets us.

"Hello, do you have an appointment?"

"Yes, it's under Ransom West," he says.

"Wonderful. If you'll follow me, Mr. and Mrs. West, I'll show you to the changing rooms."

"Um…" I don't like that.

"It's Ms. Stewart, actually," Ransom corrects casually.

"Of course," the woman says. "There are robes for you to change into here and you can place your belongings in any locker."

We're alone in a dressing room with sand for the floor and small stalls with curtains for privacy. My heart rate picks up. I didn't think this part through. I like the idea of getting a couples massage, but I'm not ready to be naked with a man I just met. I need the afternoon to work up to it.

"I can wait out here." He gestures to the atrium.

"No. It's fine." I duck behind one of the curtains and he does the same. I pull off my swimsuit and try not to think about him getting naked just a few feet away from me. "We're kind of doing this backward," I say, the idea a little assuming.

"What do you mean?"

"Normally you get naked at the end of the date."

I hear the faintest hint of a groan from him. I have to assume he's at least somewhat attracted to me, or else he wouldn't have flirted and he wouldn't be here. But I also want to know why me? It can't be convenience. It has to be something more. I don't know anything about the friends he met up with and he hasn't offered anything about them. Maybe he's slept with them all and he's just looking for someone new. He's the one who showed up here, clearly hoping something would happen, but I'm not looking for anything beyond this afternoon. I can't imagine he is either.

"We already shared a meal on the plane," he says. "So really we're halfway through the date."

I tighten the belt on my robe and open the curtain. I lean against the counter. "But that was breakfast, so again, we're doing this backward."

"Hopefully there are still good things ahead, if we're doing this date in reverse."

I'm definitely flushing. "We'll see. I'm, um…" I want to be bold. I want to have a story that I'll one day share with people. *Once I met a guy on a plane and we made love all night over the Indian Ocean. It was the most romantic time of my life.* But I need a lot more courage than I have right now.

He opens the curtain and steps out with a smile that makes me melt. "One thing at a time, darling," he says. "Let's see where the day takes us." He places his hand on the small of my back as we move into the atrium.

The robe is too thick for me to feel the heat of his touch, but I like the sense of intimacy and that he's not assuming I'm a sure thing. That we're both exploring where this goes. But I can't deny I melt a little at the pet name. It doesn't mean anything and I'm sure he uses it with lots of women he meets. But I'm holding on to the thrill of it for now.

We are led to a treatment room with floor-to-ceiling windows looking out over the ocean. It's so beautiful and bright. I pause, wanting to breathe in this beauty for as long as I can. I might live a few blocks from the beach, but I love this so much.

"Miss, have a seat please," one attendant says.

"Right, sorry." I sit down in the spa chair next to Ransom and the other attendant describes the next few hours of treatment. "This is a lot," I whisper.

He shrugs, like this level of service is nothing to him. I didn't get much about him other than he works in something money related and has friends who rent private islands.

"You didn't have to…" I start. I would have settled for a drink by the pool.

"I didn't have to what?"

"I don't know." I let out a breath as the attendant rubs mud on my calves for our toxin cleansing body scrub.

I appreciate what he's done to set me at ease. This is mostly an excuse to spend time together before it's socially acceptable to have sex. And he doesn't expect me to have made up my mind yet. I could back out, and this man would be okay with it. Frustrated, maybe. But he's not looking at me with just lust. There's something else there too. Like we're both telling ourselves this is something bigger than it should be. Even if just for the day.

"Why did you?" I ask. I shouldn't. This could expose me and all my vulnerabilities. It shouldn't matter why he's here. Just that he is.

He seems to consider the question for a moment. Maybe he's debating how much he wants to share with me. How much of *himself* he wants to expose.

"You're beautiful," he says. "And I wanted to see if I could."

"Could what?" *Get me in bed?* How far does his ambition go?

"Get here. Get you here. That's as far as I got."

"This is enough?" I'm not sure I believe him. But I'm willing to. I'm willing to spend the afternoon with him and see what happens later.

three

RANSOM

WE SPEND THE NEXT SEVERAL HOURS HAVING EVERY PART OF OUR bodies scrubbed and rubbed and draped in scented lotions that awaken our desires. It is part of the couples package, but while I expected romance, this is far and above what I imagined.

Midway through the service we're left alone with a bottle of champagne and a list of questions to ask each other to deepen our relationship and our understanding of each other. Haley is relaxed and loose as she stares at me, waiting for me to begin.

I scan the list as she pours us each champagne. Some of these questions aren't right for us. *How would you improve our relationship?* And some are too deep. *What are your biggest fears?* I need to find a middle ground. Something showing me who she is, without being so personal she wouldn't share it with an almost stranger. She hands me a glass and I clink the rim to hers. "Cheers. How do you define success?"

"Um…" She looks out the windows as she thinks. "I don't know. I guess knowing that I've helped people. I cook because I love it. And I want others to love it too."

How do I respond to that? Success for me has always been about the next opportunity. But it fits her.

I hand her the list and she takes a few moments to scan it. "What's your ideal way to spend a weekend?"

I blink. I work on the weekends. I understand the concept, but I don't take days off like most people. That answer won't satisfy her. "I usually eat brunch with my family and then I'm back at the office."

"That's how you spend your weekend. Not your ideal weekend. Come on, sky's the limit. You can do anything outside of work."

"Fine, spa day in the Maldives with you," I say.

She laughs and blushes and hands me back the list.

I pick another question, hoping to get a taste of who she is before handing the list back to her. It's almost more interesting to me what questions she asks than how she answers the ones I pick. I've been attracted to her from the moment I sat down next to her on that plane, but the need I have for her is growing. I don't want to sit through a ten-course meal with my friends just to get Haley back to my villa. I want to take her there now, order room service, and spend all night learning her body.

I think she wants it too.

I'm annoyed when the attendants return for our massages. I want more time with her alone. Even talking like this has felt like a weight has been lifted from me.

When we're done and are left to put our robes back on, she sits up and almost forgets to cover herself with the sheet. She just looks at me, all relaxed with her skin glowing and her limbs relaxed. I can almost imagine I did that to her instead of a team of highly trained spa employees.

"That was great. Thank you," she says. Her voice is husky and soft.

"It was my pleasure."

She hops off the table and grabs her robe, just letting me see a sliver of skin at the top of her thighs. God, I want to bite her ass.

We don't speak back in the changing room where she puts on

her bikini and cover-up while I pull on my trousers and shirt. When we walk out, she slips her hand into mine. This simple gesture shouldn't be so significant, but it is. It means she wants this. That she's not here because she got a free mud bath, body wrap, and massage. She wants to be close to me.

We step onto the sand and I stop, picking up a plumeria flower that fell from a nearby tree. I touch underneath her chin with one hand and place it in her hair behind her ear with the other. I'm aware the sun is heading for the horizon behind her, turning the sky the most vibrant red I have ever seen it. This beach we're disregarding is one of the most beautiful in the world. I only see her warm brown eyes looking up at me.

I cup her cheek. She closes her eyes and leans into my touch. We're close, just the barest space between us. One of us stepped into the other's space. She opens her eyes and gazes up at me with intent. She's decided something and I want to know what it is.

She moves her hands from her side, brushing up my chest. As thin as this shirt is, I want it gone. I want her skin on my skin.

The devil is in the details, and I feel consumed by them. When this is over and I'm back in London and she's in Florida, what will I have to remember her?

I'll have the flush of her cheeks when I brought up the sock comment. How I knew it would be a signal she'd brought me back to their villa and I wanted her to admit it. Was she thinking about what we'd do with her friend banished? Had she gotten new ideas in the last few hours? Do her wildest fantasies match mine? Which one of us is more ambitious in what we think we can do together? Does she feel like this is a fairy tale the way I do?

I've been careful not to rush her. I'm patient and calculating and I need her to come to me.

Her body presses to mine and that will leave a memory.

I dip down and lightly brush my lips against hers. It's a taste and a promise of something. She shifts closer than I thought possible. Her arms are tight around me. My skin feels hot, like my blood is going to burst from me. She opens her mouth and I trace my tongue along hers. She's sweet from the champagne we drank.

I've kissed plenty of women before. None of them have elicited a reaction like this. It's not just in my dick and it's not about getting her naked and under me or above me or wherever she wants as long as a part of me gets to be in her.

It's higher than that. It's in my gut and in my chest and I don't know what any of it means beyond I need to spend the night tasting her skin.

But Lena will throw me to the sharks if I miss the dinner I arranged.

I break away because I'll continue forever if she lets me. I rest my forehead against hers. "Come back with me tonight." I'll beg if I have to.

"Now?" she asks, and I pray that's hope in her voice.

I hold her gaze. "Later. We're dining at the undersea restaurant. We head back around ten p.m. Meet me at the dock. I'll bring you back here in the morning. You won't miss your whale shark adventure. I promise."

She nods. "I have to check on Sienna, but I'm pretty sure she's having a threesome I'm not invited to. I'll be there."

I give her one last kiss, something to hold me over for the next few hours. "Good. I'll see you then."

* * *

EVERYONE IS drunk by the time we're at the dock piling into our speedboat to take us back to the private island. We were a few minutes behind schedule. Haley should be here waiting. Everything about her told me she's on time for things. But she's not here.

"Come on, Ransom!" Georgina yells. "Isaac will puke if we don't get going!"

The boat driver laughs nervously.

"Give it a few more minutes," I call back. They've paired up. Georgina sits on her husband's lap. Estella is holding on to Isaac to keep him from falling overboard. Lena has her face in Myles's neck and his hands are wandering somewhere I can't see. Josephine is flirting with the deckhand.

I look at my phone. No new messages from Haley. But it's only a few minutes past ten. She could still be on her way.

I watch the beach. She has to come.

I have schemed and plotted so much in my life that it's second nature to me. It's as easy as breathing. I'm always thinking of the next move. I've had goals and ambitions fall apart before. I've been rejected by women. Nothing I've lost before has made me feel like I do now.

"Seriously, Ransom. Some of us want to go to bed," Lena calls. The way she's getting on with Myles, she doesn't plan on going to bed alone.

My phone vibrates.

COOKING_WITH_HALEY

I'm so sorry. I won't be able to come with you tonight.

ME

Is everything okay?

COOKING_WITH_HALEY

Yes. I just need to spend time with Sienna.

Thank you for today. It was really lovely.

ME

I understand. Have a great rest of your trip.

"We can go." I climb into the boat and a moment later we push off from the dock.

I don't understand what happened. We had a great time. We kissed and everything was perfect. I felt something, damn it. Maybe she was nervous about going to a different island. But I would have stayed with her or made other arrangements at this resort. I don't care if it is sold out. I would have paid someone off to have a night with Haley.

Had I done something to make her think I wouldn't take care of her? Did she not think I was worthy of her?

Whatever. It doesn't matter.

four

HALEY

THE VIDEO I'VE MADE PLAYS ON MY PHONE SCREEN. I WATCH IT carefully, noticing any mistiming or if the font doesn't look right. Should I change the outline effect? It looks clear to me, but I wrote it. I've been staring at it so long, at this point I could read the words with my eyes closed.

I send the link to my friend Carina Webb. I hesitate to bother her with something so trivial, but this video needs to be perfect.

ME

> My brain feels broken. Does this look right?

CARINA

> It's great! Those pictures are gorgeous! I can't believe you're finally posting about the Maldives. It's been ages.

It's been three months. Between Christmas and New Year's and so many people wanting to change habits in January, I had my content planned months in advance. There hadn't been a slot to post about my weeklong break from reality.

26

That's the best way I can describe it. A fairy tale. A fantasy. A few days where I was in a different world. Not the tropical location—no, that's normal for me since I live on a barrier island off the west coast of Florida. But the constant pampering and the attention to detail the staff had for everything, that was unusual for me. And I didn't have to worry about money the entire time, since everything was paid for by someone else.

This short video shows the highlights from the trip. The exquisite food. The beautiful sunsets. The shots of Sienna and me swimming with whale sharks. It's the content people will save to their vision boards and have them dreaming of their own escapes. Over the next week, I'll follow up with tutorials on how to cook some of the common fish in the Indian Ocean and a Maldivian-inspired curry.

But it's not the food or the water or the sugar sand beaches I think of when I reminisce about my trip. No. It's him.

Ransom West.

For a moment, he was my personal Prince Charming. I wasn't looking for one, but suddenly he was there, with his soothing voice and posh accent. I could listen to him read the dictionary just from the way he ordered a scotch. We'd chatted for a good part of the flight, but it wasn't going anywhere. It wasn't practical to think it would. He was staying at a different resort, and I didn't know the geography of the islands well enough to figure out the distance between them.

I would have gone back with him that night when he asked. It's not something I normally do, but I thought if I had the chance at this perfect, even temporary romance, I wanted to take it. Sienna was going through heartbreak, but I saw how much Carina and Orion had fallen in love right under my nose. I wanted my own taste of it.

Instead, I got back to our villa and found Sienna crying in bed. I couldn't leave her to go off with him. What could have been, wouldn't be. And I'm fine with that. Not every story with the potential for a grand ending is going to fall into place.

I post the video to Instagram just as the kitchen timer beeps. I grab oven mitts and pull out the spatchcocked chicken. I check its internal temperature, and when I confirm it's done, I carefully set it to rest on the cutting board I've laid out.

My mom steps into her kitchen. "Is it done?" she asks cheerfully.

"Nearly. Just needs to cool for about twenty minutes. Then I'll carve it for you," I answer.

"Thank you. This is so helpful. I set out containers for you to use." She points to the counter where there are disposable food containers. I sigh. I went through the effort of sourcing a free-range chicken from a local farmer and it's going in plastic that will be tossed away. If it was for anyone else, I'd say something. Remind my mom that there are other options. But this is for a neighbor who just had a baby so I can understand making it as easy for everyone as possible.

"Sure," I say. "And I'll be done with the mac and cheese in a minute too. That will need to cool a little bit more before you pack it up."

"Hey, kiddo," my dad says, walking into the kitchen. "What smells great? Is it for dinner?" He gives my mom a quick kiss. "Missed you, Laurel."

I smile. He just got home from work, so maximum they've been apart for eight hours.

"No, it's for Jacey," my mom tells him.

"Who?"

My mom rolls her eyes. "Really, Ken? The couple two doors down. They have the balloons on their mailbox. They just had a baby girl."

"Right. Of course," he says, but I doubt he noticed. "I'm glad you're here, Hay. I got the contract to sell those new builds on the north end of Wendell Beach. You'll love the designs of the kitchens."

I wipe my hands on a dish towel and abandon the pot I was cleaning. If there is one thing I love, it's looking at kitchens in homes I will never be able to afford. He pulls out his phone and opens the listing, allowing me to swipe through the pictures. It's concept art, but it's nearly perfect. "Where are these located?" Fantasies spin in my head of cooking for all my friends at once and serving wine perfectly chilled from the wine fridge.

"They are on the bay side. Each one has a small dock," he explains.

"Time to find you a rich husband," my mom jokes.

I laugh but look at my phone. I don't have notifications turned on for any social media post, but a part of me wanted to leave them on for that one post. Ransom and I follow each other. He rarely posts anything, but someone will occasionally tag him in their photos. I hoped this video would draw him out and he'd reach out. I should know better. He's probably forgotten about me.

"What's that look on your face?" my mom asks.

"Nothing. Just planning my week. Let me cut up this chicken for you and then I have to go. I have a meeting."

"New client?" my dad asks.

They're aware I've struggled the last few months. My social media is doing great, but I've had some private clients leave the state. Some of it is the regular ebb and flow of the snowbirds. But my biggest client left specifically because he was fed up with the way the state government is treating LGBTQ+ students and the efforts to ban books. I don't blame him at all.

"Not exactly. The Foleys want to open a new restaurant at the resort. They've asked me to consult."

Both my parents light up. "What kind of restaurant?" my dad asks.

"Not sure yet. I'll get more information later. I've never been a part of the process this early so I'm excited to see what it's like." I remove the chef's knife from my roll and begin to carve the chicken into smaller pieces.

"Are they going to hire you to be the chef?" he asks.

I groan inwardly at the question. I've worked in restaurants before and hated it. I didn't like the constant pressure. Lots of people thrive under those conditions, but I am not one of them. Of course, since I am a trained chef, everyone thinks I should be in a commercial kitchen.

"I don't think so." I've known Lisa and Mitchell Foley since I was a kid. My mom used to work at their resort, Coastline Beach House, at the front desk and then as a concierge. When my cookbook, *Fish in Florida: Easy Recipes for the Home Chef*, came out a few years ago, they were the first to request to sell signed copies in their boutique. I restock at least once a month. We were chatting on one of my visits and Lisa had asked me the same question—if writing cookbooks and posting tutorials online was what I wanted to do with my career. And I answered honestly *yes*. I like making delicious food available to people who are overwhelmed with where to start. I like sharing how to read recipes and techniques and to take the mystery out of fancy ingredients. Lisa remembers and doesn't push me toward a path I don't want to go down.

My mom kisses the side of my head. "Well, hopefully they'll pay you well."

"Unless they think they've already paid you since they covered the trip you took with Sienna," my dad says.

"That was given without strings attached," I remind him. I feel like I prepaid for it by catching their son cheating. It's an image that's burned eternally into my brain.

"I can't wait to hear about it next time you're over for dinner," my mom says. She unlocks her phone and it's clear she's pulling up the shared family calendar. "Two Sundays from now?"

"Yes, that should still work for Paige and me," I say.

I don't think my sister and roommate had mentioned any changes to her work schedule. We only live twenty minutes from Mom and Dad when there's no traffic, but it's hard for us to be in the same place often. My dad's, Paige's, and my schedules are erratic, and after years of working the evening shift as a concierge, my mom has embraced her early retirement and does everything first thing in the morning. We'd tried to do dinner every week in the past. But any instance of congestion on the one bridge between Wendell Beach and the mainland and the twenty minutes turns into at least an hour.

"I'll text Caleb too and see if he wants to FaceTime when we're here." It's been weird since my brother moved to Georgia. He's thriving there but it leaves a gap in our family time together. We try to include him whenever he's available.

I divide the chicken and mac and cheese into containers and carefully write instructions on how to reheat. I always like to explain things from the beginning without assuming the person will have any knowledge in the kitchen. Jacey or her partner might not cook at home, and since they have enough on their hands with a new baby, I don't want them to have to question any of the steps to take to feed themselves.

After I leave their kitchen spotless, both parents hug me on my way out and ask me to hug Paige for them as soon as she's home from her shift at the hospital.

I HEAD to Wendell Beach and to where Coastline Beach House takes up the entire southern tip of the island. A lot of coastal communities have hotel and condo towers along their shores, but Wendell Beach prevents that with a height restriction. Instead of nearly unlimited rooms for thousands of guests, the resort has a couple hundred and curates an experience for each guest. It's similar to what I experienced in the Maldives, but without the freestanding villas and overwater bungalows.

I hand my keys to the valet and head to the back of the building where the offices are. These halls, the ones for the staff, are like a second home to me. I've only ever stayed overnight for Sienna's engagement party, and since she was marrying the heir to the resort, we got above-and-beyond special treatment. But I feel so much more comfortable on this side.

I step into the conference room and am greeted by Lisa and Mitchell. "Haley, we're so happy you're here!" Mitchell says.

They are both so warm and welcoming to me and have always been. It's a mystery to everyone how their son turned out to be so different.

"I'm so excited you included me." I scan the half dozen other people in attendance because I had been warned *he* would be here. I spot him standing next to the far wall with an iced coffee in hand, wearing his usual polo shirt and khakis. If Beckett Foley hadn't just come from the golf course, he is heading there after. He's talking with a man with brown hair in a charcoal gray suit that's tailored over what looks like a lean but muscular frame. His back is to me, but it's so obvious how well he fills out the fabric, even if the suit is out of place. This is a business meeting, and we will be discussing something with a budget in the millions of dollars, but everyone else is dressed in business casual. I'm wearing a dress with a pink bodice that fades into an orange skirt, and a white cardigan. Part of my branding is what I wear, and I try to be consistent any time I leave the house. Just in case I have a moment I want to share on social media. It's become second nature for me to pick a bright or floral dress that it doesn't occur to me to wear anything else.

I'm still puzzled over the suit. I understand it's necessary to bring in outsiders, but I won't get excited to work with someone who doesn't know Wendell Beach. This restaurant will be part of an institution in this town. I'm protective of it already.

Beckett notices my staring and frowns. His involvement is enough to make me question mine. He fooled us for so long about who he is. I grew up with him and saw him act mean-spirited from time to time. But I thought he'd grown out of it. Some people just need longer to mature. I didn't have any hesitation when one of my best friends started dating him. Now I know the signs I should have taken more seriously. Based on the glare he's giving me, he doesn't want the woman he blames for his breakup here either.

With all these thoughts spinning around my head, I don't notice at first that the man in the suit has turned around. Even when I do see, it still takes me a moment to recognize him. Not here in Florida in a dark suit, and his sun-kissed glow faded. Not when our last interaction was laced with such profound disappointment.

Nothing on his face betrays any emotion now.

"Haley, this is Ransom West. He's the representative from the private equity fund, Spare Capital," Lisa says as the pair approaches us. "Ransom, this is Haley Stewart. We sent over her information. She's the chef consulting for us."

"Pleasure," I say, shaking his hand, because that's not a lie.

"Of course, I remember." He squeezes my hand ever so slightly before letting it go. "Is everyone here? Should we get started?"

Mitchell opens a laptop and shares his screen to the monitor at the end of the room, and I sit next to Lisa. "The Webb Group isn't funding this?" I ask her quietly, naming the investment fund owned by Carina's father. I'm not sure how I feel about being in the same room as Ransom again. Especially when I'm expected to sound intelligent about food. I'm sweating through my cardigan, while he's looking cool as a cucumber in his suit. Which should be impossible in the Florida heat, but must be some genetic trait passed down through his family. Or maybe he's underneath the a/c vent. Either way, he has an advantage that's eluding me.

Lisa shakes her head. "Didn't feel the need to have Beckett and Hamilton working on something together. Nothing would get done and we'd have a million dollars in receipts to the golf course for 'research.'"

She's likely right. Any time Beckett and his frat brother are together, things get out of hand. I open my mouth to ask a follow-up question, but Mitchell starts a video call on his laptop and we're joined by a man who looks to be in his late twenties sitting at a desk. He's also wearing a suit jacket and a crisp white shirt, but without a tie, and he looks to be in a home office.

"Thanks everyone for being here," Beckett starts. "As all of you know, I'm Beckett Foley. I'll be managing this project on behalf of Coastline Beach House. Lisa and Mitchell are only here today to show their support and enthusiasm for the restaurant."

There are more than a few glances in Lisa and Mitchell's direction. Clearly others are wondering the same thing I am: *Does he really mean that?* He makes a few more introductions—the architect and the resort's head of dining operations are in attendance. "We are providing the real estate and ultimately the clientele, so it's important the final experience is in line with our brand. But we've brought in a few others to help achieve our goals. I'd like to welcome the financing behind the project, Ransom West from Spare Capital. And joining us on Zoom is the mastermind behind everything, Will Caron, head of Lavish Entertainment. You might not have heard of him yet, but he's opened successful nightclubs in Denver and New York. This will be his first restaurant. He wanted to be here in person but is experiencing something called 'snow' in New York. Will, I'll let you explain your vision."

Beckett sits down and Will opens with an impassioned speech about what he wants to accomplish. I focus on what he's saying because if I don't, I'll be too distracted by Ransom to be of any use. It turns out I'm engrossed anyway. Will is a businessman, but it's clear he has an ethical component in addition to providing entertainment. Everything he lists is something I can get behind. I take notes on my tablet, nodding along as he talks about sustainably sourced ingredients, using local vendors, and making this a place where the food invokes a feeling of everything great about Wendell Beach in an elegant experience. He might be an outsider, but this is exactly what I would do if I ever thought about opening a restaurant of my own. He's not the chef or the financing, but he clearly has plans and ideas and is the person who will put everyone in place to execute them.

"Haley, you're the Wendell Beach food expert. What do you think?" Will asks.

I look up and around the table. Ransom locks his eyes on me while he fidgets with the pen in his hand, even as he has a laptop open. "This sounds great. We're known for Paradise Bar and Grill, and—I know I'm biased since I also consult on their menu —it's an amazing place to eat. But it's a different atmosphere. It's casual beach dining. The Lucky Oyster is our 'fanciest' restaurant, but they specialize in a raw bar and shared plates. We don't have anything resembling a chef's tasting menu or a chef's table unless you go to the mainland. And who wants to do that?" There are a few chuckles from around the room.

Will speaks from the screen. "If we hire a chef who isn't from Florida, will you be able to work with them on a menu?"

"It'll depend on the chef and their ego. But you'll want to hire someone who agrees with your vision and wants to make it their own," I say. "If they want help, I'll help."

"We can hire a chef without an ego," Ransom says, his green gaze pouring into me from across the room.

"That might be more difficult than you think. We're a notoriously difficult group of individuals." My stomach jumbles. Why is the first thing he says something related to me? How is he here anyway? I'm so surprised by him and taken by what Will is saying that I haven't asked myself the most obvious question.

Is Ransom here for me?

"You don't seem to have an ego," he says.

"No, but I don't work in commercial kitchens. There's more than one way to be a chef."

"Let's be clear," Beckett says. "I've known Haley a long time, and she's great. But she's barely a chef. She's more like a blogger. We value her input, but she'll stay in her lane."

It's not worth my effort to react. I won't get anywhere fighting with him in front of everyone. I need to impress Will, and he doesn't look like he's buying what Beckett said. I might want to turn this down to avoid working with Beckett, but I need the money and I think I have an ally in Will.

"Why don't you go over the finances, Ransom?" Mitchell asks, shifting in his seat.

"Of course." He shares his screen to the monitor, and we get a list of stats about Wendell Beach. Its tourism numbers, the size of its economy, and the cyclical flow of it. It's odd seeing my home broken down so coldly by someone who hadn't heard of it until a few months ago. Who only knows it exists because of me. "What Ms. Stewart said is correct. A fine dining restaurant will fill a gap."

"How long before we can turn a profit?" Beckett asks.

"It's hard to say with any certainty," Ransom explains. "With the renovation needed, it'll be a year before we can open." The architect grunts in agreement. "Weather is a big factor afterward. A hurricane could change things for years. And your state politics could drive people away or bring in more business."

"I've discussed this with Lisa and Mitchell," Will says. "We won't shy away from certain topics that might be controversial. Working with farmers means talking about immigration and supporting migrants. Being on the beach means we're concerned about climate change. Having a staff means fair labor practices. I come from a family heavily involved in politics. I used to hide that, but I don't anymore."

"We'll have a PR team closer to opening," Ransom says. "We'll make the message clear without being preachy."

The discussion continues. Tasks are assigned. Just before Will logs off, he asks to call me directly to discuss more. I step outside to the patio and answer while sitting on a picnic bench, the waves of the beach are my favorite working backdrop, and my tablet open to take more notes.

"Hi, Haley. I didn't want to say this in front of everyone in the room. My wife is a big fan of you. I love her to death, but she was a terrible cook when we met. She followed you and now she's halfway decent."

"Oh, thank you so much for sharing. I love hearing that from people." I'm always happy when my work has direct impacts. That's why I do this.

"I was really glad when the Foleys suggested bringing you in. I think you're a fantastic addition to the team."

"It was Lisa and Mitchell who recommended me?" I ask. I wasn't sure in this web of people how I fit in. If he knew about me before. If it was Ransom who suggested me. It clearly wasn't Beckett.

"Yes. I didn't know you were in Wendell Beach or so involved locally. And Beckett might be the main point of contact for the resort, but his parents plan to be included," he says.

"Okay. That's good to know." I'm not disclosing our past drama for the sake of our business relationship. But my one concern about being involved is how much I'm going to have to work with Beckett. I'm not sure we're going to be the best of coworkers. "How did you get involved?"

"My wife and I vacationed there a few months ago. I've been wanting to open a restaurant. We both liked the town and think it's a good place to build something new," he says.

I smile. Based on what I've heard from him, our visions align. I'll be able to work with him directly for most of my involvement and it won't matter that Beckett is representing the resort or that

Ransom is handling financing. The food and the atmosphere come from Will. "I love it here, so I'm glad you do to."

"Great. We'll be in touch in the coming weeks. Thanks again for everything."

"Of course, and if you email me your address, I'll send your wife a signed cookbook."

"That'd be lovely. Thank you. Our anniversary is coming up, so the timing is perfect."

I end the call and head back inside. In the hallway, Ransom leans against the wall and is typing on his phone. He looks up when I approach.

"Can I have a word with you?" I ask.

five

RANSOM

I DON'T THINK HALEY AND BECKETT GET ALONG, WHICH WAS NOT something I considered when I set up this venture. If she has history with Beckett, my chance at another shot with her might be blown. The whole scheme was almost too easy, so naturally a hiccup has to come when I'm this close to her. I didn't have to suggest anyone bring in Haley as a consultant. The Foleys were the ones to make the recommendation. I haven't told anyone she and I met before which is likely why she wants to talk.

I was worried I wouldn't feel anything when I saw her. I've had months of lusting over nothing but the memory of a kiss and the videos she posts online.

Now she's here. In her element, wearing a dress that looks like the sunset and all I can think about is the one we shared together. She's still so tan and I want to get reacquainted with her skin.

"Of course, darling," I say, and we head back into the conference room. Everyone else has gone about their day so we will have privacy.

"What are you doing here?" She rubs her forehead as if she can unearth the answer there. It's distracting because now that

I'm alone with her, all I can think about is how the hem of her dress hits her thighs and what I'd find underneath if she let me run my hands up her skin.

I understand her confusion. The odds are astronomically low I'd be here naturally. That I would stumble upon this restaurant project which happens to be in her hometown. The one she couldn't stop talking about and that sounded like it is out of a fairytale, complete with its own castle.

I was confused too. When I left her on that beach everything was fine. She wanted me and I wanted her. But then I was left cold standing on a dock in the night. I couldn't let her go. I still want my chance with her. I believe there was some reason outside of me that kept her away that night. That it had nothing to do with me. It had nothing to do with us.

I've lost opportunities before. I've been rejected and turned down. I always pick myself up and move on. But I couldn't do that with Haley. Everything in my body told me I needed to see her again. Or else. I still don't know what it means.

Now that she's here in front of me, in vivid color in a place filled with color, I am right to pursue this.

"What am I doing here? I'm investing in a restaurant project," I say innocently. "Did I tell you I work in private equity?" I have to let her come to me. This was a big enough move on my part. She has to meet me halfway after what I've done to get here.

"You did." Her hands drop from her forehead as she gestures to me.

I'd forgotten how much she talks with her hands. I'm curious about them. Does she have a lot of scars from knives and burns? *Can I kiss each scar better?* "Is it a problem that I'm here?"

"No, but I find it hard to believe you're here by chance in my small town."

It's not by chance. "I found this through Will. I'd been looking to invest in one of his projects. Both his nightclubs have vastly exceeded expectations."

"Oh." She looks a little disappointed.

Did she want me to be here for her? I can't read her expression. But I'm sure she's thinking things through in her mind. Would someone really move millions of dollars into a project on a different continent just for a second chance with a woman who's already rejected him? I did.

"Right. It's a huge coincidence, then," she says.

"I'm glad of it." Her eyes go wide at my statement. "I think you'll be a great addition to our team."

"Of course. Fine dining isn't my specialty, but I try to be flexible."

Don't think about her being flexible, Ransom. "You'll be great. And we'll get a chef who can work with you, not the other way around."

"I just want what's best for the restaurant," she says.

"It's fine. And we can be professional, yeah? Whatever happened with us before doesn't have to affect this." I need to earn my way into her good graces. I don't know what happened to make her not meet me that night, but I have to prove to her that I'm worth it to try again. I could come out and say it now. But I don't. I can't tell what she's thinking and don't want to risk her rejecting me again.

"Definitely. I don't want any tension between us to get in the way," she says.

"Good. We're on the same page," I say. Tension, like the lingering question I've had for months—*why did she stand me up that night?*

"Yes." She steps for the door, and I open it for her. We jump a little when we find Beckett in the hallway.

"I was about to hit the links," he says. "Care to join me, West?"

I will golf when it gets me something. But Beckett is not a real player in this venture, regardless of his title or what he said about his parents being there for show.

Plus, I have other plans for my afternoon. "I'm hoping to visit some other local spots before I head to England tomorrow. Haley, I was about to ask you to go. Maybe somewhere for a quick pint. What about the place I keep hearing about? Paradise?"

"Yes, that's a great idea," she says with more enthusiasm than I expect.

"What about the Lucky Oyster instead?" Beckett says. "It will be our biggest competitor."

"The Lucky Oyster is closed on Wednesdays. No, I think Paradise is perfect." Haley has a smile I can't determine the origins of. I know she likes Paradise, but I'm missing the subtext.

"Let's do that," I say. I don't want Beckett to join us, but it's not the end of the world. I'm not blowing my shot with Haley today. This is a long game. It's still unclear why I'm putting this much effort into this woman. Women have turned me down before, and I've moved on. I'm not trying to conquer Haley or prove a point. But I just want to be around her a little longer.

"So sorry you won't be able to join us, Beckett," Haley says.

"Why?" I ask as Beckett grinds his teeth.

"Because he's banned from stepping foot in Paradise," she offers cheerfully.

"How does one get banned from a beach restaurant?" I ask. It clearly bothers Beckett far more than I think such a ban would warrant.

"Don't say it, Haley."

"You get banned by sleeping with the owner's girlfriend a week before your own wedding."

Oh fuck. This is the bastard who cheated on Sienna.

"Fuck you, Haley," he says before storming off.

She looks back to me, an expression of exasperation on her face.

"That might have been useful information before I invested." Interpersonal relationships are everything in a project like this. We have a small team. The dynamics are extremely important.

But I still would have invested. Getting close to Haley is the goal for me. Not making money on this restaurant.

"His parents are great. He's just a bad egg," she says.

I file this away for future use. I understand people cheat in relationships. No one has ever expected me to be faithful. I've been the person people have cheated with before. And I'll never be in a place where I'll be comfortable giving myself exclusively to one person forever. I've used sex to get what I want in the past. I doubt marriage would change things so much that I wouldn't be looking to exploit every angle. I could forgive Beckett if the harm he did was contained to Sienna. But it's clear that Haley is collateral damage.

The real power behind this venture is Will. I can sidestep Beckett along the way if I need to.

"Shall we head to Paradise?" I ask.

"Sure. Do you need the address? Or a ride? I think the hotel has a shuttle."

"I hired a car," I say, mentally shuddering at the thought of public transit. It's been years since I've taken any sort of communal transit that wasn't flying. "I'll meet you there."

It's awkward for a moment as we both head in the same direction to the valet stand at the front of the resort. This place is beautiful, and from my few short days here so far, it's worth my time and effort to help improve it. I can see myself recommending Coastline to my friends and acquaintances. I've received special treatment since they are trying to impress me, but the standard experience seems to be amazing as well.

"How is it?" Haley asks as we wait for the valet to drive round with our cars. "Driving on the other side of the road?"

I actually hate it. Everything is backward and I have to think through every turn so I don't get into the wrong lane. But since arriving two days ago, I have practiced enough to not look like a complete fool if I had to drive Haley somewhere. If this turns into a real date, instead of just a meal between two colleagues.

"It's fine," I say instead. "Takes getting used to, but this isn't my first trip to America." I have an apartment in Manhattan since I'm there at least once a quarter, but I'd never drive around there.

"Right, of course."

The valet pulls up with a small SUV and hands Haley the keys. She waves goodbye just as my car arrives.

* * *

WHEN I PULL into the car park at Paradise, I'm fairly confident I'm being pranked. I've researched Wendell Beach and likely saw every time Haley posted about the town since we met. There are plenty of pictures of the Wendell Beach institution. But I'm still not prepared when I see Paradise Bar and Grill. It really looks like a sandcastle.

It's the cheesiest fucking thing I have ever seen.

Haley said this is casual beach dining, so between that and the ridiculous building, my expectations are below ground when it comes to what I can expect for the meal. I'm glad the plan is just for drinks, even though it's almost five o'clock and I'm starving. If it had been anyone else suggesting this, I would have turned them down. I'm not picky about food—though I do expect it to be edible. But this is a chance to spend some time with her. I'll take the opportunity now under any circumstance.

And Haley knows her food anyway. She told me her favorite thing to eat is fresh berries. I can't imagine she'd regularly eat somewhere that causes indigestion.

She's already here, likely taking the back roads instead of the high street with people stopping every block to peek at the gin-clear water. She stands outside the entrance talking with a man wearing a black apron over a blue tropical print button-up. It's not the ugliest shirt I've ever seen, but it's close.

I lock the door to my hired Land Rover and approach the pair. Haley smiles at me, but it's almost a wince.

"You're really helping *him* open a restaurant?" the man asks her, crossing his arms over his chest.

"It's not a competitor for you and it pays well. I'll be working with Will mostly anyway. I don't want to deal with *him* any more than you do," she says.

This must be the owner and the best man from Sienna and Beckett's wedding. Which means he used to be close mates with Beckett. I hate him already if he's making Haley feel bad for taking this consulting job, and based on the expression on her face, I wonder if she believes he's right.

Which is bullshit. I've only spent a few hours with her, but I can see her patterns. She takes care of everyone before herself. I wish I appreciated that selflessness, but instead I want it out of her so I can have her all to myself.

As soon as I'm next to them, her smile switches from forced into something genuine. Was that me? Did I make her smile?

"Alex, this is Ransom West. He's the investor I mentioned. Ransom, this is Alex Barnes. He owns Paradise Bar and Grill."

I reach my hand out to shake his. "Pleasure." He grunts in response.

"Really?" Haley glares at Alex and he reluctantly shakes my hand. I warm at her defense of me. "We're getting drinks. How can that annoy you?"

"There are no limits to what can annoy me." He opens the door. "Go on in. But he can't sit in the locals' section."

What does that mean?

"Whatever. We'll take a table outside," Haley says.

I don't love that idea. It might be February, but I'm already sweating down my back from the few moments we've stood here. I removed my tie and jacket and rolled up my sleeves before I left the resort. I don't like heat. I tolerate it while on holiday, but it's the worst part of this scheme.

Why couldn't Haley live somewhere else? Why did it have to be Florida?

But if Haley wants to sit outside, I'll sit outside. I'd sit in a closet with her right now with our knees tucked up to our chins eating by torchlight if it meant a chance to talk with her. At least the view will be lovely.

Alex points to my feet. "The outside tables are in the sand. Most people take their shoes off."

Haley looks down. "Shit."

I don't understand any of this. I'm wearing black Oxford shoes. I was in business meetings all day. This town is much more casual than I imagined. But surely people aren't running around barefoot? I didn't even do that in the Maldives.

"We'll go upstairs. Is the corner table empty?" Haley asks.

"Yeah." Alex continues to hate this. He grabs two plastic menus from the host stand, handing them to Haley. She walks toward a staircase. "Sparkling margarita?" he calls after her.

"Yep!" she replies without turning.

I follow since I don't know what else I'm supposed to do. She consults on the menus here and is friends with Alex, but she deserves to be treated much better than this. I wonder which banks this place has loans with and if I have leverage with any of them.

The second story is open to the beach below so we're outside without being in the sand. Haley leads me to a table next to the railing. It's really quite beautiful. The water is still today and impossibly turquoise. There are at least twenty tables of various sizes, with a bar covered in palm fronds on one side and a stage at the other end. We're one story up, and it feels like we're in a hut on the beach itself. I try to help Haley with her chair, but she sits before I get the chance. I sit across from her and pick up the menu in front of me. She looks at hers briefly then sets it down.

She finally gives me her attention. "Sorry about Alex. He's still really pissed about what happened with Beckett. It was his girlfriend after all, and they've been friends since we were kids."

"You've known them both that long?"

"We did kindergarten through high school together. There aren't many kids who grew up on the island and stayed."

I don't have any friendships that old. I switched schools in secondary and didn't keep any of my mates from before. When I moved on to university, I made a whole new group again. And then again with each job I've taken. I use friendships and relationships to get me where I want to go. I was impressed when Haley had told me she'd been friends with Sienna since university.

"It must have been hard for you to lose Beckett as a friend, as well." I'm curious, not just because I want to know Haley, but because I want to know what it's like to have these kinds of relationships. Lena has had most of her friends since they were young, but their parents were friends. With them, it isn't just money passing through the generations, it's also the connections.

"Not as hard as you'd think. I'd never been close with Beckett. When we were kids, he led me to believe his parents had a rule that he couldn't be friends with the staff's children, and my mom was a concierge. It was a lie."

"Kids can be such shits," I say. I wonder what armor she built to protect herself from him. Or if there were other kids who treated her as less. I wonder if this is something we have in common. I've never shared my past with someone I was dating. But I've never tried to date someone like Haley before.

She is a little different here than she was in the Maldives. She's beautiful, but there is a bit of polish to her that she didn't have on vacation. I wonder if she dressed up for the meeting today, or if this is just how she looks every day.

"Exactly. It probably sounds weird, but his infidelity shook up the island business community. As I'm sure you saw in your research, we have a few drivers of tourism. The two biggest are Paradise and Coastline Beach House. They set our strip of sand apart from every other strip of sand in Florida. The Foleys care deeply about their reputation. The news that their son almost got into a bar fight with the owner of the local distillery at Paradise did not travel well. If anything, I bet this restaurant is his last chance to make something good and turn around his reputation."

Before I can ask my follow-up questions, Alex comes up the stairs with a drink in his hand. "Here's your margarita." He smiles at her and then turns to me with a glare. "What can I get you, Random?"

"It's Ransom," I say, but Alex doesn't care. I don't know what I did to piss him off so fast, other than my association with Beckett. But if he's rude to me, hopefully he'll cut the attitude with Haley. I scan the drink menu. "I'm normally a beer or scotch drinker. What do you recommend?"

Haley sits forward, a smile across her face. "Oh, the local lager is really good. You can't go wrong with anything from Three Bays Brewing. Or if you want to try something different, this rum is aged in bourbon barrels. It's from our friend's distillery." She points to the rum list and the choices from Wendell Beach Rum Works.

This is the easiest test I've ever had to pass. I'm guessing the friend is also the local distiller mentioned almost fighting Beckett. "I'll try the rum."

"Great." Alex steps behind the bar and quickly returns with my drink and two glasses of water.

"Are you really going to be our server?" Haley asks him.

I want him gone as well. If he hovers the whole time, we won't be able to chat.

"You knew what you were getting into bringing someone here."

"This isn't a date," she says. Alex raises an eyebrow. "It's not."

"We're short-staffed. I'm working this section. The special is blackened grouper."

He walks away without saying more and I don't know what any of those words mean.

Haley shakes her head. "Again, I'm so sorry. Maybe I should

have warned him about the new restaurant. But you're leaving tomorrow, and I can't let someone come to Wendell Beach and not visit Paradise."

"It's fine. He's just concerned about his business. The new place will ruffle some feathers before people adjust."

She looks out over the beach with her arms crossed over her chest. I want to lean in closer. "He's so full of shit. He usually only works the locals' section. Never up here."

"What do you mean, 'the locals' section'?" I ask. They both had mentioned it like it was some kind of VIP area.

"Oh, it's a few tables by one of the bars downstairs that are reserved for local residents only. When this place got popular in the fifties, the original owners, Alex's great-grandparents, wanted to make sure the people who lived on the island always had a spot to eat and drink. Tourists can drive us out of our own spaces."

"But I'm not allowed in, even with you?"

"Correct. I guess in theory, if you were to hang around enough, Alex might make an exception if we were throwing a party."

"I'm guessing there's a formal petition involved. Some sort of ceremony?" I'm only half joking.

"Nothing so fancy. Just obviously dependent on Alex's mood. But it shouldn't matter to you. I'm sure you won't be in Wendell Beach often," she says.

She's not wrong. I don't intend to stay in Wendell Beach for the long term, but I'll be here as often as I can be if it means I get to spend time with her.

Six

HALEY

I GLANCE UP AT RANSOM WHEN I MENTION THE FREQUENCY OF HIS visits to Wendell Beach. I'd been avoiding looking at him since I can't wrap my head around the fact that he's here. He's real. I could reach across the table and touch him.

But he's not here for me so I keep my hands to myself.

He tilts his head to the side. His green eyes narrow and I wonder if I missed something again. Carina was convinced her new neighbor, Orion Edwards, was only in town temporarily. But she was wrong about him. Maybe I'm wrong about Ransom.

"I'll be here from time to time," he says. "Will requested I be hands-on until opening."

Likely so he can correct anything Beckett messes up. "Well, there are lots of other restaurants to check out. I can make you a list."

"I'd like that," he says.

It is part of my job to give him a sense of the community. It's nothing more. "Did you want to order food?" I want to shift the attention away from me. His gaze is intense. It reminds me too much of the time we spent together in the Maldives. I look around. Alex should have checked on us by now.

"I could eat. What do you recommend?" Ransom looks down at his menu.

The food selection at Paradise is vast. They cater to a wide crowd of beachgoers. Their specialty is seafood, and they also have chicken, burgers, and salads. Nothing is fancy. But I've worked with the kitchen over the last few years to add a little something extra to make flavors stand out. When Alex took over management, he wanted to be more than the silly sandcastle on the beach. He wanted people to come for the food and the specialty drinks.

"It depends on what you like. All the seafood is fresh and locally caught." We didn't eat together in the Maldives, apart from the breakfast on the plane, and when we spoke about food, it was about what I liked. He looks up at me, waiting for me to continue. "The grouper tacos are one of the most popular items. They come with the spicy sauce sold in the shop downstairs." I don't mention I developed it. I'm torn between wanting to brag and wanting to play it cool. This is an extension of a business meeting. They hired me because of my knowledge of food and the local food scene. But I am with a man I've kissed and who has seen me partially naked. He's used to having people trying to impress him. He probably can't be impressed. I shouldn't even bother.

"Sounds delicious." He puts the menu down and we both look around for Alex. He's not on this level, and the other tables have different servers. My friend Bristol is bartending and has had her eye on us the whole time, so I wave at her. She signals she'll get Alex.

He arrives and takes our orders with only a few more snarky comments directed in Ransom's direction. I finally know what he's doing—he's trying to get a rise out of Ransom, thinking that this is closer to a date than a meeting and knowing I wouldn't date someone who is rude to servers. Alex has a long history of vetting the men I date. At least Ransom isn't taking the bait.

I am annoyed that Alex is interfering at all. I didn't tell him about what happened during Sienna's revenge-moon. When I got back and sat at the bar downstairs, Bristol wanted a frame-by-frame recounting of the trip. Alex just grumbled about everyone's vacation stories being boring. I didn't tell Bristol, or anyone else about Ransom. As far as Alex is aware, this is a client meeting. But he could just as easily be reporting back to the Foleys about their new business partner. Like me, he's also maintained a relationship with Beckett's parents.

"Besides restaurants, what should I check out while I'm in town?" Ransom asks.

"So many places. Have you been to the pier? It's walking distance from the resort and just absolutely amazing at sunset. There are a lot of great ice cream shops along the boardwalk, and a brewery. You'll have to go to Wendell Beach Rum Works, of course. If you practice yoga, the Nebula Athletics studio is right next to the distillery."

His eyebrows rise. "I've heard of them. I didn't realize they have a location here."

"It's the original." This is my chance to brag about my friend. "Carina Webb is the owner and is a good friend of mine. She does a lot for the community too. Beach cleanups, that sort of thing. The boutique at the resort sells a few Nebula Athletics items. They have Coastline-branded sun shirts if you're looking for a souvenir." But I can't see Ransom ever wearing something that casual.

"Was it Webb, you said? You mentioned that name to Lisa earlier."

I thought we had been speaking quietly enough that we weren't overheard, but Ransom must have been paying close attention. "Yes, Carina's father is head of an investment fund, the Webb Group. I thought the Foleys would seek funding from them."

He nods, leaning forward just a little bit more toward me. "Strange they didn't."

"No, it makes sense. One of the VPs used to work for Coastline. He was frat brothers with Beckett. Lisa thought they wouldn't be a good team."

"Everyone seems to know each other in this town," he muses.

"Yes, and everyone is someone's ex. It gets very complicated fast."

"Have I met any of your exes?"

He says it almost casually. It's not an appropriate question to ask, if this is a business meeting. But we have been on a date. And I don't know what he wants going forward.

"No." The last guy I dated, Eric, likely caught the fish we are about to eat, but I don't need to share that with Ransom.

"Good."

"Why is that?" I wish I understood what's happening here. If anything is happening, or is this all in my head?

He picks up his glass and takes a sip of rum. "We work together now. I like to take care of the people I work with. I'd hate to ruin anyone financially because they broke your heart."

I laugh. It's sweet of him to think that. As much as I hoped for jealousy, I'll take this protective stance instead. He and Alex might have more in common than they want. "Don't worry. You won't have to do anything of the sort."

He looks at me with what I think is wonder in his green eyes. But before he can get out whatever question is on the tip of his tongue, Alex arrives with our plates.

"Grouper tacos and the Cajun grouper sandwich." He places them each down in front of the wrong person. "Bon appétit." He walks away without another word.

Ransom doesn't even bother to hide his puzzlement.

I hand him his tacos. "Here. Again, sorry for Alex. I think he's trying to get a rise out of you. See if you're the type of guy to be rude to servers."

"I'm afraid he'll be waiting a long time before I react. I worked in a pub when I was sixteen. No matter what he does, I've been subjected to worse."

My eyes shoot up from the plate he's just handed me. "I didn't realize you worked in the service industry." Didn't he grow up with money? Wasn't that how this worked? No one becomes as rich as he is starting from nothing.

He nods somewhat reluctantly. "Yes. Classes were easy for me. I had to do something with my free time since I wasn't studying."

It sounds like a lie, but I'm not going to push him. It's none of my business.

"Anyway. Your tacos. They are lightly battered and pan-fried grouper. It allows the flavor of the fish and the seasoning to really come through. They are topped with cabbage slaw and the secret sauce I mentioned earlier. The tortilla is corn and hand-made by a Mexican bakery down the street."

He looks at them somewhat skeptically but picks up the closest one to him and takes a bite. His eyes close and I know that reaction. It's my favorite thing to see. The way food has blown past someone's expectations, and they've just discovered something they love. A flavor they'll be chasing for the rest of their life.

"I did not expect it to be so good. I honestly had not heard of grouper before. I wasn't completely sure what it was," he says.

"It's a type of fish. And I'm glad you like it."

He looks across the table as I pick up my sandwich. "This is one of your recipes, isn't it?"

"It is. Specifically for Paradise though. There is a really popular whitefish taco recipe on my website and in my book. But that's a different one."

"How many different ways can you have a taco?" he asks.

"Endless ways." I could go on and on for hours about tacos and how I'd love to travel to Mexico and spend the whole time trying as many different kinds as I could. It's impossible to run out of options.

He smiles like it never occurred to him to think about it that way.

We continue to eat. He asks about my sandwich and seems disappointed it's not a recipe of mine. I give him a brief history of Paradise and how it evolved from the tiki boom in the nineteen fifties to what it is now. How the cocktails still come from that tradition, at least partially because beachgoers want a great rum drink, but the food options have changed. There are a few core items on both menus that Alex would burn down Paradise before giving up. But he caters to the locals more than anyone else.

I try to steer the conversation back to Ransom, so I can learn anything about him. But he keeps it on Wendell Beach. I no longer have any doubt that he wants this to be a business relationship. I resign myself to the fact that nothing will happen between us. I'm a person who knows about the town he's funding a business in, that's all. Ransom is a guy who goes after what he wants. If he wanted me, he'd go after me. And it's clear that's not what he's doing.

I wanted to see if I could.

The fantasy I had that we'd have some grand romance starting on a plane, then landing on a tiny island in the Indian Ocean, before picking up again with a grand gesture in my hometown? Is gone.

I turn when I hear loud noises and see a band setting up on the stage. If this were different, if Ransom and I were here for different reasons, I'd stay and enjoy the music with him and maybe we'd dance. But that isn't happening.

"We should go," I say before my disappointment takes over. "They'll get really loud, and we won't be able to talk."

He nods and Alex appears with the check. I try to split it, but Ransom puts his card down faster, claiming it's a business expense. We get up from the table as the guitarist strums his first chord. Ransom visibly winces at the sound. Maybe he wouldn't have enjoyed the music as much as I would.

Once we're downstairs, I point to the doors leading out to the beach. "Do you want to go for a wa—" But before I can finish the sentence, I see Carina and Orion walk in. I don't want to expose Ransom to more people without a warning. "Never mind. Let's go out this way." I turn on my heel and head out the way we came in.

"Everything okay?" he asks once we're outside.

I rub my forehead. "Yes. I was going to ask you to go for a walk on the beach, but maybe another time." The sun is about to set, and it would be so romantic if we did.

"Sure." He smiles but I can't read his meaning. "Thank you for this. I head back to London tomorrow, but we'll catch up on everything in a few days."

"Great, sounds good." Every word sounds too cheerful and fake.

He walks me to my car, and I get in without a hug or a good-night kiss or anything besides a "safe travels." I pull out of the parking lot with Ransom behind me. Then I circle the block and park in the same spot I just vacated.

* * *

ONCE I'M BACK at Paradise, I head straight for the locals' section and sit down in the booth next to Orion and across from Carina.

"Hey, I was just about to text. I thought I saw you walk out," Carina says, putting her phone away.

"Yes, I was having a business meeting. But I think I'm going a little crazy. Can we talk about it?"

Orion gestures for me to get out of the booth. "I'm going to sit at the bar, unless you want me here for this?"

I can talk to Orion about my problems. He listens and gives

great advice, but I'd rather have Carina for this one. "You sure it's not a problem?" I shouldn't have barged in. Maybe it's date night.

"It's fine." Carina holds up her hand. "I taught a handstand workshop today and my wrists are screwy. It was my night to cook, but it's not happening so we're here."

"Are you okay? Do you need anything? Have you had wrist problems before?" I look to the bar. *Maybe I should get her ice for it.* She hurts herself often. I'm always concerned she pushes herself too hard. But it's her body, so I have to trust she'll figure it out.

"Not really, but I was running behind. I didn't warm up properly."

"It was my fault," Orion says with a grin, and it's obvious what they were doing to make her late.

Which I don't need to know, but also good for her for taking some time to herself and not being so selfless. I stand and let Orion out of the booth. "Don't believe anything Alex tells you about Ransom. None of it is true."

He nods but doesn't say anything else.

"Who's Ransom?" Carina asks. A server comes by and gives Carina a daiquiri and takes my order for another sparkling margarita.

"Remember how Sienna and I went to the Maldives?" I ask.

"Yes, I remember Sienna's revenge-moon," she deadpans.

I recount the story of meeting Ransom on the plane and how we hit it off, but I didn't think anything would come of it other than maybe a few flirty DMs. Until he showed up at our resort and we spent the day at the spa.

"He was fine with spa stuff? Lots of guys aren't into that," she says.

"It was couples spa stuff. We got a mud wrap, which was fine for him since he got to flex shirtless for me, and I was basically naked next to him for three hours." I think he's a man who cares about his looks. It wouldn't surprise me if he gets treatments regularly, if he has the time.

"And you were fine with that?" she asks.

I don't date seriously much. I'm careful with the men I do. I don't jump into things. I've never had a one-night stand or a fling. Ransom would have been my first. That doesn't mean I only have serious relationships. I haven't had one in a long time. But if I'm sleeping with someone, I want him to show up for me. I want there to be trust and affection. "Yes. It was a little bit of a 'when in Rome' situation." And honestly, I was too relaxed to care if he saw all of me. I tell the rest of the story. How he kissed me on the beach and invited me back to his private island.

"But you didn't go with him?"

"No." I take a deep breath. "I'm telling you this in confidence. She didn't tell me not to tell you, but I still want to respect her privacy. When I got back to the bungalow, Sienna was crying in her bed. She'd been hanging out with a couple and I'm pretty sure they were all good to have a threesome. But they went to snorkel first. You've talked to her about it. She was obsessed with snorkeling every second we could. The resort had a reef right off the beach that was amazing. She was about to get into the water and then couldn't. She just couldn't. She swam that morning, and we had snorkeled every day since we got there. But suddenly, it was impossible. She had trouble breathing and thought she was having a heart attack."

"Oh no. That's a panic attack," Carina gasps.

I nod. "She figured it out quickly. They have a medic on staff who examined her and told her to rest. All of this happened while I was getting scrubbed and massaged with Ransom. I felt so bad I wasn't there for her and there was no way I was leaving her alone that night."

"Of course. She didn't say anything about this to me. I thought you two did lots of water sports."

"We did. She calmed down. I gave her a pep talk. The next day we swam with whale sharks. She's been fine ever since."

"I'm glad she worked through it. What did Ransom say when you couldn't go?"

"I messaged him, said I needed to be with Sienna. He told me to have a great rest of the trip."

"Okay, and then what?" Obviously, I wouldn't be telling her this story if there wasn't more to it.

"And then today I walked into a conference room at Coastline and saw him talking to Beckett. He's financing a new restaurant there."

"That was the man you were just with?" Carina blinks, doing some math and gymnastics in her head. "Hell of a coincidence."

"That's what I thought. He swears it is, and I just...I don't know. I wish it was more, but even if it was, what's the point? He lives in London. I live here." It wouldn't really matter. At least not in the short term. We could have fun while he's here and go back to our lives while he's away. But my chest tightens at the thought. I don't want to be his side piece in Wendell Beach, if that's what he wants. I don't need full commitment from him, but I need more than to be forgotten as soon as he leaves the island.

Carina pauses mid-sip and sets down her drink. "You failed to mention he's English."

"Oh yeah. Ridiculous accent. Dimples. Wears suits like a second skin. It's obscene how attractive he is."

Carina looks to the bar where Orion is laughing with Alex, who didn't crack a smile for me all evening. I'm happy for her, I really am, but I long for what she has with Orion.

She looks back to me. "But he's in private equity?"

"Yeah, works for something called Spare Capital. Have you heard of it?" She grew up in this world. She knows more than I do.

"Nope. I'm just wary of any guy who is." Her terrible ex is Beckett's frat brother and works for her father.

"I know. I know. He made it clear this is a business relationship and nothing more."

"Maybe it's for the best. I can't believe you had this whole side adventure and didn't tell me." She says it with an air of fascination at the thought.

"Like you were dating Orion for weeks and didn't say anything?" I try to play it off as a joke, but it's been eating at me.

"In my defense, I thought it was a fling and nothing serious."

"Yeah, but you'd tell me if you had a fling," I say, taking a sip of my margarita. She looks away guiltily, and I realize something. "You've had other flings you haven't told me about."

"Yes, when I traveled sometimes. It's been a while and none of those were serious."

"I thought you hadn't seen anyone since you broke up with Hamilton," I say. It had been years since they ended.

"No. I'm sorry. I should have told you about this. Orion has helped me to realize how closed off I have been. I'm trying to open up more. Share more of my thoughts and feelings and all that."

"No, yeah. I'm happy for you. And you and Orion are good together. It just hurts that you kept this from me. You used to share things." We'd been friends since we were kids. "What changed?"

She tugs on the end of her blond ponytail. "I don't know."

I nod absentmindedly. "Right. I should go. You can finish this if you want." I push my mostly full margarita at her. This thing with Ransom is nothing. There's no way he reciprocates this crush. He might have wanted a quick hookup while we were on vacation, but that ship has sailed.

"Haley, wait. I am sorry. About everything. I promise, no more secrets."

"Sure," I answer. Because that should have been the expectation from the beginning.

Once I'm back in my car, I crank the a/c and take a moment. It isn't like I've spent the last few months wishing and hoping Ransom would show up in Wendell Beach like he did. But for just a little bit of time, I thought maybe someone had put in more than the bare minimum of effort to be with me. Ransom moved oceans to take me to a spa. If anyone was going to do something big for me, it would be him.

I pull out of the parking lot to head home. I'm happy Carina has found love. But it's not happening for me.

<h1 style="text-align:center">Seven</h1>

RANSOM

I'M AWAKE BEFORE MY ALARM GOES OFF IN THE MORNING. I TRAVEL often and am used to changing time zones, but my body pulls me to London time. I'm heading back this evening on an overnight commercial flight and then have a full day at the office tomorrow. Even with the lie-flat seats in first class, I won't get to sleep until I'm in my home tomorrow night. But that knowledge doesn't help me fall back asleep once I'm up.

At a reasonable hour, and deciding to catch one Florida sunrise before I leave, I change into a pair of shorts and lace up my shoes to run along the sea. When I checked in, the front desk staff raved about the walking path that parallels the beach. I could run all the way to Paradise and back if I wanted.

The streets are empty as the sun rises over the mainland, turning the sky pink and red. This will wake me up faster than coffee as I head off at an easy pace. I jog over a rainbow sidewalk and only see a few other people walking their dogs as I get to Paradise. The facade that is normally open to the beach is closed, giving it the air of an abandoned child's plaything instead of a thriving business. I spent far too much time last night thinking about this place after I left. I played over in my head everything Haley said, and if she gave any hint at picking up our relationship where we left it in the Maldives. But even in hindsight, I can't get a read on her.

If I can't understand her, then I will understand this town. It starts with Coastline Beach House and ends with Paradise Bar and Grill. Over the last few months, I've pored over every line of Coastline's finances and business plans. But Paradise is new to me. I want to understand everything about it. Since Alex won't let me access his accounts to satisfy my curiosity, even if I asked nicely, I turned to the internet to dig up information.

I fixated on the locals' section. I searched through social media posts and message boards and travel blogs. There were lists of "hacks" to get in, but those were always followed with comments from people who tried and were turned down. Occasionally, someone suggests that since the whole place is for tourists, it's fine for the people who live there year-round to have a few seats reserved. The food and service are the same. But others always swear the people in the locals' section have more fun than everyone else.

That's because they're all friends, you wanker.

At least I wasn't alone in my obsession.

I even looked at real estate. I can afford to buy something, and then Alex would have to let me in. But I read a post about how even if you own property, you have to live there a certain portion of the year and staff checks the address on your driver's license.

Everyone in Wendell Beach knows each other. They aren't going to let people pull a fast one on them to get a different seat at the beach bar. Having spent just a little time with Alex, none of these tricks will work for me. The only way I am getting in is if Haley vouches for me. Which I want anyway.

I don't understand why this bothers me so much. I have nothing in common with the tourists trying to sneak their way in. I know people in Wendell Beach. I'm putting down some sort of roots here, even if they aren't for me. This island will change because of what I'm doing. Don't I deserve some sort of recognition?

Yes, the restaurant is an excuse to be close to Haley. I hadn't planned on asking her to consult. I wasn't aware it was something she does, and working together is proving to complicate matters since I can't just ask her out. But ours will be the best fine dining restaurant in the area. I take pride in my work and won't settle for anything less than excellence.

The real estate looked promising, even if it won't get me what I want. I can always add investment properties to my personal portfolio since the short-term rental market is huge here. I had my finger hovering over the "Contact Us" link on a property being built. But paused when I saw the name of the agent, Kenneth Stewart. It's a common enough name, but I had to be sure he is related. His social media is mostly houses on the market and a reshare of a video of Haley's with the caption "So proud of her!"

I hadn't seen this specific video yet. I'd been with her most of the afternoon and am not on social media much anyway. But there it was, in beautiful high definition, Haley's trip to the Maldives.

I saw her smiling face as she stands with a man in a chef's uniform. She's underwater with a whale shark. And sunbathing with a glass of champagne in her hand.

There are shots of the resort and a few of travel to and from. I want to believe she lingers over the spa for longer than she does anywhere else, but I'll concede that's my wishful thinking. A quick panoramic view of the business class cabin includes the seat I sat in a few minutes after she filmed.

I want our meeting to have meant as much to her as it did to me. But I can't tell, and I can't just ask her.

I try to appreciate this town before it fully wakes up and

before the heat becomes insufferable. I see the appeal of the blue waters and the way the sky turns red and then pink. Haley loves this place. She loves every grain of sand on the beach and every pastel-colored house.

I run back to the hotel but turn to the pier just before. It's quiet now. I try to see it through Haley's eyes. Would she pay attention to the seagulls getting into the bins? Or the little sandpipers running from the waves and when they get too close, letting their wings carry them a few steps?

I can charm anyone, I know that. But I thought I wouldn't have to put much effort into charming Haley. I didn't think she'd spread her legs for me the second I appeared back in her life, but I thought she'd flirt at the very least. I didn't even get that.

She's already shot me down once—I don't want to deal with that again this early in the project and I still need to keep working with her. The restaurant won't open for almost a year. Once it does, we'll be invested for a few years, but the day-to-day management will require less supervision from me. I just have to win Haley over before then. Convince her that I'm someone worth taking a chance on.

I don't have to try this hard. I could keep going with the restaurant, since I'm already involved, and simultaneously walk away from her. Anyone else and I would have long ago. But I like being around Haley when she's excited about things. I like hearing her talk about food and her town. I'm not ready to let her go yet.

I take a picture from the end of the pier and send it to my family's group text.

ME

Headed home today. I'll come by Saturday for breakfast.

* * *

I'M EXHAUSTED beyond my normal levels when I land in London. I'd spent the morning walking the location with the architect, who spoke more in grunts than in actual words. Will was on video the whole time, still wishing a snowstorm hadn't stranded him in New York. But we got an idea of what we can do with the space.

My flight was delayed over an hour due to thunderstorms. I watched through the window of the terminal as lightning streaked across the sky. Contrary to how grumpy I was about it for the Maldives, I don't fly private all the time. Just when I'm traveling with a group. For business, especially if I'm alone, it's commercial.

When I get to London, it's the start of the workday and I head directly to my office. I answer emails and check in with the partners. They are impressed with the work I've done and how fast this project is moving.

Nicolas Darlington, the founder of Spare Capital and Lena's father, is particularly impressed. "It's a tough industry. I'm surprised by your projections, but if anyone can do this, it's you."

He's the reason I wanted to work for Spare Capital. There are plenty of firms I could have set my sights on, but this one mattered to me. It's the one most attached to a legacy. I was born without much and will not inherit anything of value from my family besides a small house in the suburbs that I'll split with my siblings. But Nicolas can trace his family through generations of nobility. He might be the second son of a second son, but his family name carries weight. I want to be a part of that. I could marry Lena and bind myself to that legacy. But neither one of us would be happy for long, and the fallout would destroy any connections I build through her.

Before I end my workday and head to my flat, I call Haley. I don't strictly need to. This could be an email.

"Hey, Ransom. Did you make it back to London okay?" she asks.

I hate how much I like hearing her voice. I want to lie back on my couch and fall asleep listening to her speak. It's not just that I'm exhausted either. My assistant, Daisy, has kept my coffee full for me all day. I shouldn't be this down bad for Haley. "I did. How's your day?"

"It's fine. I just got home from the farmers market," she says.

"I'd love for you to take me next time I'm in Wendell Beach," I say.

"Yes, of course. The restaurant will want to use a lot of the vendors. I can make the introductions."

I grind my teeth because of course she turns this to work. I can't just want to go to the farmers market with her like a normal couple would. Or I assume that's what couples do. I wouldn't want to wear matching polos with her like I've seen on TV, but I'm so tired I don't rule out the possibility.

"Sure. Did you review the job posting Will sent us?" I ask.

"I did. I sent him a few notes. He approved and posted. Did we not copy you?" Her voice on the other end changes, like she's looking at her phone and tapping through to her email after putting me on speaker. "Oh, whoops, it looks like he took off your CC. Let me send you the chain."

"Thanks." The email pops up on my computer and I quickly read through the parts of their conversation I missed. Will added in the budgeted salary ranges. She added some experience requirements. None of it requires my input. Will didn't cut me out because he was trying to take control. He thought I didn't need to be involved. Yes, I'm a partner on this, but he's the one in charge. He doesn't know I need to be on every communication with Haley for my own reasons.

"Everything look okay?" she asks.

"Yes, sorry." I don't have much more to say about this. She has a handle on everything. But I want to keep her on the phone with me for as long as possible. It's so fucking selfish of me.

"You sound exhausted, no offense. I'll get alerts for the job posting. I'll let you know if anyone interesting applies." Her voice is so soothing.

I rest my head in my hand and close my eyes, just for a moment wishing we didn't have an ocean between us.

But a knock at the door jolts me upright. "One second," I call out. "Sorry, Haley, someone is at my door. We'll talk soon."

"Of course. Get some rest, Ransom."

I end the call and look up to Lena standing in my doorway. I'd walked past her office a few times today, but we haven't spoken. I'm not purposefully avoiding her, but since we've been in constant contact over email, I feel like I haven't been apart from her.

"Welcome back. Did you have a good trip?"

"I did, yes. Everything is on schedule. The location is brilliant."

"I'll check it out when it's open. A quick trip to Florida might be nice," she says. She's pretty. Anyone would agree, with her golden-brown hair and petite frame. But she's never moved me the way Haley does.

"Of course."

She doesn't leave yet. "Why did you pitch this project anyway? It's not something you've done before, and the firm doesn't fund any other restaurants."

I know why she's asking. Most places like this have such slim margins that it's a huge risk to get involved. Of course I can't tell her the real reason. She also knows I don't care about fine dining. My diet mostly consists of chicken breast and broccoli.

"Will Caron is someone to watch. His last two venues exceeded expectations. With his vision and the location at Coast-line Beach House, all we need is a great chef to make something amazing."

"I plan to check out his nightclub next time I'm in New York. I've heard good things." She hesitates. "You were talking to Haley, the chef?"

"Yes, she's consulting. But we're hiring for the actual position. She doesn't work in commercial kitchens."

"Is her social media handle Cooking With Haley?"

I shut down my laptop, wondering what her reasoning is for this line of inquiry. But Lena is usually direct, so she'll get to her point. "Yes. How do you know?"

"I was reviewing the business plan. Legal copied me by mistake. I was curious so I looked her up." Lena puts her phone in front of me. The video of Haley in the Maldives plays. "She was there the same time we were. Stayed at the resort we had to visit. The one where you went off to be with some woman. Ransom, you can't get involved with companies just because you're sleeping with someone."

I hand her back her phone. I can't tell if she's jealous or if she has some other reason to be so concerned. "You were there. You know I went to bed alone that night."

Her eyes narrow to slits. "You've been in Florida for a week. I just heard you on the phone with her. I've heard you on the phone with hundreds of people. I know what you sound like when it's a business call and when it's personal."

I hate that I'm not sleeping with Haley, but I love that I get to win this argument. "Haley and I went for dinner and drinks to get a feel for the town. We're friends. Colleagues. I'm not sleeping with her."

"Maybe not, but you want to. This is a huge conflict of interest. I should tell my father. Our investment isn't big enough that we wouldn't be able to get out. Spare Capital isn't your own personal slush fund."

"There isn't anything to tell. I want to work with Will Caron. That's what our involvement is about. I didn't bring Haley into this. The hotel owners did. And even if I end up sleeping with her, she's not a principal player. She's a contractor for the hotel. It's not against any of our rules to be involved with someone like that." I looked. I plan to end this with some sort of relationship with Haley, a promotion within the firm, and a great restaurant opened. I have to walk a fine line to get there. But I'm not going to risk my career for a gambit that might not pay off.

Half the partners are sleeping with someone's secretary. That's not against the rules as long as it's not *their* secretary. No one can punish me if something develops with a contract employee.

"Fine. Whatever. Just don't do anything to embarrass my family," she says before leaving my office.

Lena is set to inherit the firm from her father when he retires. She's deeply invested in its success. I want this project to succeed. I might not fully get the appeal of Wendell Beach, but it means something to Haley. I like Will, and I like Lisa and Mitchell Foley. I want to help them build something new in their town.

* * *

ON SATURDAY MORNING, I arrive at my parents' house with fresh flowers in hand. I order them days in advance to be delivered to my flat early in the morning so I can bring them to my mother before breakfast. When I was growing up, she'd pick wildflowers in the garden, taking great care to arrange them so they looked bigger and brighter, keeping them until they dried out before replacing them with another bouquet.

"Ransom, you don't have to," she says like she does every time. But every time, she takes a long inhale and smiles wider than I ever saw when I was a child.

I follow her into the kitchen of the house where they raised me. I want them to move to a nicer neighborhood, but they claim they are fine here. When my parents won that argument, I tried to pay for things to be renovated.

They let me buy them new toilets.

Not new bathrooms. Just new toilets. So yes, I will be purchasing my mum fresh flowers every time I see her.

"How was America?" she asks. "We were so worried about you being in Florida. Your dad was reading so many scary news stories. An alligator ate a woman's dog! Did you see any alligators?"

"I didn't, no." Gator tail was on the menu at Paradise. I wonder if Haley cooks alligator regularly. If it's just another type of protein in Florida. They'll eat fish, chicken, and instead of pork, alligator. I'll have to ask her. I pull out my mobile, but it's far too early to send her a text. I'd love to wake up to a message from her, but I doubt she feels the same way.

In the kitchen, my sister, Merit, is at the stove cooking eggs for breakfast. My brother, Victor, and my dad sit at the table with plates laid out for everyone. Mum removes the vase of wild-flowers she clearly picked herself from the center and places them on the counter so she can set the new ones down.

"Those are just fantastic," my dad says.

"It's nothing. You should have told me the last ones were dead. I would have sent more." I give my sister a kiss on the cheek.

"I don't mind going into the garden," my mum says. "I just like having the color."

The house is a mess of different colors. The walls are painted fresh every few years to match her whims. One room doesn't match the next.

I wonder what Haley would think. The kitchen I see most frequently in her videos is white and sea blue, perfectly matching the colors of the island. But she's somewhere else enough for me to wonder if she uses a studio kitchen.

"Can I help with anything?" I ask.

My mum and Merit look at me. "Oh no. Don't you have work to do? You always work while breakfast is cooking," my mum says.

I normally do. Most Saturday mornings I hit the gym first and then spend an hour or so working before I even get here. But my internal clock wants to be on Florida time, so I barely had the time to squeeze in a workout before I came. I'm starving and want to dig into a plate of beans and toast. I haven't craved any specific food in years. I only care that I'm being fed.

"I didn't bring my laptop." I could read emails on my mobile, but if I pull out my phone, I'll scroll through social media and then I'll want to text Haley. I can't do that. And I've missed my family. I want to hear about Merit's psychology courses and how applying for training programs is going. Victor's charity has an awareness campaign with adverts all over town. I want to know if he's the person who designed them. It feels like it's been forever since I've heard anything about them. "How have things been here?" I need any kind of distraction from Haley I can get.

The entire room looks at me like I've grown horns. "Fine," Victor says. "You feeling okay?"

"I'm tired from traveling and the time change, but I'm fine."

Merit puts the eggs on the table. "Everything is ready so let's eat," she says, her eyes narrowing on Victor.

"Don't give me that look," he tells her.

"Hey, no fighting," my dad says. "We're glad to have your full attention today."

We sit, and I get the answers to my questions. Merit has an apprenticeship arranged and Victor describes in detail the redesigns the adverts went through.

"Stop it, Victor," Mum says.

"What? He asked about it. I'm just giving him the information he wants."

"I don't think he needs to know every sentence of every email between you and your manager," Mum says.

"I was just seeing how much he was willing to pay attention," Victor says.

I look around, feeling like I'm missing some joke, but based on the expression of my sister, the joke is fully in Victor's head. I smile. I might pay his rent since his job doesn't pay nearly enough, but I have missed messing around with my brother.

Merit asks about my trip, and I try to sound casual. I try to not bring up Haley every other sentence. But it's hard not to when she was the most interesting part.

After helping with the dishes, again earning surprised looks but no comments, I offer to drive my sister to her flat. Before I start the engine, I check my email and have several urgent messages.

"Do you need to deal with something?" Merit asks. "I can take the Tube."

"Just one moment." I send a few quick responses. It's a temporary pause to the fire I'll be putting out this afternoon.

She doesn't say anything until we're moving and I ask more questions about what's been going on in her life. She seems hesitant to answer.

"What's with everyone this morning?" I ask.

"It's nothing," she says.

"Merit."

"Ransom."

"Just tell me. Or, I'm going to assume Mum has cancer and you haven't told me."

"You'd be the first to hear if she was sick. No, normally you're on your mobile at breakfast. Or when you call us, you're also answering email. We're not used to you giving us your full attention like Dad said. It's fine. We appreciate all you do for us. We really do. You were just different today. And we love you. We'll take you however you come. We were just surprised and thought maybe something had happened in America."

She's four years younger but has always been much more emotionally intelligent than me. I do feel different after being in Florida. I'm not sure what to make of it yet. I'm not used to missing someone. But Haley has changed that. I've never been sure what I'm searching for with her. It was never only about sex. I'm driven by goals and data, and I don't have a goal with her.

"Do you remember those princess movies you used to make me watch?" I ask.

"I didn't make you watch anything. You were just as into them as I was."

I like the way her voice shifts, getting lighter, away from her psychology tone. She knows we're about to talk about when things were simpler, and she'll get to make fun of me for something.

"Maybe. Some of them had other things besides the princesses."

"True. I did make you play princess with me. You'd wear a blanket around your shoulders like a cape and pretend you were a knight coming to rescue me."

That's the memory I was searching for. During the long summers, I was left in charge of my siblings when Mum and Dad were both working. Sometimes I hated the responsibility. I wanted to be off hanging with my mates. But I've been thinking about those days with Merit and Victor more recently.

"Why do you ask?" Merit says after I don't say anything for a moment.

"No reason, really. I saw a live version of one recently. I liked it," I say and name the film. Of course, I watched the whole thing by myself as soon as I had the chance. I was curious what made Haley so happy.

"Oh, I love that one! I saw it with some girlfriends in the theater. We did fancy dress and everything."

"I would have loved to have seen that," I say.

"I'll send you pictures. I should have invited you. Next time. You can dress like a knight or Prince Charming and pay for everyone."

"Count me in." I can't remember the last time she and I did something like that together.

"You're always one to take care of people," she says. "Even when we were kids."

She's not wrong. I've always wanted the best for my family. I've just never extended that to people beyond my family.

I drop her off and head into the office. I could work from home, but that will just lead to me thinking about Haley. And if I'm going to get any work done on my other projects, I need to put some mental distance between us.

eight

HALEY

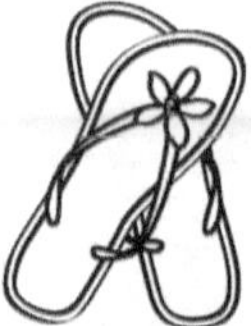

MY STOMACH TURNS IN KNOTS AS I SCROLL THROUGH SOCIAL media. Several current and former employees of the newsletter platform I use, DriverSeat Mail, have sued the CEO for sexual harassment. There are hints that more secrets will surface soon.

People are outraged. I'm outraged. But I'm stuck. There aren't many options for what I need from the service. I can't just pick up and go somewhere else. Even if I do, the steps it will take and the time needed is staggering.

People are calling for a boycott. Which turned into lists of creatives who use it and calls for them—me—to make statements and separate from the company. A quarter of my income comes from my subscriptions. With my biggest personal chef client leaving, I might not make rent.

I draft a statement and send it to Carina for vetting. The tone needs to be right, and I can't be defensive. I support and believe the women and hope they get their day in court. I add researching newsletter providers owned or run by women to my to-do list.

My phone dings, and I assume it's Carina getting back to me, but it's a text from Ransom.

RANSOM WEST

Have you reviewed the résumés yet?

I roll my eyes. We've gotten half a dozen so far, but the kind of chef we are looking for is rare. This skill set isn't going to fall into our laps. Once we find someone, we need to offer immediately. But finding the perfect candidate will take time. Of course, I have to wonder if he's just trying to micromanage me, since he does seem to check in with me frequently.

ME

Nothing promising yet.

You'll be the first to know if we get someone good.

RANSOM WEST

Good.

How is your day?

He can't just want to talk with me. I check the time in London —past five. He's likely at the office. He's not the type of person to take off early for a drink like he did while he was here unless it's for a meeting. He's probably asking because he realized it was a little rude to jump straight into questions without so much as a greeting.

ME

It's okay.

RANSOM WEST

Just okay?

I sigh. Should I open up to him? Does he actually care about what's going on with me or pay attention to social media cancellations or the news beyond his work?

ME

> Any chance you know a paid newsletter subscription provider that isn't run by harassing creeps?

I see his three dots appear and then disappear.

RANSOM WEST

> Not at the moment. But I'm sure someone is making one after today's news, and I'll give them the funding they need.

I smile. Of course he thinks money is the solution to everything. It's nice to think he'd be willing to do a little to stand up against the patriarchy.

RANSOM WEST

> I'm guessing you use DriverSeat Mail?

ME

> Yes. And it's a good portion of my income so it's not like I can just let it go.

I don't know why I'm sharing with him about my finances. He probably spends more on suits in a year than I make. It gets lonely not having regular coworkers to commiserate with. I can't complain at the coffeemaker about the boss's ridiculous deadlines because I'm always alone. And I'm the boss setting the deadlines. I talk with Carina and she's great with big-picture stuff and talking me into posting when I need a second opinion, but losing one customer is nothing to her. Even a big scandal is water under the bridge in a few weeks for her. She can't problem-solve this the way I need her to.

I doubt Ransom is the answer to this. It's inappropriate anyway since I work for him.

RANSOM WEST

You work by yourself, right? You don't have anyone managing your emails or anything, do you?

ME

No, it's all me.

RANSOM WEST

I'll do some digging and see if I can find an alternative. And if I do, I can have one of our IT people port everything over for you.

I stare at my phone. He can't possibly mean that. It's a hollow offer.

ME

I can't really afford to pay someone to do that kind of work. It's really time-consuming.

RANSOM WEST

Exactly the reason you should outsource it.

We'll cross the payment bridge when we come to it. First, we find a new platform that doesn't finance problematic cash settlements.

ME

Is that even possible?

The dots are back and then they disappear.

RANSOM WEST

In my experience, no. But that doesn't mean you shouldn't try.

It matters to me that he cares. That he thinks finding a new provider is a good idea even with the extra work. One of the freelancer forums I'm in had some guys commenting that they didn't see the problem with any of it. It's not like they personally are the ones doing the harassing.

There's rustling at the front door, causing my cat Lor to jump off the back of the couch, and Paige walks in. She's changed out of her scrubs and is wearing shorts and a T-shirt. But she looks exhausted. She's been working overnights, so I'd thought she was in bed when I woke up.

"You okay?" I ask.

"Another nurse had to take her kid to the doctor, so she was late coming in. I agreed to cover for her and then got stuck behind an accident on the bridge." She sits down and it's like she's never going to get off the couch again. "I thought about turning around and heading to Mom and Dad's, but I remembered they don't have a bed in the spare room at the moment and I can't handle Mom being a mother hen. The only reason I'm still awake at the moment is because of caffeine and I blasted the a/c as high as it goes. Look, I still have goose bumps."

"I'm so sorry." I deposit my laptop on the coffee table and go to the kitchen. "Let me make you some chamomile tea. That will help you settle."

"Thank you. Can you make sweet potato soup for dinner?"

I think through the recipe and if I have to get anything from the store for it. "Sure." I don't cook for her every day, but I'll make her comfort foods after a bad shift or when she asks.

She looks at me. "You're the best and I love living with you, but I can't keep commuting like this. I'm going to look for a place on the mainland when our lease is up."

Fuck. I don't want to live on the mainland. I grew up on this island and she'd have to pry me away with a crowbar. But shit, rent is not cheap here.

"Yeah, that'll be good for you," I say.

"You're going to stay?" she asks, sitting upright.

"Of course. I'll figure something out. Get a new roommate or find another place." Something with a bigger kitchen. But that's a long shot. At least I have a few months to figure this out before she leaves—we're just past the halfway point on the lease. The kettle sings and I pour her a cup. "Get some rest. I'll let you know when the soup is ready."

When she's gone to her room, I have another text message.

CARINA

This looks great. You should post.

Orion is on a charter. Want to go paddleboarding?

It's a few hours before I have to make dinner so the timing for this works out.

ME

Yes, I'll be right over.

It's exactly what I need to unwind from the day. I'm happiest when I'm on or near the water. I went for a walk first thing this morning, but I haven't seen nearly enough blue today. I post the statement, set my phone to Do Not Disturb, and shut down my laptop before changing into shorts and a sun shirt. I store my paddleboard at Carina's place since she has more space and is steps from the beach. I have the code to her garage and permission to drop by whenever I want, even if she's not home.

When I get to her place a few minutes later, she's got both our boards in her driveway. "Hey! How's it going?" She greets me with a hug as soon as I'm out of my car.

This is another new development for her. She used to be so closed off that it never occurred to me to offer her any type of physical affection or contact. She wasn't an ice queen, but I understood when people thought she was. Since she started dating Orion, she's been more open and warmer. I love the changes in her. She's much happier than she used to be. But I feel like I did something wrong for the years before. I've known

Carina since we were children. How did I miss so much? How did I not notice when she shut everyone out?

"It's good. This timing works out. I'm making Paige sweet potato soup for dinner." I drop my bag in her house, and she helps me with my sunscreen.

From her driveway, we cross the path leading over the dunes to the beach. The Gulf of Mexico is calm. I'm sure Orion is struggling to get any wind on his sailboat charter, but he excels at making it a good experience for the guests even if they have to use the boat's engine.

We put our boards in the water and paddle a handful of strokes on our knees before standing up once we're away from the beach. We're quiet for a few minutes. We both use this activity for stress relief, so while this might be social, it's more than that. There's something so peaceful and soothing about the gentle bob of the water. I'm using my muscles to propel me, but tension falls out of them at the same time.

"How's the restaurant going?" Carina asks.

"It's fine." I recap the chef search and how I can't get a read on Ransom, especially after his offer of help.

"Do you think he's into you?" she asks.

"Obviously there's attraction. Otherwise he wouldn't have gone through all that effort in the Maldives. But we work together. He probably doesn't want me distracted by my newsletter when I could be focused on Coastline," I say. She's silent, but it's a silence filled with thought. "What?"

"I don't think a guy like him cares about the time his contractors spend on other projects. I grew up around men like him. I dated a guy like him. Hamilton wouldn't have lifted a finger to make my life easier if it didn't mean winning something for him."

"What does Ransom 'win' by helping me?" Ransom is nothing like Hamilton.

"Maybe he genuinely wants to spend time with you?" she suggests.

"I can't tell if you're Team Ransom." We paddle parallel to the beach, avoiding getting too far out to sea. We always want to be able to get to shore quickly if anything goes wrong. Paradise comes into view, and I look across to the balcony where Ransom and I sat a week ago.

This is my home. This has always been my home. Landmarks shouldn't make me think of him.

"I'm not sure either. But I can't imagine anyone going from a romantic relationship to just friends or coworkers easily. Even if the romance was short-lived. I tried it with Orion and that clearly failed."

"It wasn't a relationship—just one kiss." One great kiss. "We haven't spoken in months. He probably didn't even think about me until I was added to the budget he had to approve."

She shrugs and it causes her to wobble, but she catches her balance quickly. "I guess I don't trust when he says it's merely professional. He might be a great boyfriend. I don't know. But if he can't be honest with you now, then do you really want to be with him?"

I don't think that's what he wants. And even if there was a romantic interest from him, it wouldn't be a relationship. A guy who tries to hook up with a woman he met on a plane isn't interested in anything long term. There have been plenty of opportunities for him to make his intentions known to me. He could have reached out at any point in the months before showing up here. But he never did.

"We are getting way ahead of ourselves here. I'm not thinking about him being my boyfriend. He lives in England," I say. Sure that's a great fantasy, that we could be in a serious relationship together, but I have to be practical. I haven't had a relationship in years. It's hard to find someone who wants to stay in Wendell Beach. We get a lot of people who come through for short periods of time. But eventually they get bored of the limited nightlife and move on to a bigger city. I can't ever see myself leaving. I don't get attached to people who are temporary. And frankly none of the guys I've been with are the type I want to settle down with.

I want someone to be a partner with me. I don't want someone to take control or try to guide me with my business, but someone who will stand next to me, support me, and offer help when I need it. I've been fine on my own for so long, but I'm wondering what it might be like to have someone to share things with.

Seeing Carina with Orion changed things for me. I want what they have. I want someone to push me to be better. Someone who will always have my back. Someone who makes me smile the way they do for each other.

"I want you to be happy, you know that, right?" Carina paddles close to me.

"Yes, of course. Maybe I'll get back on a dating app or something."

She makes a face. "I thought you hated those."

"I do, but how else am I going to meet someone? Not everyone's soul mate moves in next door," I say.

"You're right. Maybe Orion has someone he can set you up with," she offers.

"Wouldn't he have already offered?"

"It doesn't occur to him the way it does to Alex."

Alex makes it his mission to set me up with every new bartender or server that starts at Paradise, even if they are someone I'm only remotely interested in. I've had a lot of fun. But I'm ready for more.

"Maybe, yeah. Ask him. Maybe he hired a new captain and then we can both date sailors."

* * *

I TURN down Carina's offer to shower at her place, and get into my car. I check my phone and realize I have a few text messages from Ransom.

RANSOM WEST

I did some digging and found this one. They take a higher percentage of the subscription fee. But maybe it's worth it. There are a lot of useful metrics.

Of course, no pressure. You should do whatever makes sense for you and your business.

Isn't he a workaholic? Didn't he tell me that from the start? Is Carina right that he wants more from me? Why else would he have gone through this trouble for me?

ME

Sorry I didn't respond sooner. I was paddleboarding with a friend. I didn't check my messages.

RANSOM WEST
You went out on the gulf?

ME

Yes.

I send him a picture I took of the beach along Carina's house.

RANSOM WEST
That's beautiful.

ME

It was a good afternoon.

Thanks for doing that research for me. You really didn't have to.

RANSOM WEST

It was nothing. It could have been an opportunity
for me. I never know when I'm going to find the
next big thing. I turn over every rock.

Right. That's another reason it's not about me. He sees opportunity everywhere.

The sun heats up the car and I turn it on to start the a/c. I
should get home if I'm making dinner for Paige at a reasonable
hour.

RANSOM WEST

Do you have plans for the evening?

I check my watch. I've gotten good at figuring out the time
difference. It's nine at night there. Not too late. I wonder if he's
out with his friends.

ME

I'm about to make dinner. You?

RANSOM WEST

Preparing for a conference call in Singapore in 3
hours.

So, not out with friends. But he's still probably only doing this
to pass time. I scroll social media. He looks at companies to
invest in.

I wonder what he had for dinner, which gives me an idea.

ME

We never discussed if you cook.

RANSOM WEST

I can, but I rarely have time.

I flip through the recipe index in my brain. Ransom doesn't
know Florida and he doesn't know Wendell Beach. He's dug into
our economic numbers, but it's meaningless without context.

The restaurant will be in the resort and will rely on tourist money. But this town looks after its own. He needs the support of the people if he wants to make it work. He'll never care about Wendell Beach the way I do. This will never be his home. But maybe I can convince him our story isn't told with numbers.

For me that's always going to start with food.

ME

What's something you like to eat?

It takes him a suspiciously long time to answer.

RANSOM WEST

I like fish.

ME

Are you just saying that because it's my specialty?

RANSOM WEST

No. You can trust me. I'm English. I'm required to love fish and chips.

I'm not going to send him a recipe for fish and chips. I know better than to assign deep frying to someone with limited experience. I send him a different cod recipe from my website.

ME

Here is your homework.

RANSOM WEST

Why?

Because I think it's fun. Because I'm afraid he's the type of man who's used to getting what he wants, and I want to see what happens if something goes wrong for him. I'm not going to set him up for failure, but Beckett would never do something outside of his comfort zone. Is Ransom the same type of guy?

Because I'm trying to figure out how much he cares.

ME

> Because you need to learn the flavors of Florida if you want this restaurant to succeed.

RANSOM WEST

> I'm just the money. I don't need to understand the food.

ME

> Fine, then. Don't make it. But it's so easy, I give it to beginner clients all the time.

RANSOM WEST

> I'll see if I can squeeze it in.

* * *

WHEN I'M BACK HOME and waiting for the soup to come to a simmer, I do something very stupid—I open Ransom's Instagram account. I'm curious about how he spends his time away from work, if it's something he documents for public consumption.

There's very little activity. If he wasn't liking my posts, I'd assume he doesn't use it. I check to see if he's been tagged in any pictures and my stomach drops at the first one. It's a candid shot of him at a bar. His dimples are out in full force. He's talking with a beautiful woman. She's tagged as well, so I do the extra dumb thing and look at her profile.

Lena Darlington.

I close the app before I go any further. I don't need to know if he's spending his time with a rich English heiress. It's clear whatever flirtation or future possibility of continuing where we left off in the Maldives is secondary to his relationship with her.

* * *

SATURDAY AFTERNOON, I'm doing recipe research when I get a video message from Ransom. It's not late in London, but I'm not answering a video call from a guy without knowing it's coming.

ME

How can I help you?

He could be naked and masturbating.

RANSOM WEST

The fish got fucked. How do I fix it?

I chuckle and video call him back. "Okay, what seems to be the problem?"

"It's been in the oven for fifteen minutes and it still looks raw," he says. He's wearing a button-up shirt, but his sleeves are rolled up and the top button is undone. He looks good for how frazzled he is.

"Is the oven on?"

He glares at me which makes me laugh. "Yes, I can turn the oven on."

"What temp?" He gives me the number which I convert from Celsius to Fahrenheit in my head. "Okay, that's right. How close are the fillets to each other?" If they don't have enough space between them, it can take longer to cook.

He makes a face. "There was only one. Was there supposed to be more than one?"

I think I know the problem. "How big was it?"

He makes a gesture with his hands for a quite large piece of fish. "I'm not sure how much it was. It was the package in my fridge."

"You didn't do your own shopping?"

He continues to look at me with something like annoyance. But it's more frustration that this isn't working out perfectly for him than any real gripe with me. "No. I handed the recipe to my assistant, and she took care of it."

89

The recipe is clear on cutting the fish evenly if it's not purchased that way. He must have skipped that step. "You did one big piece instead of individually portioned fillets. It takes longer to cook and that's fine. We just have to wait."

"Do you want to see it?" He moves toward the oven.

"No! Don't open it!" I shout. He freezes. "You don't want to let heat out if you can avoid it. It'll take longer to bring the oven back to temperature. Set a timer for ten minutes and use the light function."

He calls out to his smart device for the timer and then props his phone on the counter and sits in front of it. "You insisted I do this so you're going to sit here with me while I finish."

"Sure, I wasn't doing anything else with my Saturday afternoon." That earns me another glare. But it's in good humor. He's not mad or anything. He's not having an outburst of rage that the fish isn't going his way. He's just frustrated.

I kind of get the whole "Orion picking on Carina" thing now. I've never been one to tease someone, but Ransom feels so easy. And really, what was he thinking calling me out of the blue?

"I didn't even realize it was Saturday. I've been at work all day," he admits.

I wonder what Lena thinks about that. "Really? Do you work every day?" I ask.

"Yes," he answers. "I told you this in the Maldives."

I have this brief thought that maybe I can save him. That we could date, and he'll learn the value of having a life outside of work and he'll take up some ridiculous hobby like windsurfing. He won't spend so much time in the office.

"If you don't cook, how do you feed yourself?" I ask.

"I eat at the office a lot. I have a service that prepares meals and delivers them." He sounds like one of my clients. "I honestly don't think about it very much."

"So why are you opening a restaurant?"

"Will is a solid investment. He owns a nightclub where everyone wears masquerade masks and it's not a sex thing. And every night there is a line and a waitlist. He might honestly be a genius at entertainment. I don't think about food much, but I know a man who is going places." He says it with enough passion that I think I've gotten my answer once and for all about what Ransom wants from me.

"Do you want to talk about the restaurant?" I ask, resigned.

"No. I honestly think my brain will melt into this countertop if I have to think about it," he says. "How was your day?"

"Um…it was good. I'm working on some new recipes so I'm doing research."

He props himself up on one hand and just stares at me like he's waiting for me to continue. He looks so tired. I almost feel bad for making him cook.

"I have clients who pay for personalized meal plans. I send them on Thursdays, so I try to have it done early in the week so I don't get behind." He's still watching me. "I hope to draft that tomorrow since I am cooking for a client on Monday."

"Cooking in person?"

"Yes. I do meal prep stuff. Make a few things in bulk so they have meals throughout the week. I only do it for a few clients and it's usually biweekly."

"Why do you work this way? With these small jobs that pile up. Wouldn't it be easier if you just did one? For instance, if you don't want to work in a commercial kitchen, couldn't you be someone's in-home private chef?"

I get this type of question a lot. Mostly from my family and friends. Sometimes it seems judgmental, like they think I haven't thought to have one job paying all my bills. But that's not how Ransom is asking it. With everything he asks me, it's out of curiosity.

"I like feeding and nourishing people. If I was a private chef, I would only help one family. This way I can help more people and in different ways. It's a lot of work, but it's fun for me." Most of the time at least. When I know I can pay my bills.

The timer goes off in the background and he gets up to pull the fish out of the oven. I use the moment to look at his apartment. It's nice, with stainless steel appliances and walls of gray and dark blue. Exactly the color scheme I imagined for a wealthy bachelor in his thirties.

"Does this look done?" He points the phone at the dish.

"Does it flake with a fork easily?" It looks done to me, but the point is for him to figure out how to do this on his own.

He grabs a fork and sticks it in the center, and a perfect flake comes off. "Ha!" His exclamation of triumph is absolutely amazing to hear. "I think I can take it from here."

"You got this. But call me again if you have any more questions."

"Will do. Thanks, Haley." He smiles and waves at me before ending the call.

I put my phone down. He's confusing me more than ever, but I still feel like there could be something between us, even if I had all but given up just a few minutes ago.

nine

RANSOM

ON MONDAY MORNING WHEN I'M ONLINE PICKING OUT FLOWERS to send to my mum, I take a leap and send some to Haley as a thank-you for helping me with the fish the other night. I wanted to impress her with my cooking but I panicked and so I swallowed my pride and called her. I was so fucking happy when she answered. I couldn't believe she was available on a Saturday, but I wasn't about to press my luck and ask her why she wasn't preparing for a date.

I choose a bouquet of tropical flowers, including a few white plumerias. They aren't the same color we saw all over the Maldives, but they'll remind Haley of the kiss we shared. When I get to checkout, I realize I don't have her home address. I fire off a text to Lisa to tell her I'm sending Haley flowers via Coastline. It's a professional thank-you gift to anyone on the outside. To Haley, I hope it awakens memories.

Several hours later, she sends me a picture of the flowers.

HALEY

You really didn't have to send this.

ME

I appreciate you. Especially dealing with my poor cooking skills.

HALEY

Anytime.

Did it taste good?

ME

Yes. It would have been better if you had made it, but I managed.

I might send the recipe to my mum. See if she can do a better job.

HALEY

So, you think women are naturally better cooks?

ME

Not inherently, but she is a better cook than I am. And she's been bugging me to come over for dinner more.

HALEY

That's nice, then. I didn't really think you were a misogynist.

ME

I try not to be.

Most of our résumés for chefs were from men.

HALEY

Yep, cooking is women's work until it's paid.
Then it's men's.

ME

Should we reach out to some female chefs? I can ask Will if we've missed something.

HALEY

I already mentioned it to him. We're trying.

Of course she's already thought this through and was already working on a solution.

* * *

ME

Please tell me this news story is fake.

FLORIDA WOMAN HOLDS CONVENIENCE
STORE CLERK AT ALLIGATOR POINT

I HAVEN'T SPOKEN to Haley in a week. I'll take any excuse to talk to her.

HALEY

No, it's real.

And while that one is intense, Florida isn't much crazier than the rest of the country. We just have looser public records laws, so the media has more access to police reports. In any other state the heading would be "Woman Robs Convenience Store."

ME

But how many states have alligators?

HALEY

More than you think.

ME

How often do you eat alligator?

HALEY

Twice a day.

Not really.

Gator bites are good, and I can make you gator tail tacos. But it's a novelty. We won't be putting it on the menu at Coastline.

ME

> I'm not eating tacos made with alligator.

HALEY

> Not with that attitude you're not.

She likes to tease me. I was teased and bullied when I was a kid. I learned how to adapt and deflect and to build armor to keep me safe. But Haley isn't doing it to wound me. She is doing it to test me. To see if she can get a rise out of me. She has to wonder if I'm like the other men in her life. If I'm the same as Beckett. I'll take it to prove that I'm not.

* * *

MARCH

I meet Haley at Wendell Beach Rum Works before I check into Coastline. My desire to see her is too strong to postpone even a few minutes. It's evening, with the sun setting red over the gulf. I'm in town for a full day to interview a chef before I head to California and then on to Asia. I want every second with her.

She's at the bar in the tasting room chatting with a blond man sitting on the stool next to her. They are smiling, and I feel like absolute shit. She wasn't dating anyone last time I was here. At least I think she wasn't. Would she have told me?

He looks up when I enter and stands as if it's a reflex.

"Oh, he's with me," Haley says as the man moves behind the bar.

She rises to greet me with a smile across her beautiful face. For a moment I think she's going to give me a hug but she changes her mind. We're colleagues, after all, but what if I want something different?

"Hey, Ransom. How was your flight?"

"Uneventful, the way I like them." I take the seat the man vacated. Haley sits, adjusting the skirt of her yellow floral dress. Her hair is down, hitting just below her shoulders, and I wonder if she was filming something today because she looks flawless. But maybe this is just how she looks. I want to reach for my iPad and draw the way the fabric of her dress drapes over her thighs, catching every dip and fold of the ruffle. I want to trace the line where she crosses her thighs until my hand disappears and she's sighing in satisfaction.

"Good," she says, oblivious to my observations or my thoughts.

She introduces the man as Christian Bailey, the owner of the distillery, and I'm brought back to reality. I keep a mental log of everyone I meet in this town and how they are connected. I had the rum from here when we were at Paradise. And the owner is the man Beckett almost got into a fight with. Looking at him now, I can imagine how that would have ended for Beckett. Christian clearly spends a lot of time at the gym, and while he isn't glaring at me, he's not exactly welcoming. Obviously, he's been speaking with Alex about me.

"What do you recommend?" I ask. People like to talk about their work. Letting Christian and Haley make this choice for me earns their trust. This isn't about what kind of rum I like. It's about Haley showing me the town she loves.

"He had the Bourbon Rum at Paradise," Haley offers. Are her legs shifting toward me?

"What do you normally drink?" Christian asks.

She's definitely shifted toward me.

"It depends. Sometimes beer. Sometimes scotch. Occasionally a gin cocktail."

Christian looks like he suspects I'm telling him what he wants to hear. But those are not lies. I drink all those things. He pulls a bottle from the shelf and pours a small amount into a glass. "Try this one. It's a spiced rum made with cocoa beans and then smoked."

I take a sip. It's good. Just sweet enough and just smokey enough. It reminds me of camping with my family when I was a child, and I'm hit with a wave of nostalgia so strong, I don't know how to react. One taste knocked me on my ass.

"Is that new?" Haley asks, turning to Christian.

I'm glad their attention is off me even as I want to reach for her to hold me steady. I need a moment to myself. I replay the countless times my siblings and I got lost in the woods only to find we were within shouting distance of our campsite.

We thought we were so brave.

"Yeah. Just finished bottling it. It's a bit of an experiment. Alex will have a blast making cocktails with it. I'm calling it Campfire Rum." He refills my glass to give me a full pour.

"It works." I place my hand on the backrest of Haley's stool. She's leaning forward enough that I'm not encroaching on her space. I need to be closer to her. I just got off a nine-hour flight. I haven't seen the woman I can't stop thinking about in a month. I haven't eaten nearly enough and all I want to do is pull her into my lap and ask her if she wants to hide away from the world with me. If we can pretend the stories we loved as children are real. I'll fight a dragon for her.

"What are you drinking?" I ask instead.

"It's an Airmail," Christian answers. "It's our small-batch, lightly-aged rum, honey syrup, lime juice, and sparkling wine. We only have it on the menu since Haley prefers her drinks to be bubbly."

I notice the flush to Haley's cheeks and the way this town shapes itself around her.

"You don't have to do that, you know," she says.

"It's popular with the after-yoga crowd too."

Right. The yoga studio her friend owns is next door. Christian moves to help another patron I hadn't noticed enter, leaving me alone with Haley.

"Are you jet-lagged?" she asks. She traces the wood grain of the bar with the tip of her pointer finger. We're close enough that I see a callus where she grips her knife.

I nod, almost out of habit at this point. "It's easier going this way than when I head home, but I travel so much I'm used to it. I'll just stay up to a regular time tonight."

She leans back a little, her arm rubbing against mine and her body turned to me. She's not bothered that I'm in her space. I don't know why, but if she rejected even this little contact, I'd feel like I'm collapsing in on myself.

We have a meeting tomorrow to go over the new details of the chef we've brought in and the plans the architect has drawn up. We don't have any work to discuss now, and I don't know what to say to her. Not because I have nothing to say, but because I have so much to say. I want to tell her she's beautiful, and how in her most recent tutorial there's a second when she's clearly smiling at someone off camera, and I wanted to pause and screenshot it so I could hold on to her joy forever.

But I can't say any of that. At least not now. I don't know how to free myself from this mess I've made with her. I want her too much to stop pulling on the threads. But instead of pulling on the correct one and getting to her, I might just fuck it up and unravel everything. She'll leave me standing on a beach, alone, again.

Instead, I ask about the one thing that always brings joy to her. "Are you looking forward to the dinner tomorrow?" The chef is preparing a sample dinner as an audition.

"I am," she says after a moment's hesitation.

"But..."

"But I haven't socialized with Beckett since I helped him plan a wedding that never happened. It's going to be a little awkward."

"He's not the best liaison for the hotel, is he?" I say. Beckett has been inconsistent. At times he's responsive and innovative. Other times it takes days for an answer to something basic.

"No. I'm trying to not let my biases interfere, but I just remember Sienna losing out on booking the band she wanted for their wedding because Beckett wasn't answering emails. I don't think something like that will happen here, but you never know."

I sip my rum, a scheme forming in my mind. I want this restaurant to succeed. For it to be one more place with Haley's mark. Maybe it's best if he's no longer involved.

I change the subject. I don't want to talk about the restaurant with her anymore. So, I ask about her week and how blueberry picking went. I'd stay here forever with her talking about how much fun she had and the things she's excited to make with her haul. But Christian tells us they are closing the tasting room and somehow several hours have passed.

Before we leave, I grab a bottle of the Bourbon Rum. I might not need it, but if I do, I want to set things in motion now.

* * *

IN THE MORNING, I greet Lisa and Mitchell after my workout and a large coffee. I wonder if the plan I made is going to hurt them. They are truly lovely people, but ultimately I take care of my people first. Haley is my people.

I find Beckett in his office. His feet are on his desk and he's on his phone. "Hey man, you golfing with me this afternoon?" He doesn't stand or glance up at me.

I don't expect formality from people. I don't think the pomp and circumstance some of my colleagues and friends in London expect is necessary. But I think you should look at the person you are talking to.

"I'll have to check my schedule. Haley and Will put a lot of appointments on it."

His nostrils flare at the mention of Haley. He puts his phone down and sits upright, his feet planting on the floor. "You talk with her a lot."

"It's part of her job," I respond.

"Yeah, but you call her when we only email," he says.

I didn't think he'd notice. "Her schedule and mine line up well for it. I adjust my communication style depending on who I'm working with." I don't, but he won't know better.

"Look, I don't know what she told you about my past with her friend." His tone is clear to me. *Whatever this bitch said, it's not true. I can call our coworker a bitch to you, right? You get it.* "It was a misunderstanding she blew out of proportion."

I school my features to be understanding. *Of course I get it.* "I like to keep things professional in the workplace. Haley understands."

"You have to be careful with her. The way she works so many jobs. I've never seen her get ahead. She probably wants a sugar daddy. Sometimes I wonder if those *clients*"—he puts air quotes around the word—"are really paying for something else when she goes to their houses and cooks for them."

I'm no longer concerned that I'll develop remorse over this. If I can nudge the toxic side of his personality to come out later tonight, especially in front of Will, it might be enough for him to be removed from the project. It's not just for Haley. It's the best thing for the restaurant. This is for everyone.

"I'll watch out. It's not new ground for me." It was a fun experience the first time a woman tried to sleep with me for my money. For years it had been the other way around. It was a sign I had finally arrived where I wanted to be.

"I mean, do what you want, man. Have fun with her. Just use your own condoms."

"Always. Anyway, I got you a gift. I do this for the managers of the companies I work with." I pull the bottle of rum out of my bag. "I normally gift a bottle of local wine, but there aren't any wineries on the island." I smile like I don't know anything. Like I don't know he hates the distiller and it's a reminder of him getting caught cheating and his subsequent downfall.

He frowns and then catches himself when he takes the bottle. "Thank you."

"We'll have to have drinks after the dinner tonight," I say. "Or before, maybe?"

"Yes. I'll definitely need to be a little buzzed tonight."

"We will crack that open tonight, then."

* * *

ME

Sorry, I'm on a call to Singapore. Pour me a drink and I'll be there in a few.

BECKETT FOLEY

Be quick. This booze won't drink itself.

I HOPE he takes the bait. That he's sitting in his office staring at the bottle of rum waiting for me. He'll pour two drinks, and when he realizes I'm not coming he'll down both. If I'm lucky, he'll show up to dinner drunk and make an ass out of himself. Management of the new restaurant on the resort's end can go to a different employee or one of his parents. He won't be an obstacle to success and Haley won't interact with him anymore.

I wait for her in the Coastline lobby. She knows where we're having the dinner and doesn't need an escort, but I want to see her first. I spent most of the morning with her and everyone else involved in the project. It was torture being in the same space as her and not be able to inch closer the way I wanted to. To not be able to see if she's inching closer to me. We've formed small jokes in the past few weeks, and I want them out in the open for everyone to see. But we're not ready for that. Not when she's so deliberately acting professional in front of Will. So, I'm taking this moment, this short walk, where I can be a little bit more than just her colleague. I want a few minutes with her all to myself.

I notice the flash of color when she enters through the revolving doors. She's wearing a bright blue floor-length dress made of almost sheer fabric. It's covered in white lace flowers with a slit up to her mid-thigh and from there the fabric is opaque, and I hate everything about that. The top is a V-neck showing off her slight but perfect cleavage along with a few dainty necklaces.

I open my mouth when she's walked up to me, but I can't think of anything appropriate to say.

"What?" she asks.

"I was just going to say you look lovely, but that's probably not something one says to a colleague." It's the tiniest sentiment, when she has become my whole sky. My sun and everything. I want to take her home to London so that on the darkest days of winter, she lights up my life.

She smiles and it is pure brightness. "I promise I won't report you to HR."

"Good. Well, you look lovely." *And beautiful. And perfect. And I want to take you to my room and hide from the world with you.*

"Thank you. You look great yourself."

I'm wearing a black suit with a white shirt and an emerald tie. She's blushing just the faintest amount. I'd give anything to know what she's thinking.

I have time. Time to win her over. Time to prove this could be a relationship. It's not just about sleeping with her or making up for the lost opportunity from the Maldives. It's become something more important to me. I know what I'm chasing now.

"If you say so, darling." I offer her my arm.

"Oh, we're being formal," she says.

"Of course. We always enter a dining room based on rank. It's time you Americans relearned a thing or too." I pitch my voice ever so slightly to make it posher than it already is. I didn't grow up speaking like this. I taught myself how to sound like my class-mates. Now I can go between the two as much as I want. But really, the reason I offered her my arm is because I want to touch her.

I lead her to a room at the back of the resort with windows overlooking the beach. I imagine they use this room when the weather turns and weddings can't be outside. It is decorated in the same style as the rest of the resort with subtle but luxurious ocean embellishments. One corner hosts a bar with a lone bartender. At the center is a rectangular table set for seven. Next to the bar, Lisa and Mitchell chat with Will Caron.

They look over when we walk in. I let go of Haley's arm, because here she's not mine anymore. I'm just the guy who's financing a project she's working on.

"Ransom! Haley! So glad you're both here," Will says.

I've only met him in person once before today, when I was in New York in January. It was a quick meeting to establish a business relationship. He's younger than I am by a couple of years, with deep brown hair, and wears an expensive black suit and tie.

"We were just talking about Paradise," Mitchell says. "Will and his wife went there for lunch today."

"Oh lovely." Haley's eyes light up. "Did you sit outside? The weather was great for it."

"We did, yes. It was a lot of fun." Will continues, "The food was great, and the owner stopped to ask us about how this restaurant is coming along."

"Alex has grown into a real steward of the community," Lisa says. "We've known him all his life. And he can be gruff at times, but that's when he's being protective."

I shift on my feet. I'm not sure how I feel about Alex. Maybe I should give him a chance. Maybe our instincts and interests are in the same place.

"Do you want something to drink?" I ask Haley.

"Dinner has a wine pairing, right? I think it'll be better if I wait," she says.

"Of course." I gently squeeze her shoulder before stepping to speak with the bartender. I order a gin and tonic with a light pour on the gin. I can't make the same mistake I'm pushing Beckett into making.

"We're just waiting on Alma and Beckett," Lisa says. "You know Beckett, Haley, so I don't have to apologize for his tardiness."

"It's fine," Haley says. "I'm sure he'll be around soon."

I check my watch. We were supposed to start five minutes ago. It's not really late, but considering he's in his office only a few feet away…

Maybe he'll prove me wrong and show up sober.

I hand Haley a glass of water and the smile she gives me feels like ice is melting somewhere deep in my soul. This isn't a date, but I wish it were. Even if it was still for the new restaurant, I want Haley to be here with me. Fuck, I just want to be here with Haley as something more than colleagues. Food is her world, not mine. I wish I had arranged for the two of us to join Will at Paradise. I would have worn boat shoes and shorts and we could have sat at a table in the sand. The women could laugh together while Will and I share a look about how lucky we are to have them in our lives.

But none of that is happening. At least not this trip. I just need some time.

"Yes, I'm here for the chef dinner," a feminine voice says in the hallway. I turn and see Beckett walking a little too close to a brunette.

"I didn't know we were going to be joined by someone so beautiful. I would've made sure you were greeted sooner," he says.

I cough on my cocktail. I thought he'd get an early start on drinking and he'd have bad manners. I didn't think he'd hit on a woman who is clearly flashing her wedding ring, especially when he knows everyone on the guest list.

"Beckett." His father's tone is unmistakable.

Beckett steps back when he realizes he has an audience. I watch for any sign of intoxication or any sign of his mood. Is he mad I stood him up? Will he see right through me when I say I lost track of time?

Instead, I watch as the woman nearly runs to Will, and he hugs her like it's been ages since he's seen her instead of a few minutes.

Haley leans in close to me and pulls on my jacket sleeve. "That's his wife?" she whispers, turning us away from where everyone else is talking.

"Yes." He's mentioned her a few times to me, and I always make the effort to ask after her when we talk.

"Okay, I can't believe this. I mistakenly assumed they had the same last name. But that's Alma Blake," she says. She can tell I'm not following her. "She's an actor. She was just cast in *The Stained Crown.*" I still don't follow. "She's a big deal. Or will be a big deal."

I nod and look over to where he's introducing her to the Foleys. But Beckett steps into my line of vision.

"West, what happened to pregaming?" He claps me on the shoulder, like there's no hard feelings.

"Sorry about that. Had to put out a fire in Singapore. By the time it was done, I had to be here. Next time." I feel exposed when I realize Haley has taken a step away. She must assume I'd been looking forward to that drink. I hate it, but I can't exactly tell her what I've done.

"Of course," Beckett answers before Will walks over to introduce us to Alma.

"It's such an honor to meet you," Haley says. "I'm a big fan of *The Stained Crown* book and I think you're just the perfect casting choice."

Alma smiles warmly. "Thank you. And thanks for the signed

cookbook. I swear I burned water before I met Will, and your recipes and tutorials are the only ones I can reliably follow."

"That's wonderful to hear—not that you're a bad cook, just that you were able to find something that works for you." Haley is delightfully adorable when she's nervous.

"We ready to eat?" Beckett asks, having gotten a beer, and sits at the head of the table.

I love challenges. The more difficult the better. It's so *boring* how easy it was to manipulate Beckett.

ten

HALEY

I shouldn't judge anyone's beverage choices, but Beckett is drinking a national brand beer when they have a keg of Three Bays Brewing. Sienna would have never let him order that at Paradise and neither would Alex.

"Of course, let's all find our seats," Mitchell replies to Beckett and takes the chair next to him.

The rest of us follow suit and settle in. Somehow it ends up with the women on one side, and I'm in the middle between Lisa and Alma, across from Ransom. I wish I was a little farther from Beckett, but I didn't want to admit to Ransom that I'm nervous about socializing with him. I want to believe we can have a professional relationship, but it's on Beckett to figure it out. I'll be on my best behavior. With the added alcohol in the mix, I'm not sure how he'll act.

Ransom, on the other hand… I want more than a professional relationship. We've been texting a lot, but none of it is strictly personal. I don't know anything about his personal life other than what I've found on his social media, which is minimal. It's also not strictly professional either. He calls me about emails I've sent him, seeming to prefer to work out the details over the phone. That probably doesn't have anything to do with me.

Then yesterday…

I swear we almost had a moment in the tasting room. He gave me a look I've been replaying in my mind ever since. It wasn't lust, although I caught him checking me out. It was like I was his heat source on a cold winter's night. But he was tired. Maybe he just has resting longing face.

Today he'd planned to drink with Beckett before dinner, and I don't know him well enough to trust that they aren't the same.

I feel Ransom's eyes on me when the servers present our first wine pairing and the first course, before the chef walks in. She's a Black woman in her late thirties and wears the traditional white chef's coat. I take a quick picture of the plate so I can remember it later and make notes.

"Thank you all for coming. For the couple of you who I haven't met yet, I'm Norah Grand. I'm incredibly grateful for the opportunity to cook for you all tonight. Especially you, Will."

"I'm glad everyone gets to taste what I already know will be amazing food," Will says.

"You won't be disappointed. I promise," she tells us. "This first course is beer-battered snapper, so fresh it was swimming in the Gulf of Mexico last night. Enjoy."

We are silent for the few moments after she leaves, and we take a bite of fish. She's right. It's so flavorful and the coating is done just enough to give it a little crunch and not overwhelm the small portion.

"Well. What's the verdict, chef?" Ransom asks.

I look up, startled to see everyone watching my reaction. It's been so long since anyone has called me chef, it took a moment for me to react. "Right, I'm working. I got so caught up in the food, I nearly forgot. She's exceptional."

"I've had better," Beckett remarks.

I sigh at the first sign that he's going to act like a child all night. He must have pregamed without Ransom.

Lisa grimaces before smiling and turns to Will. "How do you know Chef Norah?"

"She was an in-home private chef for my mother a while ago," Will says.

I thought Will was good at convincing other people to fund his ideas, I didn't know he also came from money. He has several other venues and is a few years younger than me. *Am I the only one who struggles to make ends meet?* Coastline has been in the family for several generations, and even with the challenges during the pandemic, if they're expanding, they must have rebounded.

"Was this when she was mayor?" Mitchell asks.

My eyes shoot up to Will.

"Yes." He must notice my surprise. "My mother was mayor of Denver for a term. Alma's father is currently mayor."

He'd mentioned his political family, but I hadn't bothered to investigate what he meant.

"Thanksgiving dinner must be interesting," Lisa quips.

Alma laughs. "There's a reason we moved to New York."

We get another glass of wine and the soup. Alma turns her attention to me, and we discuss her favorite recipes. She's in her late twenties as well, but considering she's the daughter of a politician and famous in her own right, she's incredibly easy to talk to. I was so nervous when we were introduced but she's more than set me at ease.

"I'm going to New York in May," I tell her when we finish the salad course. "A few friends and I are going to the Ashley Ferris concert."

"Oh! That will be so much fun. I'm trying to get tickets but haven't been able to yet," Alma says.

"I'm sure you'll make it happen," Will says, breaking away from the conversation on the other side of the table.

"When will you be there?" Ransom asks, pulling his phone out of the inside breast pocket of his jacket.

"The twenty-second through the twenty-fourth," I answer.

"Huh. I'll be there that week for a meeting," he says. He looks at me hopefully. Like he's excited for a chance to spend more time with me.

"It's a girls' trip. No boys allowed," I say with a bit of flirt in my voice.

Beckett barks a laugh. "You and your fucking girls' trips."

"Beckett," his father cuts in. "Watch yourself."

Will and Alma exchange surprised looks at his outburst.

"Whatever. I'm getting a drink." Beckett stands up and walks out of the room.

"He knows that's what the server is for, right?" Will asks. The bartender left when we sat down, but the server has been bringing him drinks throughout the meal.

"I'm so sorry for our son's behavior," Mitchell says. Beckett had been getting more irritable with every course. "He's been difficult since his engagement ended."

I cough on my wine, and Ransom quickly hands me a glass of water.

"He wasn't engaged to you, was he?" Alma asks.

"Oh god no. My best friend," I explain.

"Haley was the maid of honor," Lisa says. "She was really involved with the planning, right up until the end."

"He's exceptionally good at project management when he wants to be. Frankly, this restaurant is his last chance to get his act together," Mitchell says. "We value this partnership, and we want to preserve it. If you have any concerns, we want to know before it becomes an issue."

"I'll be sure to keep my eye on him." Will takes a sip of his wine.

I cringe inwardly, wondering if it's judgment I hear in his voice. If he's having second thoughts. Could he pull out altogether? Do the higher-level contracts allow that? This doesn't happen without him. The money I make through consulting for them is important, but it's more than that. I've fallen in love with the idea of this restaurant. Of having a place I helped build become an institution on the island.

And Ransom. I'm not ready to say goodbye to him. But this project is the only thing keeping him in Wendell Beach.

Beckett returns in time for the second fish course. Chef Norah comes out again, explaining the sauce she created and how impressed she is with the quality and freshness of the fish. She retreats to the kitchen as we prepare to take our first bites.

"I bet Haley fucked the fisherman."

The room starts to spin.

"That's uncalled for." Mitchell's voice is a hair's breadth below a shout, the tone clear. The next words out of Beckett's mouth better be an apology.

"For god's sake, Beckett." Ransom shouts. He even looks panicked.

I should have seen this from the start. All those things I brushed aside from when we were kids, I should have seen them for what they really were. I can't go back in time and save Sienna from his damage, but I know now that some people never change.

"Beckett, you can apologize to Haley and then you can leave." Lisa is cold as she dismisses her son.

"I'm not apologizing to that slut," he yells.

My eyes are glued on Beckett, but I swear Ransom flinches.

"Watch yourself." Ransom says it in a voice so icy I'd be afraid —if I wasn't sure he was on my side and way too fancy to get into a fight.

"Fuck you." Beckett throws his napkin on the table and walks away.

Once he's gone, I speak to the table, everyone's eyes wide in horror. "I'm so sorry about that." Beckett is the one who did this.

I didn't do anything wrong, but I still feel the weight of everything he's done to hurt the people around me.

"You're not the one who needs to apologize. *We're* sorry," Mitchell says to everyone.

"I fear this might be slightly my fault," Ransom says. "I suggested we share a drink beforehand. Didn't think he'd struggle to pace himself or be such a git to Haley."

"I think it's safe to say he's off the project," Lisa announces, fidgeting with her napkin. "We value integrity in our work. If our son can't honor that, then we will have to go in a different direction with him."

"Fine with me," Will says. "Haley's contributions have been invaluable. I'm sure between the rest of us we can fill the gap Beckett has left."

A server enters the room with timing so precise he had to have been waiting just outside the door for the drama to wind down, and pours everyone the next wine pairing.

I rub my temples.

"Are you okay?" Ransom asks.

"Yes, I just need a minute." I walk out of the room.

* * *

I TURN the corner and head straight into the ladies' room.

Alma follows. "I'll go, but I thought you might want a friend. And I figured I'm better than Ransom," she says.

I bark a laugh. I kind of do want Ransom with me, but that's not happening.

I'm increasingly regretful we missed our night together in the Maldives, if only because we'll never have the opportunity again. The *would've, could've, should've*s are ringing loudly in my head. His interest in me has passed. I'm afraid I've been feeling myself fall for him in the last few weeks. It's more than my attraction to him. Now I want to jump ahead to the part of the relationship where I only need to share half a thought and he knows the rest.

It's the relationship Carina and Orion have. And the one it looks like Will and Alma have. I've never been jealous of relationships before. I never envied Sienna when she was dating Beckett, or Carina when she was with Hamilton. Maybe I knew then they weren't the type of men to be counted on. But something inside me is aching that I'm alone all the time, and I wish I could reach for Ransom.

I face the mirror and pull lipstick out of my bag to do something with my hands. "I know I'm not responsible for Beckett's behavior, but it feels like I am."

"He's an ass. He has everything he could ever want and doesn't appreciate any of it." She leans against the wall and examines the basket of toiletries on the counter.

"He's still upset he had to pay for me to go on his honeymoon with Sienna," I say.

"I'm sure he deserved to. But don't think about him. Think about the guy who's waiting for you in the dining room," she says.

"We're just colleagues." I pause holding my mascara, but my skin warms at the mention of Ransom even if she didn't say his name.

"Sure, Haley. So why can't he keep his eyes off you, then?"

"He's watching for my reactions to the food."

"Maybe." She pauses. "Are you not into him? I don't want to make you uncomfortable. I genuinely thought you two were dating since you were standing so close to each other, and how he reacted to Beckett."

I drop my makeup into my bag, thinking back to the Maldives. Even if we had gone to his private island that night, we wouldn't be dating now. I'm under no illusion about what that was to him and to me. We haven't talked about it, other than the first day, not even when it's just the two of us on the phone. There weren't expectations then. There aren't any now. "I wouldn't want to get involved with someone I work with. The last guy I dated probably did catch the fish we ate. It's been awkward since I still use him as a supplier."

"Either way, Beckett is an ass who just lost his job. Ransom is definitely into you. And no matter what, you're amazing at your job. You're having a great meal. And the people who really matter think the world of you."

"Thanks." I've always wondered how people make friends as adults, grateful I've known Carina since we were kids and met Sienna in college. But having a half cry in the bathroom at a work dinner seems just as good as any other way.

When we return to the dining room, Alma plants a quick kiss on Will before sitting down and I'm hit with another wave of jealousy.

I lift my gaze to where Ransom is watching me.

You okay? he mouths. I nod and smile in return.

* * *

NORAH PRESENTS our next course and the rest of the dinner proceeds smoothly and deliciously. Once dessert is done, Lisa and Mitchell declare they are happy with Norah if Will and Ransom are. It's a huge relief we secured a chef this early in the process. We have someone to build their vision around.

"How are you getting home?" Ransom asks as we gather our things to leave.

"Cab," I answer. Paige dropped me off on her way to her overnight shift since I don't drive when I have wine pairings. I'm close enough that I could walk, but it wouldn't be particularly pleasant in these heels.

"Good. I'll wait with you by the valet stand."

We step outside into the humid air. After being in the air

conditioning for so long, I love the heavy feeling on my skin, like I'm wrapped in a weighted blanket.

"Did you enjoy dinner?" he asks. "Apart from Beckett being a bellend."

"Apart from that, yes. I should be more used to it. Him, I mean." *Should I tell him about the fisherman? That I did probably sleep with him? Would Ransom even care?*

A cab is waiting. I should climb in and leave this all behind. But I want to sit in this moment with Ransom. The surf crashes on the beach and a band plays at the pool bar. But here, it's almost quiet between the two of us. My attention and focus are on him.

He stands close to me. He's in my personal space, right where I want him.

"You and Alma seemed to get on well," he says.

"We did. She's one of those people who could charm a bridge troll."

"I think you're selling your participation short." His mouth is turned up into a half smile, but I can't decide if the other side is a half frown. "Let's go sailing next time I'm in town."

I smile but it feels more like a reflex than anything else. Will and Alma mentioned they are chartering a boat tomorrow. Ransom wants to experience the same things. I step back. "Um… sure. I know the owner of Lost Craft Charters, the company they are using. I can get us a reservation on one of his boats."

"I was thinking private." He steps forward.

"Right. It's annoying to have to deal with American tourists. I get it." He's used to having everything he does be exclusive.

He chuckles and shoves his hands in his pockets. "Sure, that's it."

I look up at him. God, his eyes are so pretty. The way the fairy lights hang from the ceiling of the portico makes everything about this moment feel more romantic. It's been months since we kissed and I'm sure he's seeing other people, but for this moment

I don't care. It's not relevant that we work together or that he's leaving in the morning. I can't pretend anyone else has made me feel the way he does. No one else gives me butterflies.

It's a mistake since I'm falling fast. And despite what Alma said, I don't know how he feels about me. If I'm a colleague or a friend. But I remember what he told me at the spa that day.

I wanted to see if I could.

He really can't blame me if I want to see if I can spend the night with him and not lose my heart. One night to believe in the romance between us. Not to believe it's going anywhere, but just to indulge.

I lift up on my toes and kiss him.

He doesn't react at first, and I've clearly made a terrible mistake. But then his hand is on the nape of my neck, and he holds me close to him. I open and trace his tongue with mine. I've kissed a lot of men on this beach, but this is different. He's deliberate and consuming and clearly the type of man who goes for what he wants.

I melt into him. My skin is already damp from the humidity, but my entire body flushes. I let out a soft moan when he squeezes my hip, and if it weren't for my long dress I'd have already jumped into his arms. I tease him with the softest bite of his lip, letting him know I want more. That this can continue. He grows hard against my stomach. This can keep going. We can go to his room. I don't have to take care of anyone else tonight.

We can take care of each other.

He releases my mouth and rests his forehead on mine, just like he did in the Maldives. I close my eyes and memorize everything about this. The sounds. The way he smells like some kind of woodsy cologne mixed with the salt air. The pounding of my heart in my chest, and when I rest my hand over his, I can feel it's the same for him.

"You should get into the cab, Haley."

Oh.

I step back and his hands fall away, leaving me cold in the night air. "Sure. I'll see you later. Or not, since you're leaving in the morning." I walk to the waiting cab and the valet opens the door.

"Let me know when you get home," Ransom calls after me.

"Yep!" I yell back as I slide into the rear seat. I give the driver my address. "Yes, I could have walked, but it's been a night."

"No judgment from me," he replies before leaving the hotel's circular driveway.

I can't believe I did that. The one time I've done something bold outside of the kitchen and it blows up in my face. I thought kissing a guy I'd already kissed wouldn't be a big deal.

Once I'm in my dark apartment, I send Ransom a text.

ME

Home.

Sorry about the kiss. I've clearly had too many of the wine pairings.

RANSOM WEST

It's fine. I just don't want you doing anything you'll regret.

We'll be in touch.

Is there anything colder than "We'll be in touch?"

Eleven

RANSOM

I hated putting her in the taxi. All I've wanted since coming to Wendell Beach was some indication she is still interested in me. Then she was kissing me, and my entire body demanded I take her to my room.

Women have used me as an impulse before. As a reaction to a bad day. I can't be that with Haley. We'd both been drinking, and while we were functional enough to not embarrass ourselves, I want to be more than a drunken act with her. When we do sleep together, I'm going to take my time with her. I won't be rushing out the next day to catch a flight.

It was an act of chivalry I regretted the moment she walked away.

I text her a couple of days later when I'm on the West Coast. I don't have a place here like I do in New York, but my hotel suite has a full kitchen. She sends me a recipe for a sweet potato and black bean salad and tells me to try as many different taco places as I can. It becomes another challenge.

For the first time, maybe in my life, I'm paying attention to the food I'm eating. It's never been something I cared about before. It's been fuel for my body and nothing more. I'm particular about what I eat only because my looks are a tool I use to get ahead and I need to keep my body in shape. But I told the meal delivery service my requirements years ago and haven't thought about it since. It's never been fun or exciting or joyful. It's only now as I'm asking every local in the office where their favorite spot is that I realize I was deprived for the last few years.

Lena is in LA as well and finds the mission ridiculous. She's not used to me doing anything while we're traveling other than work and the gym. She bribed me once to go to dinner at a restaurant when I wanted to order from room service alone. But I can't tell Lena I'm doing this to feel connected to Haley and as an excuse to reach out to her.

Our text and email exchanges aren't enough for me. Apart from discussions of tacos and salads, they are mostly professional with only the odd comment about English Premier League football. Haley shares that she's a fan of Liverpool since her roommate in culinary school was from England. She asks me for my team one night when it's late in Florida, but early in Singapore. I wonder if she's alone in her bedroom thinking about me and watching that day's game on replay.

ME

But Liverpool? I guess you have one flaw.

I wait for some kind of response. Like she's annoyed at me or I've taken it too far.

HALEY

Ha! I'll have to send you the blooper reel of my next cooking video.

ME

I'd love that.

She sends me a gif of a woman rolling her eyes before she shifts the conversation back to work.

I shouldn't be gleefully happy. I should temper my excitement. But I got what I wanted. Haley was miserable and I made things better for her. I was furious Beckett took his frustrations out on Haley. I should have expected it, and I felt so fucking terrible he hurt her on his way down. And when she kissed me, it almost felt like I didn't deserve her. I'm not sure I do on my good days. But I'll work hard to convince her I'm worth it.

* * *

APRIL

I'm finally back in Florida in mid-April. The builders start the teardown of the space, and I'll be working in Wendell Beach for a week. I convinced Haley to cook me dinner at her home. I'd told her it wasn't fair I spend all this time cooking for myself when I hadn't really had something she'd made. It's a gap in our friendship.

It feels like a gap in her affection. She cooks because she cares for people. I want her to care for me. It's so fucking selfish because I want so much from her. But I'm taking this.

I don't understand any of this—that I'm jealous of the way other people get to eat what she's prepared. I've never been jealous before.

My parents love each other. I grew up in a loving home. But they are one of the only couples I see who feel that way about each other. I've never wanted nor seen the appeal of giving myself completely to another person. Amongst my friends, they talk about how in love they are one minute and the next they are hooking up with another person. Or me, even. I've been the guy they fucked to get back at their husband and I never cared about the ethics of it. Love was never going to be a part of my future. It's a luxury only afforded to the lower classes who have less to gain from a beneficial financial arrangement.

I've had girlfriends give me something. Sure, sex is great, but so is getting promoted my first year out of university because I was dating the senior partner's daughter and got close to him. I showed him just how good I was at my job. I could have gotten noticed on my own because I am the best at what I do. But it would have taken so much longer and I'm not a patient man.

Plus, I'm a great boyfriend. Gifts, expensive dinners, my complete undivided attention when necessary. I give them what they need in bed and frequently what they haven't gotten from previous partners. I always leave them better than when we started. No one can accuse me of being a heartbreaker. I'm far too measured for that.

I'm not in love with Haley. But I feel more for her than I expected to. Even before we left the spa that day, it became more than attraction. I have nothing to gain from dating her. No new promotion to win. No deal to be signed. No step closer to a long-planned goal. She's just a woman I think about every second my mind drifts from work. Who inspires me to rearrange my schedule to hear her voice.

I pull into the driveway at the address she gave me, cheering at finally having it so I can send flowers here instead of the resort. It's a beautiful house close to the beach with the same wraparound porch all the houses in the area have. It's much larger than I thought she'd have. I've done my deep dive on real estate in the area, and even with some of her revenue streams drying up like she mentioned, she must be doing better than she's let on. I know what we're paying her and wonder if Coastline is one of her lower-earning projects.

I knock on the door and she answers a moment later, somehow brightening even this sunny Florida day. She's wearing a frilly floral apron over a solid blue dress. Her hair is piled into a bun on her head. She's perfect and put together with every stray strand of hair like it was placed where it is on purpose.

"Hi," she says, after a slight pause. "Come on in."

I step inside and hand her a bottle of wine. She likes sparkling, so I brought a bottle of champagne.

"This is too much." She looks at me with her brow furrowed.

It's a good bottle and cost twice as much as retail since I got it through room service. I stopped pinching pennies years ago. "It's nothing, Haley. Unless it won't pair with dinner?"

She rolls her eyes. "Come into the kitchen and I'll pour us both a glass." She leads me down a hallway to the open kitchen which features in so many of her videos.

"Did you move recently?" I ask. "You used to film your videos in a different kitchen." I show my hand a little. *Yes, Haley, I pay a lot of attention to you.*

She opens a few cupboards before grabbing champagne flutes. "Um…that was my friend's place so I'm still there from time to time. But I cook here when I can."

She must have just remodeled because everything looks new. "It's beautiful."

She looks a little unsure. "Thanks."

She expertly pops the cork and pours us both a glass. We toast and I take a sip of mine, hoping this is the first time I get to be alone here with her. No spa attendants. No owners of local establishments. Just the two of us.

"Dinner will be ready in just a few minutes."

"No rush. Is there anything I can help you with?" I lean against the counter out of her way and watch her move around. She's laid out several cutting boards and has a clear system in place.

She gives me a side look. "You're just being polite. You don't have to do that."

"I want to help. I've been getting much more practice, thanks to you."

She thinly slices pears while she speaks to me. "Have you made it to your parents' place for dinner more?"

"I have when I'm in London. My mum made the fish I needed your help with. It was loads better than mine. My brother made fun of me for a week." I hadn't minded. We hadn't messed around in ages.

She smiles as she adds the pear to a bowl. "How many siblings do you have?"

Fuck yes. This is what I want. I want to talk with her about her family and her friends, the ones who don't hate me, and I don't want to spend one single second of this night discussing the restaurant. "Two. Both younger. Merit is finishing a graduate program in psychology. Victor is a graphic designer for a charity. What about you?"

"Same, actually. My sister, Paige, is a nurse at the hospital on the mainland. And my brother, Caleb, is an engineer and lives in Georgia."

"Parents? You said your mom works at Coastline?" I'll take this one mention of the resort if it gets me a window into who she loves the most.

"She did. She retired during the pandemic. My dad is a real estate agent. They both live on the mainland."

I knew about her father already, but I love hearing it from her. "You keep saying 'mainland' like it's some distant place," I say.

"You haven't had to sit through Sunday afternoon traffic yet," she says, pointing her knife at me. "You'll think it's as far as the moon soon enough."

I smile at her because she's so adorable the way she talks about the island. It's clear she loves this place. That's always been so apparent to me: she loves things fiercely. I've never been passionate about one thing the way she is about so many.

She turns away when a timer goes off and she pulls a pan out of the oven.

"Both my parents retired a few years ago," I continue. "Before that my dad was a builder, and my mum worked in an office."

Haley stops what she's doing and looks up at me. "Oh."

"Oh?" But I know what she's thinking. She thought this had always been my life. That I grew up with expensive champagne and trips to remote tropical locations. But I didn't have any of that as a kid.

It's a relief to share this with her and trust she won't judge me. I've spent so much energy avoiding these conversations, like my background was something I should be ashamed of. Haley doesn't care where I came from. I don't need or want armor around her.

"I just assumed your parents were also in finance or something," she says.

"No. We weren't poor, just working class. Most of our vacations were camping, and once we went to France."

"That sounds like me. We took a few trips to Disney World or the Keys."

I want to pull her into my lap with the way she's reassessing everything she assumed about me. I want to take her to her bedroom and strip down everything between us. I don't have expectations of where this night is headed, but I have hopes.

"Why don't you have a seat and I'll bring everything to the table." She gestures to the long kitchen table with two place settings arranged so we both can see across the neighbor's yard and to the beach. It's amazing to know this is what her life is like. This is the view she sees every morning. This is a taste of what she loves.

She brings a salad bowl and a plate of chicken. "Okay, there is a fresh avocado and pear salad. And this is chicken in a white wine and lemon sauce."

I hold out my glass toward her. "Cheers. Thank you so much

for cooking for me." I serve myself some salad and a piece of chicken. I take a bite and swear my life changes. "Wow. That's brilliant," I say.

Her face lights up, like she feared I wouldn't be moved by her food. "Thank you. Chicken isn't fancy, but it can be great depending on the preparation."

"I've had a lot of pretentious meals, but I'll take this any day," I say. I've never understood why people pay so much for food cooked by expensive chefs with weird frills and servings the size of a thimble in rooms without any soul. I take part because it's expected of me, but I'd rather have this—Haley and me eating in her home. Or in my home. I don't even care which one, as long as it's just the two of us.

After we're done eating and she's told me about culinary school, she brings out a pie. It's off-white with a graham cracker crust. "This is Florida Key lime pie." From her tone, this means something. "It's amazing," she continues while opening a few drawers in the kitchen before grabbing a spatula. I thought she would have a serving utensil just for pies, but apparently not. "And we'll kick you out of the state if you don't like it."

"Really?" I can't imagine they kick people out of the state for not liking dessert. But this is America, and Florida specifically. They do a lot of dumb things.

"Not literally, but it's good. We have a lot of flaws but pie isn't one of them. And this is the best recipe for it. It's not even one that I developed."

"But you baked this?"

"Of course. There are great bakeries on the island I can take you to if you want to do some comparisons."

I only want her pie. "I'll give it a try."

She cuts a slice and hands it to me on a plate with a fork before getting herself one. It's polite, but I'm constantly impressed by how selfless she is and how she is always taking care of others first.

I take a bite and am hit by the creamy texture and then the tartness of the custard. It finishes with a sweet crust. She's watching me and I don't want to be kicked out of the state.

"It's really good," I say and mean it. It's not something I normally eat, but if I'm going to have any pie, it's going to be this.

"Good. I'm glad you like it. We'll keep you around after all."

* * *

WHEN I'M HELPING her with the dishes and feeling like the night can pick up where we left it after our last kiss, I hold up a cutting board I dried. "Where does this go?"

She gazes up from where she's drying her knife. "Um."

"Um?" I repeat.

"That cupboard." She points, and when I open it, it's full of cleaning supplies.

This isn't adding up. She puts the knife into her knife roll and that's when I notice several others in a block on the counter. Does she have two sets? I turn and see she's watching me. We stare at each other, wondering who's going to break first.

It's clear she's stubborn. "Haley, what's going on?"

"I can explain," she says, holding up another knife before setting it down. "You wanted me to cook for you and I wanted to cook for you. But my apartment is tiny. And I live with my sister."

"This is a rental?" That isn't the view she sees every morning? This isn't her space?

"Sort of. It belongs to my friend Orion. He owns the sailing company we're going out with this week. He moved next door with his girlfriend, Carina, a few weeks ago."

I look out the window to the house between us and the beach. A couple sits on their deck. "That them?"

She nods. "They're probably waiting for your car to leave so they can ambush me and ask me everything."

"Do they do that every time you entertain your colleagues?" I sort through my feelings. I'm a little proud of her. I would have done the same thing. But I don't know what it means when she won't open up to me.

As I look around, it's obvious in hindsight. There isn't enough color. Everything is too polished. This isn't the house of a woman who's been on this island for years.

"No, I haven't entertained here before like this," she admits. "And it's not like we're just colleagues."

"We're not?" I try to be neutral, but I'm sure I'm failing.

"Well, you know. We have kissed."

Fuck. This could be my moment to put it on the line for her. To figure out if she's really involved here with me. I don't know what to do with these knots. I've been lied to before. I've lied plenty. But I didn't think it would come from Haley.

"Why didn't you just tell me?" I hate how desperate and hurt I sound. I look at the half-empty bottle of champagne on the counter. I'd imagined finishing it in bed with her. Now that I know this is her friend's house and it's her friend's bed—it's not happening.

Was having an off-limits bed another reason to host me here?

"Honestly, my apartment is terrible for entertaining. And Orion offered. This is a vacation rental, and they didn't have a booking. I thought you expected a nice house."

She's not telling me the whole truth—that she thought I'd judge her for wherever she does live. But I just want to know her.

"You can be honest with me, Haley. We're friends, yeah?"

She nods and the tension between us eases. "Yeah. I'm sorry. It was better here, I promise." She sighs. "Speaking of Orion, and since we're friends, I have no excuse not to ask—instead of doing a regular charter, Orion wants to take you out on his boat with Carina. As like a double date, except not since we're not dating. It's just because we're spending a lot of time together around town and people talk. Orion and Carina want the chance to get to know you."

"Right, should I bring anything?" I ask. I'll call it a date if she will.

"No. Carina is an overplanner, so she'll take care of drinks, and I'll bring food. We'll probably go paddleboarding or swimming so just wear swimming stuff and bring a change of clothes."

The tension has eased, but it's not gone. She might not admit it, but this is important to her. This is another test. *Can I spend the day on her friend's boat with her?*

"I'll be there," I say and thank god she smiles at me.

twelve

HALEY

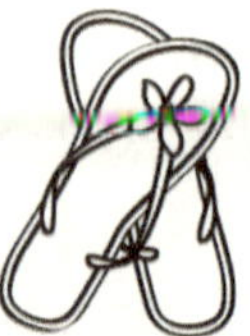

ORION ALWAYS WANTS TO SAIL IN THE MORNING WITH THE SUNRISE, and this trip is no exception. I thought Ransom would be opposed, but he confirmed the details when I sent them. This was supposed to be his private charter where he dictated the terms, including sailing time. Instead, we're telling him when and where to show up. He'll probably have half his mind on work anyway. I can't imagine him giving up an entire day to spend with me and my friends.

I groaned at the thought of getting up before the sun. But I prepared my cold brew coffee last night, so when I park my car at Carina and Orion's place, I'm feeling somewhat awake. In the past, Carina would have insisted on walking to the marina since it's not that far. But we can't walk and carry the food we need for the trip.

In their kitchen, the two of them bicker over which wineglasses to bring. "Can you two not do this right now?" I ask. It's foreplay to them and it grates on my nerves today.

They both freeze. "You know we're just messing around, right?" Carina says.

Carina wasn't silly when we were children. Sure, she had fun playing on the beach and we'd go to parties and clubs once we were old enough. But this is different. This is new.

I'm happy for her. At the same time, I'm a little bitter it was Orion who brought out this side of her. That for all the love and support I've given her over the years, it wasn't enough for her to break out of her shell.

"Yeah, I know. But this is kind of a business thing for me," I say. It's not, and they know it. Ransom doesn't need to know Carina or Orion for the restaurant to be successful. In the fallout of Beckett's affair, they both came out on top. Carina supplies the resort staff with sun shirts and Orion is the dedicated charter company for all guests. There's a direct shuttle from the resort to the marina, which conveniently means Ransom doesn't have to drive.

They nod at me. I swear Orion sees through everything I'm thinking. "We're getting it out of our system. No fighting on the boat," he says.

When we arrive at the marina, I head to the galley on the *Twisted Rigging* to stow the food from the coolers, while Carina and Orion set up the sails. In two days, they leave for the Bahamas for a few weeks. Today's trip is a practice run for them. And my last chance to spend time with Carina before she's off the grid for weeks.

Orion climbs down the stairs and I move to get out of his way, assuming he's headed to their cabin.

"You okay?" he asks, leaning against the wall.

"Yes, I'm fine." I adjust the cheese I carefully arranged on a plate last night.

"Haley." He takes his time saying my name.

"I'm just nervous," I admit, looking up at him. Last year, Carina chartered this boat to reward some of her staff and brought me along for the ride. It's how we first met Orion. For a few months after that, when I thought he was just Carina's neighbor, he was also my friend. The first person to call me on any bullshit I threw his way.

"I thought this is a business trip."

"It is. But I'm confused. I don't know what he wants from me." I filled them in on what happened after the dinner at Coastline and when I cooked for him.

"Have you tried asking him?"

"It's not that simple." The cheese is as perfect as it'll get, so I put it in the tiny fridge and move on to the plate of fruit. But the dragon fruit doesn't look the way I want.

"Explain that to me," he says.

"I've already kissed him, and he put me into a cab when his hotel room was right there. If I ask him if he wants to date me and he says no, then I'm still spending the next eight months working with him. I don't want my rejection staring me in the face every day." I don't mention that I looked at his social media again. This time it wasn't a picture of him, but that same woman, Lena Darlington, posted a picture of some tacos and tagged him. I'd been so excited that he'd taken my suggestion and all the updates he'd sent me, but it felt twisted to know he was with someone else. I don't think they're dating—she mentioned a work trip in the caption—but she's enough of a mystery to me that I'm concerned about his loyalties.

"How drunk were you when you kissed him?"

"Drunk enough to need a cab. Not drunk enough that we couldn't have a conversation about consent." I lean against the counter because I'm out of things to do with my hands. "And I don't understand why he seemed so upset about me cooking at your place." He left quickly after that.

"People don't like being lied to, Haley." Orion crosses his arms over his chest.

"I know. I never said it was my place. I just implied it."

"If he was just your business associate, he wouldn't care."

Orion shrugs. "You can learn a lot about a person from their house. He probably thought he saw a part of you and it was a lie. He cares."

"Fine. I'm still not asking him anything. I made a move, and he rejected it already. The ball is in his court."

"Okay. Fair enough. I got your back, you know that?"

"I do. You're a good friend. Thanks."

"You and Carina are good, right?" he asks.

I'm startled. "Yes, why do you ask?"

"You just seem a little distant lately."

"We're fine. I was with her when she got her new tattoo. You taking up half her time is an adjustment. I'm giving you both space. Plus, searching for new clients is more work than retaining them. I'm busy."

"Great, glad that's settled."

"We're good." I don't think he believes me. I'm not even sure I believe me.

I hear voices on the deck, so I follow Orion up the steps as Ransom hands Carina a bottle of wine.

"You really didn't have to," she says.

It takes a few blinks for me to realize that it is him. He's wearing board shorts and a Coastline Beach House sun shirt. I spot the Nebula Athletics logo near the hem. I wonder if he remembers it's Carina's brand. I didn't expect him to wear a suit on the boat, but I also didn't think he'd look like he fits in so well.

"It was nothing. I thought Haley might like this one," he says as I step into the sunlight and he turns to me.

Carina is impressed. "He knows what wine you like."

It doesn't mean anything and he probably doesn't know how to show up somewhere without a bottle of wine. "Everyone knows what wine I like," I say. "Now that you've met Carina, this is Orion Edwards. Orion, this is Ransom West."

"Pleasure." Ransom reaches for Orion's hand to shake.

I wait for any indication they're going to have some sort of manly show of strength. I'm sure it happened when Orion met Beckett. But they both just smile and let go after a second.

"Welcome aboard. We're almost ready to push off if you're good?" Orion looks between Carina and me.

"I'm all set," I say. This is old habit for us at this point. I go with them as often as they invite me. I'm used to staying out of the way while Carina and Orion prepare the boat. "Ransom, I'll give you a quick tour."

"Of course." He follows me below deck.

"Here's the galley. Everything here is something I brought, so help yourself to whatever snacks you want. The head is there, and if you need to change or anything, the smaller cabin is a good choice. You probably want to avoid the primary. They spend a lot of time in there."

"Right," he says, getting the hint. "This is a nice boat."

I wasn't going to say anything, since I assume Ransom has been on far fancier ones. Even if he hadn't grown up with wealth like I thought, he's now friends with people who rent entire islands. Someone has to own a superyacht.

"Yeah, she's Orion's baby. It's surprising he lets Carina touch her at all." There was a time when he wouldn't want a guy he'd just met to come aboard. It shows how much he has loosened up over the last few months that he even offered. I look around the cream interior at the small shelf with a few sailing books and pictures of the two of them.

"But the name? The *Twisted Rigging*? Should I be concerned something will go wrong?"

I've often wondered about Orion's naming strategy between the boat and his charter company, Lost Craft Charters. "No, he's incredibly good at this. He has tons of experience. Orion just likes to laugh in the face of danger. That type of thing."

"I'll bear that in mind," he says with a smile that shows off his dimples.

He's removed his sunglasses, and I want to lose myself in his green eyes. Since the end of our dinner the other night was awkward, I was worried about what it would be like once we were here with my friends. But everything about him now makes me feel at ease.

I open the bottle of sparkling rosé and pour us each a glass. "What about the two of them?" he asks.

"Carina might have some later, but Orion can't drink and sail." The boat shifts, and I motion for us to head up to the deck.

Carina takes the lines off the dock while Orion steers the boat from the helm. He's relaxed as he does it, completely in his element, with his chin-length hair blowing in the breeze. The two of them call out distances to each other, while Ransom and I get comfortable on opposite bench seats.

Once we make it out to the Gulf of Mexico and Carina has raised the sails, I speak up. "What's the plan for the day?"

"I thought we'd go to the spot where we went the first time I took you two out. It should be good this time of day, before places get crowded," Orion says.

"It's beautiful. You'll love it," I assure Ransom.

He shrugs. "Works for me. I'm looking forward to seeing Wendell Beach from a different perspective."

"And Haley just wants to be out on the water," Carina says. She settles in with her back against Orion's chest as he leans on the bench behind the helm. His arms wrap around her as she steers. I have no doubt the two of them will be locked in that position for a long time over the next few weeks on their trip. Since their relationship became public, they can hardly keep their hands off each other.

"We brought paddleboards. Have you done it?" I ask. I'm almost testing Ransom. I can't imagine dating a guy who doesn't want to spend all his time on the water. Maybe if I find a fatal flaw in him, I'll be able to move on and won't have to ask any direct questions.

"I'll give it a try," he says.

"Didn't you two meet in the Maldives? You didn't paddle-board there?" Orion asks. "That's basically all Sienna and Haley did as far as I heard."

"That and swimming with whale sharks," Carina adds in. "Which takes so much skill and bravery."

"Right! And didn't they go deep-sea fishing and then prepare the catch with the chefs? Haley, did you tell Ransom about that technique you taught those very experienced chefs?" Orion asks.

"Very subtle, you two," I say. Those things did happen, but they are just talking me up to impress Ransom because I never will.

Carina turns her head to look at Orion who smiles lovingly down at her. I look across to Ransom whose expression is so neutral, I wonder if it's the same one he wears when he fires people or rejects a business proposal.

"I'm going to sit on the bow." I stand and inch my way to the front of the boat.

"Sure," Orion says. "Just watch the boom."

"Got it!" I'm always careful of the long beam that runs along the bottom of the sails, but Orion is always concerned about safety. Since he deals with so many tourists, he's seen too many almost-misses because people don't listen to him.

When I get to the front, I realize Ransom is behind me. I sit with my feet dangling over the side and hold on to the metal railing in front of me. He sits next to me.

"You never did tell me how swimming with whale sharks went," he says.

I look away from the horizon and toward him. I think about the night before the whale sharks, when I was supposed to meet him. Is he thinking about that? Does he feel anything about me not showing up? "It was good. Did you end up going?" That day has my stomach in knots. I felt so guilty for being off with him when Sienna needed me. And I haven't told anyone else Sienna almost had another panic attack right when we were about to jump in with the sharks. I had to talk her down. She was fine a few minutes later and we got the experience we wanted. But I thought everything had gone wrong. That Beckett had damaged her so much she couldn't do the things she loved.

I've never truly regretted not meeting up with Ransom that night because I'll always pick my friend over a guy. And maybe it is for the best since he ended up here. I wouldn't want to work with someone I had hooked up with.

I only wish I could have it all.

"No. Not nearly a good enough swimmer," he says.

"And if you didn't paddleboard, what did you do?" I don't mention the day he spent wooing me. I wonder if he tried to woo anyone else and my skin prickles with waves of jealousy. I feel seasick for the first time in my life. He's swept my sea legs away from me.

"Loads of things. I spent a lot of time on the jet skis and went parasailing. The resort had a whole itinerary of activities set up for us. I didn't have to think or plan anything. Someone showed up and told me we were taking dance lessons."

"You must have been miserable." I pull out my phone and film the water and the way my feet dangle over the side of the boat. I'm careful to keep Ransom out of the shot since I didn't specifically ask him for permission. And I never feature anyone in my content unless they are a permanent fixture in my life. This is just B-roll that I can never have enough of.

He looks at me with a Cheshire cat smile. "There was one day that wasn't so bad."

I want that to mean all my fears about him should burn away. That I should feel stable again.

But I can't look at him right now. I can't talk about that day. Not here on Orion's boat where I'm stuck if I get rejected and we can't do anything if I'm not. My worst fears repeat in my head, and I can't get them to stop.

"This trip will be worth it, I promise." I bring us back to the present moment, instead of dwelling on the past. "Carina is really influential in Wendell Beach and Orion is charming to everyone." Maybe I can turn the conversation to the resort and the restaurant. Back to safe territory.

"I don't mind being so disconnected today."

He can't say that lightly. Every time we've talked in the past few months, he's been working. Except for when he's calling me about cooking. We're separated by so many time zones, and he always answers me right away. Even if my email or text isn't time sensitive. I hadn't wanted to be too friendly after I kissed him, but he initiated, and I felt like I was in too deep to pull myself out.

"Oh yeah? Your phone's not burning a hole in your pocket?"

"It's in my bag downstairs," he says.

"Didn't want to risk falling overboard with it?"

"Sure," he says. But I feel the way he's inched closer to me.

Without warning, a dolphin breaks the surface alongside the boat. "Oh my god, did you see that?" I shift to get a better look as a second one joins the first.

Ransom joins in my excitement as we call back to Carina and Orion. I start a new video to catch as much of this as I can.

"This isn't fair! I have to steer the boat!" Orion yells as Carina makes her way to the bow. "Hold on to something, princess! I don't want to have to jump in after you!"

"I've never seen them like this before," Carina says, laughing from pure joy.

"Neither have I," I say. The two of us lean over the side, watching as they jump and swim along with the boat. I tear up watching them, amazed by their beauty and grace.

"You okay?" she asks.

"Yes, don't know why I'm getting emotional."

She wraps her arms around me. "I get it. I wish Sienna was here."

"Me too. She'd love this."

The dolphins move on, and at some point Ransom headed to the helm and stands next to Orion. The two of them are chatting amicably.

"Is he trying to impress Orion?" Carina asks.

"I don't know. He has no reason to," I say, wondering what they are talking about. The wind is blowing in the wrong direction for me to be able to hear them. The two of them make quite a pair. They're about the same height and both attractive, even if I've never been interested in Orion. They even have nearly matching sun shirts on and it's hard not to notice the way Ransom's shirt pulls against the muscles I know he's hiding.

"It's because he likes you and needs your friends to like him. Alex has been dismissive at best, outright hostile at worst when I'm at Paradise and mention Coastline."

"He's not interested in me," I say.

She looks at me sideways. "That might have been the case a few months ago, but something's changed. This isn't a 'business sailing' trip. This is 'I like her, and her friends are important, let's not fuck this up' trip."

"I don't know. Maybe. But I don't want him to reject me again any more than I want to be his Florida side piece." This is the same conversation I had with Orion, and close enough to the one I had with Alma. But none of them have been there with me in the moments alone with him. They can't see inside this.

"Do you know if he's dating other people?"

"No, but I can't imagine he's been alone this whole time." She's seen his face. If he's single, it's his choice. I don't know who the woman in the pictures is, but she's someone.

"He probably can't imagine you're single. You don't have to do anything, but talking helps. Telling people how you feel helps. And if you put it on the line and he rejects you, that'll hurt. But I'll be here to pick you up when you need it."

She's right. What really is the worst that can happen? I don't correct her that she won't be here to support me. She's leaving in two days. But I know what she means. Regardless of what happens, I still have my home. And the Foleys will still want me to work on the restaurant. Ransom wouldn't fire me. He's too practical for that.

I look back at Orion and Ransom. I have all day with him. Maybe by the end of it, I'll have figured this out.

thirteen

RANSOM

I prepared for Haley's friends to not like me. I assumed Carina would be hard to impress. Lisa went on at length about how much volunteer work she does when I was in the resort's boutique. I thought bringing the wine and wearing one of her company's shirts would go a long way toward showing her that I'm putting in effort.

Lena even mentioned I should check out her yoga studio. She doesn't know that I have any connection to Carina, but she loves the leggings and the brand on social media. I doubt she's aware of the dynamics of small towns where everyone is connected to everyone else.

"How are you liking Wendell Beach?" Orion asks.

"It's quaint. Not entirely what I expected, but it's growing on me."

"I get that. I moved here last summer. I quickly learned how fiercely protective they are of their own," he says.

"This is the 'don't mess with Haley' speech, is it?" They waited for me to leave the other night, so I'm sure she's given them most of the details. But I wonder how many. If she told them about the kiss at Coastline. If they realize every time I call her it's because I want to hear her voice. I'm fine to conduct most business over email, but I'll call her every chance I get.

"I got it from people when I moved here. It's my duty to pass it on," he says.

We both watch as the women chat at the front of the boat. I want to spend time with Haley, but the moment with the dolphins seemed like something she wanted to share with her friend. I don't need to be involved. Of course I loved seeing the animals, but it felt more important to take care of Haley than to indulge myself.

I could deny I'm interested in her. Tell Orion this is strictly professional. But he might be an ally. Alex doesn't like me on principle. Christian was ambivalent at best. "I like her. But I want to give her space since we work together."

He nods. "Space can be good, so I respect that. But I think you can be honest with her. Tell her how you feel and see if she feels the same. Carina and I can give you time to talk once we get to the anchorage."

"You're not going to tell me to back off or anything?" *Does he know something I don't?*

"No. But I'll be watching. The last guy she dated wasn't good enough for her, but you seem like you'll treat her well. Just be forewarned, if you date her, you'll have to become an expert in photography for her social media. I do it for Carina all the time. It's a great perk really. She poses and I get to stare at her. Win for everyone."

I love everything about that idea. And he makes it sound so easy. Just tell Haley I like her, and we'll sail off into the sunset like Orion and Carina. But I've never told a woman I had feelings for her even when it's been true. My heart has never been exposed. It's uncomfortable and I don't like it. I don't understand why anyone does this willingly, and often.

I want to ask more about the other guy, the one who didn't

deserve her. Haley hasn't mentioned past relationships to me, but I'm curious. Did he hurt her? Does he miss her? She's at the other end of this boat and I miss her.

Orion calls out to Carina for help with the sails since we've arrived at our destination. A few other boats dot the water, but it's open and quiet. Spring break is over, the snowbirds have headed home and school is still in session, so this is their slowest season. This information came up in my research on the area, but I didn't give thought to how it would feel.

After they drop the anchor, Haley pulls out paddleboards and sets them in the water. There is a frenzy of action as cover-ups and shirts are removed and sunscreen is applied. Haley looks at Orion while Carina sprays her back.

"I hadn't seen your updated tattoo yet," she says. "It looks good."

He has several I can see, but the anchor and floral design on his left pec has the brightest ink so it has to be that one.

"Thanks," he replies. "I have to make sure this one knows I'm committed somehow."

"Hey, no fighting on the boat," Carina shouts with a smile.

"I'm not fighting. Are you fighting?" he replies.

"Picking a fight is the same as fighting," she says.

This must be a game.

"Let's get you off the boat then, princess." He picks her up and tosses her on his shoulder before jumping into the water. They both surface a moment later and she swims for a paddleboard while he goes to the lone kayak.

"We're going to head over to the mangroves, if the two of you are going to stay around the boat." Carina points to a cluster of trees along the shore.

"Works for me." Haley waves as they take off.

"All set?" I ask. She's quiet. I know her well enough to know she's hiding something from me. What had she and Carina been talking about? And what was that look at Orion?

"Yes, I can help you get on the board, and then I'll show you how to stand. It's much easier than it looks."

I pull off my shirt and toss it onto one of the benches. Haley freezes and for that second, the time spent in the gym is worth it. Her attraction to me has never been in question. But does she want to do more than just look at me? Right now, if all I get is her attraction and her attention, I'm going to appreciate every second I get it.

I do as she describes and kneel on the board. It takes a couple tries, but I'm able to stand and I take a few tentative strokes with the paddle.

"Perfect. Just like that!" she calls from behind me.

She's gotten on her own board and paddles ahead of me with confidence. She's wearing a beautiful geometric print one-piece that shouldn't be as sexy as it is. I look away, otherwise I'll fall over staring at her ass, thinking about the way I want to take a bite out of it.

We keep the boat in sight but paddle in circles getting closer to the mangrove forest her friends are exploring. "Want to stop here for a moment?" she asks. She sits down and opens the small cooler she has tied on the front of her board. I get close and she hands me the end of her paddle. "If you put this in your ties on the nose of your board, we'll stay together."

The boards make a little raft as we get comfortable sitting. She hands me a can of the Three Bays Brewing golden ale and opens one for herself.

"Cheers," she says.

"Cheers." I take a sip. "Is 'going out on the boat' code for day drinking?"

"Not entirely. Like I said, Orion can't drink, and Carina is always going to be responsible. But it's hot out and you and I aren't working, so why not?"

"You make a compelling argument."

She smiles. "You and Orion getting along okay?"

"We are. He gave me some tips about being new in town," I say.

"But you're not really 'new in town.' You're visiting." She says it in a way that's not fully judgmental, but is curious. She's thinking something else.

"You're right. But my involvement has grown since Beckett is out."

"It's still only temporary," she says.

"You know how restaurants work. We're not opening until December. And after, Spare Capital will be invested for several more years. I'm not leaving any time soon."

This has never been about a one-night stand or a hookup. I wouldn't commit years of my life for something so fleeting. Even before I admitted it to myself, Haley has always been more to me.

I want to get in the water with her and feel what it's like with her legs wrapped around me. We're alone. We could go to the boat and into the guest cabin. But I don't know how long her friends will be gone and I want to take my time.

"Right, that makes sense." She looks off into the distance in the direction her friends went.

"You seem close with Orion." I wonder if there's more to the tension I feel between the friends. Did she have a thing for him before he dated Carina?

"Yes, he's great. Really easygoing most of the time. He's a good friend."

That doesn't explain why she was staring at his chest a few moments ago. "How long have they been dating?"

"Over six months." She sighs. "But it's still new being around them. We met him, and they hooked up right away and he moved next door to her. They continued to see each other but didn't tell any of us for months, even though we were all hanging out. I'm feeling a little petty. We've talked about it and I'm happy for them. But it's weird to see my friend go from single to getting coordinating tattoos almost overnight."

"Coordinating tattoos?" I didn't see any anchors on Carina. I noticed she had some ink, but didn't get a close look. I was too focused on Haley.

"He had the anchor before and got the orange blossoms added. They're her favorite flower. She already had the Carina constellation and got the Orion constellation to match."

I nod in understanding. It's beautiful how they changed their bodies to symbolize their love for each other.

I want that too. Maybe not tattoos, but the commitment.

I reach for her hand. "You know what you should do to get back at them?"

"Have a secret affair?"

I don't mind that idea as long as it's with me. "Don't worry about what they're doing. Let it go. Live your own life."

"You're right. It has more to do with them than it does with me," she says. "Plus, they're going away for a few weeks and Carina needs a vacation. I love that Orion brings this out of her. She's happier."

I'm curious about her reaction. I don't fight with my friends. They fight amongst each other all the time. Georgina picks fights with anyone for any reason. I stay out of it. I don't have the time or energy to deal with any of it. When they are fighting, walls are built. People are blocked on social media only to be unblocked later. And far too often there are long crying sessions I hear about for hours.

This isn't any of that. There's no drama here. She clearly loves Carina and is putting her friend's feelings above her own. My instincts tell me to do something to protect Haley. But I don't know how to help. She's protective and cares about them. Anything that hurts them would only hurt Haley.

We float, letting the wind and currents drift us around. Haley visibly relaxes in a way I've never been able to. She tells me stories of growing up in Wendell Beach and the mayhem she and Carina got up to during the summers.

I should feel aimless drifting. We're not headed anywhere on purpose. But it has the opposite effect. This time on the water is circling me closer to her.

I take a few mental pictures. I'll return to this moment and this place when I draw next.

On the sail back to Wendell Beach, I let Carina and Haley spend time together, while Orion tells me about the trip to the Bahamas they have planned. They'll be back before my next trip out here, so I see the irony in giving Haley time with her friend, when Carina already has so much more time with Haley than I get. But all I want is for Haley to be happy. I watch her from time to time, excited to see her smiling and laughing. And occasionally, she sees me watching her and smiles at me.

I've never felt this way before. It's amazing and terrifying and I can't wait to get her alone.

We get to the marina and I reluctantly put my shirt back on. I'm not ready to say goodbye to Haley. I look to Orion, hoping he realizes I didn't have enough time with her. He exchanges a meaningful glance with Carina, who nods.

"I know we drove you, Haley, but we're going to stay here and go over our prep lists one more time. Are you fine to walk back?" Carina asks.

She looks intently at the shoes she's putting on. "Sure. You'll bring my cooler by tomorrow?"

"No problem," she says.

"Is your car at your place or…" I ask Haley.

"No, I parked at their house," she says.

It's still hot as fuck out so I wish this happened a different way, but I'll take the chance I get. "I'll walk with you," I offer.

She looks up at me. "You don't need to. Take the shuttle."

"I'll walk." I extend my hand to help her stand. She takes it. "You can drive me to the resort from there." *Please don't be done with me the way I'm not done with you.*

"Okay, that's fine. I was going to stop by the pier and get ice cream."

"Sounds like a plan," I say. I can't remember the last time I had ice cream.

We walk along the streets toward Carina and Orion's house. Every few moments she tells me some bit of local lore about who lives where, or which houses they were convinced were haunted growing up. I don't add much—I just like listening to her talk.

Once we get to her SUV, she unlocks it and we toss our bags in the boot. I almost make the mistake of getting into the driver's seat.

"You're not one of those guys who can't handle a woman driving, are you?" she asks, playfully.

"No, I truly forgot which side you drive on over here," I say.

I climb into the passenger seat—aware that I smell terrible. I'm covered in seawater and sweat. Even when we were in the Maldives, every two hours we were freshening up for something. I didn't stay dirty for long. But Haley doesn't seem to mind.

With the air conditioning blasting, she drives me through town. As I assumed she would, she takes side streets, until she pulls into a car park around a condo building.

"Is this where you live?" I ask.

She nods. "Yes. My sister, my cat, and I are on the third floor."

"There's a cat too?" I ask. She's never mentioned one.

"She hates people." She nods. "I didn't think you cared about my apartment or my cat."

If it's important to you, then I care.

"Am I going to meet her?" I ask. We're here anyway. The pier is a few blocks away and Coastline is close as well. She was this close to me the whole time and I had no idea.

"Maybe. After ice cream."

"Okay." I step into the street. It's late afternoon and humid and hot. I follow Haley past several shops until I see the beach. We arrive at a small storefront with a teenager managing the till.

"It's all locally made so you can't go wrong," Haley says as I examine the menu.

I pick one at random and get a cup while Haley gets a cone.

"Come on, let's walk to the pier." She takes a few licks of her cone and I have to adjust my shorts.

We've spent all day in the sun and on the water, but it's still not enough for her. There is a promenade out to the pier over the water. She takes the lead and we walk to the end. She looks around, like she's the new one instead of me. I'd wanted to see this through her eyes and now instead of looking around, I can't keep my eyes off her.

She looks down at the water over the railing. "I always hope to see something interesting. Some rare fish or a turtle. Maybe a small shark," she says.

"How often do you come here?" I ask.

"Almost every day."

She grew up here. Anyone else would take it for granted. This place is a piece of her. "I find that hard to relate to."

"Really? There's not one thing in your life you love so much that it's a part of your every day?" she asks.

I rack my brain. My schedule is so busy, there's little I can count on every day. "I go to the gym."

"Because you love it? Or because you think it makes you sexy."

"Your words, not mine, darling," I say.

"Well?"

I think for a moment. "I don't do it every day, but I try to talk with my family most days. Not all of them. But at least one person."

"Loving your family is the bare minimum," she teases.

"How often do you see your parents? All the way on the mainland?" I ask.

"Not nearly often enough."

"And your siblings?"

"Again, not nearly often enough. Even though we live

together, my sister is a nurse and our schedules don't match. And Caleb only a few times a year, but we talk plenty."

I look at my watch. It's almost half five. "Is she working now?"

"Yes, she's on days this week. She'll be back in a few hours." She finishes her ice cream and looks into my eyes.

"Guess I should meet your cat," I say with a smile.

fourteen

HALEY

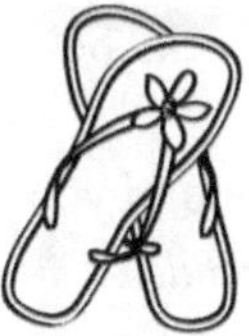

I SHOULD BE NERVOUS ABOUT SHOWING RANSOM MY PLACE. Something shifted today. Neither one of us has mentioned the restaurant, and while I regaled him with tales of Wendell Beach history, it was about sharing stories of my past with him. This isn't a work trip. There's no professional reason for him to be in my home.

We grab our bags from my car. The resort is right around the corner. He probably wants to head to his room to shower. We haven't discussed how long he'll stay. But I hope this isn't a quick tour and a wave goodbye.

I'm glad I spent time with Carina today. She told me everything she's excited about for the sailing trip and how it feels good to walk away from Nebula Athletics for a month. She'll have internet sporadically and wants me to text her whenever I can. But she needs time to disconnect from the world. I'll be here when she gets back.

Now, I'm excited for the time I get alone with Ransom.

I step inside my apartment and take off my flip-flops. We'd rinsed our feet when we left the beach, but they are still grainy. In the air conditioning, my body feels different. There's lingering salt from jumping in the gulf mixed with my coconut-scented sunscreen. Everything is tight and hot, but that might also be Ransom in my small space.

He removes his shoes and looks around. I wait for him to say something. I trust him enough to not be overly judgmental about its size. He might have more money than I can dream of, but he's not as pretentious as I once thought he was.

"Where's the cat?" He peeks behind the couch as if he'll find her there.

"Lor doesn't like strangers. If you stay a while, she might poke her head out." *Please stay a while.*

"I look forward to it." He steps into the kitchen. "How do you cook anything here?"

"It's a pain. I wash a lot of dishes as I go. And try not to drive my sister crazy." I have a two-foot section of countertop that isn't covered by appliances or a dish rack. I'm lucky if I can spread out one cutting board and the ingredients I need.

He smiles. "I like it. It suits you."

My chest warms at his approval. It's cozy here. Everything is dated, but I like the bright orange tile on the floor, the mish-mash teal backsplash, and walls that have been repainted a hundred times that are currently a shock of bright yellow. We've hung art on every wall space available. Paige can't help herself—she buys something every time we go to a community art show.

"I had an interesting conversation with Orion today, while you and Carina were watching the dolphins." He leans casually against the sink with his hands in his pockets.

I take my spot across from him next to the counter. The one section of tile I've spent more time in than any other. "Oh, really?"

He's going to explain himself in a moment, but I can't imagine where this is going. I appreciate Orion trying and the advice he gave me, but those men have extraordinarily little in common.

"He told me I should be honest with you, about wanting to be more than friends and colleagues with you."

My heart jumps. I thought I had missed my chance. "Um. Yeah. That is something you should be honest with me about." I don't know how to make sentences anymore. I'm not just leaning to match his stance. I need the counter to keep me upright.

He steps closer. "Is that something you'd want?" I can smell the seawater on his skin. I'm used to this scent. But on him it's better.

"I thought you wanted to keep this professional. That what happened before didn't matter." I want his answers out in the open. I don't want any misunderstandings. I want to be sure of what he's thinking.

"That's normally how I operate. It's neater. But with you, I can't. I haven't stopped wanting you, Haley." His eyes are intent on mine.

"At all?" I ask, my voice quiet. Is he saying what I think he's saying? That he wanted me even when he showed up all those months ago and I was so confused to see him? When he said this was a coincidence?

He steps in closer and cups my cheek, holding me so I'm looking into his emerald eyes. "Not for a second."

"I didn't know." Our lips almost touch. This kiss will be different. We don't have to say goodbye. We don't have appointments to keep or anything stopping us from moving to my bedroom. Or shower, preferably.

"Do you still want me?" he whispers.

I nod and his lips touch mine.

It's nothing like before. Any uncertainty we had is gone. This is slow and precious, like we're taking our time to learn each other. Like we have all the time in the world to explore.

I press my body into his and he steps us into the counter. We get bolder—my tongue delving into him because I want more, and he does too. My hands go around his back to feel his strength and pull him to me because I've been keeping my distance from him, and I don't have to anymore.

He kisses my neck and his hands sweep down my sides to lift the hem of my cover-up dress.

"God, you taste good," he says.

I laugh because I haven't stopped thinking about the shower I need.

He lifts me up and sets me on the counter and steps between my spread legs. I can feel his hardness against my center, and I crave more from him. I moan as his hand travels up my thigh until he's almost at my swimsuit.

Then a key turns in the front door.

"Shit. She's early." I push him away enough so I can jump off the counter and angle my body to cover him. My sister will know what she's walking in on, but I don't need her exposed to the evidence.

She steps in a second later. "Haley, I got the mail. You have a —" She stops when she sees Ransom. "Package."

"Hey, Paige. This is Ransom."

"Hello. It's a pleasure to meet you," he says, his voice strained.

She's still frozen. She knows everything that happened between us. She knew we were spending time together and how confused I was by him. But neither one of us brings people here often.

"Yes. Great to put a face to the name." She turns to me. "How was sailing?"

"It was good. We stopped by the pier after for ice cream."

"Fun! Did you fish? Any chance you can make dinner?"

"Do you always cook for your sister?" Ransom asks.

"Not always and no fish." I don't want to disappoint my sister. But I want to spend time with Ransom. I open the fridge to find a few vegetables from the farmers market the other day. "How does shrimp sound?" Before either one answers, I remove some from the freezer. "You can stay if you want, Ransom. It won't be anything fancy. You have a change of clothes, right? You can shower. Get comfy." *Please stay so we can finish what we started.* "I'll prep dinner and then shower after you."

"That would be lovely. Do you mind if I check email while you cook?"

"That's fine. Let me show you the bathroom." I take his hand as he grabs his bag, and we go to my bedroom. I shut the door behind me. "You really don't have to stay." My voice is low since I don't want Paige to overhear this.

He kisses me. Deep and hard, pressing me against the three different cardigans hanging on the back of my door. "I'm staying as long as I get to keep kissing you," he whispers into my lips.

"Kissing is good. Bed is good too." God, I want him.

"We don't have to rush anything." His hands dig into my hips like he hates every second I'm not flush with him.

"I know. Let's do dinner and see what happens after." I'm not entirely sure I want to have sex with my sister in the next room, but I can't let this moment pass.

"I like that idea." With a final press of his lips against mine, he heads for the bathroom and turns the shower on.

I step into the kitchen before I can think better of it and join him.

"I interrupted something, didn't I?" Paige says.

"Maybe. But it's fine." I run cold water into a large bowl and place the bag of shrimp in it to thaw.

"I thought nothing was happening with him."

"So did I. But I was wrong." I grab ingredients from the pantry for a grain salad.

"He lives in England," Paige says.

"It doesn't have to be anything serious. We can just have fun while he's here and see what happens." I'm saying that just to say something. I want more than just fun. I want commitment. But I don't know what he wants. With barley added to my rice cooker, I chop some vegetables.

"Okay, I'm clearly getting ahead of things. As long as you're happy."

Paige goes to her room to unwind a bit, and a few minutes later Ransom appears in my doorway. He's wearing jeans and a T-shirt, and I swear I drool. He dressed casually on the boat, but I thought it was a one-time thing. I didn't think he owned anything like this.

"I'm all set. You mind if I work in your room?" he asks. He smirks, my thoughts obvious to him.

"No, that's fine. Everything is as prepped as it can be. I'll shower and then finish up." I follow him to my room and immediately close the door to the bathroom, because if I don't, I'm going to attack him.

I shower as fast as I can, getting the saltwater and lingering sunscreen off me. I towel dry my hair and pull it up into a messy bun so it's not on my face or neck. I'm wearing a short robe and realize my mistake. I don't have any clothes in here, and to get to my closet I have to go into the bedroom where Ransom is.

I take a deep breath. *I need to make dinner. My sister is in the next room. I can't climb on top of him naked and have my way with him.*

I open the door and peek out. He glances up from his seat on my bed, leaning against my pillows and headboard with his iPad on my lap desk like he belongs there.

And he's wearing glasses.

"You wear glasses?" I blurt out because I can't think.

"Blue-light blockers." He takes them off and looks over me slowly. "Are you wearing anything under that?" His accent changes. It's rougher now.

At some point I'll ask him about it, how I notice he's not always refined. But right now I can't form words. I can't believe that this man wants to be here with me. In my tiny, cluttered room when he could have anyone he wants.

I shake my head. *Clothes, Haley.* "I need my closet."

He sets aside his device and stylus and crosses the room to me. He places his hands on my waist, feeling that I don't have any underwear on. "Are you trying to tempt me?" he asks.

His face is close to mine. But if I kiss him, this will be over. We'll be on the bed, both of us naked in no time. "Later. We're hungry." My stomach growls. "We have time, right?"

"I leave in two days." He rests his forehead on mine. Somehow, he wants me. "I meant what I said though. We don't have to rush this."

I wonder if he's trying to make up for the Maldives when all we had was the one night. If this is a promise that this is more than physical. "Then you should probably stop grabbing my ass," I say.

"It's a great ass."

"Later."

He takes a step back with a groan. I grab the dress and underwear I need and return to the bathroom, skipping a bra since the dress will hold everything in place. When I step out, I'm fully dressed. He again looks me up and down and smiles, like he's a little disappointed I'm not naked, but this is a second best option.

"Do you want me to sit out there with you?" he asks.

"It's up to you," I say. "I'd rather have your undivided attention later. If you need to get work done now so you can relax later, that's fine."

He smiles. "I'll sit out there if it won't distract you."

If we only have two days right now, then I'd rather not waste any time with him in a different room. "You're not a distraction."

"That's insulting, love," he says.

Fuck. It's that word, *love.* It's like his voice is connected to my pussy. My desire for him is stronger than it has ever been. But he doesn't mean it. It's just a term of endearment. I don't want him to mean it literally now. *But do I want it someday?*

* * *

I BUTTERFLY the shrimp before tossing them in melted butter and a few seasonings. I question my judgment making a food we'll eat with our hands if we're going to be hooking up later, but my options are limited. At least I wear gloves when handling it raw.

Dinner doesn't take long to make, and Paige comes out for the last little bit to set the table. We almost never have company, so we rearrange things on our table. Ransom sets aside his work to help, turning his charm on Paige. It's different from the charm he used on me. He's honest with her, but polished. He asks about her job and is perfectly impressed by everything she does.

It's charming me.

She tells us about another nurse she'd like to ask out. But the two of them are rarely on the same shifts so she can't tell if she's interested.

"Wouldn't hurt to have a conversation with her," Ransom says. "I'm a fan of telling people you want more with them." He winks at me.

I don't suppress my laugh. "Okay, we have broiled salt-and-pepper shrimp with kale and barley salad."

Ransom looks at his plate and then to me. "I saw the inside of your fridge. How did you just whip this up?"

"I've seen her do more with less," Paige says.

"I have a stocked pantry and freezer. Plus some things lingering from my trip to the farmers market," I say.

Paige digs in while Ransom and I look at each other for a moment. This meal that we share is different from all the other ones we've shared. We're really in my home and my sister is here. This matters to me. I hope it matters to him. I smile before I start eating.

After we eat, he helps Paige with the dishes, giving me the chance to post a few things to my social media. I answer comments and delete the trolls who ask how big my boobs are under my apron. I review what I filmed throughout the day. I didn't shoot as much as I normally do—not wanting to mine for content my day with Ransom. Most of my life is, but occasionally I want something just for me.

"I'm going to head to my room and put in earplugs," Paige says. "It was nice to meet you, Ransom." She doesn't normally declare her earplug usage.

"I'll see you again soon," he says. He's always been cocky, but it's earned. He turns to me. "You still need to get work done?"

I shake my head and close my laptop.

He's on me in a heartbeat as we kiss and stumble our way to my bedroom. I manage to close and lock the door. He kisses down the side of my neck and pulls the strap of my dress off my shoulder with his teeth, before pushing down the bodice so my breast pops out. His thumb brushes over my nipple as I press deeper into him.

"God, you feel good," he moans. He's everywhere at once. His tongue and lips are on my skin, making me wet for him. His fingers leave goose bumps in their wake.

"Bed. Naked. Now," I order. "Please tell me you have condoms."

He freezes. "I don't. Shit."

This is truly one of the most disappointing moments of my life. "Um. We can run to the store. It'll be quick." Was he not planning this?

"Haley, it's fine. We can do other things. I've been tested since my last partner. If you're not on birth control, we can wait."

I place my hand on his chest and push back just enough to look him in the eyes. "You really mean that?"

"Of course. We have tomorrow night." His smile is so reassuring.

"Then we can return to my original plan. Bed. Naked."

He picks me up and turns to walk us both to the bed. His hands are on my ass, and I pull the dress over my head so I'm in my thong and nothing else. He lays me on my back and braces himself over me. I arch into him and pull at the hem of his shirt to get it off. He goes for the button on his jeans, shoving them down and almost falling to get them off his legs. Then we're both in just our underwear.

He pauses for a moment, looking me in the eyes. We didn't bother to turn on the lamp, and it's already dark out so the room doesn't have much light. I don't know why he's hesitant. There is something more in his reaction than wanting to savor the moment.

I push up on my elbows. "Everything okay?"

He kisses me. "Yes. It's been a while since I've been with someone I care about."

What does that mean? Is it a while since he's had sex, or is it that he's been having so much meaningless sex? It doesn't matter. His past doesn't matter. All I care about is him, right now.

I don't know why he picked me. He could have any woman he wants. But he's in my bed and he wants to be naked with me so badly, he practically falls out of it.

I reach down and remove my underwear. "You said we can do other things. What exactly did you mean?"

He smiles his wicked grin. "Oh, I plan to feast on you."

It takes a moment to register he means oral. I haven't been with many men, and none of them have shown enthusiasm for the act. But he takes his time, moving down my body with kisses. He licks one nipple while caressing the underside of the other breast. He switches and I'm aching all over. But mostly between my thighs where I need contact. He traces down my belly until he's so close to where I want him, but he doesn't move. He just waits.

"I've wanted this for so long," he says as he spreads me open with his thumbs.

He's teasing and slow, sucking my clit and caressing me with absolute perfection. It usually takes a while for me to come this way. I'm too in my own head, worrying if my partner likes it or if he's just humoring me. But Ransom clearly loves every second of this. This is as much for him as it is for me. I try to be quiet, but it gets harder when he eases one finger and then two into me.

"Fuck, Haley. Tell me what you like."

"Just like that," I gasp. "Please."

"What are you asking for, love?"

God, his voice is going to kill me. This is what I've fantasized about with him. Since I first heard him ordering a scotch on the plane before I had even seen his face I've loved his voice.

"Please make me come. Ransom, please."

"Anything for you."

He picks up his pace with his tongue on my clit and thrusts perfectly with his fingers. His end-of-the-day scruff adding just enough friction on my thighs that I'm pushed over the edge, crying out in pleasure, failing just a little as I try to be quiet.

I'm panting when I open my eyes. We're not done yet. This can't be done.

He kisses the inside of my thigh and looks up at me.

"Come here." I reach for him because he's too far away.

He lies on top of me, the soft fabric of his boxers rubbing my clit in the most perfect way. I want them gone. I want him inside me. We had a good reason we couldn't. But I can't quite remember it right now.

But there's something else itching in the back of my mind. On my wall is a corkboard covered in postcards from places I've traveled to. The one in the center is from the Maldives, and I specifically bought one with a picture of the resort's spa. I've looked at it every day for months and thought of him. "If we had done this that night—if I had gone back with you... Would we still be doing this tonight?"

He's slow in the way he kisses me, the taste of me sweet on his lips. It's not an answer to my question, but I'll take the way he maneuverers himself between my legs so my thighs are tight around his hips.

This isn't sex, but he's devouring every part of me.

"I don't know," he says finally. "But I'm grateful we're here now."

"Me too." It would have been good that night. I'm sure he had condoms, and we would've had a lot of fun. But as attracted as I was to him that day, this is better. This is a connection. This is real.

"Your pussy might be my favorite thing I've tasted," he says between kisses.

"You're ridiculous." I giggle.

"Yeah?" He moves his hips against me and I moan. "That feel ridiculous?"

I reach between us. "Boxers off."

He grabs my wrist. "No. If they come off, I'll fuck you."

"Don't threaten me with a good time."

"Haley. We can be smart about this."

I move out from under him and sit up. "Fine. At least let me return the favor."

"That wasn't a quid pro quo," he says but rolls onto his back. His fingertips gently brush along my shoulder, making me shiver.

"But I want to."

He looks at me like I imagine he looks at a spreadsheet that's not working. Like he's trying to find where the formula is broken. "Fine. But you're sitting on my face while you do it."

"I've never…"

"Good. I love showing you new things. Get your pussy over here." He pulls off his boxers and his cock springs free. He's hard, and strokes it a few times like he can't wait to have me around him.

"I don't know if I can come again," I say as I maneuver myself so I'm straddling his face and then lean forward to take his cock in my mouth.

He spreads my moisture around with his thumb. "I'm patient," he says softly.

I lick around the head and work him with my hand at the

same time. He continues to feast on me, eliciting groans of pleasure from both of us. This is harder work than I expected—to balance and not collapse onto him. But years of watersports and cooking have made me strong.

Even as I concentrate on the way he tastes on my tongue and the way he fills my mouth, I'm still overwhelmed by how good his tongue feels. He's building a second orgasm faster than I've ever experienced before.

"Oh fuck, Haley. I'm going to come."

I pull him deep to the back of my throat one last time, holding on so he can come in my mouth, his body shuddering underneath me. I expect him to be done with me—to not care that I was so close. But as soon as he's spent, his tongue is back on me and his fingers are in me.

It's waves again, breaking hard against him. He holds on tight and I need his support. It's so much more intense than I've felt before, and I collapse onto his legs. He pulls out of me and caresses my hip. I open my eyes and look back at him.

He's not smirking like I thought he would. He's not gloating that he got me to come twice. There's something in his expression I can't read.

I turn, and he pulls me to rest on his chest while our breathing slows.

"Can I stay?" he asks.

It's a vulnerable question. Was that his expression—vulnerability? Was it more for him with me than it was with others? Does he feel moved the way I do?

"Please." It's a bad idea to try to pack so much emotion into a few short hours because he's leaving, but I don't know how not to.

"I have terrible insomnia. If I sit up and work, will that bother you?" he asks.

"No. I just want you here."

fifteen

RANSOM

I watch Haley as she sleeps. She's curled on her side, one arm reaching for me. She's adorable and sexy and all I want is to lie down, face her, and drift off.

My email is open, but none are important enough to bring into the sacred space of Haley's bed. I tap over to my illustrating app, but I freeze here too. The only image I want to draw is Haley. But I can't do that without her permission.

I set my iPad on the nightstand and do exactly what I wanted in the first place. Fuck it if I don't sleep. A strand of her hair crosses her face. I resist the urge to brush it away. I want to see her whole face, but I don't want to disturb her.

* * *

I wake early in the morning. My body is sore from our night together and the day on the water. I have a conference call between Singapore and London that I need to get to. On a different day, I would go to the gym first, but I don't want to leave Haley a second before I need to. I kiss her forehead and pull myself out of bed. I hope I have plenty of time with her this evening.

She stirs. "You're leaving?"

"Conference call. I'll see you after work?" I need more time with her. I need to be in her. I could stay now and lose myself with her again, but I need to be sensible.

"Yeah." She half presses up on her elbow. "I can drive you to the resort."

"Stay in bed. I'll walk." It's not far. It'll feel good to loosen up moving. I kiss her and she gently pulls me to her. "Haley. I'll see you later. I promise."

She releases me. "Fine." She sinks to the mattress and her eyes flutter closed.

I want to stay with her. If I didn't have the guarantee of tonight, I'd call in sick, something I've never done before. But I dress in my jeans and T-shirt and leave her behind.

* * *

HALEY

Bad news.

ME

Last night was a mistake?

HALEY

Absolutely not.

Carina and Orion are having a last-minute going-away party at Wendell Beach Rum Works tonight.

We'll go. I'll say goodbye and then we can order room service at Coastline.

I GROAN. I don't want to wait any longer to be alone with her. But I can't come between her and her friends.

ME

You'll stay as long as you need. Your friend is leaving. You should be with her.

It's fine if I gate-crash?

HALEY

Yes. You'll know half the people anyway. Just don't tell Beckett.

ME

No chance of that.

I'm not surprised that I'm overdressed when I walk into the distillery. I left my jacket and tie back at the resort, but even with the sleeves rolled up on my shirt, I stand out.

I find Haley immediately in the crowd of people. The place is packed, but I see her talking with Alex and a blond woman who looks familiar. His eyes narrow when he sees me. Haley catches his expression and looks to me. I'll take his glare any day as long as she keeps smiling at me the way she is.

I don't know how she wants to play this. We haven't talked about what we are, besides two people who really want to have sex. But she walks up to me and wraps her arms around my neck. Thank fuck because I need to kiss her.

It's quick, but it's enough. It's a declaration. It doesn't matter what they thought of me before. She's with me now.

"Hi," she says.

"Hi." I brace one arm around her lower back to keep her body flush against mine.

"How was work?"

"Took too long. Wanted to see you," I admit.

"We don't have to stay," she says.

But I shake my head. "This is important. We can wait."

"They'll be up early in the morning, so it won't go long anyway. Let's get you a drink." She takes my hand and leads me to the bar. "Do you want the same thing you had before? Or Alex made a specialty cocktail. Sailor's Warning."

"Really?" But it's appropriate for Orion.

We reach the bar where Christian stands talking with the same blond woman. Haley introduces me to her as Bristol Bailey, his sister.

"It's so nice to actually meet you," she says. "I bartend at Paradise. I saw you there a few months back."

That's where I recognize her from.

"And she's the friend I'm going to the Ashley Ferris concert with," Haley says.

I'm about to ask about her trip again, but Christian interrupts.

"Is this official now?" he asks.

Haley answers before I can. "Not relevant."

I don't know what that means, but I hope it's Haley not wanting to put me on the spot. We haven't discussed anything besides getting into bed.

"If you say so," Christian says. "What can I get you?"

Bristol waves at a redhead and moves through the crowd to greet her.

"I'll take the specialty," I say. I'm willing to try anything to win points with Alex.

"Great choice." He pours a glass from a pitcher and hands the red cocktail to me. "Want to open a tab?"

"Please." I hand over my credit card. "And obviously, her drinks are on me."

"You don't..." Haley starts while Christian runs my card to start the tab.

"Is this really an argument you want to have with me?" I ask her. Up until now, my income hasn't been a factor in our interactions. I've been able to pay for her and claim it's a business expense. But this isn't work related. She's clearly struggling with it, so I lean close. "Let me spoil you."

"Fine," she relents.

We clink our drinks after Christian hands back my card. Before I can have more than a taste, Carina and Orion come over.

"Haley, I have to show you something over here," Carina says, putting her hands on Haley's shoulders.

"Really?"

"Yes."

Carina drags Haley away and Alex appears in the spot she vacated. Christian stands behind the bar and I realize I'm surrounded.

"This is an ambush, is it?" I ask.

"Haley is a sweetheart," Alex says.

"I know."

"She doesn't deserve to be messed around with," Christian says.

"I'm not messing with her." I look at Orion. He's the one who told me to go for it.

He takes my side. "I told you all I handled this yesterday."

"Look, I get you care about her, and I respect that," I say. "You might have reservations. But Haley knows me and you should trust her."

Christian rolls his eyes. "Why are you two so difficult to threaten?"

"Probably because we both actually like the women you're trying to protect," Orion answers.

"How much time do you spend with Beckett?" Alex asks. His eyes narrow at me.

"I don't. Haven't outside of work. And he's off the project now, so I have no reason to."

"Haley mentioned that," Alex says. "Do we want to know how that happened?"

There's a simple answer. He was drunk and rude in front of Will. I don't have to tell any of them it was on rum I gave him, hoping it would send him over the edge.

Why do I think Alex suspects?

"He's an ass. He couldn't hide it. Will Caron has exacting standards for the people he works with," I say.

"Will reached out to me about carrying my rum in his nightclubs." Christian leans back so his physical intimidation is lessened.

"I made sure he tried it when he was here last month. Sent him home with a bottle." I say it like it was nothing. Like it wasn't another step in my plan. "He's a big fan of local and small-batch liquors. It'll be the same at the restaurant."

They lay off me then as I talk about the restaurant. It's the same curious questions everyone asks. What's it called? When is it opening? I answer quickly and direct the conversation back to them. This isn't new for me. I want something from everyone I interact with.

Christian talks about the future of the distillery and his big plans. "We're looking at expanding the facility. But we might need a new location. Unfortunately, our neighbors won't let me buy them out." He leans over to say the last part to Carina who's returned with Haley.

"Ha! Never going to happen," Carina says.

Haley stands next to me and wraps her arm around my waist. "They didn't threaten you, did they?"

"Nothing I can't handle," I say.

"Really? You never did this with Eric," she says to Alex.

"Yeah, but I know Eric," Alex says.

She rolls her eyes. Eric must be the last guy she dated. The one Orion thought didn't deserve her.

My phone vibrates in my pocket. I had turned off notifications, except for calls. I retrieve it and see Lena's name. She's in Singapore and it's the beginning of her workday.

"This is a coworker. I have to take it," I tell Haley. She nods, and I step to the back hallway to get some silence. "Lena."

"Ransom, I've texted you seven times. The other side of the Relevance deal just backed out."

"Shit."

"Did you just swear at me?" she asks.

"Sorry darling, I'm with a vendor. I'll head back to the hotel and log in," I say.

"Good. You're going to need to travel here," she says.

I end the call and hate everything. I know how this goes. I'm not going to get any time with Haley and won't be in Florida for a few months.

Back in the tasting room, Haley looks up and her face falls when she sees me. It's the same expression I have on my face. She knows I'm leaving. I gesture to the front door. She follows me and we step outside.

"I have to work. Things are falling apart with another project. I might have to fly to Singapore instead of London." I *hate* this.

"Okay, um… If that's what you have to do, I understand."

"I don't want to leave," I say. I kiss her because I don't know what to say. I've never felt this way about ending a date to work, even if we planned to have sex.

"When will you be back?" she asks.

"Not for a while. But I'll be in New York the same time you are and I have an apartment there," I say. She said it was a girls' trip and I wasn't allowed, but things have changed. Maybe she will want to see me.

She nods. "We'll figure it out. I can go early or stay late. Even if just for a night?"

I want more than a night. "I'd love that." I kiss her again. "My tab is open. You can charge whatever you want to it and then close it out for the end of the night. Tip well. Hell, the whole party can be on me."

"You don't have to do that," she says.

"I can afford it, and it'll put me in your friends' good graces. It's basically a foolproof investment."

I have years of experience getting people to care about me because I can buy them things. That's not Haley, but I'll try anything with her friends right now.

She looks like she's going to protest so I kiss her instead. "I'll text you every day."

She nods. "Okay. Safe travels."

I let her go and walk to my car.

* * *

I CHECK my card later and see several hundred dollars' worth of charges for the night.

It takes nearly two full days of commercial flights before I'm in Singapore, and I am so jet-lagged it takes me a few days to text Haley. I'm lying in bed when I do. I check the time. Florida is twelve hours behind me. She's likely awake and going about her day.

ME

Hello, love.

HALEY

Hey. Did you make it home okay?

ME

I'm in Singapore. I honestly don't know what day it is.

HALEY

Oh, that sounds difficult. There's great food there. Have some chili crab for me.

ME

I wish. I've barely left the office. I'm exhausted.

HALEY

You should sleep. Call me when you're rested.

ME

Okay.

I want to say more about how I miss her and can't wait to see her. I've been great at text conversations in the past. I know how to keep women at the right distance. They get attached to me enough to get me the connections I want and still feel like it's their idea to let me go as soon as I need to move on. But with Haley, I want to pull her closer. I've never been with someone where I've needed to be honest about my feelings.

I catch up on sleep and feel like a normal person once Lena and I are on a private flight back to London. She sits down across from me as I catch up on emails related to Coastline Beach House. I reach out to PR operations to build buzz in the next few weeks. I see the magazine profiles in my head. Will, Norah, and Haley highlighted, bringing this experience to life. A wave of jealousy courses through me thinking about Haley cooking with the two of them. I want to be there for this. Will is spending more time in Florida as things ramp up, but I don't have a business reason to be there.

"You're making a face," Lena says. "Everything okay?"

I look up at her. "Yes." I haven't told her things changed with Haley.

"You haven't responded to Josephine's invitation to the Hamptons," she says.

I blink. I have no idea what she's talking about. "I don't think I got that."

"You did. I confirmed with Daisy. Your trip to New York was planned around it."

I planned this trip over a month ago. How have I been unaware of something else going on the whole time? I search my email and find the invitation, along with a reminder from my assistant informing me she spoke with Lena about it. Apparently, Josephine is dating an American who owns a house in the Hamptons. They invited a group for a week following my New York meetings.

I don't have a good reason to decline. They won't accept that I want to spend time with Haley, alone. But now I'll be forced to be in a beach house with my ex, her sister, and a few other friends. I like Josephine, but this is going to be a repeat of the Maldives. Everyone too drunk to function while I'm bored and forbidden from working.

"You've been distant the last few months," Lena comments.

"I've been traveling more." I continue to type away on my keyboard.

"It's not just that. Even when you are in London. When was the last time you went to the club?"

"It wasn't long ago." I comb through my memories and realize it was back in winter. I was on the waiting list for the private club for so long. I love going. So why has it been so many months? I haven't even seen the rest of the group in ages. But I don't miss them the way I miss Haley.

I'm not ready to tell her about my relationship. At least not here. I'll talk to Josephine and tell her I'm bringing a guest. I've brought dates in the past. Quick flings that were over before we even unpacked at home. Haley will be different. I've met Haley's friends and her sister. She should meet my friends. I'll give Lena the details at some point.

* * *

A WEEK LATER, I finally get Haley on FaceTime. The time difference between London and Florida is rough but not as bad as Singapore. I need to see her. It's late for me and I'm in bed, but even though we haven't slept together yet, this is a relationship. She's going to be my girlfriend if she doesn't already consider herself so. I don't need to perform "polished" for her the same way I did before.

"Hey, how are you?" I ask.

She sits on her bed. "I'm good. Just busy with my newsletter as always. How are you?" she asks.

It's the first time I've heard her voice in weeks, quite possibly the longest I've gone without it since I first came to Wendell Beach. I didn't realize how much I missed it. How used to her I've gotten. "Tired. But I'll be home for a few weeks, so it won't be so much turmoil," I say.

"Is it nice to be in your own place?" she asks.

I shrug. "I'm used to traveling. A comfortable bed is a comfortable bed. Now, if you were here…"

That makes her smile. "I couldn't travel like that. I need access to a kitchen."

"When we travel together, I'll make sure we stay in a suite with a full kitchen," I say. I can't quite read her face. "What's wrong?"

"Nothing. Or I don't know. The distance thing is weird. I'm adjusting," she says.

I've been busy and she's going about her life wondering if I'm thinking about her as much as she's thinking about me. "I'll be a little freer now. We'll work this out, yeah? You know I like you and you're important to me."

"Yes. I do. But it's good to hear you say it," she says. "It didn't help that Carina and Orion left the next day, so I've just been talking Bristol and Paige's ears off."

"Carina will be back before you know it. And I'll see you in New York next month."

"Right." She shifts and her laptop comes into focus. "I was going to ask you what days you wanted to spend with me so I can change my flight."

"Actually, I was wondering if you can extend a week after the concert. My friends are holidaying in the Hamptons, and I'd love for you to come with me."

She looks back to me. "You want me to meet your friends?"

"I met yours. We'll be staying at my friend Josephine's new boyfriend's family house. We can have separate rooms if that's what you're concerned about…"

"That's not the problem. I'm just surprised."

"I know. It's soon. But you'll be close, and if I'm on holiday, I'd rather it be with you. These people are important to me. Obviously, you can visit me whenever in London. I'd pay for you to be here tomorrow. This is a chance to meet everyone when we're all together."

She looks uncomfortable. "You don't have to do that. I want to see you, and maybe a week away from work will be good for both of us. Can I look at my schedule and get back to you?"

"Of course. And no pressure. We can stay in our room the entire time." I want her to meet them, but I also want to keep her to myself. My time with her is so limited and I want her undivided attention.

"I'm sure that will make your friends like me," she says.

"They'll just think I'm working and boring you with spreadsheets."

"We'll leave your laptop in the kitchen or something."

"That would be unthinkable to them."

"You might be getting overexcited about this. We might not be good at sex together," she says.

"Oral sex is sex, Haley. And we're very good at that."

She rolls her eyes. "So is phone sex *sex*?"

It takes me a moment to process what she said. Haley, my Haley, the woman who is always polished in a way that appears effortless depending on the setting, who is reserved and careful, wants to be naughty on the phone with me? She blushed when they kissed during the very family-friendly film on the plane.

It's not that's she's a prude. She's just not one to take the first leap. But if she's going to trust me with her body and her mind and all of her deepest desires, then I am going to protect them and cherish them with every fiber of my being.

I get hard in my boxers. "It's close enough for us now."

She props her phone up and puts headphones in.

"Have you done this before?" I ask.

"A little," she admits.

That surprises me so much more than it should. "I haven't," I say. Why would I have? I've never missed someone when they weren't around before. I unbutton my trousers and take my cock in my hand. "Tell me where you'd want me to touch you, if you were here?"

Her hand travels to her panties. "Why would I be there?"

"I've already been in your bed. I want you in mine." Did her sheets smell like me after I left? Did they smell like us?

I want my bed to smell like her even when she's not here. I remember the fruity scent she had when I first met her on the plane. The airline gives passengers small fragrance samples. I discarded mine, but she wore hers on the plane and I swear I smelled it when she kissed me at Coastline. Did she buy a full bottle? Should I send her one? Should I have one for here for when she visits eventually? I need a part of her here with me.

"Fine. You'd touch me here." She gives a small tilt to her hips and meets it with a moan.

Fuck. I love that sound when she makes it.

"I can't wait to lick you again." I don't think it's going to take much encouragement for me to get off. Not with her cheeks flushing and her back arching against her pillows. "I'm going to take my time again. Get you worked up over and over before finally letting you come after hours of teasing."

"No," she says. Breathless.

"No?" I repeat. "You want it fast?"

"Don't make me wait."

Good, I like the way she thinks. I stroke myself faster now. I don't care that I can't actually see what she's doing since her shorts are still on, but her hand is moving faster. "Tell me how you want it, love?"

"I don't know. I just want you close."

"You want me over you? Your sexy thighs tight around my hips?"

"Yes!"

"Do you want me to be gentle with you?"

"No," she says.

"You never have to be gentle with me," I say.

It's amazing how many miles separate us, and still we come at the same time.

sixteen

HALEY

MAY

TWO DAYS BEFORE WE LEAVE FOR NEW YORK, I'M AT THE BAR OF
the locals' section in Paradise editing videos. It's been a rough
month since I last saw Ransom. He's busy, and I understand that.
But I feel like we're talking less than we did before. I spend as
much time as I can distracting myself. It's not hard. I'm trying to
track down more meal prep clients and expand my subscription
service. I still have months before my involvement with Coastline
winds down, but I have to look ahead.

I should trust Ransom about us. We haven't established
boundaries, but I have to believe that he wouldn't bring me to his
friend's place if I didn't mean something. But that doesn't stop
the thoughts in my head when it's days between messages.

I wanted to see if I could.

Maybe now that he got me, he's done. Maybe I was just
someone who turned him down and it made him feel things he
didn't like so he stalked me across the globe and as soon as he
saw my tits he was done with me.

I don't know how I feel. I like him and it's clear he likes me.

But what does this mean for him? I wonder if I'm the only person he's with or how committed he is. I haven't seen any new pictures of him with the other woman, but that doesn't mean he hasn't seen her. Even if he wants to be exclusive and define our relationship for the twenty-four hours we were together in person, he could have met someone else. I've seen how fast everything changes. He could be saying those lines about how he hasn't stopped wanting me to a lot of women.

He's reassuring on the phone, and I want to pretend these feelings will last forever. And it's clear we have amazing chemistry. We've masturbated together a few more times and it's great. It feels way more vulnerable with him than being in person. I don't have anything to hide behind when I'm exposing my desires.

Bristol approaches me from the other side of the bar. "You'll never guess who tested positive for Covid."

I look up. "Autumn." She's Christian's wife and is going to the Ashley Ferris concert with us. She's a huge fan of the singer and this trip was supposed to be a gift from Christian to his wife and sister.

"Yep. And the friend she was bringing. It went around graduation or something. Now we have two extra tickets to the concert." She's a teacher and this was the one thing she'd looked forward to as the semester dragged on.

I rub my forehead. "That sucks so much for them. Has Christian already left for his conference?" I'd thought it was strange he was spending so much money on a trip and not going himself. But he has a distilling conference in Kentucky each May.

"Yeah. She doesn't want him to come home unless it gets bad, but it's mild and she's vaccinated. I asked if she needs help with anything, but she says she's fine with Netflix and DoorDash."

She's going to be devastated she's missing this trip. Especially since she wanted to go to an earlier concert but didn't get tickets. "Okay, are we going to sell the tickets?" I ask.

"Or we can offer them to Carina and Sienna," she suggests, adjusting the knot on her shirt.

Carina returned from the Bahamas a few days ago. She's tan and relaxed and even more in love with Orion than she was before. I'm happy for her, I really am. But this last month has been so confusing for me. I wished she was around so many times. With Ransom gone and me not knowing where we stand, I wanted to talk through my feelings with someone. I brought it up a few times to Sienna, but every time, it seemed like she wanted me to drop the conversation as fast as possible. I don't blame her. She went through a rough breakup. She doesn't want to hear about two people falling in love. And I'm increasingly missing Paige. She's working the overnight shift more and crashing on our parents' couch. It just added to my stress about finding a new place to live. I've settled on the likelihood that I'll stay in the same place and try to make it work on a month-to-month lease. Moving is expensive, and I don't need the extra stress.

"Yeah, that would be fun. I don't know what their schedules are like, but we might as well ask." It's better to have them than two strangers next to us.

She pulls her phone from the back pocket of her shorts, and I get a text a moment later.

BRISTOL

Do you two want to go to the Ashley Ferris concert in NY in two days?

SIENNA

Yes.

Obviously. What gods do I need to sacrifice to?

BRISTOL

Just thank my brother and whoever gave Covid to Autumn.

CARINA

I really shouldn't, but what's another few days off work?

SIENNA

Who are you and what have you done with Carina Webb?

Me: Orion has turned her mellow. It's great.

CARINA

I'll work on the plane. I won't be completely detached.

BRISTOL

I'll send Haley's and my flight info so you can coordinate.

"Did I tell you I changed my return flight? I'm spending the week after with Ransom," I tell Bristol.

She looks up from her phone. "No, you didn't. Won't that violate girls' trip rules?"

Girls' trip rules originated between Carina, Sienna, and me in college. We added Bristol a few years ago when she moved to Wendell Beach.

"Not if the trip is already over. I won't meet him until you're on your way to the airport." I decided to leap and spend time with Ransom and his friends. I don't know what I'm getting into, but I want to be with him and know the people who matter to him. Just like he's done with me. The fact that he's invited me should ease some of the anxiety I have about him. But I'm never not going to feel like he's far out of my league.

"It's going better, then?" she asks.

"I think so. The distance is hard when he's so busy, but when we talk it's great."

"Good. You deserve someone great. Maybe the distance is a good thing. Then you're not rushing into a relationship."

She bounces off to take another customer's order while I'm left wondering if we are rushing things.

* * *

WHEN WE LAND in New York two days later, I'm busting with excitement to spend the day with my friends before the concert. We check into the hotel and lounge around, showing each other our outfits and the makeup we have planned until it's time to get ready. I'm helping Carina put some artful rips into her T-shirt when I get a surprise phone call.

"Hi, Will, how can I help you?" I email daily with him, but I'm out of the office. There can't be a restaurant emergency requiring my attention. And if there is…it's not something I'm going to deal with. I've been looking forward to the concert for a long time. I'm not giving it up.

"I'm good. Listen, I'm told I'm playing by some very tricky rules, so apologies in advance," he says.

"Okay?"

"Alma was able to get VIP tickets to the Ashley Ferris concert —the one you're attending tonight. In addition to the two tickets for two of us, she was given an extra five."

"We already have tickets," I say.

"Right. But these are VIP tickets. I'm guessing your seats aren't as good, since these are the absolute best in the house," he explains.

I look at Bristol, who's putting on eyeliner.

"Um…what exactly are you saying?"

"You and your friends are welcome to join us," he says.

"And the fifth ticket?" I have a feeling who gave Alma Blake the tickets and who will be using the last, odd one out.

"Ransom is going to take it. He's in town too. Did you know he's a huge fan?"

"No, that hasn't come up in our conversations. Can I get right back to you?" I hang up the phone and call out to my friends. "That was Will Caron, the mastermind behind the restaurant. His wife, actor Alma Blake, was given VIP tickets to the show tonight and wants us to join them."

"Are you kidding me? That's amazing!" Bristol jumps up and down.

"You're not as excited about this as you should be," Carina says.

"I'm excited. No really, I am. There is a catch." If it were up to me, I would be overjoyed. This would be the best thing to happen. I'll get to spend the entire show with Ransom. But this is a huge departure from girls' trip rules, and they might be upset about that. "One of the extra tickets will go to Ransom."

"There's not enough for all of us?" Sienna asks.

"No, it'll be the four of us, Will, Alma, and Ransom."

"She was given seven tickets?" Carina asks.

"I highly suspect they were given to her by Ransom."

I wanted to see if I could.

They look between each other. "I think we can agree we don't like him doing this on principle, but I'm willing to overlook some red flags for Ashley Ferris tickets," Sienna says.

"Agreed," Bristol echoes.

"I'm clearly in my fuck-it era, so sure," Carina says.

"Great, I'll call Will back."

* * *

A FEW HOURS later as the doors to the concert open, we approach Will, Alma, and Ransom on a crowded street outside the arena. I'm aware of the hundreds of other people around, including one of my bosses, but all I see is Ransom. I play it cool, when I want to jump right into his arms, my legs tight around his waist as he spins me around.

Another time.

"Do I get to threaten him?" Sienna asks as we approach. "I feel like we didn't get to properly vet Orion." Carina shakes her head.

"Don't worry," I tell her. "The guys have already been through it with him. And you've met him. He's a good guy."

"We still get your full attention tomorrow, right Haley?" Carina asks.

"Of course. He'll be around for the show and then it's back to girls' trip rules."

This concert is supposed to be the center of the trip. This should be the time they have my undivided attention. While I'm annoyed Ransom went behind my back to do this—and I'll talk with him about it—I remember when we were on the boat and he let me have a moment with Carina. He knows how important this is. He values my friendships. We have next week together. As much as I'm going to block out the world and only be with him, we have time. I'm unsure about so many things with him, but he gets this.

"Hi," I say when we're finally close enough to talk, and wait for his reaction. He looks me up and down. I'm wearing something so different from what I normally do, jean shorts and a white T-shirt pulled over one shoulder, exposing a pink bralette strap. It's cute and a copy of something Ashley wore in one of her music videos. Any fan will recognize the homage.

"Hi," he replies with a smile. He brings his fingertips to my jaw and lowers his lips to mine. It's brief but a promise of so much more. All my anxieties melt away.

"We really need to talk about what you did," I say.

He smirks in response as I turn to introduce everyone to Alma and Will. She gives me a big hug and mentions how excited she is to try a new recipe I posted.

Inside the arena, the energy is palpable. Through the opener, we're loose and we dance, already having the time of our lives. Then Ashley takes the stage and we all lose our minds.

Will and Alma lean against each other for the entire show.

Carina sends selfies to Orion between songs. I'm here with Ransom and I want so much more from him. He's behind me for most of the set, his arms draped over my shoulders. I worried for a moment about singing and showing him just how much this means to me. Am I exposing too much of my soul?

The lyrics are full of hope and promise and love and it's exactly how I'm feeling.

He looks at me and it's clear he's never heard half of the songs, but his body is warm against mine and I know, deep within my soul, that he cares more about me being in his arms than he does about anything happening on stage.

When the show ends, Alma looks down at her phone. "I'm meeting a friend. Will, I'll see you back at our place?"

"Sure," he says, kissing her.

She hugs all of us and promises Carina she'll order a new sports bra from her.

Ransom whispers something in Alma's ear that I don't catch. But she looks up at him and smiles. "That would be fun. I'll see."

Will addresses the rest of us. "Our place is only a few blocks away. Want to go there for drinks? I also own a nightclub, but it's a little farther."

Everyone looks to me. They know what's going on here. If we go to either place, Ransom will come along. This is supposed to be just us friends. We could go back to our hotel and call it a night.

But Bristol nods. "Yeah, I'm not ready for this night to end. Your place sounds great. I want to make the drink I mentioned."

Alex came up with a custom cocktail for the trip, the Ferris Wheel. Will is sure he has the ingredients and since his first job was bartending, they could have a contest to see who makes it better.

As we walk, Ransom holds my hand. It's nice to be with him, but we haven't been alone together since he left my bed all those weeks ago. I can't ask him about us. I can't ask if we can put a label on things. Not until we're alone.

Will and Alma's apartment is small, but not crammed or cluttered like mine. It's set up for entertaining small groups like us. I look around at the pictures on the walls of the two of them. One catches my eye of Alma in a knee-length white dress and a flower crown. Will wears a suit as they kiss on the street.

Bristol and Will move around the kitchen measuring ingredients and doing math aloud to make the drink in a batch. Sienna is more than a little interested in the drink. She's always loved the custom drinks Alex makes for her. It's been a part of their friendship since college.

I sit on a barstool with Ransom at my back rubbing my shoulders, watching the two of them work. "Are you going to join in?" I ask. "Didn't you work at a bar?"

He kisses my neck. "Yes, I was a server at a pub. But it was mostly pulling pints. Let them make the cocktails."

He engages with Carina and Sienna. Asking how they enjoyed the show and about Carina's sailing trip. They both open up with him, and I'm content to soak in the activity around me.

Will passes out the drinks and we toast to the night. I lean into Ransom, feeling warm. I have my friends with me and this man who I care about and things feel like they are looking up.

The front door opens, and the sound of women laughing carries into the kitchen. I turn and we freeze.

Alma walks in with Ashley Ferris.

"Hey!" Alma says. "I met up with Ashley backstage and invited her back. That cool with everyone?"

Ashley is still wearing her stage makeup, but she's in ripped jeans, a white T-shirt, and an oversized cardigan. "I want a night away from tour stuff," she explains.

The door closes behind them as a man follows them in. I recognize him from on stage. He played guitar in her backing band.

"We can be cool," Carina says.

My brain is still trying to catch up to what is happening.

Ransom squeezes my shoulders. "We can talk about things besides the tour," I respond.

Bristol stands with her mouth open, so Carina nudges her. Bristol quickly smiles. "We're very chill people."

"Totally," Sienna agrees.

"Great. You must be her husband," Ashley greets Will. "She said you make a great cocktail, and I really need a drink."

Will takes this in stride and makes another round of the Ferris Wheel. We introduce ourselves. Of course she recognizes Carina and swears her leggings are the only ones she wears. Tristian, the man with her, is acting as her temporary bodyguard. He has dark hair and would be in the dictionary next to the entry for brooding rock star. He keeps his eye on Bristol, and I want to jump in and say she's harmless and not a threat. She's just trying to keep her cool.

"Why don't we go out to the terrace?" Ransom says to the men.

"You okay with that, Ash?" Tristian asks.

"It's fine. The door is locked and no one saw me come into this building. You can relax," Ashley says. He grunts.

"Have fun, love." Ransom kisses my neck.

I don't want to be apart from him, but this is a once-in-a-life-time opportunity. So he bows out, just like he did on the boat.

The rest of us pile onto the couches in the living room.

"How do you two know each other?" I ask, surprised I'm able to find words. Alma didn't give any indication during the show that she knew Ashley, or when we talked about the concert when she was in Wendell Beach.

The two of them exchange a look and then laugh. "We can't go into details," Alma says. "But we met recently and hit it off."

"I'm trying to make sure Alma doesn't go through what I did when I got famous. Granted, she has an amazing husband so hopefully there won't be news stories about her love life every five minutes." She turns to Alma. "I'm so glad you made it tonight. It's so much more fun performing when I know I have a friend in the audience."

"So, you got her the tickets?" I ask. Maybe this wasn't Ransom after all.

"No. I mean, I would have if I had known she wanted to come."

"The tickets came from where you think they did," Alma says. "And we're not allowed to talk about it for some reason."

"Okay, girls' night rules. No talking about men," Sienna asserts. She's always comfortable being the life of the party. "We're normal people with normal jobs getting to know each other."

"Oh! Drinking game!" Alma says. "Never have I ever. I'll go first. Never have I ever performed in front of fifty thousand people."

Ashley rolls her eyes and then drinks. "Fine, never have I ever gone cliff jumping."

Carina looks up with a jolt. She had just posted pictures from Eleuthera. "Wait, how did you know?"

Ashley shrugs. "I told you I'm a fan."

Carina drinks. "Never have I ever swam with whale sharks."

Sienna and I both drink. We continue to go around, using each of our turns to share a fun fact about a different person. Ashley is instantly obsessed with everything Sienna has done in her graduate program, and Alma can't stop asking Bristol about working at Paradise and the kayak trips she takes around the state.

We go through hours and rounds of drinks without discussing the men in our lives more than a passing mention.

"Ashley, what's something you miss?" Alma asks as the night lingers on, the topic turned from fun to a little melancholy.

"Honestly, normal things like this. Right before I moved to

LA, I was a camp counselor. I really miss those long nights spent by the campfire. I did some of my best writing that first year. I've grown as an artist, sure. But back then the emotions were raw and fresh. I haven't been the same since."

I look out to the terrace where Ransom is sitting. I can only see his profile, but I know he's been checking in on me every so often. I can feel his eyes on me. I understand what she means. The concert would have hit differently if I wasn't in the process of falling in love. How long do I think I can hold on to this?

Seventeen

HALEY

Brunch the morning after is mimosas and espresso martinis on a patio with overpriced eggs. I've traveled to enough big cities, but I prefer the quiet of Wendell Beach. The crash of waves soothes instead of the aggravation of car horns. I'm not the only one. Sienna has a chip on her shoulder about how Boston is better and gets into a fight with Orion over it through Carina texting him. We've forgotten the no-boys rule.

After last night, our other plans are anticlimactic. We can't talk about the undercurrent of energy we all share. We signed nondisclosure agreements last night—we're willing to protect Ashley. But there are other upsides. Autumn would be devastated to know she missed this. It's a kindness that we can't tell her. Even with her precautions, Ashley didn't open up about herself. We got hints. Enough that I'm confident most media stories about her love life are wrong. Our game of sharing felt like we could go on for days. It felt like the first page of a real friendship. I won't get my hopes up. Not because I don't think she's genuine, but we have such different lives. She followed my social media and promised to share my content.

I could feel Ransom's brain spinning when he walked us back

to our hotel last night. I waited for him to say something about exposure or increased revenue, but I cut him off before he did. "Not everything has to be monetized."

"Says the woman who films nonstop." It was a tease and I took it in stride, shutting down the camera app.

"This was enough for me. If nothing comes of this and we never speak to her again, I'll still be happy. Thank you."

He squeezed my hand three times. "I didn't do anything."

I didn't call him out on his lie. If this was what his secrets and his scheming led to, I wasn't going to complain. I should look closer, and maybe I will in a few days. But right now I don't want to know what other manipulations he's done.

I'm on my second mimosa when he texts me.

RANSOM WEST

What's your dress size?

ME

Why?

RANSOM WEST

We're attending a gala later this week with a black-and-white dress code. I'm sending my assistant to pick you up a dress.

I bite my lip. If he had told me, I would have made time to go shopping. But Ransom will spend more money on me than I will ever spend on myself. I'm not interested in him for his money, but I can't deny it's a nice perk. I don't need him to spoil me, but I can accept a dress.

I send him the number.

RANSOM WEST

Shoe size?

ME

I only wear Louboutins.

RANSOM WEST

I know you're kidding, but I'll buy you a pair.

ME

You know this doesn't matter to me.

RANSOM WEST

Yes. But I can do this for you, and so I will.

"What's that look for?" Sienna asks.

I glance up. I was biting my thumbnail as I texted. *Shit.* I'll need a manicure if we're doing something fancy. The kitchen turned my hands rough, and I didn't think about it before. "Ransom is buying me a dress for a black-and-white party. He's asking for my sizes."

Carina's eyebrows rise. "I thought you two haven't even slept together yet, and he's buying you clothes?"

"Depends on your definition of sex." I tuck my phone into my bag.

"You're getting the full Cinderella treatment, then?" Bristol asks.

"I don't know about that," I say. "It's one dress for a specific occasion." Which I guess is Cinderella.

"Has he sent you other gifts?" Carina asks.

These questions are simple, but their tone makes me feel like I'm being interrogated. "He sends flowers."

Sienna scoffs. "He probably has his assistant do that."

That doesn't make me feel better, especially since he just said he was sending his assistant for the dress. "Either way, no, he hasn't sent a ton of gifts."

"I realized after the fact that Beckett sent me gifts when he was cheating. Maybe it's a good thing you're not getting many." Sienna's tone is almost whimsical.

I open my mouth to defend Ransom, but I come up short. I don't think he'd cheat on me, but we haven't talked about being exclusive. "Beckett and Ransom aren't the same person." That I believe. I am confident Ransom doesn't secretly admire Beckett or what he did. They aren't having clandestine happy hours together. They had plans for drinks once and Ransom didn't even go. *And then Beckett showed up to dinner already drunk.* Did Ransom do that on purpose? I'm realizing the extent to which he can manipulate things, and I wouldn't put it past him. "They don't get along."

"That doesn't prove anything. How do they know each other?" Sienna asks.

Carina and Bristol look at me confused. I don't understand why. I don't understand Sienna's question. Then it hits me—I never told Sienna the restaurant's location. She doesn't know I was working with Beckett.

"Okay. Hear me out. I didn't tell you this at the beginning because I didn't think my involvement would be as in-depth as it is. And I didn't want to upset you."

"What the fuck, Haley?" Sienna sits up.

"The restaurant I'm working on is at Coastline Beach House. Beckett was involved until he was fired."

"Are you fucking serious? The one with Will?"

I nod.

"Help us understand why you're so upset, Sienna," Carina says in her most soothing, end-of-yoga-practice voice.

"I'm upset because your new boyfriend is hanging out with my piece of shit, two-timing asshole ex-fiancé." She raises her voice, and while we're outside and there is plenty of street noise, the table next to us gives us a collective dirty look. "He took six years of my life from me. And I find out it wasn't for someone he cared about. She was just convenient. Now you're telling me he's working on an exciting project with Alma Blake's husband and Haley's boyfriend. He can rot in hell and the only thing I want to hear about is him rotting in hell. Did you know about this?" The question she directs to Bristol and Carina.

They both nod.

"I'm sorry," I say. "I didn't think it was a big deal at the beginning and then we kept calling it 'the restaurant' and it doesn't even have a name yet and I forgot you didn't know." I rearrange the silverware on my empty plate. "Ransom hasn't liked Beckett since I got involved. I told him that he was a cheater, and he believed me."

"Oh, I'm so glad he believed you when you told him something you witnessed with your own eyes. That's really big of him. So brave. How did Ransom get involved anyway?" Sienna asks. "How can you trust him?"

"Because he's given me no reason to doubt him. And he knows Will. That's how he's involved."

"I thought he came because of you," Bristol says.

"No, that's what I thought too at first. But it's a coincidence," I say.

"Hell of a coincidence," Carina repeats what she said when I first told her about him back in February, all those months ago.

"So, you're saying he meets you on a plane, happens to come to our resort for the day and has a spare spa package. Then he happens to invest in a restaurant in your hometown, by coincidence?" Sienna asks.

"The resort thing was obvious. That was to get with me. But Coastline was a coincidence." I flash back to when I first saw him in the conference room. "He's wanted to work with Will for a long time. It had nothing to do with me."

They all look at me like I'm crazy.

"Or did he just say that to not come off as a stalker?" Carina asks.

"Why would he do that? We didn't even hook up in the Maldives." Ransom could get any woman he wanted. Not just because he's rich and attractive, but he's a thoughtful and caring person. He wouldn't have done this just to get with me.

"Wait, I thought you did. What happened exactly?" Bristol asks. "He didn't make a move on you?"

"It's complicated," I say. Sienna is fuming. "We spent the day at the spa and planned to go to his island after dinner. But I decided to spend time with Sienna instead."

Bristol can tell something isn't adding up but doesn't press. Thankfully, Carina is quiet on the matter. I don't want Sienna to know I told her about the panic attacks.

Sienna drains her espresso martini and signals for another. I hadn't told her about the plans to go with him. She was so upset when I got to our villa, I didn't mention it. Girls' trip came first. "So, let's get this straight. He manipulates a ton of things to spend the day with you in the Maldives. And he was behind the tickets and meeting you know who last night. But you believe him when he says he didn't come to Wendell Beach just to see you again?"

I can't argue with them. I need to talk with Ransom first. "So what if he did? What's the point of this?" My chest is tight and my stomach churns and it's not the alcohol.

"We want you to make an informed choice," Carina says.

"Like I said the other day, it's good that you're not rushing into things," Bristol echoes.

"I don't understand why you'd believe him when he says things like that," Sienna says.

"I believe him because I believe people when I ask them a direct question and they give me an answer." My gaze turns to Carina, and she freezes.

She looks guilty and hurt, and I know she didn't mean to hurt me when she lied about her relationship with Orion. I'm not mad about it anymore. But I'm feeling a little petty. I don't understand why they can't support my relationship the way they support hers.

"Haley, I'm so sorry we lied to you," she says.

"I know." I stand up from the table. "I don't think I can do this right now." I don't know what to think anymore. They've poisoned my mind, and I won't be able to rest until I get answers from Ransom. "I'll send you money later if you cover my portion."

My phone vibrates and a picture text comes through from him. It's a black gown with an off the shoulder tulle collar. It's pretty. Not necessarily something I would have picked out myself, but I can try new things. And I'm not paying for it, so what the hell, right?

"Where are you going?" Carina asks.

"Back to the hotel and then to meet Ransom."

ME

I can't do girls' trip anymore. Can I come over?

RANSOM WEST

Yes. I'll meet you at my apartment. Or I can come to you?

I plug the address he gave me before into maps. I knew generally where it was, but not specifically in relation to where I am right now.

ME

I'll get a cab. I need to stop by the hotel first. 45 minutes?

RANSOM WEST

I'll be there.

"You can't," Carina says, her voice breaking.

I'm done catering to their feelings right now. This is against girls' trip rules, but so is staging an intervention for something they know nothing about. I need space.

"What more do you want from me, Carina?" I ask.

"Let me walk with you so you're not alone," she says. She hands Sienna her credit card to pay and follows me onto the street.

We're silent for a few minutes, trying to not look like clueless tourists, but probably failing miserably.

"I didn't realize how upset you were about Orion. I didn't think it was going to last, and I was terrified," she says after a few blocks.

"Terrified of what exactly? That I would judge you? That I'd disapprove of him?"

"I clearly know better now. I don't want to fight with you."

"I'm not mad about him anymore. I lashed out and I'm sorry. But you're doing to me exactly what you were afraid we'd do to you."

We get to the hotel and take the elevator up to the room I'm sharing with Bristol.

"I don't want to fight either," I say. "I need to sort some things out with Ransom first." I gather my things from around the room and put them into my suitcase.

"I'm sorry, Haley. Can we talk about this?"

"We'll talk it out when I get home."

"Will you at least tell me when you get to him safe? Or let me go with you."

"I can manage the city on my own." I look at her as she holds back tears. She never cries. But I'm angry and she can't distract me from what I need right now.

Back on the street, the bellhop flags me a cab. "I'll text you when I get to Ransom." I'll at least give her that, so she's not worried about my safety.

"Okay, thanks. We'll talk when you get back from the Hamptons?"

I nod. This isn't the end of our friendship. I'm not worried about that. I just need a few days to calm down and think about things. I need my questions about Ransom answered. "Tell Sienna and Bristol that I'm sorry and I need a break."

"Of course. If you want to meet up later, just let us know…"

"No. It'll be fine. Have fun without me." I sound so bitter, and I don't know how I got here.

eighteen

RANSOM

I SHOULDN'T LEAVE WORK EARLY TO SEE HALEY—I'VE NEVER DONE it for a woman before—especially after the time I took off yesterday. But I have my assistant cancel my meetings anyway. They can all be emails. Haley wouldn't leave her friends without something drastic happening. This trip and this time are important to them. I can't imagine what happened for her to break their sacred rules.

I wait for her in my building's lobby. I dropped my jacket and tie in my apartment and made sure everything is presentable. My space is kept clean thanks to the housekeeping service I hire, but I need to make a good impression on Haley. This is the first time she'll be in my world. I need her to want it, but all the arrangements I made are for tomorrow. Tonight will be an improvisation. I'm caught on my back foot without a plan.

I almost run out every time a cab pulls up, hoping it's the one she's in. As soon as I see her, I'm out the door and on the pavement. My chest tightens at her red, puffy eyes. She immediately falls into my arms and wraps herself around me. I lift her off the ground ever so slightly so that she knows I've got her. It doesn't matter what is going on, I'll handle it. I love that she needs me in this moment. And I'm selfish enough to be happy about it. I'll be a perfect boyfriend for her.

"Let's go inside so you can tell me what's wrong," I say into her ear before setting her down.

She nods but doesn't say anything in response. She smells so good, like berries and flowers and the faintest hint of her. She pulls away first, realizing before me that we're blocking pedestrians.

"Did you pay the driver?" I ask, taking her bags from him.

"Yes, it's taken care of," she responds. She laces her fingers with mine and lets me lead her inside. Once we're in the elevator she pulls out her phone. "I need to tell Carina I'm here safe."

I'm silent, not wanting to push her yet. This is fresh territory for me. I'm not used to caring about the problems of the woman I'm with. I've listened to more than my share of meaningless drama. I know when to nod and agree and proclaim things terrible. Usually I'm not paying attention. It never mattered to me who blocked whom on which social media platform. Or who didn't get an invitation to someone's birthday party. With Haley, I want more. I want to make this better. If I need to march over to where her friends are staying and fight on her behalf, I will. I will fight all her battles for her.

I unlock the door to my apartment and let her step in before me. I watch her take the space in. This obviously isn't my main residence. It's here for my long trips to New York and so I can say I own property in Manhattan. It's a one-bedroom condo with Central Park views. Everything is gray with hard lines. I think of her apartment, with its color and its clutter and the cat I never met despite staying the night.

She's the only color in sight, the lemons on her sundress taking up my focus.

"It's nice," she says.

"It's functional." I take her luggage to the bedroom. I wasn't prepared for it to be awkward between us. We haven't been alone together since I left her in bed a month ago. I'd planned on being able to flirt and charm her when I picked her up tomorrow so by the time we crossed the threshold we were tugging at each other's clothes.

She stands in the living room staring out my floor-to-ceiling windows.

"Can I get you something to drink? Tea?" I ask.

"That sounds lovely." She follows me to the kitchen and sits at the island while I put the kettle on the stove. No fancy electric kettle with different temperature settings?"

I smile. It's the way my mum made tea growing up. Loads of people use the electric version, but I can't. "No, some habits aren't worth breaking. The stove is the only way to make a cuppa."

She smiles back, but she's so sad.

I've never felt so incredibly powerless. "Tell me what happened, love." I face her with so much space between us and the island barrier. It's nothing I've done to cause this. This isn't about our relationship, but I don't know how to bridge the gap.

She shakes her head. Was it so bad she's still trying to process? "We were at brunch when you texted."

I suck in a breath. I hate that I had anything to do with this. That her friends could use me against her. "They didn't take that well?"

I wait for her to explain. She laid out girls' trip rules for me in the Maldives. Phones are for documentation purposes only. Never for scrolling or messaging. The world could fall apart, and they would be unaware. When I'd reached out earlier, I'd expected a delay. It wasn't an emergency. I could have waited.

"I don't think it was about you. Sienna brought up Beckett and there were some unflattering comparisons." She goes on to explain Sienna's outburst and her own lie of omission.

Haley stares at her hands while the kettle screeches. I pour her tea and set a timer for it to steep. She finally looks up at me.

"When you got interested in the Coastline restaurant, was it because you wanted to work with Will?"

She looks doubtful. I think back to our conversation in the conference room. What exactly had I told her? No one else knows the truth. I had reached out to Will. It was a huge stroke of luck that I was able to find a venture requiring direct management and that gave me enough deniability.

I can repeat what I've already told her. I wanted to work with Will. It was a coincidence the restaurant is in Wendell Beach. That I thought she wanted nothing to do with me. I would have respected her space if the Foleys hadn't hired her.

But I can't keep digging this hole. Not with Haley.

"I wanted another shot with you." The truth feels weird. "I like you, and I was confused with how things ended. I couldn't figure out a way to see you organically. So I found something to invest in. I was aware of Will, so when I found out he wanted to open a fine dining restaurant in your hometown, it felt like fate."

"Why didn't you tell me before?" she asks. Her voice is even and controlled. She's not going to share what she's thinking until she's ready.

The timer beeps so I remove her tea bag. "Milk and sugar?"

"Please."

I keep talking as I prepare her tea. "You came at me guns blazing. You were clearly upset about something. Honestly, love, I thought you weren't going to give me a chance. I took a step back to take my time."

"What if I had been dating someone? What if I hadn't been interested in you?"

I can't tell her that I wouldn't have cared if she had a boyfriend. It had crossed my mind. But I'm patient. I would have waited for her. I would have fought for her.

"If he made you happy…" I throw my hands up in surrender. I don't believe anyone else could truly make her happy. "And if my affection was never returned…getting to know you and be your friend and see you work…" I can't say it would be enough. I can't lie to her face right now. I'm trying to say the right thing and the honest thing, and it will break me if I hurt her now.

She steps to my side of the island so there's only a foot of space between us.

"Why?" she asks.

"Why what?"

"Why me? You could have any woman you want. Don't deny it. I was just another woman you met. Why did you go to this level of effort just to sleep with me?"

"If this was truly about sex, I'd have moved on a long time ago."

"That doesn't answer my question, Ransom."

"I don't know. You're beautiful and I love your smile and how your voice changes when you're passionate about the subject, and I thought *fuck, I wonder what it would be like if someone was that passionate about me.* I wanted that someone to be you."

She watches me for a moment, and I can't tell what she's thinking. Was that too much? Is that a good enough reason? I don't know why she's the person to capture my attention fully. No other reason than she's the person I want to be around.

She moves suddenly. She presses her body to me and her lips find mine. I open, needing to consume her fully. I thought this could be the end. That she'd say I lied too much and she couldn't get over it. Instead, her arms are around my neck and she's letting me pick her up, her legs tight around my waist and my hands under her dress on her perfect ass.

"Bedroom," she moans while I kiss across her cheek until I find a sensitive spot just below her earlobe. "Please tell me you have condoms this time."

I walk, stumbling a bit when she pulls my hair. "Yes. Not to be presumptuous, but we did discuss this."

I deposit her on my king-sized bed, loving the way she's looking up at me. I've seen her in lust before, but it was dark and we hadn't turned the lights on. We'd touched ourselves over the phone, but I couldn't see nearly enough. Now I'm here with her and I get her pleasure in the daylight.

She's so fucking beautiful.

I want to stay in this moment longer. I want to hold this space of anticipation. The lead-up to when everything changes. It's intimacy after she knows my lies and knows I'm willing to do whatever it takes to get what I want. She isn't pushing me away but pulling me closer. I've never been afraid to use people to accomplish my goals. For the first time, Haley is my goal. I only want her and nothing else.

But Haley wants more from me than this pause.

She pulls me down and I fall to my back. She's on me at once, straddling my hips and reaching for my belt buckle. Her hands grazing my erection, but not giving me nearly enough contact. I let her remove my belt and undo the buttons on my shirt as I lift up and kiss her. I haven't kissed her enough. For all the time I've spent getting to know her and being in this relationship with her, touching is new. Kissing is still new.

Her lips are soft and warm, and I love the way she smells.

I rub my hands up her thighs until I can grasp her hips and feel the soft skin of her ass. She grinds into my erection and I'm afraid I'm going to lose control long before I'm ready to. I sit upright. "Dress off. Now."

"Yes, sir." She reaches behind her and pulls down the zipper, revealing a simple beige bra, one she likely picked so it wouldn't show beneath her cream dress. It's not meant to entice or seduce, but because it's on her I love everything about it.

I still want it gone. She unclasps it and I take my shirt off.

This is the moment that makes the trips to the gym worth it. When she sees my abs and traces each ridge on my stomach with her fingertip.

She looks me in the eyes. "You know this doesn't matter to me?"

"Sex?"

She rolls her eyes. "I find you attractive with or without your muscles."

"But the muscles do have benefits." I pick her up effortlessly and flip us so I'm over her. I'll think about what she said later. It might not matter to her, but it mattered to everyone else in the past. But I don't want to think about that now. I only want to make her feel good. She might be thinking about how her friendships are falling apart and whatever insecurities she's having about us. But I can give her orgasms and that's enough for now. I've always been good for that.

She giggles and opens her legs so I can settle between them. I brace myself over her, every muscle in my upper body flexing for her. But she's only looking at my face.

"Pants off now," she says.

"You're bossy, you know that?" I say as she works the button and zipper.

"Ha! That's something no one has accused me of. But you're going to do what I ask anyway because you want this as much as I do."

I really do. We're both down to our underwear, and I still want to stay like this for a little bit longer. I want to hold her and cherish her. I want to appreciate her body with its soft curves. This moment is perfect. No one is going to interrupt us. I don't have to get on a call for work. Her friends aren't hovering.

I take my time then, lowering my lips to hers and learning which stroke of my tongue drives her wild. I tilt my pelvis so my cock rubs her clit in just the right way to make her moan. I learn her body so I can always do this for her. No matter how she's feeling outside the bedroom, I can bring her pleasure in it.

After a few minutes of making out and grinding against each other, she groans in frustration and reaches down to pull off her underwear. "I need you inside me."

I kiss her. "I'm never going to be able to deny you anything."

Anything she wants. Whatever it is, I'll give it to her.

I grab a condom from my nightstand, roll it onto my dick, and then I'm over her again. I rub my cock between her folds just for a second to test her readiness and because it feels so fucking good. I should have gone down on her or done something to make sure she can take me, but it's too late now. We both need this.

I press in just an inch and watch her eyes go wide. "You okay, love?"

"Yes, oh god. You're just big." The expression on her face changes to pleasure.

"Relax. I'll make this good for you."

It's never felt like this before. I've never felt connected. I've cared about my partner's pleasure because it got me something. But I care about Haley coming because even if I get nothing, she deserves to have everything good.

I bottom out and my hips hit hers. "Fuck," I moan.

We've talked about this so much over the last few weeks. I've imagined it a hundred times. What she wanted. How I'd give it to her slow. How she'd need to hold me close since we've been far away for far too long.

She does what she promised she'd do and more—her legs are around my waist and her nails dig into my shoulders.

I nibble on her earlobe. "God, Haley, you are perfect." It makes her clench around me, and I almost come.

I am consumed by her. I want everything from her.

"Come on, love. Tell me what you need."

"Just like that. Keep going."

Her heels press into my back and her pussy pulses around me. She has to be close. Her entire body tenses under me. I hold her tight because this is going to change us both. This is too good. Too vulnerable. Too intimate to be anything other than real. To be anything less than love.

She moans into my shoulder. Her pussy squeezes around me

through her orgasm. I have to hold on until she's done. I can't lose myself until she's taken care of. It's too fast. It's not long enough.

She finally stills under me and I look her in the eyes, watching her come back to life. "You okay there?"

She nods. "I'm fine. I just…did you?"

"Not yet." I nip her bottom lip. "I needed to take care of you first."

She laughs and it sounds like a half sob. "You did that and more." She looks at me. "Do you need me to…"

"No. Just let me look at you." I swivel my hips into her and her legs fall to the sides. God, she so fucking wet now. Her mouth opens in a gasp of pleasure. I thought I was going to come instantly but if I can get another orgasm out of her, I'll deny myself a little longer. "One more. Do it for me, love."

"Oh god, I can't," she moans, reaching between us to rub her clit.

"Yes, you can." I give her a few more strokes in the spot she likes so much.

This time she shatters and doesn't muffle her cries into my shoulder. She lets me hear it. And then I'm coming like I never have before. Like this is heaven and I've never done anything wrong in my life.

I need Haley in my life forever. I was right to go to these lengths to be with her. And there's nothing I won't do to keep her.

* * *

MY PHONE PINGS with an alert from the concierge desk. My assistant dropped off packages for me and they are bringing them up.

"Supper is still a few hours away," I say. "But do you want to cook? I know it makes you feel better. Or we can go out. We have reservations tomorrow night. But I'm sure I can find something last minute."

Haley looks around my kitchen. "I don't need to cook. But it might be nice. What do you have?"

I open my fridge like I expect to find groceries. "Um...I haven't been eating here so I don't have much." She steps between me and the fridge as I hold the door. She leans into me, and I love the way her body feels against mine. She's in my shirt and nothing else. I undo a few buttons so I have easier access to her breasts. She moans as I gently rub her nipple.

"Stop distracting me." She laughs. "Ketchup." She's correctly identified the only thing I have. "This is worse than me."

"We can always order grocery delivery," I suggest.

"Ew. No. I don't trust anyone to pick out produce for me."

There is a knock on the door and I answer it, retrieving the garment and shopping bags. "Can you try this on? Make sure it fits."

"You just want me to take my clothes off," she says.

"I do want you naked again," I say. I drape the garment bag over the back of the couch and put the rest on the floor.

"Then you can take the dress off me."

"I'll definitely do that in a few days." I step closer to her, hoping to feel the heat of her body. "I don't mind waiting for the experience."

"Did you only buy the dress and shoes? Or is there something more?" Her eyes drift to the bags I don't have the attention for.

"My personal trip to the store was going to be this evening. So no, Haley, I didn't have my assistant buy you lingerie."

She smiles but then her expression turns dark. "They seemed to think it was odd you were buying me clothes when we haven't slept together yet."

I really don't like her friends killing the mood right now. "Technically, I'm giving you clothes after we've had sex."

"Of course you'd find a loophole," she says. Her fingers trace the edge of my trousers—the tips barely touching my stomach. "I just want to make sure we're on the same page and you aren't hiding anything from me."

I understand why this is a sensitive subject for her. Carina was lying to her. She was keeping things from Sienna. Beckett lied to Sienna. She wants to be sure of one thing.

"I'm not keeping anything from you. We still have a lot of getting to know each other to do, but there's nothing about me I won't tell you. We just haven't had enough time." For the first time in my adult life, this feels real. This is what honesty feels like.

"Good. I'm not keeping anything from you."

Then she undoes my trouser button, and we barely make it to the bedroom again.

nineteen

HALEY

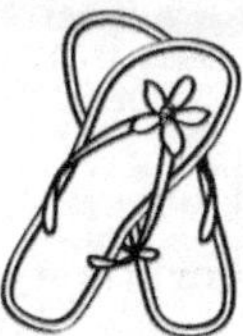

I SIT ON RANSOM'S BED, WRAPPED IN A BEDSHEET LIKE SOME woman in a rom-com, scrolling restaurants on my phone. "This place should be good. Have you been?" I show him a Michelin-starred ramen spot a few blocks away.

"You really want to wait in line for an hour to eat soup?" He leans over me and nibbles on my ear. He's put his boxers and suit pants back on. I keep waiting for him to put on something truly casual. Sweatpants or something. I'm not sure he owns any. It seems like so much work to keep getting dressed when we keep getting naked. "I'd rather order delivery and eat you while we wait."

"Funny. But yes. I want to explore a little. It's not like I get to New York often. If you need to work, that's fine. I can go on my own and bring it back to you."

He growls. "No. I'll go with you." He pulls slightly away and looks at me. "I'm in New York often. You could be here every time I am."

I brush my fingers up and down the line of hair between his pants and his belly button to watch him shiver. I'm sure he grooms because no one is this naturally sexy. "I know. I'm not

209

saying that's not going to happen. But I don't want to let this trip go to waste either." We haven't talked about what us dating will look like. Time on the phone has felt too precious—I didn't want to waste it asking about the future when I didn't understand our present. Does he think I'm going to split my time between London and Florida? With side trips to New York and Singapore tossed in? I don't know if I want that. I can technically work from anywhere. But Florida is a part of my soul. I won't give it up for anyone.

"Fine. We can go. And when we come back, we'll look up places you can order from next time so I can keep you naked."

It takes us a long time to get dressed. He gets distracted and kisses me every time I'm in his field of vision. I don't mind at all. I've never had someone want me this much.

When he told me he wanted this the whole time, I was shaken. Yes, it was intense and maybe I would have run away if I had known then. But now I want to steep in this feeling. This amazing, smart, thoughtful man moved mountains for a chance with me. I dated a guy on the mainland once who complained every time I asked him to come to Wendell Beach. I would have appreciated far less effort from Ransom.

I'm glad the ruse is up and we can be together as ourselves without any pretenses. It's a breath of fresh air. This relationship is new, but it's deep. We both have too much on the line to not make it work.

Once we are on the street, he expertly navigates us through the crowd. I've traveled through Europe and to a lot of big cities, but I've never gotten the hang of the hustle and bustle of so many people walking. I'm afraid to do something wrong or be obvious. I'm sure I have a sign on my back saying *small-town girl*. But Ransom holds my hand and doesn't let go. He probably glares at anyone who gets too close, but I don't care.

While we wait in line he asks me about my business. What parts of it I like working on the most. Which parts are the most profitable. What's the most time-consuming but doesn't make me much money. I don't mind having this conversation with him. He's listening to me intently and isn't making assumptions or talking over me. He knows how to be successful. My business isn't as big as he's used to working with—it's not a multimillion-dollar restaurant or whatever tech startup he has his fingers in. But I need fresh ideas. I'm stuck and things have been so hard lately, I need extra insight.

Plus, I'll never tire of the way he looks at me.

This is exactly what I want. I'm tired of doing everything by myself. I want someone to share the burden with me. Not someone to take over, but someone to help.

Ransom could be that person. But he's so perfect, I'm afraid this isn't real.

Sienna and Carina have their reasons to be suspicious of him, but I know him. He's not either of their exes or their crappy fathers. He's special and he's good to me.

And that's separating everything away from the mind-blowing sex.

I was so afraid it would be anticlimactic with him, but it was the opposite. It was better than with anyone else. He paid attention to what made me feel good. He remembered the fantasies I whispered to him over the phone. I'm sure he could have finished long before I came the second time. But he was patient and sexy and just thinking about it is getting me hot while I'm waiting for ramen.

"Why this place?" he asks when we get our table and order.

"We didn't need reservations," I answer. Not all the best restaurants are fine dining, despite what some food critics think.

"That's not all," Ransom says.

I look up at him and away from the chopsticks I'm fiddling with. It's the truth, but I didn't realize how much of it was only a half-truth. "No. Ramen is one of my favorite foods. When we were kids, we always had packages of instant ramen in the house.

It was a quick meal I could make for myself when no one was home. I got bored of the seasoning packets quickly, so I experimented." I laugh. "I made some truly horrible food. But I figured out what I liked eventually. Between ramen and mac and cheese, I fell in love with cooking. Of course, what I made was a far cry from anything authentic, but I learned that too in time."

"Have you thought about traveling to Japan to get some direct experience?"

"No, I'm happy with what I cook and how I cook. And that's a luxury I can't afford."

"I could—"

I put my hand up to stop him. "I know. It's not just the money. It's also the time and energy. Maybe someday in the future."

He wants to insist. I can read it all over his face. But this isn't a problem and he can't fix it by throwing money around. I could spend my whole life studying, but that's not what I want. I change the subject instead. "What about you? You must have some favorite foods from childhood?" I want to know who he was as a child. Who he was before he became this.

"Buttered noodles with peas." He smiles as if he can't believe his answer. "It was what my mum made on busy nights. She'd be tired from her job, but we'd sit down and she'd ask about our day."

I wonder if I'll get to meet his family. If I'll go to London at some point. But I'm getting ahead of myself. I haven't even met his friends yet. My parents live twenty minutes from me, and I don't know when he'll meet them.

I want to spend the rest of the night exploring the city, but it doesn't last long. He pulls me into a kiss on the sidewalk and then we're back in his bed as fast as we can be without running through the streets of Manhattan. I'm not mad about it. He's right—I'll have more opportunities to see the city.

I don't want to get caught in what he's offering me. I could lose myself in him so easily and the fantasy of a life with him. I don't want to give up my job, but being with him would make so much of my life easier. I wouldn't have to worry about money so much. I could cook for people because I love it. Isn't that what everyone wants?

The ache in my stomach would go away because I wouldn't have to worry about clients leaving. I could take the time to explore new platforms for my subscription. Maybe I could travel and spend more time learning. I could film videos in his apartment instead of moving around Carina's and Orion's schedules.

My gut twists at the thought of her. She acknowledged my text, but nothing else. I know Carina—she'll apologize the second she gets the chance because that's her nature. But I don't want that from her right now. I want to fight with her. I want us to work through these issues and her lack of trust and maybe even my jealousy that she's fallen in love. Our friendship will be better for it. That's what I want from her.

* * *

THE NEXT DAY, Ransom takes me to the museums I missed seeing with Carina, Bristol, and Sienna. I get emotional in front of *Starry Night,* and he presses his chest to my back and wraps his arms around me.

"I can take you to Amsterdam," he whispers. "We can go to the Van Gogh Museum. There's great food. It'll be perfect."

I nod, not bothering to correct him that I'm having a moment about my friends and not the art.

I like the idea of going to Amsterdam with him.

He won't tell me what we're doing for dinner. Before I'd left Wendell Beach, he'd told me where we're going doesn't have a dress code, but he will be in a suit and for once won't be overdressed. I packed a knee-length lace emerald green dress with an exposed back. The sweetheart neckline gives the illusion of more cleavage than I have and the heels I pair it with are a little unsteady under me. I'm not used to them and normally I'd go with flats, but I like how they look. Maybe I'll adjust over time. Or maybe this will implode, and I won't wear them again.

"You look absolutely amazing," he says when I step out of the bedroom.

"Thank you. You going to suggest we order takeout and stay in?" I ask.

"No." He stands from the couch. "I love having you all to myself, but I'd never deprive you of what we're about to experience."

"Do I get a hint?" I rub my hand down his black silk tie. Sure, suits are sexy, but now it's too many layers between us.

"You have to trust me, love."

I do trust him to sweep me off my feet. It's what he does best.

A car waits for us downstairs, but it only takes us a few blocks. "We could have walked," I say. Although then I would have definitely opted for the flats.

"What's the point of having all this money if I can't spoil you?" He plants a kiss on my lips.

We've stopped in front of an elegant restaurant. I looked it up but knew I wouldn't get a reservation unless I had called a year ago. "How?" I ask.

"Again, if I can spoil you, I will." He winks.

I shake my head, but he ushers me inside. The maître d' greets Ransom by name and leads us up a flight of stairs and to a small room with a table set for two. The walls have large windows overlooking the kitchen. We'll be able to see everything happening as the chefs prepare our food.

"This is amazing," I say as he pulls out my chair for me to sit down. A server is already present and offers us a choice of waters. I barely get my preference out when the chef de cuisine walks in and introduces himself, going over the menu we'll have tonight.

Once they leave, and the blur of the last ten minutes fades, I'm alone with Ransom. I speak. "You really didn't have to do this. I want to explore and see and try new things, but I mostly want to spend time with you. You don't have to try so hard to impress me."

He smiles, but it's a little sad. Does he think this is all he has to offer me?

He takes my hand across the table. "I know. I know I don't have to buy you things or take you on trips to impress you. But I can do those things and so I will."

"You forgot you bought me clothing."

"We never did get around to you trying on that dress," he says.

"Guess we just have to cross our fingers it fits."

He waves me off. "We can call a tailor if we need to once we get to the house. The fundraiser isn't until the third night we're there."

Right. He can just call tailors on demand.

Dinner is amazing. The food is French and delicious and every single time we get a new course, it's better than the last one. I'm in absolute heaven.

We head back to his apartment, and I jokingly ask if he has any more surprises for me planned.

"At least one more." His dimples are on full display.

I notice it as soon as we step into his apartment as we both toe off our shoes, the scent of vanilla and amber. And beneath everything, roses. The lights are off, but a glow comes from his bedroom. I look up to him when we cross the threshold, and I see the candles and the roses and he's once again holding me close.

"This was supposed to be our first night here. I had plans."

"I'm sorry for ruining them."

"No, you aren't," he whispers darkly into my ear.

"How did you do this?" We'd left his apartment together, and these were recently lit.

"Will helped. He knows a service."

"Of course he does." He owns a nightclub named after the god of love, Eros, after all.

"He's rooting for us," Ransom says.

I didn't know I needed to hear that. When it feels like the rest of the world is against us, it's reassuring that at least one person is on our side.

"Let's not talk about my boss right now."

We've exposed so much of our skin to each other before we even admitted to having feelings. It should feel raw and vulnerable. But it never has. I'm at peace with my body, knowing it's full of softness and strength. It allows me to do so many things that bring me joy. I don't need to compare myself to anyone else in order to know my value.

But Ransom, now that I know him, I know he has masks and shields and his body is another one. I don't doubt that he likes to go to the gym, but it's more than that. I want to know what he's hiding underneath everything. Will he let me close enough to show me?

I take my time with him. We have all night. We have all week. He sits on the edge of the bed with me straddling his lap. He's always in control of everything. Will he let me take control of this?

I remove his tie slowly, undoing the knot before sliding it out from his collar. Then it's each button of his shirt. He watches my eyes the whole time—his hands on the skin of my upper thighs holding me in place. I'm safe here with him and in his bed. I know he's not in this space very much. It's not like my bedroom which is also my office and the only place I can call a sanctuary. His essence isn't everywhere, but it doesn't matter because he's holding me.

By the time I get to the last button and untuck it from his trousers, his torso has erupted in goose bumps. He's hard beneath me and I know this is killing him. He wants to flip me under him again. I told him that's what I wanted. I thought I wanted things to always go fast with us. But he was right—slow is good.

"Haley," he whispers into my ear. "Please."

I take pity on him and let him shift so that he can move to the center of the bed. I grab a condom from the nightstand as he undoes his belt. I know the romantic fantasy is for him to lay me down on a bed of roses, but somehow I like this better.

We're quiet, when all we had was our words before. He shoves his pants and boxers down just enough to free his cock so I can roll the condom down its length. I should remove my dress. We should completely strip down, but maybe now's not the time. Maybe tonight is the night for the fairy tale. The pretty dress and the suit and the layers between us that don't actually mean anything at all.

I pull my dress up over my hips. Ransom takes control then, delving his hand into my panties to feel my soaking center. I fall forward with a moan and it feels so good to have him fill me. For weeks all I had were my fingers and they'll never be as good as his. I bury my face in his neck. He's going to push me over the edge in no time at all. His thumb rubs my clit, stretching my panties against my skin.

My climax comes fast and hard. Fireworks explode behind my eyelids. It's never been like this for me before.

He removes his hand and holds me above him. My pussy is resting on his condom-covered dick. I'm already sensitive but I'm chasing every moment of pleasure I can get tonight.

"Haley," he whispers again.

I turn my head so that I'm looking into his eyes. We're so close to each other. I feel his breath against my lips. He brushes my hair back from my face and cradles the nape of my neck.

We weren't even kissing and we aren't having sex. But this look in his eyes tells me everything I need to know.

We've found something here between us. Something wonderful and precious and worth protecting.

I reach for his cock because I'm terrified of what happens next and how this happened so fast and slow at the same time. My panties are pushed to the side and I sink down around him, loving the pleasurable stretch I knew was coming. For what feels like the first time in my life, I have the power to take from someone.

My orgasm builds slowly and then fast. His hips rock up into mine. It's only been a day that we've been doing this, but he knows all the spots to hit.

I press my lips to his as I come, letting him sense the full force of everything I feel for him. Not just what my body is doing around his, but the way my heart is collapsing into him. He shudders beneath me and I know it's the same for him.

I wonder if this can last forever.

I pause for a moment as our breathing returns to normal. He's still inside me as we gaze into each other's eyes. Neither one of us wanting to break whatever spell we've fallen under. This was more and bigger than we shared before.

But after a moment I slide off him and he rolls over to dispose of the condom. I sit on the side of the bed, thinking I should stand and do something about my hair, but he comes up behind me.

"Let's get comfy." He pulls the shoulder of my dress down my arm, kissing each inch as he exposes skin. His voice is still soft and reverent. We strip to nothing and I arrange myself against the pillows and the headboard, noticing the mess we made of the rose petals.

"We're doing this backward again," I say.

"It works for us," he says before kissing me deeply. "Give me one minute." He leaves the room and comes back with his iPad.

"Really? You're going to work now?" The thought feels like a betrayal of what we just shared. I'm sure he'll want to work if I fall asleep before him, but I'm not ready for that yet.

"No, this is another surprise." He sits behind me, allowing my back to rest against his chest. This is becoming my favorite way for him to hold me. He opens the device in front of me. He taps an app and hundreds of thumbnails pop up. "I've never shown anyone this." He kisses my neck. "I don't have a lot of free time, but when I do, I like to draw."

He taps one and it expands to show a beautiful landscape of a beach with huts on stilts over the water.

"The Maldives," I say, looking at him. It's beautiful, with just enough detail, and the colors are perfect.

"It was forward of me to show up like I did. But I couldn't stop thinking about you. Yes, I was bored, but it was more than that." He kisses my bare shoulder. "It was always more than sex with you. I wanted you badly, but I wanted to know your thoughts on everything. If the sand was as soft in Wendell Beach. If the food was good or if we were drunk and only thought it was amazing."

He flips through more drawings. He's good. It's clear this is something he's passionate about. The scenes are mostly land-scapes. I recognize a few from the resort I stayed at. The spa. The undersea restaurant.

"We never talked about the rest of your trip." I see connec-tions to me in each drawing.

"We went deep-sea fishing and then the restaurant helped us cook the fish we caught."

"We did that too. It was a lot of fun," I say. He's scrolling through more pictures. Pausing to give me time to examine each one.

"Carina and Orion mentioned that, remember? You taught the chefs a thing or two." He nibbles on my ear as he says it. "But my friends were drunk the whole time, so they didn't really help with the deep-sea fishing. Half of them were still sleeping when it happened. And when we got in the kitchen, the staff decided it was too risky to give them knives so they mostly ripped apart lettuce."

I laugh. "These are the same friends we are spending a week with?"

"Yes. Don't worry. They'll love you," he says. "But while we were doing that, I was so focused on how you would prepare things. I wanted to sit with you on the beach. Now I wish you had shown me how to paddleboard there. I wanted everything from you even then."

I kiss his arm. "You're just saying that because you want to get laid again."

"I won't lie to you to get you into bed. Not anymore." He whispers the last bit—the part that feels like a confession.

It's a risk for me to really get involved with him, knowing what he's capable of. But I'm going to trust him now.

We scroll through more pictures. I recognize the London skyline in the rain. Then it's Paradise.

"I honestly thought I was being pranked when I saw it in person," he says. He swipes again and it's the stretch of beach from Coastline with the pier in the background. "I knew it wouldn't be easy when I came here. I didn't expect you to fall over me. But you made me work for it." He holds me tight, and I realize he's been holding on to his own insecurities.

"I thought about you. I wanted to go back with you that night, but Sienna needed me. I wanted a second chance so badly."

"So we could have been doing this a long time ago?"

"I thought you wanted a one-time thing. I didn't want to put myself out there for a crush you didn't reciprocate."

"I did." He chuckles darkly. "There's nothing I wouldn't do to be with you, Haley," he says.

We flip through the rest of the pictures. There are ones of every spot in Wendell Beach I've taken him to. In a few of the recent ones, I notice the outline of a brunette. She's done in shapes without details. She sits on a paddleboard, her feet dangling in the water, and a beer in her hand.

"I want to draw you, fully and detailed. But I won't without your permission."

I lean farther into him, his cock pressing against my back, getting hard again even though we just exhausted ourselves. I know what this moment is for us—it's a promise of more. He wants to create an indelible record of me in his life. This isn't a passing fancy to him. This is something he wants to work for. He'll adjust. He'll change for me. It's everything I've ever wanted in a relationship.

How can I say anything other than yes?

twenty

RANSOM

In the morning, I cut my workout short to get back to Haley faster. I don't like being away from her any longer than needed. I get this week with her and then I don't know when I'm going to see her again. Time is too precious to waste.

When I get back to my apartment from the building's gym, she's making coffee in the kitchen. I embrace her, needing her touch the way I've never needed it before.

"Ew…you're stinky." She giggles, leaning into me. "I was surprised you went to the gym this morning. I thought we had a busy enough day ahead of us."

"I feel weird on the days I don't go." My life is so chaotic, but getting some kind of workout in helps me to feel centered. I protect the time whenever I can. "How about tomorrow you stay in bed and wait for me there?"

"We'll see. I don't normally sleep well in unfamiliar places." She scrunches up her nose like she's feeling the accumulation of so many days away from her bed.

"I don't normally sleep well, so we're a good fit," I say. I take a mug from the cupboard and press a few buttons on the machine to make an espresso for me.

"I noticed. Let me finish this coffee and we can shower together. What time do we leave?" she asks.

"We have a few hours before our flight is scheduled."

"Our flight?"

I look at her. "Did you think we were driving?"

"It's not that far, is it?"

"No, but traffic is terrible. I chartered a helicopter."

"Of course, why didn't I think of that?" Her voice is light with surprise.

Now that we've made everything official and she knows why I came to Wendell Beach, I don't have to hide my intentions. I can fully sweep her off her feet. Romance her beyond what she's ever had before. Money isn't going to buy her affection, but it can go a long way in showing her the kind of life she could have if we are together. This week is my first chance to show her my world.

I'd never drive to the Hamptons anyway—what should be a couple of hours' drive is elongated with congestion I'll never have the patience for.

After our shower, Haley puts on a dress with blue and white squares on it. Her hair is down and lightly curled against her shoulders. She takes my breath away every time I see her. I want to stay here in my apartment with her alone so I don't have to share her with the outside world.

But I want to show her off to everyone.

My phone vibrates in my hand, forcing me to look down at it as I maintain my opposing thoughts. "The car is here."

"Great." Haley moves for the front door but I stop her.

"The driver will get our bags. We can wait here," I say.

"I don't think I'm going to get used to traveling the way you do." She fiddles with the strap on her bag.

"What if I hope you do?" I take her hands and look into her eyes. "I've spent weeks now getting to know your world. Let me show you mine."

"Fine. That seems fair," she says.

When this started, I wasn't sure what my endgame was. It was the first time I'd done something only caring about the next steps. I wanted Haley. There was no mountain I wouldn't climb to get there. Now that I have her, I want more. I want it all. Haley is my endgame. This time with my friends is my chance to convince her to join me and my world. She's attached to Wendell Beach, and I don't expect her to move to London soon, but eventually I want that. I need to convince her to want it too.

This is my chance to show her the possibilities for us are endless. I can give her anything she wants. I'll stretch her imagination to its limits. This is only the beginning of our fairy tale.

The helicopter ride is standard for me. Haley does her best to not appear fazed. But she squeezes my hand throughout the trip. I forgot she didn't like takeoff and landing of the flight we shared. I should have thought about that before booking this trip. I wonder if there is another company with better helicopters and a smoother flight.

Her phone lights up in her lap and Carina's name appears.

"Send her a selfie." I want her friends to be jealous of her.

She shakes her head. "I don't want to rub it in her face. We're in a fight. But not broken up."

"But if you weren't fighting, you'd send her a picture."

She leans close to me and takes a quick selfie. "I'll show her when I get home."

I kiss her forehead, looking forward to the day when we share a home.

* * *

"Do you have a fleet of black cars on retainer or something?" she asks when we land and I'm handed the keys to a black luxury sedan.

"At least I'm driving this one." I open the passenger door for her. I use a driver plenty. I value expertise and specialization. If someone can navigate daytime traffic, allowing me to answer emails, then I'm going to hire that service. But I like the freedom of being able to drive when I want to, without having to wait on anyone else.

"Whose place are we going to?" she asks while I connect my phone to the car's system.

We haven't talked much about this trip. We haven't had nearly enough time together. I wasn't going to waste any of it discussing what is coming when I'm so focused on appreciating the moment.

"My friend Josephine is dating a man named Daxton. His family owns a stock exchange. We're visiting one of their summer homes and attending a charity fundraiser for underprivileged children later this week."

"Are we the only ones there early?"

"No, besides Josephine and Daxton, there will be Estella, Myles, Isaac, Georgina and her husband, Thomas, and Lena. It's the same people I went to the Maldives with."

"That's a lot. What should I know before I meet them?"

"Lena and Georgina are sisters and their father owns Spare Capital. Thomas, Lena, and I work together. Estella is lovely. She works for a Labour MP and will love to discuss American politics with you. Myles and Isaac live on their trust funds. I used to date Lena." I hope the last bit goes unnoticed. There isn't much to explain. Lena was someone I was with when it was necessary for my career. It didn't mean anything more to me than a nice time for a little bit. Haley is the only person who matters. But someone might bring it up and it'll turn into a fight if she doesn't hear it from me. It will be the Carina and Orion situation all over again.

"Oh. That's information I would have liked earlier," she says.

I reach for her hand across the center console and squeeze it. "It was a long time ago. I didn't have strong feelings for her." I kiss her fingers. "Don't worry about her. I'm yours."

"You're very charming, you know that?"

I never thought I'd feel this way, content and happy with the person I'm with. I have plenty to gain by being on my own. Marriage would be a business arrangement more than anything else. My parents love each other and I have a great family. But I don't see that with the people I share my life with now. No one is faithful. And I didn't expect that from previous partners. My relationship with Haley is different and unexpected. It's about companionship and affection, and just being in her presence warms my soul.

Haley speaks and breaks my thoughts. "You work with Lena, you are friends with her, and you used to date her. Is that weird?"

"No. She decided we're better suited as colleagues and as friends than anything more. It wasn't a long relationship anyway." Lena and I had lengthy conversations when I started working for her father. I'd liked her enough and enjoyed spending time with her. But I had gotten what I wanted. I didn't see a reason to stick with her for my future loveless marriage. In the process, I might have let on that I'd be open to casual sex with her. It never panned out, but it felt like the incentive needed to help Lena feel like our breakup was in her best interest.

Haley wrinkles her forehead. "We haven't talked about past relationships."

Her fingers are still intertwined with mine, so I give them a squeeze. "We can at some point. I'd much rather think about the future with you."

"That's evasive. But you're right, we have time," she says. "Anything else I should know?"

"You might be wary of Isaac and Myles. They'll probably offer to have a threesome with you, but they're harmless. Tell them to bugger off and they will."

"That makes me feel super comfortable." Her tone of voice is clear she means the opposite.

"Don't worry. I won't leave your side. I see these people all the time. I don't get to see you nearly as often as I like."

"You're not feeding me to the wolves?"

"Never."

"You should know, I don't share," she says.

I've stopped at a red traffic light, so I take the moment to really look at her. I don't understand why this trip is stressing her, but I'll do anything to put her at ease. Including making a promise I've never made before, but one that is natural with her. "I don't share either. You're all mine and I'm all yours."

She smiles and I feel so content I can't imagine this weekend going anything other than perfectly.

* * *

WE PULL up to the ultra-modern house. It's entirely glass and we can almost see directly to the beach. The gate opens, and in the circular driveway a line of staff waits for us.

"Hello, Mr. West. Ms. Stewart. Mr. Whitman is expecting you."

We step out of the car and I hand the keys to the valet. They grab our luggage before we can say anything, and Haley is doing her best to not be flustered again. I'm used to this. She'll get there eventually.

"Welcome." A woman wearing a knee-length black dress with a high collar leads us into the house. She must be the household manager. I rest my hand on Haley's low back to keep her close to me. "The rest of the guests are out by the pool. If you'll allow me to show you to your room, you can settle in before you join them." Another woman offers us warm hand towels once we've stepped into the air-conditioned atrium.

"Lovely. We'll follow you," I say. I don't know who else is here. I haven't received any new emails from Lena since yesterday, which likely means she's not working and might have arrived from England.

Our guide takes us up a grand staircase and down a hallway. At the end we step into a large room with a king-sized canopy bed covered in white linens. Past that are glass doors leading out to the balcony.

"Your bags will be up in just a moment. Please let me know if you need anything."

"Are you okay?" I ask Haley once we're alone. She hasn't said anything.

"Yes. Normally when I visit someone I'm greeted by my friend and not their staff."

I kiss her forehead. "Don't worry. They're going to love you." I honestly don't know how anyone couldn't.

She moves to the balcony doors. "Wow. The view is beautiful."

I open them and we step out. The whole estate is magnificent, with a perfectly maintained lawn until it hits the sand dunes. Down below is the expansive pool where everyone else is lounging. We appear to be the last to arrive.

Haley changes into a stunning one-piece pink-and-white swimsuit. Over it, she has on a sheer white dress. I want to keep her in the bedroom longer. But she's nervous and if we get this meet and greet over with, then she's all mine.

We step out onto the pool deck.

"Ransom! You finally made it!" Josephine shouts, standing up and rushing over. She gives me a hug, almost spilling her drink on me. "And this must be Haley. So happy you're here too. You're so pretty!" She gives Haley a hug and does spill some of her drink on her. "Oh. I'm so sorry. This is like my fifth one of these. They get a little away from me."

"It's fine. It'll wash out," Haley says, looking down at the pale pink spot.

"Haley, this is Josephine Frost," I offer since Josephine is too far gone to be much more help.

"It's nice to meet you," Haley says.

"You must meet Daxton. This is his house. Daxton! Come here!"

A tall, tanned man with blond hair stands from the pool area as the rest of the group notices our arrival.

I make introductions to everyone and catch Myles checking out Haley's legs. They are gorgeous, so I can't blame him. I keep her hand in mine as if to say *you can't have this one.*

"Haley, you said?" Lena asks. She's wearing a hat and sunglasses, but I'm sure I saw a hint of a stony glare before she turned on her smile.

"Yes," Haley says, looking at me with a nervous glance. I wrap my arm around her waist in a way I hope is possessively reassuring.

"I didn't realize you were bringing anyone," Lena continues. "Especially a colleague."

"She's my girlfriend." My tone is probably cold. I never did get around to telling Lena that Haley and I are dating.

"What a fun surprise! If you'll excuse me, I need to get out of the sun. Georgina, would you like to come with me?"

"Of course," her sister responds.

"Why don't we sit?" I pull Haley toward an empty cabana and we sit on the couch. I glance over to where Daxton and Josephine climb into the pool. In another life, I would have made sure to get plenty of time with him. I'm not looking to move jobs, but he has more connections in America than I could dream of. But I'm not sacrificing my time with Haley.

Another member of the staff brings us a bottle of sparkling rosé. I specifically asked for them to have it on hand for Haley. It's not her preferred bottle, but a little pricier. I'm hoping she'll enjoy it.

"Why didn't they know I was coming?" Haley asks.

Is that why she's uncomfortable? She thinks she isn't welcome?

I kiss her forehead. "I talked to Josephine about it. I don't know why she didn't tell everyone else. The staff knows so clearly Daxton welcomes you."

She nods but still looks doubtful. Her eyes focus on the waves on the beach. "But if they're your best friends, why didn't they know you were dating anyone?"

"Haley, love, we just started dating. It wasn't a secret like Carina and Orion. You know how busy I've been these past few weeks."

"But Lena? You work with her."

"Yes, and I try to keep things professional in the office. I truly have not socialized with any of them in the last month. And I clearly wasn't going to say anything before we were official. I'm not keeping secrets, I promise." She needs this assurance from me. She needs to know this isn't a pattern for me.

"Okay, I guess that's reasonable. But Ransom, you said you don't have feelings for Lena, but she's clearly upset I'm here."

"She doesn't like to be out in the sun. She's always been this way. It has nothing to do with you," I say.

That doesn't seem to satisfy her, but we go silent as Myles and Estella enter our cabana.

"Mind if we join you?" Estella asks.

"Of course not," I answer as I drape my arm around Haley's shoulder.

"Lena said you are colleagues. What is it that you do, Haley?" Estella sounds genuine and has always been the nicest of us.

"I'm a chef," she says.

"Is that what they're calling it these days?" Myles asks, leaning back against the other couch. He gets close to Estella who inches away from him. "I guess homemaker is a little old-fashioned, but I can't keep up with the changing titles these days."

"Um…no, I went to culinary school. I cook for people and for events, professionally," she says.

My blood boils, but I know Myles isn't worth the effort to fight back right now.

"Ignore him," Estella says. "Are you the chef at the restaurant in Florida? Lena was telling me about how different that is from your usual investments, Ransom."

"I'm consulting there, but I'm not working in the kitchen," Haley explains.

"She's a great chef," I say. "Loads of followers on social media. And her cookbook was a bestseller."

Haley blushes.

"This I have to see." Myles pulls out his phone. He finds her easily enough. "Meh. My dentist has more followers."

"For fuck's sake, you are the worst," Estella says.

"I'm just playing around," Myles says. "She's clearly nothing like the usual girls he brings around."

Haley turns to ice next to me. I should have prepared her more for this. I should have made time to go over every bit of my past so she could feel secure in me now.

Myles continues. "I'm just looking out for everyone. Can't have her using us to get more likes."

"Oh piss off, Myles," I say. I'm not going to let him or anyone else make Haley feel less than.

twenty-one

HALEY

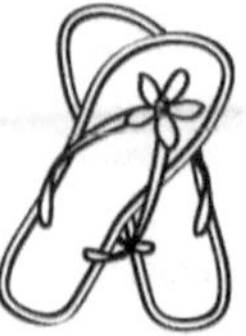

WHEN I WAKE ON THE THIRD DAY THERE, RANSOM IS STILL IN BED with me. The weight of his arm on my torso keeps me locked in place. I want to stay here for as long as I can, with him at peace and my heart rate low and restful.

"Morning, love," he says, giving me a squeeze.

"Morning. How long have you been awake?" I ask.

"Not that long. I woke up earlier. Watched the sunrise, then came back to bed and fell asleep again," he says.

I roll to my side to face him. He hitches my leg over his hip so that I'm pressed to his erection.

"See, you just needed an incentive to stay in bed." I grind into him.

Waking up with him has been everything I wanted. Here in our room, in our bed, however temporary our stay is in this house, is our sanctuary. Last night, Estella and Daxton got into a fight about universal health care and so I'm not looking forward to a day with the group after that. I drank way too much wine in order to feel less anxious about the whole thing. And while Ransom didn't say anything during dinner, afterward he called Daxton a wanker who could not comprehend that life could be any harder than he had it.

So this morning, I remove my clothes and Ransom's shorts and straddle him. I pull him into my body and love every second I get this stripped-down version of him.

* * *

MY PEACE only lasts when we are in the bedroom.

I shower and put on makeup, wearing just a little bit more than I do when I film. Cameras can be harsh, but I know how to use lighting and filters to my advantage.

I have none of those protections around Ransom's friends.

"We could stay in the room," he says, coming up behind me and placing his warm hand down the bodice of my dress. I love knowing how much he wants me and all that he does to keep his hands on me whenever he can.

This physical connection we have is so important to me. I need to hold on to it for the weeks and months when we aren't able to see each other.

"Later. I'm hungry." I spoke with the household manager last night who promised me that breakfast would be avocado toast with poached eggs and every type of fresh berry they could source. I haven't been able to stop thinking about it since.

"Fine, but this afternoon when everyone is napping…"

"I will take my clothes off, climb into bed, and artfully cover myself with a sheet so you can draw me."

He gives my nipple a light pinch, just how I like it, and then pulls away. "Deal."

We hold hands as we descend the stairs in the quiet house.

"Breakfast is on the patio this morning. Can I get you anything to drink?" one of the housemaids asks.

We order our coffees and step outside. I'm aware the table has been set, but I only have eyes for the ocean. The waves roll in heavy and powerful in a way they almost never do in Wendell Beach unless we have a storm coming in.

"You should have seen the sunrise," Ransom says. "It was the brightest reds and pinks I've ever seen."

"Maybe tomorrow I'll get up with you and we can watch it together." I love watching the sun over the water, but one benefit of Wendell Beach is that since it's on the west coast of Florida, we get sunsets over the water instead of sunrises, and I'm not a morning person.

"We have the gala tonight. There's no way you're getting up early tomorrow."

"Maybe we'll stay up all night then," I suggest.

"I like the way you think, love," he says. He gently tugs at my hand. "Let's sit." I follow him to the table as the staff brings out trays of food.

"This looks so good," I say, pulling out my phone from my dress pocket and opening up the camera app.

"Oh, there she goes again," Isaac says, stepping out of the house. "Got to get those likes."

My stomach twists. These remarks have been happening all the time over the past few days. They are still convinced that I'm using this trip as a way to grow my social media following. Taking my phone out to photograph food is just habit at this point. I have it down to a science so that the food doesn't get cold. And right now, I just want to remember these beautiful details of a time when it's someone else taking care of my every single need.

I put my phone away. "Just trying to record memories," I say.

Ransom kisses my temple as we sit down. "Ignore him, Haley."

It's so easy for him to say that. So much harder for me to follow through.

Estella arrives next as I wait for someone else to start taking food so I'm not seen as the one to dig in first. She sits next to me and immediately reaches for the platter of berries.

"Ugh, I love a raspberry. Don't you, Haley?" she says, popping one into her mouth.

I smile since she has been the most nice to me all weekend. We've chatted about the weather and she gave me some suggestions about where to shop in town, but the whole time I've wondered if she's just trying to get close in order to report back to Lena, who has been surprisingly scarce.

I couldn't believe that the woman from those social media pictures I saw was here. I understood they weren't dating when she posted them, but now I'm still confused about their background.

We're brought the avocado toast and I start eating as the rest of the group slowly joins. I listen as they talk, but a portion of it I don't follow. They've dropped into some form of British slang that I don't fully understand. Daxton doesn't seem to care—he's too focused on his phone to pay any attention. Ransom is playing with the hair at the base of my neck with one hand and eating with the other. He's not involved in the conversation any more than I am.

I haven't figured out yet how he fits in with this group. They don't appear to share many interests, and the only things I note they have in common are money and being tied to Lena or her family in some way. Ransom is the newest addition to the group from what I can tell—everyone else has known each other most of their lives. I have to wonder what made them bring him into their fold.

And why Ransom wants to stay in it.

This man who is so forward in so many things in life cannot be content to be so completely passive with these people.

* * *

CARINA ANSWERS on the second ring. "Haley, I'm so glad you called. I'm so sorry about everything."

"Thanks…but that's not why I'm calling," I say. I'm in the bathroom, wearing a silk dressing gown and letting my hair air dry for the few minutes I have before the stylists arrive. Ransom is in the bedroom working, but I'm far enough away from the door that he shouldn't hear me. I can't believe I've resorted to hiding from my boyfriend to call my best friend.

"What's wrong?"

"I think I'm in a nightmare," I admit. I knew Carina would answer my call, and after those months of feeling like I had no one to talk with, I'm taking the risk and reaching out. I've known her since we were kids. If we can't put our brief argument aside, then I don't know what to do. Plus, she texted me to check in the other day.

"Hang on, let me go to the other room." I hear fabric rustling and the slap of her feet on hardwood floor. "Sorry, I was with Orion. What's wrong? Are you safe?"

"I think so. I don't think they're going to kill me." I say it with a soft laugh because otherwise I'll cry. "I kind of hate them. The friends. Not Ransom." I don't hate him.

"You, Haley Stewart, the world's nicest person, hate Ransom's friends?"

"Yes. A few of them are okay. But they are constantly making jokes at my expense. I understand we are speaking English, but I swear they use British slang just to go over my head," I explain. I'm about to cry. I feel like I haven't slept in days. "Remember when we were kids and went to camp, and we both woke up so early because we were excited but all it did was make us cranky after the long drive? Then when we arrived most of the other girls were already friends and they didn't want to hang out with us?"

"That was the worst! I would have died if it hadn't been for you," she says.

"Yeah, well, this feels like that, except then I knew I could count on you. I'm not sure I can count on Ransom."

"Oh, Haley. Is he not with you?"

"No, he is. He promised he wouldn't leave me alone and he hasn't. I'm just hiding in the bathroom since I'm getting ready for this fundraiser."

After breakfast, we took a trip into town to get away from all of them. He was back to his normal self. I like that version of him. Walking down a pretty small-town street feels natural with him. But I knew that waiting for us back at the house were people I just didn't want to be around and I can't see that he does either.

When I finish explaining the dynamics to Carina, she's silent for a moment.

"Okay. You don't have to stay there if you don't want to. I know you like him, so I'll give Ransom the benefit of the doubt. But you need to tell him you're not having fun. If he cares about you, he'll be on your side."

"You're right," I say, wiping away tears.

"I always know Orion is on my side, even when we're bickering or he's picking on me, okay? It should be the same with Ransom. He needs to be Team Haley."

"I'll talk to him before we go to this infernal gala." I'm sure it's a worthy cause, but I hate everything about it. I like catering for fancy parties, but I'd much rather be at a cookout in someone's backyard or be barefoot in the sand.

"Is this the fancy black-and-white party?" she asks.

"Yes, turns out it's a charity event with hundreds of guests." So much of this week has been a surprise to me. I don't understand why he didn't prepare me.

"Ugh. Hopefully, the food will be good," she says.

"Hopefully. Thank you, Carina, for talking to me. I'm sorry I yelled at you. I am happy for you and Orion. I just feel like a bad friend since you felt like you couldn't tell me," I say.

"You've never been a bad friend. I was terrified. And I should have listened to you instead of assuming the worst of Ransom."

"The funny thing is he did come to Florida to see me again," I admit. I don't know how she'll react to that information. She saw it as a red flag. But after years of just wanting someone to put in the smallest amount of effort, this grand, sweeping gesture meant everything to me. It would have been a different story if he had come on strong at the beginning, but he hadn't. It was every bit the fairy tale of the prince going to the ends of the world to be with his princess.

"Oh. Well, that's intense," Carina says.

"I know, but we've talked about it. He's being honest with me, and I trust him."

"Good. Go talk to him. We'll catch up about everything else when you get home. I'll kick Orion out and we can sit on my porch and split a bottle of rosé."

"Sounds like a plan to me."

We hang up and I hear voices in the bedroom indicating the stylists have arrived. My conversation with Ransom will have to wait until after my hair and makeup are done.

For the next hour and a half, my hair is pinned and combed and curled, and my face highlighted and contoured. Every so often Ransom pokes his head in to make sure we're doing okay, offering to get me water or a drink. I appreciate that I don't have to do this myself, but I hate this much product in my hair or on my face. I wear makeup daily since I'm constantly filming myself. I try to be polished. I know this is a one-time thing but I can't get over how much effort it takes.

"Do you need help getting into your dress?" the makeup artist asks when she applies my final lip color.

"No, I'll get it for her," Ransom says. His voice is low and full of heat. He leans in the doorway, already dressed in his tuxedo, as handsome as the devil.

"Okay, we'll be off."

They exit the room, leaving me in nothing but a dressing gown with a boyfriend who looks like he wants to eat me.

"The event has already started," I tell him.

"Everyone who matters will be late," he assures me. He takes a long breath out. "I can wait until later to get you back in bed. Let's get you dressed."

In the bedroom, the dress is draped over the foot of the bed, along with the lingerie he bought me and the red-soled heels.

I take a deep breath as he wraps his arms around me from behind. "Are you okay?" He kisses my neck.

"Yes. Just nervous. But can we talk for a second?" I turn to face him. "I called Carina."

"Yeah?"

"Yeah. I don't get your friends. They haven't been exactly welcoming and they're kind of mean."

"It's a defense mechanism," he explains. "You have to understand people are always trying to take advantage of them and what they have. Someone always wants something. They're closed off for self-preservation. They need to weed out the charlatans. It took me forever to earn their trust."

"But I don't want anything from them. I just want you." He pulls at the collar of my robe, kissing down my shoulder. At this rate we won't make it to the party. Honestly, a night in bed with him sounds better.

"I know. But people will go to extreme lengths to get close to them. They don't know you aren't after my money."

I laugh. "You're the one who chased after me, remember?"

"I did. You're right. I should have prepared you more. I'll make sure everyone knows you are mine, and a part of this group."

I nod with him. I have a thousand more things I want to say but keep them quiet. I don't want to be judgmental of his friends. I'd be devastated if he thought about Carina, Sienna, and Bristol the way I'm thinking about his friends. But maybe everything will change tonight, and I'll see the side of them he gets to see.

Ransom undoes the ties of my robe and helps me into my

undergarments. We're silent as we do it, like this is foreplay. A taste of what's to come later when we do this in reverse.

Physically, he's always made sense to me. I've always loved the way he touches me and how my body reacts to him.

I stand in front of the full-length mirror in my dress. Ransom is behind me as we admire how perfectly it fits. I don't think I've ever intentionally worn solid black outside of a kitchen uniform before. It's gorgeous and the cut is stunning, but I feel like I'm wearing a different woman's skin.

"You look absolutely amazing." His voice is low. If I moved even a hair's breadth away, I wouldn't hear him.

"Thank you." The dress pools at my feet since I haven't put my shoes on yet.

"I have one more present for you," he says, wrapping his arms around me and placing a small box in front of me.

"Ransom, you really don't have to do this."

"I know, but I want to."

I open the red box to find white gold diamond earrings. "These are beautiful, but you really can't do this." I turn to face him. "I love them. But what if instead of you spending your money on me as presents, we spend it together."

His eyes narrow. "What do you mean?"

"I'm not saying I want to go pick out jewelry and dresses and shoes just for the sake of it. I just want to be around you," I say. "Next time you want to buy something for me, bring me along." We can window shop and leave the expensive things at the store.

"Do you not like them?"

"No, I love them. They're perfect. But I like you more."

He kisses me. I know what I almost said. I'm not sure if he's ready for it, but this feels right to me. He pulls me in tight and I want to skip the party. I want to drown in the perfect heat of him and the woodsy smell of his cologne.

He abruptly lets me go. "Shoes."

"What?" I'm still a little dazed from the kiss.

He points to the floor where the shoes rest. "If we don't leave soon, then the dress is coming off and we'll never get to the party."

"Don't threaten me with a good time," I say. But I sit on the ottoman anyway while Ransom retrieves the shoes and kneels in front of me. The pumps are silver and covered in sequins. The heel isn't too high that I'll have to worry about my balance, but higher than I usually wear. I can do this. I can dress like this for events if I get to be close to this man.

He takes my foot in his hand, running his palm up my calf until he gets to my knee. If he goes any higher, this is over. He'll find my wet panties and he'll have to remove them.

"Ransom," I say breathlessly.

"Haley, fuck." He kisses the spot just above my ankle that I didn't know was so sensitive until now. "I adore every inch of you."

He blinks and it's like he comes back to himself, but I want him to go back. Not because I don't want to go to the party and because I want to stay here with him. But because I know that man. The man he is beneath the suits and the money and the helicopter rides. That is the man who cares about me. Who would give anything for me. Who could make me a better person. Who might just be everything I need.

He eases my foot into the shoe before moving on to the next one and then helps me stand.

"You and me tonight? That's what's important," I say. I need to be on the same page as him. I think we are, but I'm so deeply terrified we're not.

"You and me," he echoes.

* * *

THE PARTY IS on the roof deck of the house. It's beautiful as the sun sets over land behind us, making the clouds magnificent shades of red and purple. I never get tired of sunsets and sunrises, especially when I'm near the beach.

A few heads turn when we step outside with Ransom holding my hand. I scan the crowd for any familiar face, like somehow Carina will show up. I would die for the unlikely event that Will and Alma are here too. Maybe they somehow know this same crowd of people. Every woman wears either a black or white floor-length dress and the men are in tuxedos. There is a bar set up on one side, with servers walking around passing out champagne and canapés. At the other side of the rooftop is a long table with people walking slowly along it.

We're greeted by Daxton and Josephine, who gushes over my dress and tells us to help ourselves to the drinks and food and, of course, to visit the silent auction table.

"It is for the children, after all," Josephine says sweetly.

"Come, let's get a drink." Ransom keeps his hand on my low back as we move through the crowd.

With a glass of champagne in my hand, I walk down the silent auction offerings. I don't know why I expected anything here to be in my price range. It's luxury vacations, private yachts, and jewelry I could never imagine wearing, let alone casually placing on a table. But then again, there is a burly man standing at each end, so maybe they are concerned about someone running off with the diamonds.

Based on the way the bids increase in value, it seems more like a way for guests to brag about how much money they can spend.

Toward the center of the table is an offer of a dinner party with a seven-course chef's tasting menu, provided by chef Zach Evered. Current bids are in the thousands of dollars.

"Oh, I know him!" I tell Ransom, who hasn't let go of me. "We worked in a restaurant together in Paris."

He looks at me with a tilt to his head. "You've never mentioned working in Paris before. Or restaurants."

I place my hand on his chest. "Not a fun part of my life," I answer. "I didn't like the head chef yelling at me every dinner service."

He kisses my temple. "I hate him already."

"Zach was good though. We relied on each other to get through the internship. I'm happy he's doing well." I can tell Ransom is digging through some feelings. "It was strictly platonic."

"I wasn't jealous," he says, looking away.

I dig my hands into his hard pec. "Yes, you were. But if I'm not jealous of your ex-girlfriend staying in the same house as us, you don't need to be jealous of someone I used to work with."

He plants a gentle kiss on my lips. "You're right. I'm curious if he's here. I'd love to meet him and hear more about the restaurant you worked at."

"Haley, you should have donated your services for the night." Georgina steps up next to us with Myles and Lena at her side. Lena is stunning in a white dress that manages to not look like a wedding dress, paired with a simple diamond necklace. Everything about her is understated and beautiful.

Myles stifles a laugh but I just roll my eyes. With Ransom's hand on my waist, I know I have nothing to fear from these people. We'll put in our time and then go back to our room.

"I'm sure a meal prepared by Haley is worth quite a lot," Lena says with a fake smile that she manages to fill with a glare at her sister.

"Whatever, still the help," Georgina says.

I turn to Ransom, waiting for him to say something to her, but he's frozen looking at Lena who is doing her best to ignore him and look at me.

I am missing something here. I get that they used to date, and something isn't resolved for Lena. I understand her sister is being protective of her. But I hate that I'm being dragged down in the process.

That doesn't mean I have to subject myself to this.

Being polite isn't winning them over to me. "If you'll excuse me, I have to be anywhere but here." I remove myself from Ransom's grip and take a few steps before he grabs my hand and pulls me into a kiss.

My soul melts the way he takes over me. His mouth is on mine and his arm braces my lower back as he dips me. Almost as if he's trying to fully invade my body through our clothes. The world falls away, and I only feel him. I'm afraid I'm going to topple in my heels, but he holds on to me with all his strength. No one else matters. It's just him and me and this love that's blooming in my chest.

He ends the kiss and we shift upright. He cradles my face in one hand, looking at me like I'm the sun lighting up his universe.

twenty-two

RANSOM

I HAVE SEVERELY MISJUDGED THE SITUATION.

Lena and I spent one Christmas together. We traveled to her family's estate in the countryside with Myles Ainsley's family. That's where I first met her father and made my pitch to work for him. I got the job and we broke up. We weren't involved long enough that I thought any real feelings had developed.

So why is she wearing the diamond necklace I gave her that Christmas?

I've barely talked to her this week, except for her admonishing me for sending her work-related emails when we were supposed to be on holiday. She's more closed off than usual, but she gets like this when she travels.

"I'm all yours, and you're all mine," I whisper into Haley's lips after the very public display of affection I gave her. I need to mark my claim on her and have her claim me. I'm not interested in anyone else. Haley is it.

"I'm all yours, and you're all mine," she says. She looks kiss drunk but that might be the champagne. Either way, I release her so we can at least get a crab cake before the formal sit-down dinner.

For the rest of the cocktail hour, I keep Haley close. I should take the time to get to know the other guests. Someone might be a useful connection, but I only want to focus on Haley. I'm bored throughout our conversation with Daxton and Josephine until the emcee asks us to find our tables.

We're seated with Lena, Estella, and a few others I don't know. They're American and somehow seem even stuffier than most English I've met.

Lena is silent for most of the meal, but Estella engages with Haley and soon the two of them are chatting like old friends. Estella asks about Wendell Beach and Haley's friends there. To my surprise, it's Estella who brings up Carina Webb for the first time.

"I've been wearing her leggings for years. I didn't realize she's from the same town as you," Estella says.

"She's actually one of my closest friends," Haley replies.

"Really?" Lena asks, leaning forward.

Haley nods. "Yes, we met as kids. We were roommates in college together."

"University," I correct. Americans use the two almost interchangeably, but in Britain there is a difference. Haley can stand on her own, but I'll give her any armor she needs. Including making sure my friends know she is as educated as they are.

"Right, university," Haley echoes.

"Did you meet her?" Lena asks me, as if wondering how involved I am in Haley's life.

"I did. We went sailing on her boyfriend's yacht."

"That must have been beautiful," Estella says.

"It was. We saw dolphins," I say.

After dinner, on my way back from the restroom, I turn a corner and almost bump into Lena. She nearly spills her drink over her white dress, but steps back enough to avoid it.

"Fuck." She brushes a hand over the skirt to make sure there aren't any lingering drops.

I smile. She doesn't swear often in my presence, but it's endearing when she does. "Here, let me." I grab a cocktail napkin from a nearby table and hand it to her.

"It's fine. Don't start to care about me now," she says wearily.

"I beg your pardon?" I must have heard her wrong.

She looks at me full of exasperation. "You never really cared about me, did you? It was about getting a job. Nothing else."

I want to roll my eyes and dismiss her, but I need to shut this down. I work with her. She holds my career in her hands. She has the power to completely crush me.

"Let's talk somewhere private," I say, moving inside and down the stairs to the second level. I step into the gaming room. Lena shuts the door behind her and then moves to the other side of the room.

"It's true, then," she says, her posture stiff and her eyes cold.

"Just because I want to speak privately doesn't mean anything."

She rubs her eyebrow in a move that reminds me so much of Haley, I want to leave immediately and find her. "What are you doing, Ransom?" Lena asks.

"Enjoying a fundraiser for a children's charity," I answer.

"No, with Haley. We talked about this. You can't date her," she says.

I adjust my cufflinks. "There is nothing in our policies that states I can't date a contractor who doesn't report to me."

"For fuck's sake, Ransom. Is any of this real? Is any part of you real?" She raises her voice. I don't know how much she's had to drink tonight, but throughout dinner she drank wine faster than she normally does.

"Yes, Haley and I are real. I care about her deeply."

"I should have seen this coming. But I thought…" She doesn't continue, but idly adjusts the necklace at her throat.

"Lena, darling, we broke up years ago. We were barely

together to begin with. I don't understand how you're still upset about it," I say.

Her eyes go wide and I wait for some cutting remark.

"Ransom?" I turn to find Haley standing behind me, having pushed the door open. "What's going on?" She looks concerned and I wonder how much she heard. But there wasn't anything I said that I wouldn't say directly to Haley. There weren't any secrets shared or lies told.

"It's nothing, Haley. Just give us a minute and I'll be right up," I say.

"Actually, I'll head upstairs with you, Haley," Lena says. "I have nothing more to say to him."

"Lena, wait…"

"Wait, what, Ransom?" Lena exclaims. "What more do you want from me. I don't owe you anything. There's clearly been a misunderstanding between us. We can leave it at that."

"What kind of misunderstanding?" Haley asks.

I don't want Haley to hear Lena's answer but silencing either one of them is a bad idea.

"I thought there was something between us, but all he wanted was a job and somehow was able to convince me we had a chance after we broke up."

"He what?" Haley asks.

"I didn't mean for you to wait for me," I say. "You thought it was a bad idea for us to date and work together." I might have led her there, but Lena thought it was the right choice. "You said no one would take you seriously if we were dating."

"But you left the door open. There was a chance we could have something again. Once you settled in and earned everyone's respect. I shouldn't have expected you to come around. I knew none of the other women you dated meant anything. You were just passing time. I thought we were real. But I was just someone else for you to use."

I turn to Haley as if she has the answer I need. She's still looking at Lena. "I'm sorry, Lena. I shouldn't be here."

"Take care of yourself, Haley. I promise he's using you just the same as he used me."

Haley opens the door again and leaves.

"Fuck." I move to follow her.

"Is she really worth this?" Lena asks. "I'll go to my father or Will Caron. Tell them this is because you can't keep it in your pants. How do you think that will go over? That man wants commitment in his partners. How do you think he'll react if your commitment is first to her and not to the restaurant?"

Fuck. She might be right. Will wouldn't blame me if I found love in the process, but he might object if he thought I was fucking around with his dream restaurant to get my dick wet. Which is exactly what Lena would tell him. And if the Foleys find out after they gave their lecture on integrity, they'll convince him to end my involvement.

"Is it because she turned you down? Is that what this is about?" Lena asks. "You just don't know how to lose."

No. It's always been about more. "You wouldn't understand." I leave her fuming behind me and head back to the party. I do a quick lap, but Haley's not here. I get to our room and she's nowhere to be seen, but the lights are on and the door to the bathroom is closed.

I knock. "Haley. Please talk to me."

"I will. Just give me a minute."

I lean against the door. I don't know what she's thinking. I don't want to have to explain the whole situation with Lena. I can dance around the edges for Lena, but with Haley I need to be honest. I refuse to believe Haley will accept everything Lena said without discussion. Not my Haley. Not the woman who values loyalty above everything else.

I'm all yours, and you're all mine.

I hear rustling of fabric and a zipper. Then the door opens

and I almost fall forward. She looks up at me when I catch myself. She took off her dress and is wearing shorts and a tank top.

"Why did you change?" I ask. It's clear she's not going back to the party. I hoped we could resolve this quickly and then return to the terrace. I'll smooth things over with Lena as soon as I take care of Haley. Then we can enjoy the rest of the night. It was supposed to be perfect. We were going to dance under the stars until the sun came up.

"I felt like I was playing dress-up."

"You said you liked the dress."

"I do. But I don't dress like that normally. It's not something I'm comfortable with." She sits on the sofa with her legs tucked under her. I sit down next to her and face her.

Right. She's much more used to Florida and its flip-flops than she'll ever be to black tie. "Okay. That's fine. Next time you'll pick something out you're more comfortable in. I'll get you a stylist."

"I'm not so sure there is going to be a next time."

"What do you mean by that?" Of course there is going to be a next time. Just like she's allowed to fight with her friends, I'm allowed to fight with mine. She accused Carina of lying and they dealt with it. I didn't even lie to Lena. We'll get through this.

She takes a deep breath. "I like you a lot and I really care about you. But what Lena said rang true. You're going to say and do whatever you need to get what you want. I don't know that I can trust you."

"Lena is just upset. She'll get over it," I say.

"No, that's not good enough. I'm not asking about her behavior. I'm asking about yours."

"I'll tell you whatever you want to know." I take her hand, and I'm comforted that she doesn't immediately pull away from me.

"Tell me about your relationship with Lena," she says.

"I will. But it doesn't matter. It's in the past. There are plenty of other things I can share first." I'll plead. I'll beg. I'll do anything to get her to ask about anything else.

I'll find a list of questions to get to know your partner like we did at the spa.

But she's looking at me like I'm missing the whole point. "I can't shake the feeling that you used her. And if you've done that to someone before, you could do it again."

"I'm not using you, Haley."

"But you used her?"

"You didn't listen to the nonsense your friends said about me. You shouldn't listen to what Lena said."

"Ransom. Did you use her?"

"It's complicated."

"'It's complicated' isn't no." She stands up and paces. "Tell me what you did." She pauses between each word.

"I am good at what I do." I watch as she moves around the room, completely and utterly mesmerized by how beautiful she is. I'll do anything to keep her, but I need to be truthful with her. I must do the right thing. She won't accept anything else. I need her to accept all of me. "I've earned all my successes. But it was nearly impossible to get in the door. There was no way for me to get a job at this firm without a personal connection."

"So, you made a personal connection."

"Yes."

She nods without looking at me. "You picked a company you wanted to work for, discovered the owner had a daughter your age. Then staged some meeting so you could date her?"

"No!" She's making me sound like a complete stalker. "No. I was working for a different firm. One that was good, but not quite as elite. I met Lena at a social club. I liked her. I didn't know who she was at first."

Now she looks at me. "But you wouldn't have called her if she couldn't get you the connection you wanted."

"Haley, you have to understand..." But I have no idea how to finish the sentence. I don't know how to make this better.

"Had you done this before? Are there other women you treated as stepping-stones?"

"You are not a stepping-stone, Haley."

"Answer the question, Ransom."

"Yes. There are others."

"You called her 'darling.'"

What? "Her last name is Darlington. Everyone calls her darling."

"You called me darling." Haley's voice has gone cold.

What? I'm sure I didn't, but I can't remember the last time. I call lots of people darling. It just comes out. It's not the connection she thinks it is. "Love, I..."

She grabs her phone from the nightstand. "I need some air."

"Haley, wait."

"No. I need a few minutes. I can't think clearly when you're around."

I don't want to, but I let her go. A thousand terrible ideas run through my head of how to keep her here. But she's right. If she stays, I'll get her in bed. And as much as I want that to solve things, I know it won't.

<h1 style="text-align:center">twenty-three</h1>

HALEY

Leaving is probably a mistake. But I meant what I said—I can't think around him. I want him too much and I feel too much for him. I can't trust myself when I don't trust him.

I don't understand what's in this for him. Why did he go to these lengths for me? He's always been too good to be true. Too charming. Too polished. I should have seen it sooner. But I swore I knew who he was beneath that facade. Now I'm left wondering if he's turned me into the villain in Lena's story.

The party is in full swing, but most people are upstairs so I'm able to take the main staircase down without anyone spotting me. I exit out the back door and skirt around the edges of the pool deck, avoiding the few people who have come down for privacy. I follow the pathway lights out to the beach. At least the ocean calms me. I sit on a bench Ransom and I passed earlier and watch the outlines of waves in the distance. The Atlantic is much more violent than the Gulf of Mexico. The water is colder too.

What would have happened if I hadn't left the partition open between our seats on that flight? But I was enchanted by the way he thanked the flight attendant for his scotch. I felt so desperate for something magical to happen. I wanted my fairy tale for even a few hours.

He can get anything he wants using that charm. He got me to believe that we are something real. That I was safe to believe in a happily ever after.

It's the fight with Carina, Bristol, and Sienna all over again, just so much worse. This might not be reparable.

I don't think he's using me now because he doesn't get anything from being with me. I don't give him status or connections. His feelings for me are real, but how long before they change? Or before he realizes someone else could get him what he wants? He's not going to stop being ambitious because he's with me.

I want to be in this relationship with him. I saw a future for us take shape. It was only the outline, but I started to hope. Now I don't know if he's on the same page as me.

I feel rather than hear someone approach. There's a shift in the noise of the sea and the sand. It must be Ransom, and I'm so annoyed he followed me here, but then I smell a cigarette and turn quickly to see Zach Evered standing beside me.

"Sorry, didn't mean to startle you. May I sit?" He does when I nod. "I saw you leave the party. You were down the stairs before I got the chance to say hi."

He always had an impeccable sense of intuition. It helps him in the kitchen when he knows which rare ingredients pair well together. Or what risk to take with a dish for a particular person. I appreciate that more than ever now as he sits and doesn't ask me anything.

"I saw your silent auction item. I looked around for you but didn't see you," I say after we've been watching the waves and his cigarette has gone out.

"I was in the kitchen for most of it," he answers.

I look at him more closely. What I thought was a suit is black pants and an unbuttoned chef's coat. "I didn't realize you were the chef tonight. Everything was excellent." Even with Lena staring Ransom down the whole time, I still tried to appreciate the food.

"What did you think of the fish?" His face turns to me. It's too dark to really see his expressions, but I know what he's thinking.

"Magnificent."

"Even to a Floridian?"

"Yes, even to my standards, it was amazing."

"Good," he says. "I'm surprised you're here. This doesn't seem like your set."

"It's not really. I'm dating a guy, Ransom West. He's friends with Daxton's girlfriend, Josephine." But is he? Are they still friends now that Lena has realized he won't date her again?

"She's a piece of work. Had me change the menu three times," he says. "Other than storming out of a party and ending up on the beach with an old friend, are you doing okay?"

"For the most part, yeah. Business is good. It's hard. I make it work."

Zach helped me realize working in a commercial kitchen wasn't a good fit and to accept that it was okay. That there are a million ways to be a chef.

"Good." He stands. "I'm heading back to the city. Do you want a ride out of here?"

I turn to him and contemplate his offer. I should put space between Ransom and me. I could get a flight back to Florida tomorrow and be done with this. But I can't leave my things in the room. I don't even have shoes, let alone an ID.

I could walk away from Ransom. I'm not in too deep. I'll only get deeper if I stay.

But letting go of him feels worse than anything waiting for me back in that room.

The last few days with just the two of us have felt so close to love. It was magical and easy, and the quiet moments have been better than any other relationship. I'm not ready to call it love, but it's what we both want.

I don't want to run like I did with Carina. I want to figure this out with Ransom. I trust him enough that if I decide to leave, he'll take me to the airport in the morning. But we both deserve closure.

"No. I'm fine. But thanks for the offer."

"Of course. If you're ever in New York again…"

"Sure. And you should come to Wendell Beach sometime."

He laughs. "I have been meaning to check out the sandcastle restaurant you're so fond of."

"The drinks are amazing and the food is fantastic. It's not just the tourists who keep it open," I insist.

"Whatever you say." He lightly squeezes my shoulder and walks away.

I take a few deep breaths of ocean air. I wait for the noise of the party to die down before I head back in. The only thing worse than sneaking out of a party in shorts and a tank top is sneaking back in.

The pool deck is quiet. Staff moves about, picking up discarded glasses and bottles.

"Is there anything I can get you, Ms. Stewart?" one woman asks me.

"Some water would be wonderful, please."

"There are bottles in your room. We made sure everyone had extras. But I can have some more sent up if you'd like," she responds.

"No, thank you. I'm sure there's plenty," I say. The excess I've seen this week is staggering, but right now I wish I always had someone looking after small things for me.

I enter our bedroom and find Ransom on the couch with his iPad open. A few days ago, I'd have assumed he was working. But he's likely drawing. He's drawn me at every chance over the last few days. He's talented and it's been wonderful to see myself through his eyes—the parts he chooses to highlight and where his attention falls.

It makes my heart hurt knowing that if we can't get through this, he'll have physical evidence of our good moments and I'll have nothing of him. I wouldn't keep the diamonds or the dress. Even if I did, those would only remind me of this night.

"Oh, thank god." He stands and approaches me. "Haley, I can't change the past. But I'm a different person. I won't do things like that now."

"When exactly did you become a different person?"

He crosses his arms when it's clear I'm not going to fall into his embrace. He's taken off his tuxedo jacket and tie and rolled up the sleeves of his shirt. I shouldn't want him as much as I do.

"I don't know. When I met you," he says.

"That's not a good answer."

"I've changed. I've become a better man for you."

"That sounds really romantic, Ransom. But that's not how this works. I can't be responsible for your personal growth."

He recoils at the statement. "Why else would I have changed?"

"To not be someone who uses others."

He blinks a few times. "Okay. Can we sit and talk about this? If we can talk through this…if you just let me explain everything from the beginning, you'll understand and we'll be okay."

I nod and sit at the other end of the couch from him, holding a pillow in my lap.

He runs his hand through his hair. This isn't an elaborate long con where he's trying to get something out of me. He cares about me and wants to be in a relationship. But his past can come crawling back to him at any time. Does he even know what he truly feels? Has he been lying so much that he believes it and this house of cards is going to come crashing down on me? I can't trust him.

"You know I grew up in a family that always struggled with money. But I got into private school with a scholarship. I was around these other boys whose allowances were more than my parents' income. I was top of my class academically, but I couldn't keep up socially. Not when their outings cost money. I couldn't even afford to go to the cinema. It matters differently in England."

I nod. We've talked around this. I may not know all the details, but this isn't a surprise.

"I was relentlessly teased and bullied about it by the other kids."

I close my eyes and see little Ransom trying to fit in and never being good enough, and none of it was his fault.

"When I reached secondary school, girls took an interest in me. My parents don't have much to give me, but they have good genetics. My first girlfriend, Margaret, was the most popular girl in school. At first, no one could believe she was giving me attention. But she did. The teasing stopped and my entire world had changed."

I don't respond and just let him continue. I see where this is going.

"I'm smart and I work hard. I got a job after school to afford better clothes and got into Cambridge with my grades. I set my sights higher than just fitting in."

"You didn't want to get by like your family did—you wanted to never worry about money again," I say. I understand the feeling.

He nods. "And I did. I wore the right clothes. I changed my accent to be posher. I did everything I could to fit in with the wealthy and upper class. To never remind them that I wasn't the same. Including dating women to get access to their connections or because they elevated my status. I got the jobs I wanted. I got the money and the status, and I use it to provide for my family. My sister's schooling is from me. My brother's flat—I pay for it so he can work for a charity that helps immigrants get jobs. In

America, I would be someone to look up to. But in England, I'm one misstep away from losing everything."

"Further proof we were right to separate ourselves," I quip.

"Now you get patriotic on me?" he says with a smile.

"Okay, I get it. Money and status save you from bullying. You'll do anything to prevent that from happening again. Including using women for gain. So how do I fit into this? What do you gain by dating me?" His friends think I'm the help. I don't elevate him.

He smiles and it's so sad. "I like you, Haley. I met you on the plane and I wanted you. The way you are. Your passion for everything. The way you love your friends. I want that."

"Just because I love some people doesn't mean I feel that way about everyone."

"I know. But I wanted to be part of your world."

"And you'll do anything to make it happen?

"What exactly are you mad at me for? Do you think I'm lying to you or are you mad about how I've treated Lena?"

I take a very deep breath. "I don't think you're lying to me about your feelings. But it makes me deeply uncomfortable how you've used women in the past. And I'm not sure I can be a part of your future knowing that. I'm not sure when you're going to lie to me or when you'll realize you can gain something by sleeping with someone else."

"I won't lie to you. I know you value the truth."

"But you don't. See, I know you'll do or say anything to me to get what you want right now. I don't know anything about your own morals."

He stands, looking resigned and betrayed. "You really do think the absolute worst of me, don't you?"

I don't answer. I just nod.

twenty-four

RANSOM

I'M TRYING TO GRIP WATER IN MY HANDS, AND IT KEEPS SPILLING out until I have nothing left but the memory of what was once there.

I stand frozen in front of Haley. Her warm brown eyes are full of tears. I can tell she doesn't want to end things with me and that she feels something for me. But it's possible what I've done in the past, what I've done to get me to where I am—a place where I could meet her in business class on our way to a luxury destination and give her the earrings she's still wearing—might be unforgivable.

"It will never happen again," I promise. "I'm faithful in relationships. I'll be faithful to you."

She doesn't look convinced.

"I know this sounds like I've been terrible. But I treated those women well. I was attentive. And at the end of the relationship, I made sure they weren't brokenhearted. It was always their idea to end things."

"You manipulated them into thinking it was their idea. Will you do that to me?"

"No!" I take a deep breath.

"Until you find someone else who can get you something you want," she says. She looks utterly defeated.

"No." I can't. How can she think I'd toss her aside for a new job? Or access to higher status? I hadn't thought about it this way before with her. In the past I had put values on my relationships. I had my parents and my siblings. There isn't anything I won't do for them, no price at which I would turn on them. Then I had my friends, girlfriends, and colleagues. Those had a pound sign above their heads for the amount I was willing to cut them loose.

But with Haley, there is no amount. How do I get her to see that?

I am so deeply stuck. She won't take anything I say to her at face value. No confession of love or devotion.

I step closer to her and she doesn't move away. "We're good together, Haley. My past doesn't have to determine our future."

"How can I possibly trust you?" she asks.

Great question.

"Name anything," I say.

She cringes. "That's kind of the problem."

"Okay, give me something measurable. A target I can hit."

"Fine. Do you really care about Lena as a friend?"

"Yes."

"Then you have to make up to her what you did," she says.

I grind my teeth. I don't have anything to say to Lena. I was a great boyfriend. I told her the truth. I never lied to her. It's not my fault she hung on. Everyone else I dated moved on. Why couldn't she?

"I'll speak with her in the morning." I'm not sure Lena will listen to me, but I have to smooth things over at some point. We still work together. If she wanted, she could get me fired from my job. I'll figure out some way to make it up to her without breaking any promises to Haley.

"Good. Also, most of your friends are fucking terrible."

"Excuse me?"

"I get that you want money and you want to provide for your family, and now I guess me. But why do you need to be friends with *these* people? And if your answer has anything to do with money or status, it's wrong. Tell me you love being around them and your memories with them are precious. That they'll stand with you no matter what."

She knows I can't.

I should fight back. Remind her she hasn't spoken with Sienna since she left the city. But I won't sully her friendships with my mess.

"Are you going to make me choose?" I ask.

She rubs her forehead. "I don't want you to pick. But these last few days haven't been fun for me, and I don't think they make us a stronger couple. They want to tear us down. That's not good for us. You aren't even the same person around them that you are in private with me."

"You know me, Haley."

"Maybe. But you haven't convinced me to stay."

It feels like a knife to the gut. This knowledge that she might walk away in the morning. I'll do anything to keep her, but everything I've done in the past will just push her away. I have no more tricks left. I have nothing to offer her.

For once, it's just me.

"Okay, we won't do trips like this again." A trip like this brought me to her, but I leave the irony alone.

Haley nods but doesn't say anything further. I don't know if I've convinced her yet. I lay it out on the line in the best way I can. I give her the most honest thing I can. "I wish I could tell you that if I could go back in time and change everything I've done, I would. But then I wouldn't have met you. I would have done a lot worse things if it meant getting to you sooner."

"I don't want that, and I don't want to be with someone who thinks it's okay to step on people to get what you want."

I'm fucking this up. "I don't know what you want from me."

"I don't think I want you," she says.

My world feels like it's shattering.

"No. We're not ending this here. Not like this." I'm not letting *them* take from me the one person who matters.

"Then show me who you really are, Ransom. Not this man who will do whatever it takes to get what he wants. Not the man with the money and the jewelry and the apparently fake accent. Show me who you really are. God, that dramatic kiss was just to prove a point to them too, wasn't it? Do you mean anything you do?"

I don't know who that man is. For the first time I realize I don't know what she sees in me. That I might not be the type of man she needs. I've always been ruthless and gone after everything I want. I might be the opposite of everything she is, but I'm not giving up on her.

"I've always been someone who takes. That has never changed. I don't know that it can. But every time I've touched you, it's been about us."

"So show me that. Then I can decide if I'm staying." The challenge is in her eyes. "Show me who I'm really with and not this fake person."

I step forward into her space and take her hips in my hands. "This is what you want?" I press my hips to hers. I can get hard in an instant around her.

"Is this all you have to give me?" Her eyes trace mine, pleading for me to say something.

I honestly don't know what else I have to give her. But I can give her this.

I can give her pleasure she's never felt before. I can give her a reason to keep me around that's not trips and jewelry and fancy meals. If that's all I can give her, if that's the only reason she wants me, then I will take those scraps.

Sex with Haley has been easy. The pleasure, the connection,

and the joy. But it's simultaneously terrifying. She sees through me, even when she doesn't realize it.

I nudge her onto the bed, and my hand skims underneath her tank top to the bralette she's wearing. She pulls off both while I climb onto the bed with her, straddling her hips. She reaches for the buttons on my shirt.

"This off now," she says.

I take her hands and place them above her head. "No." I deliver a gentle nibble to her lips. "Let me."

I release her hands and sit back so I can undo the buttons slowly.

"I don't want a show," Haley says, her eyes full of disappointment. "I just want you." She reaches up and pulls as buttons go flying.

I kiss her until we're both panting and my cock is aching in my trousers. We've done this before—holding on to each other while I'm still outside her body. We drag out the moment of anticipation because we're both so afraid that reality won't match up with the expectations we've built.

But I can live up to any expectation that's created for me.

I sit back again so I can get her shorts and panties off and then my mouth is between her thighs. I want to drown in the taste of her. She's better than any rare wine or aged scotch. I could survive on her alone.

She's not quiet. She doesn't blush around me anymore or hide her desires from me. I thrust two fingers into her channel, harder than I have before, but *fuck* she takes them so well. She's wet and I'll fight with her every day if it gets her this turned on.

She comes hard and fast, and I want to take a moment to sit with her as she comes down. A gentleman would. But I don't.

I grab a condom from the nightstand and flip her onto her stomach and lift her hips up. "Is this how you want it, love? You want it rough, like me?"

She moans as I enter her. God, she so loud, she's going to wake the whole house.

I lean forward so my chest is against her back and I'm able to rub her clit and whisper in her ear. She holds me up as I hold her. "I've wanted you since I first met you and I don't let anything stand in the way of what I want." I thrust hard, drowning in the saltwater smell of her. "Not distance. Or money. I would have done anything to have you, Haley. Please let me keep you."

It's both always been about sex with her and never at the same time. I've always wanted her body and her mind and to know everything she keeps hidden.

I hit the right spot inside her and she screams "Yes!" as she comes.

I follow her and it's good, but I still feel hollow. I know her yes doesn't mean what I want it to.

I remove the condom and roll over to look at her. She's watching me intently.

"What do you think is going to happen when the restaurant is open and your involvement is over? Are we just doing long-distance forever?" she asks.

I brush her hair back from her face. At least now she's thinking long term and not ending everything. "I hope you'll move to London. Since you can work wherever, you could travel with me. We wouldn't have to be apart."

She rolls onto her back and pulls the sheet up to cover herself. "I don't want to move out of Florida. I love Wendell Beach. I can't imagine living anywhere else."

This is what I had feared, that even if I was a better person there is still too much standing in the way of our happiness.

"Okay. We can work with that. I'll buy a house in Wendell Beach and we can come back once a month. We can make it work." I'm based out of London, but I have money. I will fix this. I've made so many things work in the past. We can do this too.

"I don't know." She turns her head to me. "This feels too hard. I don't know if I can trust you."

I pull her in close. "You can, Haley. You're the only person I can be myself around. You're the only person I don't perform for. Please don't end this."

She nods. "We'll try it. It's not like we're getting married tomorrow. But you have to apologize to Lena. You need to make that right."

I groan. "Fine."

I hold her as we both fall asleep. I'm convinced that in the morning things will be better.

twenty-five

HALEY

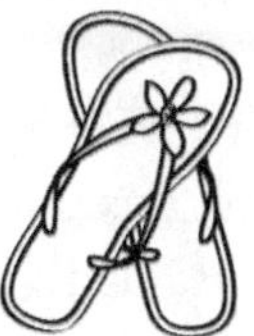

In the morning, I feel Ransom leave bed. Our plans to watch the sunrise together shattered with our fight last night. I don't blame him for wanting to get out for a run before the heat of the day.

We spent the night tossing and turning, eventually giving up the ruse twice and reaching for each other. He's trying to prove something to me with sex. I think it's his way of showing we're good together and I shouldn't walk away. I reach for him now, wanting him to stay just a little bit longer. I don't think we're doomed, but if we are, I want to spend as much time with him as I can.

"Go back to sleep, love," he whispers as he kisses my shoulder.

I nestle in deeper to the mattress and pull the sheet over me. But as soon as he's gone, my brain turns on and I need to move. So I get up and head for the closet. I change into yoga pants and grab the mat I took from the house's gym yesterday, not wanting one of his friends to walk in on me while I was practicing. On the balcony overlooking the ocean with the sun rising bright yellow and orange, I move through a yoga flow Carina taught me to relax.

It doesn't fucking work. I'm on edge. We agreed to stay together, and we'll figure out the details. I believe he wants to do things differently than he did in the past. He's not lying to me about how much I mean to him. He'll put in effort to be with me. No one has ever done that before.

And it's more than that. He values me and my work. If I choose him, then he will be a partner in the ways that matter to me.

Maybe when I go back to Wendell Beach and he goes back to London, I'll get time to think this through. We're not making any unchangeable commitments. This is serious, but we're not married. I'm not moving tomorrow. We have a few more days here and we'll take it slow. We've been trying to pack everything we feel into such short amounts of time. We haven't had the chance to simply be with each other.

When I finish my yoga practice, I step into the room and find Ransom, shirtless, staring at his phone and leaning against the bedpost.

He looks up at me and smiles. "I didn't want to interrupt you," he says. "Want to shower with me?"

I nod because I want closeness with him. I want him to hold me and tell me he cares and to feel his skin against mine.

My relationships have always ended because it was time for one of us to move on. I've always been so sure of my decisions. But I don't feel sure about this one.

He takes his time washing my hair and being so careful and kind. And I know I love this man, but I'm not convinced he deserves my love.

I've never wanted to change someone. It doesn't work. It's not my job to be a part of someone's redemption. I already absorb more than my share of other people's burdens—I don't want that in my relationship.

But underneath everything, Ransom is a good man. He's caring and loving, and he has had so many chances to make me believe something that wasn't true. He could have chosen the easy path, but he hasn't. He's being raw and vulnerable and taking the chance that I won't stay.

I understand the bar is on the floor right now.

When we get out of the shower, his phone vibrates. "This should be quick." He answers wearing just a towel around his waist.

I don't eavesdrop, but it's clear it's a work call. I've never asked what his other projects are. For all I know, he's investing in oil refineries. I add that to the long list of things I need to find out about him.

He looks at me and the joy he had before drains from his face. I wonder if he's already seeing consequences from last night's fight with Lena. If she's so hurt that she got him fired.

"Yes, sir. We'll be on the next flight out." He ends the call, but before he can tell me anything, there is a knock on the door.

"Ransom, we need to head to London." Lena's voice carries through.

"Yes, I heard. We'll be out in a few minutes. I'll tell Daisy to arrange the flights."

"Fine." Her steps retreat.

"Everything okay?" I ask.

"Negotiations fell apart on a tech deal. We're back to the drawing board."

That's better than him losing his job. "Okay. We're headed to the city, then? Should I switch my flight?"

He's tapping at his phone and grabbing clothes. "Just get dressed and packed. I'll have my assistant sort out your travel."

"Okay." I select a dress from the closet, and after putting it on I go through the room and place everything in my bags. Ransom and I work without talking to each other. But he's on his phone so much, we'll be here forever if he tries to do both. So, after I finish mine and place it next to the door, I pack his clothes.

"You don't have to do that, Haley."

"It's fine."

He stands behind me and wraps his arms around me. His phone is still in his hand, but I love the way his warm body feels against me. He kisses the top of my head. "You are absolutely perfect."

I smile weakly even though he can't see it.

Lena waits for us in the atrium. The household staff take our bags and place them in Ransom's car.

"Should we say goodbye?" I ask. I liked Estella enough in the end.

"It's fine," Lena says. "Most are sleeping, and a few are on the boat." She already has her sunglasses on and refuses to look at us.

I'm willing to try for Ransom, but I can't imagine a life where I'm friends with these people. I'm so glad he agrees that we won't do this again.

In the car, I sit in the passenger seat while Ransom drives us to the airport. He holds my hand across the console again. I know it's not to make Lena jealous, but I can't help but wonder if it happens anyway. But I hold on since he's leaving me and we don't know when he'll be in Wendell Beach next.

The helicopter isn't ready for us when we get there, so we wait in a lounge. The two of them have their laptops out and share notes. Lena's eyes are red and while she's doing her best to hide it, she looks exhausted. I'm not sure I look much better.

This feels wrong. She knows him well and for much longer than I have. I don't think for a second she's forgiven him. This is just what she does to survive.

He keeps rubbing his eyes while he looks at his screen.

"Are you okay?" I ask.

He looks up at me confused. "Yes, I'm fine."

I know him better. "Where are your glasses?" I ask, opening the pockets on his briefcase, trying to remember where I packed them.

"Ransom doesn't wear glasses," Lena says, not bothering to look up.

"He has blue-light blocking readers." I pass them across the table. He looks at me like I've missed some point. "Right. You've never worn them in front of anyone else, have you?"

"No." He takes them and puts them on.

I will bet our entire relationship he was bullied for glasses in school or saw someone get bullied for them.

Lena lets out a disbelieving chuckle and shakes her head in amazement. "Men," she mutters under her breath. She doesn't care that he wears glasses.

He looks good in them. I take the time to appreciate him. Now that we're out of the house and I feel like I can breathe again, things feel better. I remember the good.

He smiles and looks up at me. "I'll send you an email about this later, but I just got confirmation a food journalist will be by Coastline in a few weeks to interview you, Will, and Norah."

"Why me?" I ask. I'm supposed to be a background person.

"It's as much your baby as it is theirs. Will agrees. This will be good for you. You can talk about your business. It'll be great media exposure."

"Of course. I'm just surprised Will and Norah are good with it," I say. I instantly think about what I'll wear. What do I own that still is in line with my brand and makes me look like a competent person?

He reaches across the table and squeezes my hand. "You know what you've done for the restaurant. And someone needs to be there to defend the presence of alligator on the menu."

"Excuse me?" Lena had been trying to ignore us.

I shake my head. "No. He's kidding."

He smiles to another eye roll from her. Maybe that's his version of an olive branch.

I appreciate that he's included me in this. I'm not used to

someone looking out for me. For finding me opportunities and allowing me to shine on my own.

* * *

THE RIDE back to the city is uneventful. I still don't like flying, so I focus on appreciating the views. I text Carina a picture.

ME

On my way home.

We land at the airport. I'm bound for the commercial terminal, while they're headed to the private planes. Lena looks impatient to be going.

Ransom pulls me into a tight hug. "I'll text you when I land and call you as soon as I can."

"Okay. I understand you're busy and this is important." I don't want a repeat of that month when we were together but I spent so much of it afraid I didn't understand what was happening between us. He'd promised he'd call when he went to Singapore, but it was days before I heard from him.

"You're important to me. You are my priority."

"Thank you. I appreciate that," I say.

"Ransom, they're waiting for us," Lena calls.

He rests his forehead on mine. "I...I'll see you very soon. I promise."

I kiss him because I know what he was going to say. But we know it's the wrong time for those words.

Once I'm past security, have found my gate and am sitting at the bar across from it, I call Carina.

"Please tell me you're not hiding in another bathroom."

"I'm not hiding in another bathroom."

"Oh good."

"I am drinking at an airport bar."

"It's eleven in the morning."

"Time doesn't matter in airports," I say.

"You sound like Sienna."

I cringe. I still haven't talked to her. I'll text her as soon as I get off the phone. "Any chance you can pick me up from the Sarasota airport? I know this wasn't the plan and I can get a cab or wait for Paige."

"I can get you. I was wondering what was happening when I got your text. Orion has plans with Christian and Alex tonight. It'll be good to spend time together, just the two of us. We need it."

"Yeah, I think so too. It's been a while since we've done that and I haven't been filming something."

"Send me your flight information. I'll be there."

As soon as we hang up, I send her the information and text Sienna.

ME

I'm sorry I didn't tell you about Beckett. I was trying to protect you, and I should have known you're strong enough to handle it.

SIENNA

I'm not sure I am.

I'm angry and I hate him. But some days I miss him so much.

ME

I didn't know you felt that way.

SIENNA

I know. Because what kind of person still loves the man who ripped out her heart?

I break down crying at the airport bar because I had no idea my friend was in so much pain and I can't fix it for her.

Am I making the same mistakes she did?

* * *

CARINA PICKS me up with a bottle of water and reusable wipes to get the stale air of the plane off me. "I know I'm not supposed to say this, but you look terrible," she says.

"Thanks. It's been a rough few days." I spend the drive to her place going through everything that happened since we spoke yesterday. About the conversation Ransom and I had, the fundraiser, and our fight.

"What are you going to do?" she asks after we've gotten to her place and are sipping rosé on her deck overlooking the gulf.

"I honestly don't know. I'm glad I have space to think things through. I think I'm in love with him, but maybe that's not enough."

She nearly chokes on her wine. "Sorry. Orion said something similar to me once. I know I've been skeptical of Ransom, and I don't like everything you've told me about him, but maybe he has changed. Orion did. Our pasts don't have to define us. But you're right. No one is moving continents today. You can get to know him a little better. Give him a chance to prove himself."

A few hours later, I get the text that he's finally at his flat in London.

RANSOM WEST

> I can't wait for you to visit here. I have so much I want to show you.

twenty-six

RANSOM

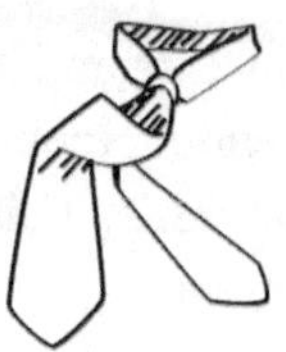

I SPEND THE NEXT FEW WEEKS IN LONDON SORTING THROUGH THIS tech deal and trying to give Haley the attention she deserves. But none of it is easy. I don't have much free time usually and it feels like every second is going to preserving a project I'm not sure I care about.

This job has always been about money and status, but after spending months working on Coastline Beach House, getting close to Haley, and learning Wendell Beach, these other investments seem meaningless.

Jesus fuck. Do I actually like Wendell Beach?

Once upon a time, I'd have sent her expensive gifts, but Haley insists I can't spend money on her. This relationship needs to be about caring for each other and nothing else.

But the time I'm not with her, I'm missing her. I reach for her when I wake up. When I can't sleep, I wonder what she's doing without me. I can't wait for her to come to London so I can show her the things I love about this city and hope she loves them too.

I'd always planned to get married—at some point it would be

"

a good decision. But I never thought I would feel like this. That I would feel so much. Haley consumes me.

I do what I can to be close to her. I've been cooking my way through her cookbook and sending her pictures of each dish. I refuse to call her, panicked, when I make a mistake—she doesn't need to be dealing with my ridiculous questions on top of everything else. And I'm getting better at it. I watch and like every video she posts. I buy T-shirts from Nebula Athletics because she can't get mad at me for spending money on myself even if it's her friend's company. And honestly, I like them so much I don't know why I didn't do it sooner.

The time difference is the worst part. I'm working when she's not, and I'm trying to sleep when she's free. She's working harder than ever. Ashley Ferris posted a video of her making Haley's fish tacos, and Haley's follower count exploded. As a result, she's getting approached by brands who want to partner with her. I'm so fucking proud of her and everything she's accomplished.

My phone rings and it's her. I sent her a package and it should have been delivered.

"Love, how are you?" I ask.

"This counts as spending money," she says. But I hear a smile in her voice.

"No, it's homemade."

"It's professionally printed," she counters.

"But do you like it?" I ask. I took a sketch I had made of the two of us on paddleboards with Orion's boat in the background and had it printed on canvas. It's not even that big. She has plenty of art on her walls. I wanted to add something. I wanted her to have a piece of us.

"I do. Thank you. It's perfect."

"Good. I have another one hanging in my office," I say. "But it's just the boat. I didn't want to expose you to everyone I have a meeting with." I want her in my space. She hasn't been here yet, but I want the memory of her wherever I go.

She laughs softly. "That's thoughtful on a few levels."

"I'm glad you're happy. I mean it, Haley."

"Thanks. I…um…have to go. I'm in the middle of recipe testing. But I'm free tonight if you want to FaceTime?"

"Of course. I'll text you when I'm home."

We hang up and I finally feel like I'm turning this around.

* * *

THERE IS something I need to do that I've been dreading. It mattered to Haley, and I'll do it for that reason alone.

It's past the end of the workday a few days after Haley received the package, but Lena and I are both at the office. She's been polite and professional since we left the Hamptons, but we haven't spoken about anything personal. We haven't shared a meal or done anything to suggest we are friends.

The door to her office is open. I knock and she looks up, irritation flashing on her face. "It's late," I say. I have my bag on my shoulder. I'm leaving the office regardless of how she answers my question.

"It's only half seven."

"Care to join me for a drink?"

"Why would I do that?"

Ouch. "Because I owe you an apology."

"Haley's making you do this, isn't she?" Lena asks.

"She's not making me," I say. An apology won't mean anything if it's forced. It's why I took a few weeks to do this. I had to want it too. "Since we work together, we should clear the air between us."

"Fine." She shuts down her computer and grabs her handbag.

We enter a pub a few blocks from our office. Far enough away that we won't run into any of our coworkers who might have gone out for a pint after work. It's not a place she'd usually frequent, but I like it here. We grab two stools by the bar where she orders a wine and I have a lager.

"First. I'm sorry I wasn't honest with you about my intentions. That I led you to believe we had a future. I thought you'd find someone else and move on. Or after enough time, you'd get the message."

She shakes her head. "Was it all a lie? Did you care about me at all?"

"I think you're a beautiful, amazing woman and I genuinely enjoyed our time together. That afternoon we spent in Kensington Gardens? It was truly lovely."

She looks disappointed. "I was so enamored with you. You are smart and handsome and everything I want in a partner. I got swept away in you."

It is truly a surprise to me that she felt that way. I thought Lena could have anyone she wanted, and I'd assumed she wanted to be with someone in her own social class. That I was a blip on her long history of being perfect and polished and doing everything right. "But I didn't grow up like you."

"No, but I never cared. My father didn't care."

"I am truly, deeply sorry for having hurt you. For dragging you down the way that I did."

"I don't think I've ever heard you say the word 'sorry' before today. Not for any reason. Now twice in one conversation," she says.

"It's very un-British of me," I say. I also can't remember the last time I said that word. It doesn't come naturally to me anymore. I've fought to be on top for so long that apologizing means admitting to lowering myself. I never felt the need to do that before. I could never admit to weakness.

"I know it wasn't long, but I wanted you to be the one. Now I realize I just wanted someone to look at me the way you look at Halcy."

"You'll find someone," I say.

"Don't say that. You don't know that," she says.

I take a deep drink. This is what I didn't think about. I am supposed to leave everything better than I found it. But I didn't with Lena. And she is right. I was a good boyfriend, but I still did damage.

"You are truly amazing. I shouldn't have done what I did. And I can't make up for it," I say, "but I'm trying to do and be better. Whatever you need from me, I'll do."

She looks at me over the rim of her glass. "If I asked you to quit the firm?"

I swallow. "If that's what you really want…" My mind races. I could recover from the loss. I'd find some way to land on my feet.

"I don't. You make us good money. But maybe we shouldn't socialize as much," she says.

I don't like that idea, but then I wonder if any of them are really my friends. If I'll really miss them when I don't see them. They've always been tools for me to climb in my career. I don't have the same relationships that Haley has. Ones that are for the sake of the time spent together and nothing more. Yes, Haley's friends all seem to help each other out, but that's because they want to. Not because they're expecting anything in return.

Do I give a fuck about any of my friends? And do any of them give a fuck about me?

"Helena!"

She turns at the sound of her full name as Myles's brother approaches us. "Sebastian, it's good to see you. You remember Ransom West?"

"Sorry, I'm not sure I do," he says.

We've only met a handful of times. He works for a rival firm. At one point I would have wanted his friendship, but now instead of wanting to sit in a room drinking scotch with people, I think I'd rather be on a boat. Or at a table in the sand with my shoes off. "No worries. I did Christmas with your two families a few years back," I say.

"That's right." It's clear he doesn't remember me. "Lena, I'm doing drinks with your father later this week. Will you be joining?"

"I don't think so, but I'll check with him."

"I hope to see you then." We exchange a few more pleasantries before he leaves.

"How many people call you Helena?" I ask.

"I think just him. I was always closer with Myles growing up. Sebastian would get annoyed when we tried to follow him around."

"What about Myles?"

"No. Yes, we sleep together, but it's not anything real. For the last few years it was a way to get your attention. Clearly it didn't work."

"Is that why you wore the necklace I gave you? You wanted to get my attention?"

"What are you talking about?"

"The necklace you wore at the fundraiser, it was the one I gave you for Christmas."

"No, that was a different one. I don't think I still have anything you gave me." She looks like I've lost my mind. Like she's finally realized she's better off without me.

I was mistaken. How have I misinterpreted so much with this woman? I'm not sure what I'm going to do next in our professional relationship. But at least now, I feel like I've done what I need for us to move forward and to show Haley that I can make amends for my past.

She finishes her drink. "Well, I appreciate this, but we never need to speak about it again." She stands up. "You'll get the bill?"

* * *

I'D WANTED to be in Florida for the interview with the journalist, but I'm stuck in London. We've spent so much time producing a strategy—making sure everyone has their talking points and has a cohesive and concise vision. The food is high-end, but accessible for a range of palates. We know few people go to Florida for the food. But we want to create something special.

We're unveiling the name in the article—it certainly took Will long enough to come up with one—officially introducing Arrow's Table to the world.

I'm nervous about this in a way I haven't been with other companies I've managed. I've never had a personal stake in something before. I've never wanted it to grow for the sake of someone I care about, only for how much money it could make.

Will is in Wendell Beach and taking the lead showing the journalist the space. Everyone has to use their imagination since it's far from finished, but he has the drawings the architect did, so they'll have a clear idea of what the space will look like when it's done.

I spent last night going through everything with Haley. Practicing answers with her so she won't be nervous. She is good on camera so this should be easy for her. But I'll do anything to ease her anxiety.

I pace my office since I can't concentrate on any of my work, another new experience for me. I stare at the drawing of the boat. I'll be in Wendell Beach in two days and maybe we can go out with Orion and Carina again. She's made up her fight with them, but I also need to make sure they are supportive of our relationship. I have no intention of going anywhere.

I have big plans for when I'm in town. I have one secret I haven't shared with Haley. She might get mad at me for it, but it was a sort of impulse decision. I'd already told her it was something I was considering.

My phone vibrates and Haley's name pops up on my screen. I answer immediately. "Love, how did it go?"

She's quiet for a breath longer than usual. "I think it went well for the restaurant."

I sit, my nerves not able to die down. That's not the way I was expecting her to respond. "Yeah?"

"Yeah. He seemed infatuated with Chef Norah and was very impressed with everything she said."

"Good. That's good, right?" Her voice tells me something else is still very wrong.

"Yes. Um…why this journalist?" she asks.

I want to ask her what's wrong, but she'll get there eventually. She'll tell me in her own time. I can be patient. "His publication is well respected. He has awards for food journalism. Why? What happened?"

She sniffles. She's been crying. *Fuck.* I will destroy him. "Like I said, he was great with everyone else, and he was fine with me when we were talking about the restaurant. A little dismissive about my role in everything, but I get that. If you're not in our group and haven't been around this whole time, it's hard to see what I bring to the table."

"We all know what you've done," I say.

"Yes. Will and Norah talked up my involvement. How Norah and I worked with flavors, and introduced both you and Will to the local scene."

"But?"

"But when he asked about my business, he was very dismissive." *Fuck.* "He said I was nothing more than a second-rate influencer and didn't understand why anyone would listen to anything I said."

"Haley, I'm so sorry." I'm already making a list of everything I can do to bring this man down. *How dare he say that to her?*

"He also said that if I didn't have a brainless pop star posting about me, I wouldn't have nearly the following I do."

Jesus fuck. "He really said that? About you and Ashley?"

"Yes, it was so weird. Like a switch flipped in him as soon as Will and Norah were gone."

I want to say something to comfort her and make this okay,

but I'm not sure what. I've never been the caretaker of someone else's emotions before. Not in this way. I'm good with platitudes that don't mean anything, but telling the woman I love that someone well respected in her industry doesn't matter isn't in my skill set.

"I'm sure he won't put any of that in the article. His editor won't let him talk down to Ashley Ferris like that. Her fans will make their lives hell." I make a note to reach out to his editor and make this explicit.

"Of course. It's unprofessional of them." Her voice is distant as I type the outline of an email.

"I'll be in Florida in two days." I close my laptop. "Why don't I talk to Lisa and see if we can do some sort of private dining on the beach? Just you and me." I can see it already—we'll sit on cushions in the sand while the sun sets, with a chef working nearby to bring us the best seafood available. It'll be perfect.

"I'd like that. I just really wish you were here," she says.

"Me too, love." Maybe on the beach I'll finally tell her what I've felt this whole time. Share how I want to make her a permanent part of my life. "Was Will present for that part of the conversation?" I'll get his perspective on the matter. If he thought the journalist was being fair for the rest of the interview. Or if he was shady in private with everyone and not just Haley.

"No. I haven't talked to him about it yet. I needed to call you first." She sniffles.

"I'll talk to him. It's so vexing. I pulled a lot of strings to get this interview. No one should diminish your accomplishments."

She's quiet again.

"Haley?"

"You 'pulled a lot of strings.' What does that mean?"

The hairs on the back of my neck rise. "I worked hard to get it. I called a lot of people. Used connections. These things take work. What do you think I meant?"

"I don't know." Her voice is a pitch higher than normal. "I just reacted. With your history—"

"Fucking hell, Haley, I'm not going to sleep with someone to get you an interview," I almost shout. I should be more sensitive to her while she's feeling vulnerable, but my gut is sinking. Is this how it's always going to be?

"I know that. But when you say things like that it makes me wonder."

"Wonder what?"

"If you're still manipulating things," she says.

"Of course I'm still manipulating things. That's my job. But it's not a bad thing and I have lines that I won't cross."

"Okay, I get it. I'm just always going to wonder how far you're going to go to get what you want."

Fucking hell. She's always going to think the worst of me. I didn't fix what was already broken. She's always going to think I'll step over everyone else. And wonder at what point I'll cut her out to get something I want.

Doesn't she realize she's what I want now?

"What more do you want from me?" I've given her absolutely everything I have. My time. My money. My body. And it still isn't enough.

"I just want you! And I want you to stop all this scheming for personal gain!"

"You have me! It's not for my personal gain anymore. It's for ours. That interview was for you. I'm pissed it didn't go well. But the next one will. I'll make sure of it." I'll vet the next person more. I'll do whatever it takes to give Haley the opportunities she needs to make her business succeed.

"I don't want that. I don't want you moving pieces on a chessboard. Have you been listening to me at all?"

"I have been listening to you. I hear you, Haley."

"You were just on your computer on this call! I heard you

typing. You're such a liar! How have I not realized this sooner?" The last bit is quieter than the rest.

"For fuck's sake, Haley. I can type a note to myself and listen to you at the same time." It's pointless to argue with her. She's never going to believe I'm doing this for her, and I have a code of ethics I won't cross when it comes to her.

I can't keep putting myself out for her to reject me again and again. She's already made up her mind about where she wants this relationship to go.

"You're not a pawn. I have been listening to you," I say calmly. "But I don't think I can do this anymore." I thought I had fixed things or at least made progress. But it's clear I never will.

"Wait, what does that mean?"

"I can't be with someone who doesn't trust me," I say. "And you never will."

"Oh, that's rich! You're the one who's been lying for so long, you don't even know what the truth is anymore. Of course I'm not going to trust you. You haven't done anything to deserve it. I'm not going to let you make me doubt myself anymore."

I should have seen this earlier. I'm always going to be putting in effort when it comes to her. I've moved so many mountains. I've crossed oceans for her, and what has she done for me? I only met her friends and her family by chance. I brought her into my world. I would have given her everything, but she's given me nothing.

I won't do this. Not again. I was not good enough for so long. I won't be again.

"I've done everything I can to get you to believe me. I've bent over backward. I'm not doing this, Haley. I'm not going to spend the rest of my life wondering when you're going to decide I've crossed some imaginary line I don't know about. We're done."

I fucking hate saying those words because I don't want this. I don't want to end things with her, but it's only going to lead to more pain in the future. I'm not going to let her mistrust turn everything I love about us toxic.

"Fine. That's the best idea you've had in a long time." She ends the call.

I drop the phone on my desk. "Fuck!" I don't care who in the office can hear me. I regret everything. I acted on impulse. I never do that. I want to take it back. We can still work this out. I can get her to trust me again.

But when I tap her name again, the call goes directly to voicemail.

twenty-seven

HALEY

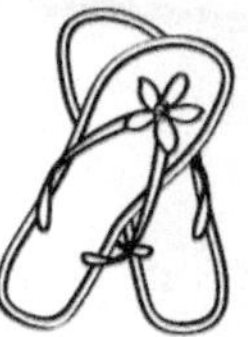

Ransom's name appears on my screen immediately after I hang up. I don't want to hear any more excuses or lies or whatever bullshit he is going to feed me. I send it straight to voicemail with the echoes of the journalist's words running through my head and my hands shaking as I reach for a tissue.

"Chef Norah has cooked for international dignitaries. What gives you the audacity to offer her advice?"

I'd just wanted to complain to my boyfriend about my day. I didn't think it would end with him breaking up with me. And I can't believe he ended things. I was thinking it, but I thought we could give things a little bit more time. He's going to be here in a few days. I thought maybe we'd calm down and talk things out in person.

Maybe he's right and we're never going to be able to trust each other.

My phone vibrates and I'm sure it's going to be Ransom again, but I see a text from Will.

WILL CARON

As soon as you're done talking with Ransom,
can we discuss your takeaways? I'm in my suite
but can come down to the offices. Or meet you
in the lobby.

ME

Can I come up to your suite?

WILL CARON

Sure. 515

I leave the conference room, checking first that the hallway is empty. The employee offices are on this level, and I don't want to run into anyone. I stop in the bathroom to fix my makeup, but it feels useless. Will is going to see right through me. Which is the reason I want to have this conversation in private.

He has become a friend in the last few weeks. It's not just that we're working closely together, but something changed the night of the Ashley Ferris concert. He's been supportive of Ransom and me since the night Norah cooked for us. I don't know how he's going to react to our breakup. He might take Ransom's side on things.

"The only people who follow you are teenage girls."

I don't know what "bro code" these two might have. If they are ready to be ride or die for each other. There was a time when I thought Alex and Beckett would do anything for each other. But Ransom didn't cheat on me and I'm just a contractor—there is no reason for Will to stand up for me.

I manage to skirt through the corridors of the hotel without running into anyone I know until I get to Will's floor. I knock and he answers right away, ushering me into the sitting room where he set up his office. He's changed into jeans and a T-shirt in what seems to be the casual uniform of every man I know, except Ransom.

"I'm curious what you thought— What the fuck happened?" Will hadn't seen my face until I walked into the light. Clearly, makeup doesn't cover it up.

I sit on the couch and he hands me a bottle of water, sitting next to me while I relate to him everything that happened with the journalist and then with Ransom's phone call, omitting the details, but stating that he was mad that I didn't trust him. "And of course, now he won't stop calling me." I've put my phone on Do Not Disturb to silence him.

"He obviously thinks he made a mistake," Will suggests.

"Do you think he made a mistake?" I ask.

"I made your shrimp ceviche, just to give you a fair shot. It's out of balance. Too much salt and avocado. You should go back to the drawing board on that one."

"He cares about you and that's probably terrifying for him."

I stand up because I don't want to be around someone who is going to take Ransom's side without question. "I should go."

"Haley, wait. I'm not saying take him back or even take his calls. Especially when your emotions are high. I'm trying to hear you out. But I saw him around you. Did he really give you that many reasons to mistrust him? You didn't say he ever lied to you."

I sit back down and think over the last few months. It's never been about what he has said or done to me. It is always been about what he is capable of. How I'm never going to feel secure in our relationship knowing how easily he manipulated me. "No lies that I know of since his first day here," I say.

"What did he lie to you about then?" Will asks.

"I asked if it was a coincidence that he was here in Wendell Beach. He said it was. He told me later that he didn't want to come on too strong."

I fidget with the ruffle on my dress and so it takes me a moment to notice Will has gone still. "What do you mean it was a coincidence?"

I look up. "Oh shit. I shouldn't say anything. I mean there's nothing to say." I don't want to fuck up Ransom's job. I don't want to put Arrow's Table in a difficult situation. I'm not a vindictive person to my ex just because we broke up.

"No, Haley. You need to tell me."

"I'm telling you this as my friend and not as my boss," I plead, hoping we can draw enough boundaries to salvage this.

"It doesn't work like that."

"Fuck. Ransom and I met in the Maldives back in November. We flirted. We had a connection. It was a whole thing. Nothing happened, which was my fault, but not because I didn't want him. I was with Sienna. It was right after her breakup and she was a mess." I pause, feeling like I purged too many secrets and none of them are my own. "I thought it ended there. Then he showed up here."

"He orchestrated his involvement and could fuck with my dream to date you?"

"He wouldn't do anything to jeopardize your restaurant. He cares too much about his reputation."

"You're probably right. I've just had investors attach personal strings to money before. I didn't think that was the case here, but clearly I was wrong."

"I know this sounds bad, and maybe it is. But you know him— he wouldn't screw you over if it didn't work out with me. He gave me space and let me come to him when I was ready. I know we just broke up and I don't trust him. But I'd bet on him to take care of his reputation and his career. He won't walk away from this now. He'd look bad."

"Yeah, I guess. I don't know. We both have some things to think about." Will leans against the side table. "Also, the journalist was an asshole. Probably can't tell a snapper from a scallop either."

I smile weakly, not sure if I believe him. He did have some

accolades. It could be an important article for Arrow's Table. "We'll see what he writes."

"Of course. Let me know if you need anything. I'm going to stay in town for a few more days. Obviously, your contract with us is safe. I'd cut Ransom loose before I'd let you go. He's replaceable. You're not."

"You're not a real chef."

* * *

My APARTMENT FEELS empty even though I'm used to being home alone. Lor jumps off the back of the couch the second I step in, rushing to Paige's open room.

"Great, even my cat doesn't want me." This is her normal behavior, but it still hurts.

After showering and crying, I open my fridge to find nothing fresh. I groan. I'd hoped chopping vegetables would heal something in my heart. Instead, I add salted water to a pot on the stove to make spaghetti with white beans. I've never doubted my chef skills before and I'm not going to let anyone take that away from me now. I can make something delicious with barely anything.

While I'm waiting for it to boil, I look at my phone. I have an endless to-do list for my business, but I had planned to take the day off after the interview so I don't have anything pressing to do. It's an ambitious thought anyway—to think I'd be able to work right now. But I want something, anything to distract me from what I'm feeling.

SIENNA

How did the interview go?

We've been talking more these last few weeks. I felt bad I missed so much about what was going on with her. Of course, she hadn't been open with me either, but this is a two-way street. We hadn't been deliberately withholding anything from each other as much as we were trying to figure out so many things on our own. I now understand what Carina had been trying to do too. But we're not alone. We have each other.

ME

You up for a call?

I don't get a response—the phone just rings with a FaceTime call.

"Hey! I'm cooking so there might be a lot of noise." I prop my phone up on the counter where we can see each other while I'm working.

"No problem. Just be careful talking and chopping," she says.

"I'm not using knives. But you know I can talk and cut." When I worked in commercial kitchens I had to work fast with chaos around me. Catching up with a friend is easy.

"I know, but I'm always concerned. Well? How was it? No offense, but you look terrible."

I feel numb at this point. I've already cried and talked it out with Will. I believe this is for the best. It's good, actually, that Ransom broke up with me. I would have dragged it out a few more months and it would have been terrible longer.

"I'm so sorry, sweetie. I always liked the two of you together," Sienna says after I tell her everything that happened today.

"You did?" She had never shared that with me. I feel like I've been getting so much conflicting advice from my friends. The guys harassed him and my girlfriends have all been wary. Has everyone been hiding their true feelings? And why does everyone think I can't make up my own mind?

"Of course. I was the one who pushed you to go off with him. I wish I had known you made plans with him that night. I can't believe you stayed back to hang out with me."

"I don't know what would have happened if we had hooked up in the Maldives. But it was a girls' trip. I couldn't abandon you." Our connection could be fate. Or it could be that we were able to get to know each other slowly. Would Ransom still have wanted me as much as he did if we had slept together earlier?

"I felt like I had the rug pulled out from under me when the wedding didn't happen. I should have seen through Beckett so much sooner than I did. You remember my surprise visit last fall? Remember how you and Carina drove me to the airport because Beckett had a work emergency?"

I nod while draining water from the spaghetti. We spent the whole weekend on wedding preparations. Beckett had been the perfect fiancé up until the end.

"There was no emergency. He joked there was nothing in it for him since he wasn't getting laid later."

"Fuck, that's cruel. But you didn't say anything! You seemed fine." I search my brain for any indication she'd been upset that day but come up empty.

"I know. I've always been good about pretending things are better than they are. Beckett and I fought about it. But his parents had already spent so much on the wedding. I thought things would get better once we were married and I was done with school. I should have seen right through him."

I toss the spaghetti in the pan where I've made a quick sauce before putting it on a plate. I don't take a picture before I dig in, even though it would be easy content. *This twenty-minute pasta will heal your heartbreak.* I pick up my phone and food and move to the living room to sit on the couch. I take a bite and wonder if I put too much salt in the pasta water.

"I'm not telling you this because you missed Ransom's red flags. I obviously don't know him as well as you do, but I was on that plane too. I had my headphones in, yes. But I saw the way he looked at you when he thought no one was watching him. It wasn't just lust. With Beckett, not even the good times felt like a fairy tale. I'd hoped one day they would, but I was wrong."

"So, you think I should ask him to get back together?"

"Do you think that's what he wants?"

"Why else would he have called me right after hanging up?" Ransom would not dig in deeper. He wouldn't want to make the wound sharper.

She shrugs. "I don't want to dunk on him. Have the guys do that. But you are feeling pretty terrible right now, and it is his fault. Remember that part."

I don't know what I'll do. But I'm grateful for the space I have.

twenty-eight

RANSOM

I FUCKED UP. I KNOW I FUCKED UP AND I WILL DO WHATEVER I need to unfuck this. I'm in Florida by noon the next day. Haley prefers to spend time with me rather than me spending my money on gifts. Well, dropping everything for a last-minute charter should be exactly what I spend my money on.

I check into the resort and change into clothing appropriate for Florida in the summer. I only packed one suit for this trip. I'm tired of being overdressed everywhere I go. I can adapt to my surroundings and change my style to match where I am.

I drive to Haley's place. I hope she's had enough time to cool down. If I can see her—if she lets me explain things—we can work this out.

There isn't an answer at her door. I check my watch. She could be anywhere. I know her habits enough to have an idea of where she could be, but she doesn't have a set schedule. I don't think she had a client today, but she might have changed things and not told me. I wasn't supposed to be here until tomorrow.

I pull into the parking lot at Paradise. I haven't been back since the first afternoon with her. Alex never warmed up to me. I'll never be good enough for Haley in his eyes. A part of me wants to believe him. But another part of me knows Haley and I are good together. We make each other better.

She won't be upstairs or on the patio. If she's here with friends, she's in the locals' section. I head in that direction and I see her at a table with Carina, Orion, Christian, and a redhead I've seen around, but I don't recall specifically meeting her.

I step toward them but Alex moves into my path. "You're not allowed in this area," he says.

"Oh for fuck's sake. I'm here to talk to Haley."

"She doesn't want to talk to you." Orion steps up behind Alex, and Christian is right with him. "She wants space." He's really going to prevent me from stepping foot in the locals' section.

I know the story. I know what happened when they caught Beckett cheating and how it turned into a fight here. I'm not going to be that guy.

I look over their shoulders. Carina is holding on to Haley who is clearly upset at my presence. "Fine. I'll go." I close my eyes. He's right. If she wanted to talk to me, she'd wave me over or come to see me. I'm not going to yell across a restaurant to get her attention or to make a point, and Alex won't let me through to her. "Just tell her I fucked up and I'm sorry."

Alex grunts in response.

It's more than their eyes on me as I leave the restaurant.

Back in my car, I drive aimlessly. I know the area well enough that I won't get lost for all that's possible on this island that's only a few kilometers long. I end up in the only place I want to be.

I park in the public car park by the pier. I remove my shoes and socks and roll up the hems of my trousers so I can step into the sea. The sand is hot beneath my feet after baking in the sun all day. I wish I had my iPad with me to draw but it's at the hotel. My brain is too scattered for it anyway. I wish I had something to help me process what I'm feeling and expel these emotions.

I thought if I could get in front of her… If we could talk about this, we could work it out. But she wants nothing to do with me.

I'm not sure I blame her. I'm not ready to believe that is truly over.

I walk to the end of the pier and sit down. My legs dangle over the edge and I rest my arms on the lower railing. I don't know how long I'm here, but eventually I lie back and close my eyes.

Soon after, someone sits down and lies beside me. I'd know her scent of flowers and berries anywhere.

"I didn't come here because I thought you'd be here," I say. She wanted space. I tried to invade it. But I am giving it to her now. Even though I hate it so much.

"I know. I had a hunch you'd be here." Her voice sounds calm and strong. This is not the same upset person I saw at Paradise.

I sit up to look at her and she does the same. We sit cross-legged facing each other. The pier is empty—it's too hot for any sane person to be outside. Sweat covers every inch of my body. Haley looks beautiful in a purple dress. I wish she wasn't wearing sunglasses so I could see her eyes, but the sun is blinding. I want to know if she's been crying. I don't want her to be hurting, but if she's as upset about this as I am, then maybe we have a chance.

"I'm sorry about how things ended on the phone," I say. "I was upset for you and then you were mad at me. I reacted. I don't want us to be over. We can work through this."

She shrugs. "I thought a lot about what you said, about how I'll never be able to trust you, and I think you're right. We're not a good fit. We're too different."

"We're not that different," I counter.

"We want different things," she says.

"Do we?" We both want a stable relationship. I didn't know at the beginning that I wanted to fall in love, but Haley did. Now that I have, I won't settle for anything less.

"Why me, Ransom? You must have met thousands of beautiful women who could have been your path to redemption. Why did you pick me?"

I stare at her because the answer is so obvious to me: I'd never thought I needed redemption before. "I found you when I was ready, and I wanted you. You make me a better man. I will try, Haley. I'll do better. I promise."

She shakes her head. "I'm sorry, Ransom. I can't do a promise for better. I might love you, but I don't need you. I can walk away now, and you haven't given me reason to stay."

I bark a laugh. "Only you would say you love me for the first time while you're breaking up with me."

She smiles and it's so sad. "I said 'might.'" But we both know that's a lie. "Please don't say it. I'm trying to protect me. And if you love me, you'll do this."

I nod and look to the horizon. It's a double-edged sword. If I tell her I love her, she won't be able to resist and she'll be in my arms seconds later. I'll get her back. But it won't last. She'll believe the worst of me, that I'll lie and manipulate. If I don't say it, then she knows I mean it. I won't manipulate her into getting her back. But then she'll be strong enough to walk away.

"I—I care about you deeply. I don't want this, Haley. We're making a mistake. But you seem very sure on this, so I'll let you go."

I stand up and brush the sand from my pants. I hold out my hand to help Haley up. She takes it and I let go as soon as she's standing. I want to pull her into me, but I don't get the privilege of holding her anymore.

"I'll stay away from Paradise," I say. "Any other places you want me to avoid?"

"I doubt you'll be at the yoga studio. I'll avoid the resort in person. Do everything I can through email."

"I'll have a conversation with Will. Make sure your work goes through him. I don't want my cock-up to affect your employment." I nod. "You know how to reach me if you change your mind."

"I do, but don't wait for me."

I can't respond to that. So instead, I walk back to the beach, leaving her at the end of the pier.

* * *

THE PROBLEM with ending things with Haley as soon as I arrived in town is I still have a week left in Wendell Beach. I still have to be in this town where everything reminds me of her, and I can't have her.

There was always a chance this was going to end poorly. I'd prepared for that. But I thought it would have been in the early stages. That I'd show up in Wendell Beach and Haley would have a boyfriend and wouldn't want anything to do with me. That I could turn on my charm and it would have no effect on her. In those scenarios, I would have worked for Arrow's Table and left with my heart and soul intact. And I thought if a relationship would have run its course with her, then it would be the same as all the others I'd been in. We'd split amicably and we'd both be better off for it. But now everything is in tatters.

To my surprise, Will is in the lobby of Coastline when I get there. I need to shower and sleep before I have a real conversation with him, but I can't avoid him now.

"I thought you were headed home," I say.

"I extended. I wanted to talk to you in person," he says.

He gestures to the lobby bar where we get a booth and order a golden ale each.

"Have you seen Haley already?" he asks.

I nod. "I did. We broke up."

"She said that yesterday. She also told me something else."

I look up after taking a sip of my drink.

"Is this whole thing a joke to you? Just a game to play?" Will asks.

"She told you? That my involvement is for her?"

Will nods. "This restaurant means something to me. Haley is

my friend and she's friends with my wife. If this doesn't mean anything to you, then leave now. I'll figure out the money somewhere else. I've done it before. I can do it again."

"I would have never fucked you over. Even if she had rejected me from the beginning. I want this to succeed. I want her to succeed."

"I thought you were the one who ended it."

"I made a mistake. I was upset in the moment. I never did anything to break her trust, but she holds everything I've done in the past against me. I'm not sure this is something we can get over. But I want to try."

"At least you didn't lie to her," he says.

"Yes, but my whole past is toxic to her. I don't know how to get her to trust me once it's broken."

"When did she stop trusting you?"

I think back to the time when we were in my apartment in New York. I had exposed my one lie, and she jumped into my arms. It was only afterward when doubt crept into her mind. I explain what happened in the Hamptons to Will. He's happily married. He might know how I can fix this.

"I think she's right," Will says. "Those people sound toxic."

I raise my eyebrows, not expecting that from someone who grew up with a private chef.

"Look, you clearly have worked hard to get where you are. But what more do you want? You can always chase more money. And if that's the most important thing to you, you wouldn't be upset about Haley."

"It's not the money," I say. "It's the people too. I have a connection with them." That sounds hollow. I'm only connected to them through my job. If I had a different one, would I even bother to stay in touch?

"Think about it. I don't know how much you make currently, but I'm spreading myself too thin. I need a partner. Someone who is good at raising money. Someone who wants to expand and build something. You fit the bill."

"You just found out I lied to you and now you're offering me a job?"

"I believe in second chances, and you need one. I would want you to work in Florida for the foreseeable future. Arrow's Table needs someone more hands-on than I can be at the moment."

"This will just piss off Haley more. She doesn't want me in this space. She doesn't want me on this island for longer than I need to be." And even if Haley was okay with it, her friends won't be. She's made up her mind about me. I can't do anything to try to get her back.

"Maybe. If it's a problem for her, we can reassess. Maybe you want to stay in London at the job where you have everything you could ever want, but it costs you the one thing you want most."

It might not be the worst idea. I think they're right about my friends. I've already lost Lena. I haven't tried to socialize with anyone else. I'm not sure they'd take my calls. *Would I even take theirs?*

"Let me think. I haven't slept in two days and I'm covered in sand." I down my beer and stand up. "I appreciate you not thinking the worst of me."

"I've been where you are. If Alma hadn't seen through my bullshit, I'd be in a worse place than you are."

* * *

ON MY LAST day in Wendell Beach, I still haven't decided about Will's job offer. He's right though—I can't keep living my life the way I have been. I don't care about the private clubs or the exclusive parties or anything else that used to drive me. I care about taking care of my family and making sure Haley is happy.

I'd give almost anything to sit in the locals' section at Paradise eating fish tacos with her.

Mitchell mentioned he needs to run some contracts over to Wendell Beach Rum Works. I offered to take them since I have a meeting on the north end of the island and it's on my way.

I enter the tasting room and the woman behind the bar greets me. For the first time, I'm here and Haley isn't. I look around and can appreciate the wood-grain bar and the bright and warm atmosphere.

"Is Christian around? I have contracts from Coastline Beach House for him," I say.

"He is. Hang tight and I'll grab him." She comes back a moment later. "He's on a call but will be out in a moment. Can I get you anything?"

It's the middle of the day, but who cares? "I'll take an Airmail."

She gets to work on Haley's favorite cocktail, and I sit on a stool at the end of the bar.

When Christian comes out, I'm sure he was deliberately making me wait since my drink is half gone.

"Didn't think you'd still be in town," he says. He looks a little bit more haggard than I've seen him before. Like I'm not the only one having long nights without sleep.

"I'm still invested in the restaurant." I hand him the documents.

"Thought you'd dump that as soon as she dumped you," he says.

"I'm not going to risk my professional career because life got awkward for me." I let him read over the contracts for a moment. "You always seemed to hate me the medium amount, so will you at least tell me if she's okay?"

"Why do you think you deserve that?" he asks, not even looking up.

"This isn't about what I deserve. It's about what she deserves. I might move here. Not for her. For me. I have a job offer that might be exactly what I need. I haven't decided yet. But if my presence is going to be a source of pain for her, then I won't. Tell me she's moved on. That everything is fine, and I'll be able to decide for me."

He looks at me sideways as if trying to tell if I'm lying. "She's hurting. But she'll be okay. She's strong and her friends will take care of her."

"Good. I'm glad she has you all."

"Is this the part where you tell me to not tell her you stopped by?" he asks.

"No, this is the part where I ask you to sign these contracts and then for a bottle of your long-aged rum."

He smirks and grabs a pen.

An hour later, on a quiet street with half-finished houses, the real estate agent hands me the keys to unlock the front door of my impulse purchase. I step into the custom kitchen and place the bottle of rum on the counter. I'll be back for it eventually.

twenty-nine

HALEY

JULY

"What if we go to Boston for a few days?" Carina asks. "I have some points we can use for flights."

We're in her kitchen and I'm concentrating very hard on the salad I'm making, but I'm not flowing the way I normally do while cooking. All my proportions are wrong. My instincts are off. I've never felt like this about cooking since I first experimented with noodles when I was a kid. But even then I was able to approach it with a sense of curiosity and not judgment. Now I'm wondering if I ever had any skills.

"I can't. I have so much to do. Even if I work while we're there, I'll be overly stressed getting ready." I'm behind on everything. My social media is taking up more time than it ever has been. My paid subscriptions have gone up, making me feel like I should be delivering a higher-quality product. I've even fallen behind on the regular maintenance for my knives. They aren't nearly as sharp as they should be. Most home chefs wouldn't notice the difference, but these blades are an extension of my hand. I can tell when they are even a little bit off.

"Okay. Want to go out on the boat this weekend?"

And be around two perfectly in love people? "I'll have to see what's on my schedule." I know she's trying, and I appreciate it, but none of it is helpful. I want to crawl into myself. It's been weeks since Ransom walked away, and it hasn't gotten easier. I know I made the right decision, but I feel like there's a different timeline where he is perfect for me. He was such a good partner. He challenged me in the ways I needed to be challenged. He wouldn't let me sit still in my career. I'm still working on the ideas he gave me. I'm a better person because of him.

I wish he could be a better person.

When he showed up at Paradise, it was like my dreams came true—the perfect moment in the story where the prince comes to win the princess back. I wanted it so badly. But if I took him back, it would only be a matter of time before something else happened to make me mistrust him again.

I needed him to know that and I wanted to end it on my terms. It was a huge risk on my part to search for him that day, but I wanted to look him in the eyes one last time before it was over. I couldn't do that at Paradise in front of all my friends, especially the guys who had made their feelings on him clear. So I bottled up everything I was feeling to put on a brave and calm face. Now it feels like those emotions are overflowing and will never stop. The well is endless.

I haven't heard from him since. Even at the restaurant, I work directly with everyone but him. And now I'm sure all the times he reached out to me for work were just an excuse to talk with me.

I can't decide if I miss it.

"Fuck!" I get the angle wrong on an onion and the blade slips, cutting through the back of my finger.

"Oh fuck." Carina grabs a towel.

I slide down to the floor, my back against the cabinet.

"Let me see."

I take the towel and squeeze as tight as I can. "It's fine. I just need to put pressure on it." I've had more than my fair share of cuts and burns. Every chef has. But this was a careless mistake.

We sit on the floor in silence for a few moments with nothing but the sound of the waves of the gulf out her window.

"You know, Orion and I broke up once."

I look her in the eye. "It worked out and you two are happy. Not the same thing."

She takes a deep breath. "I know we've been hard on Ransom." I groan at his name. "But maybe you've been hard on him too."

"You're the one who said him opening a restaurant in town was almost like being a stalker."

"Yes, but he's listened to you at every opportunity. He's given you space. He gave you a choice. He tried with the guys. He could be different if you give him another chance."

"But I can't do that. He lives on a different continent."

"I don't know. You were happy when you were with him. And maybe that freaked us out. It made us protective when we didn't need to be. We knew if his intentions weren't good, then you'd be brokenhearted, and we didn't want that. You're such a good friend. We let down Sienna and we weren't going to make that mistake again. But we ended up causing the exact situation we were trying to save you from."

"It wasn't your fault. It wouldn't have worked even if there wasn't a good reason for me to doubt him."

"Maybe. But we should have listened to you."

My finger throbs. I pull it out of the towel. "Shit, this looks deep."

Carina stands. "Let's get you stitches. I'll drive."

"Ugh. The mainland. I'll text Paige and let her know to expect me."

She helps me up and we turn off the stove before grabbing our flip-flops and our bags.

Orion passes us in the garage coming home from a sail. "Hey, princess, where you headed?"

"Hospital," Carina answers cheerfully.

"Have fun!" He steps toward the door. "Wait, what?"

I hold up my hand. "Knife. I'll be fine."

"Can you clean the kitchen?" Carina asks. "Maybe don't eat any of it."

He shakes his head but Carina waves him off with a kiss.

* * *

EMERGENCY SURGERY TO repair a tendon was not on my bingo card for the year, but neither was falling in love with someone I couldn't trust. It's truly going to be a rough recovery. I can't use my left hand for six to eight weeks and then it'll be only for some things. I don't know how I'm going to be able to cook. I itch to open my laptop and search through my library of videos for things to repost. But I know better than to post on social media while on painkillers.

I sit in my living room with my family the day after the surgery. Paige is discussing her plans to move out soon and wondering if she should delay to help me. I don't want that. I don't want anyone to upend their life because of me. We Face-Timed with Caleb who debated about driving down to visit, but I told him to wait for a long weekend like he had already planned.

"What about the man you were seeing?" my mom asks. "Is he on his way?"

"No," I answer. I'd told them we'd broken up, but my mom is still holding out hope. "Ransom won't be showing up."

My dad sputters as he sips his iced tea. "What did you say his name was?"

"Ransom West," I answer. My stomach turns at his name. I'd wanted to reach out to him if for no other reason than I wanted him to care. But he's in England and would probably end up flying here in an instant if I asked. It's just a bad idea. "Why?"

"No reason. Just don't think you ever mentioned his name to me."

He looks uncomfortable and I glance between my sister and my mother. But neither has any more information for me. Dad looks relieved when there is a knock on the door that he can answer. My heart beats fast for a moment, hoping we've summoned Ransom. But it's Carina, Orion, Alex, Bristol, and Christian instead.

My mom ushers my father and sister out the door. "We'll be back later."

Carina unpacks the tote bag she brought in the kitchen. "I made you meals in single-portion containers. You should be able to open them with one hand, but if you want to try now, I'll figure something out if you can't."

"I'm sure it's fine, Carina. Just come sit," I say.

Everyone else has piled into the living room. I sit with a blanket on my lap even though it's July in Florida and the a/c is blasting. It's a comfort more than anything else. Orion gives Carina a look, and after she puts everything in the fridge she joins the rest of us.

"How are you feeling?" Bristol asks.

Carina and Orion are on the love seat while Bristol has taken the recliner and Christian sits on the floor next to her. Alex is at the other end of the couch.

"I'm okay. Just annoyed with myself."

"You can't blame yourself," Orion says. "These things just happen."

"I know. But I could have taken better care of my knives and paid more attention to what I was doing. I've been distracted lately."

"Oh, so we can blame Ransom," Alex says.

"Really, Alex?" Carina says. "Let's not bring him up right now."

"She's right. Can you all distract me?" I feel like I've been in my own world and I've fallen behind with them. "What's been going on with you lately? Christian, how have things been since your magazine feature?" Last month a national lifestyle magazine featured Wendell Beach Rum Works. It was about the distillery mostly, but also about him and his grandparents.

I realize Autumn isn't here. She doesn't always spend time with us, and the two of them have separate friend groups. But it feels a little weird she's not here for this. She came to Paradise the day after the interview when Ransom showed up. Maybe school started and I haven't noticed? No, it's way too early for that.

Bristol rolls her eyes. "The only thing more annoying than people coming up to me at Paradise and asking about Wendell Beach Rum Works is the follow-up questions asking if my brother is single."

He barely laughs at that. "I didn't have any say in the pictures they used. It was the editing anyway." The spread featured high-resolution photos of him in the distillery looking more attractive than necessary in a T-shirt with his tattoos poking out. The piece had gone somewhat viral because of it. #DistilleryHottie was trending for a bit. "But yes, things have been good. Distributor orders are up. The tasting room is at capacity most days."

"I have to keep ordering more rum," Alex grumbles.

"How'd that happen anyway?" I ask. Maybe he has some marketing tips I can take advantage of in my downtime.

"The magazine reached out to me," Christian says. "It was a surprise."

A thought niggles the back of my mind. Ransom has already shown he's willing to work hard to get people or restaurants featured in magazines. Would he do something similar for Christian?

No. It must be the painkillers. That article had been in the works for months. The Arrow's Table article won't be out until the fall. These things take time.

"I was able to ditch my dad's firm as an investor," Carina announces. "Our latest profits made it possible for me to buy them out." This has been something she's wanted for a long time. He never understood her vision, and pushed profits over her values.

"Which is great timing because a yacht owner approached me who wants to offer his boat for charter. It's big enough for overnights with crew quarters. He wants Lost Craft to manage it," Orion says, securing his hair into a bun on the top of his head.

"Is that something you want to do?" Alex asks.

"I've always wanted to offer more services, but I'm limited by the boats I have. Now I can do what I want, without having to buy a new boat. Win-win."

"Will you captain overnights?" I ask.

Carina laughs. "Not if I have anything to say about it."

"How did you find him?" I ask.

"I didn't. He found me," Orion says.

That's the second big, random stroke of luck one of my friends has had recently. Am I reading too much into this?

My dad had also mentioned that he sold one of the new construction houses at the north end of the island recently.

Fuck.

I grab my phone and type slowly using only my right hand.

ME

Did Ransom buy a house from you?

DAD

You know I don't give out client information.

ME

Just tell me if you've met him.

DAD

I've met him.

I groan and sink into my seat.

"Are you okay?" Carina asks, jumping up. "Where are your pain meds?"

"I'm fine. I just figured out how you all are doing so well suddenly." They wait for my explanation. "Ransom."

"You really think that?" Bristol asks.

"It could be a coincidence, but it makes sense that he's been moving these pieces behind the scenes for months now."

"Why would he do that?" Alex asks.

"To make Haley happy," Christian says. "He knows her friends mean the world to her. We succeed, she's happy."

"This is kind of his whole thing," Carina says. "You broke up with him because he does things like this."

"Yes, but I thought it was for his benefit. Promoting the restaurant makes his investment better. He doesn't get anything out of this."

"When we were out on the *Twisted Rigging*, I mentioned wanting to do overnight charters," Orion says.

I don't know how to feel about any of this. He's clearly done so many amazing things for my friends. But it was also because of him that the journalist was able to get me to doubt myself. He lifted everyone else up. Should I blame him for sinking me, even if it wasn't directly his fault?

"Okay." Carina rushes to my bedroom and grabs a notebook from my desk. "Pro and con list."

"Really?" Christian asks. "We're going to judge him with that?"

"Do you have a better suggestion? Pros: likes Haley a lot. Respects her space. Does nice things for her friends. Cons: has a long history of manipulation. Lives in England."

"He bought a house on the island," I say. "At least partially lives in Wendell Beach." I'm less bothered by that than I thought I would be. Buying property might not be a big decision for him.

"That's intense," Alex says.

"When we were fighting in the Hamptons, he made an offhand comment about buying a house. I didn't know he had gone through with it."

"Con: makes real estate decisions without consulting girlfriend," Carina narrates.

"Even if these add up to Ransom being a great guy," Alex says, "I still don't think Haley should take him back after he's hurt her. He's the one who ended it first. Not everyone deserves a second chance."

It feels like a vent. I didn't expect that from him. But maybe this isn't about Ransom. Maybe it's about Beckett still wanting to be friends with Alex after everything that happened last year. Maybe Alex's girlfriend wanted to get back together with him after she cheated on him. Maybe, like me, he doesn't want to be a part of someone else's redemption.

"You're just bitter because you didn't get anything," Bristol says. "Maybe you should have been nicer to him."

"That's not it," Alex says.

"I like second chances," Orion says. "Carina is doing very well with hers."

"Thank you." She kisses him on the cheek. "And really, Alex? Weren't you the one who told me to get my head out of my ass?"

"Yes, but I like Orion."

Christian rolls his eyes and raises his hand. "Ransom came to the tasting room. He has a job offer to work in Wendell Beach."

"Pro: is in high demand in the job market. Con: might not respect Haley's space," Carina continues.

"He told me he wouldn't take it if it hurts Haley," Christian says. "It's not about getting her back. I may have been skeptical of the guy, but if you have something good, you should hang on to it. You know, when their soul lights up your universe."

We all turn to him and are silent for a moment. "You know that's an Ashley Ferris lyric? Not some romantic poet," Bristol says.

"Yes, I know. I don't know where the rumor started that I don't like her."

"You groan every time her music comes on," Orion says.

"You put in earplugs when Autumn and I talk about her," Bristol says.

"You change the channel in the tasting room when a story about her comes on one of the TVs," Carina says.

"You don't like the videos where I use her music," I say.

"You notice that?" Christian asks me.

"I did a test when you missed buying the tickets last year," I say. "I used her songs three times in a row. You liked all the videos except those ones."

"Maybe I didn't see those videos. You know how the algorithm is."

"Now that you mention it, I have noticed you mouthing the words at Paradise," Alex says.

I let them debate Christian's taste in music. But I can't stop thinking about the list Carina has made. Will I regret giving him up for the rest of my life?

* * *

AUGUST

It's been over a month since I've seen or heard from Ransom, unless I count the get well soon tropical flowers that I received from "Coastline Beach House." But the next day Lisa and Mitchell visited me and brought a gift box with bath bombs and candles. Will and Alma also sent a separate gift. So obviously the flowers were from Ransom.

It's gotten easier. I can handle being around the places I

showed him and not get upset or annoyed. But I still miss him. There are things I want to share with him that I can't. When I'm struggling on a certain day with the business, I want to know what he would suggest because I know he'd help me. But I don't get to do that anymore. I know there was a good reason why I couldn't trust him, but sometimes it's hard to remember why. Especially after I've seen the effects of his scheming.

I wasn't surprised when I found out it was Will who offered Ransom the job. He assured me that I still came first in his eyes for Arrow's Table, but he was thinking long-term expansions. It would have felt like a hollow sentiment if Will wasn't the first person to put a wall up at work between Ransom and me. I have the feeling he's still rooting for us but is giving me the space I've asked for.

My hand is doing better since the stitches came out and I've graduated to wearing a brace to keep the finger immobile. I can't lift anything heavy, but I take myself to the farmers market hoping I will get my head on straight. I need to get over him, but I don't know if that's going to happen. Some local produce or a new handmade apron will fix me.

When I exit my car, Ransom stands at the entrance to the market, holding a tote of his own. I never thought I'd see him here. Since I knew he was in town more, I'd been waiting for a moment like this. A sign from the universe I could call fate.

It's silly because it's a small island and the odds we'd run into each other are high.

He doesn't move toward me, but he looks as surprised as I am to see him.

I approach. "Hey, how are you?" I ask. It's a normal question. I can hide how much I miss him.

"I'm well. How are you? How's your hand?" He looks concerned, like he wants to reach for me.

"It's better. How did you know?" I hadn't posted on any of my socials, wanting to wait until it was more healed before opening it up to the world. I couldn't handle the internet criticism I know will come when I'm feeling so emotionally and physically vulnerable.

"Christian messaged me, thinking I would care. Alex messaged me, wanting me to feel guilty for it. And then Orion told me, thinking I should drop everything and fly here."

"But you didn't do that," I say.

"No, I didn't think you'd want that," he says. He sent flowers instead.

"You bought a house," I say.

"Haley, this isn't an effort to get you back. You made me a better person and I needed a break from the places and people that made me someone you couldn't be with. If you want me to go, then I will. I don't want you to be uncomfortable," he says. "As soon as Arrow's Table opens, I can work in New York. I'll turn the house into a rental property. I bought it for us, as a surprise for you, but that was before."

"You helped my friends," I say.

"I don't know what you're talking about."

"Don't lie to me, Ransom."

"Fine. Most of that had been in the works for months. Since before we started dating. I've done a lot of things to get ahead. I thought I could take care of my family, and that by providing for them all my selfishness was cancelled out. But since meeting you, it's been about you. You helped me remember what's important."

"Right." I'm not in a place to address any of that right now. "What did you buy?"

"Just some vegetables. I bought an air fryer. Thought I'd experiment with zucchini," he says.

I nod. I don't have any recipes for the air fryer, since I definitely don't have the space for one. So he's getting his recipes elsewhere. "Not doing a meal delivery service?"

"No, I want to use my kitchen."

I nod. Should I offer to help him? I want to, but I don't want to be waiting for him to call me with a cooking question. "I need to get going. Maybe I'll see you around."

"Did you want some help?" he asks. He gestures to my hand. I'm sure it kills him to see the brace and to not do anything about it.

I'm almost desperate enough to say yes. "No. I'm fine. Thank you though."

"Of course." He nods. "It's good to see you, Haley."

I walk into the market and try to put him out of my mind.

thirty

RANSOM

Will you be at the house in the next hour or so? I want to swing by with your closing gift. I can't believe it's been in my office all month. So sorry about that!

Sure. I'm here all evening.

WHEN I SIGNED THE DOCUMENTS FOR THE HOUSE, HE GAVE ME A cutting board in the shape of Florida engraved with his name and phone number. I'm fairly certain he called it a closing gift, so I don't know what he's bringing over. But it sounds important to him.

I won't bring up Haley unless he does. I haven't heard from her in the few days since we ran into each other at the farmers market. I wanted more time to talk with her, but it was clear she didn't want to. I wanted to know how her hand was feeling. If she'd let me kiss it better. She should be seeing a physical therapist, so how is that going? Is there one on the island or does she have to go to the mainland? I wanted her to know how proud I am of the work she's been doing. But this only gets better if I back off.

I took the job Will offered me, severing ties with most of my life in London. I thought it would feel like cutting out a part of my soul, but it didn't. I felt relief more than anything. I trust Will to not throw me out the second I make some social misstep or because he found out I didn't grow up with a silver spoon in my mouth. I'd always thought I wanted to align myself with a long legacy. But I find the challenge and ownership of building from nearly scratch to be more rewarding. I need to be in Wendell Beach for Arrow's Table, but it's clear Will wants to help Haley and me get back together. I want that more than anything. But I'm willing to wait. And I'm prepared for it to not happen. I just need her happy. My family is the only thing I miss. But I'll take a few days each month to go home. They'll like this more anyway. I won't work when we're together, and they'll have my full attention.

Almost an hour after the text, the doorbell rings and I'm surprised to see Haley when I answer it.

"Hi." She extends a box toward me. "This is a closing gift from your real estate agent."

I recognize the box. I take it and lean in the doorframe. It's hot and humid as fuck, but I don't care. Haley is here. "He must have made a mistake. He already gave me a gift. At closing."

"Oh. Well, this is highly impractical anyway. There aren't any grooves to catch drippings."

"Also, odd shape."

"It's not terrible for charcuterie if you entertain." She smiles.

"Do you want to come in?" I ask. "We can see if I have any cheese in the fridge to dice up."

"Sure, if you're not busy." She steps under my arm and takes off her sandals as soon as she's in the entryway.

The house is large and open, but nothing extravagant. It's a new build, but since I came in late to the process I only picked the final paint colors, bright white with splashes of blue. I've furnished it with the help of an interior decorator, but it still lacks the personal touches to make it feel like a home. I've been waiting for some indication from Haley that it's okay I'm here. Doesn't she realize she holds my entire life in the palms of her hands?

"You could have called," I say. "Or emailed. Texted. You know where I work." There are a thousand ways she could have reached out to me. I don't want to assume her showing up at my house means anything.

But I want to believe.

"I know. I was curious about the house you bought," she says. "And my dad wouldn't just give me your address, so I had to 'run an errand' for him."

Now who's the scheming one? "Let me show you the kitchen." I take her through the open living room to the kitchen. "Like I said, I've been doing a lot of cooking lately."

"Are those..." She points to the knife set on the counter.

I know knives are important to a chef. I'd decided to invest in my own. I spent hours late one night, reading reviews and watching videos to pick what I hope is the perfect set for me.

"Yes. But they aren't for you. I know better than to buy a chef a knife. You know what you like." She's still looking around at the counter space that's double even what's at Orion's house and the six-burner stove. "You're more than welcome to cook or film videos here. The lighting is great."

"Yeah? And what do you want in return?"

"Nothing. Maybe we could be friends in time." She's here in my house. She clearly wants something more from me.

"Maybe," she says. She peeks into the yard. It's not on the beach like Carina's but there is a dock leading to the canal.

"I bought a paddleboard too. I go out on the water first thing in the morning a few times a week. Or sometimes I see dolphins while I'm having tea," I tell her.

"It's not safe to go out by yourself," she says.

"You should come with me." It spills out before I catch myself. I sound so desperate. But I don't know how else to be around her.

"I'm not much of a morning person," she says.

"Right, maybe some other time of day."

"What if I was already here in the morning," she suggests, springing to face me and sounding as desperate as I feel. "What if I woke up here?"

I want that more than anything. But— "Haley, you need to mean that. I know I screwed up in the past and I don't want to screw up in the future. But I can't have you toying with my emotions either."

"I know. I'm not. I mean this. I miss you every day. I know you've changed, and I know you aren't doing to me what you did to other people. I'm sorry I didn't trust you. That I didn't believe you knew your own feelings. And you've made amends. I'm ready for this."

"Oh, thank god." I step to her and cup her cheek, kissing her.

The kiss goes on and on. We're both grasping for what it used to feel like and finding our memories don't do the present justice.

"I love you," I say. "I wanted to say it on the pier. I honestly thought about it, because I knew I'd get to keep you for a little longer. But you were right. You needed the space, and I'll give you everything you ever need. I promise."

"I love you too." She jumps up so her legs wrap around my waist. "How about you show me to the bedroom?"

"I can do that," I say, carrying her up to the primary bedroom. I'm careful of her hand, which is still in a brace. I remove her dress and kiss down her body. "I've missed you so much. There will never be anyone else for me."

She props herself up on her elbows and looks down at me as I remove her underwear. "I needed you, Ransom. So much. I was standing still before you came into my life and I was standing still after you were gone."

I kiss the inside of her thigh. "Never again, love. I'm here for you, I promise."

I pull her panties down and find she's already wet for me. I want to take my time. I want this to last all day. And I also want this fast. I want to skip to the end, to when I know this isn't a blip. That I have her forever.

It feels like ages since we've done this. Last time there was so much mistrust between us. Now we're free.

We're careful since she can't use her left hand. But I don't mind putting in the work for her. I take my clothes off just to feel her skin against mine. My cock is hard between us, but I don't reach for a condom yet. I want to kiss her for as long as I can.

"I went to the doctor last month," she says.

"I know." Why is she mentioning her surgery now?

"No, the gynecologist. I'm on birth control," she says.

I stop kissing her neck and look at her. "Does that mean we can skip condoms? I haven't been with anyone else since you came into my life."

"There's no one else for me," she says. She reaches between us for my cock and lines it up with her entrance.

"No need to rush, love."

"It's been months, Ransom. Just fuck me already."

"When you put it that way." I sink into her wet heat, moving the way she likes it.

Everything is better than I remembered. Not just because I've never had sex without a condom, but because it's Haley and we're in my bed that I hope will become our bed soon enough. We're building a life here.

"I love you," I whisper into her ear.

"I love you too." She comes hard around me and pulls me with her.

* * *

HAVING Haley back is everything I have ever wanted. Will was right about that. We spend the next few days in bed when we're not working. I tell her about my new job and the plans Will and I have for expansion. He wants his own hospitality empire and I'm more than happy to help him build it.

Haley is working on balancing the new endorsements she's getting and how to capitalize while staying true to her message. She does an Instagram Live with Alma Blake where Haley walks her through a basic sheet pan dinner for two. She banished me to my home office, and I watch the feed on my phone. The two of them have so much chemistry. It's fun to watch them play off each other even if I'm not cooking along like they encourage their audience to. Alma is a terrible cook, but Haley is patient as she works with her. She can't demonstrate so it's an extra challenge. Will only steps in once to help Alma. I laugh knowing he's been off camera the whole time.

She's had to stop doing in-home cooking for private clients while she's been injured. She was afraid that they would find other chefs and the business would dry up. While it hasn't been easy for her, she's working on arranging contracts for as soon as she's cleared for full use. She's working her ass off, scripting and researching for everything she's going to do once she's healed. I could take care of her financially, but she doesn't want that. We discuss her moving in with me since her apartment lease has ended and the month-to-month terms are terrible. But we're determined to not rush into anything.

Haley's getting ready for happy hour on Friday when she comes out of the bathroom wearing the same pink-and-white dress she wore when I first saw her. My mouth goes dry. I want to flip the hem up, pull her panties aside and be inside her in a heartbeat. I put my iPad on the nightstand and think about dragging her onto the bed with me.

"I think you should come," she says.

"Yes, coming is always part of the plan," I say, rubbing my hardening cock through my trousers.

She glares, but climbs on top of me anyway. "Not that kind of coming. You should come to Paradise."

"They don't want me there," I say.

"That's not true. What's the point of moving here if you don't take advantage of the established friend group?"

"They don't like me," I say.

"Still not true."

"Do you want to see the text messages from Alex saying that?" I'm still partially hard because Haley is on me, but it's not easy to maintain an erection while we're talking about her friends.

"I'll talk to him. Everyone else has come around. They know what you did for them. And it's fun to leave the house."

Staying in the house is also fun, but she's right. I have to prove to them I'm not going anywhere. "Fine. But I'm not wearing flip-flops." And we'll be at the house later. I can get her dress off then.

"No problem. We'll get you a pair of boat shoes this week. It'll still scream 'Florida' while still screaming 'rich white man.'"

"Always the goal."

I drive us to Paradise and spend five minutes searching for a parking spot before we see someone leaving. We walk in with Haley holding my hand and she leads me directly to the locals' section.

Alex stops us. "He can't sit here," he declares.

"Alex, you know he bought a house and has a job here. By your criteria, he can sit in the locals' section," Haley says.

"Why'd you move here?" he asks.

This is a test. He wants to know how much I'm gaming Haley. "I thought some sun would do me good. I wasn't waiting around for Haley."

"If you hurt her…" Alex says.

She steps between us. "Alex, Ransom and I are good."

"You were crying over him a week ago. You have to forgive me if I'm a little skeptical of the whole mess."

"I know. We talked. I was being unfair, and we're both committed to working on this relationship."

"Fine, but it's probationary access."

"As expected," I say. I can respect that he's protective of his bar and of Haley.

We approach the table where Carina, Orion, and Christian sit.

Orion notices us first. "Looks like we need an extra chair."

"Wait, what's he doing here?" Carina asks. She manages to keep accusation out of her tone.

"Sorry, it's been a busy week, but we're back together," Haley announces.

Carina raises her eyebrows. "Okay. We might as well do a round of sparkling."

"I think Bristol is already on that," Christian says, pointing to his sister who has a bottle of sparkling rosé and pours it into five glasses.

We sit and toast, and Carina immediately pulls Haley aside to get the details.

"You took the job?" Christian says to me.

"I did. It's with Will Caron expanding his hospitality group. Once Arrow's Table is open, we'll work on a new place. But I'll continue to be based in Florida." I have an office now at Coastline Beach House. It's next door to Beckett's, but he's barely doing any work these days so I don't see him often. Lisa and Mitchell are more than happy to see me frequently. Spare Capital hired Sebastian Ainsley to take over my portfolio, but he's content to only need status reports once a month. Once the restaurant opens, I'll transition to my home office. As much as Will claims he wants me on-site, we both know it's not necessary. It's a pay cut and change in my lifestyle, but I still make enough to keep Haley happy.

"How did this happen?" Orion gestures between Haley and me.

"I ran into her at the farmers market. Then she invented an errand to get my address out of her dad. I gave her the space she needed."

"I was waiting for you to get your head out of your ass. She was miserable without you. The two of you were the only thing standing in your way," Orion says.

"Yes, thank you, we figured that out." I relax into my chair and drape my arm over the back of Haley's. She was right to make me come out since this is what I wanted.

"We'll be over tomorrow for the housewarming party," Orion declares.

Haley looks up from her conversation with Carina. "No."

"Yes. You did it to me, I'm doing it to you," he says.

"Why don't we go fishing tomorrow and then housewarming Sunday," she suggests.

He narrows his eyes. "Fine. I agree to your ridiculous counteroffer."

"What just happened?" I ask.

"We're throwing a housewarming party at your place. It's fine. I'll take care of everything. You can just show up."

"Does this mean I get to help?" Carina asks. "I have a new spreadsheet template for party planning."

"Yes," Haley says.

I don't understand, but I trust she'll fill me in later.

We spend the rest of the evening chatting like we've been old friends. With both Premier League football and American football starting their seasons, we have plenty to talk about. It's easy to be with them all now that I'm not worried about them kicking me out of the state.

That night, I curl up in bed with Haley at my side, feeling relaxed, happy, and content. It's all I've ever wanted.

epilogue

HALEY

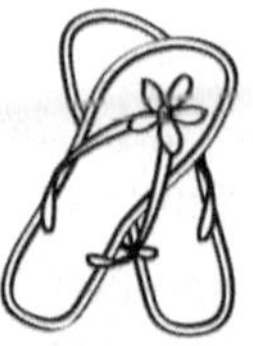

DECEMBER

"Which cufflinks should I wear?" Ransom holds two nearly identical sets. Both are mother of pearl, but one set is round and the other square.

"Your shirt studs are round, so the round ones," I say.

"Thank you."

He kisses my cheek as I try to finish my makeup. I've already kicked him out of the bathroom several times, but he keeps finding excuses to see me. He was always going to wear the round ones.

"You need to let me finish getting ready or we won't be on time." We'd been up late last night and had accidentally slept in this morning. It's friends-and-family opening for Arrow's Table. My part has been over for weeks now. Chef Norah has a vision that aligns with Will's and a team to help her achieve it. They've brought on an excellent manager who wants to spend all day solving the problems that come up on a routine basis in any restaurant, and the full staff has been training together for weeks. Tonight is the final test before it opens to the public this weekend, just in time for the holidays.

We are booked well into the new year. The article that caused so much agony came out and it was completely glowing. I looked at the byline and saw it had a cowriter added. I didn't ask Ransom, deciding I didn't need to know the details, but I assume he gave the editorial staff an earful and they added someone else in to smooth any rough edges.

"I know, but you look so beautiful, I don't want to miss a second of it," he says before leaving the room, Lor on his heels, rubbing herself on his leg. She's decided that she still doesn't like anyone, except for Ransom. I think it's because he bought her a fancy self-cleaning litterbox when we moved in with him.

I'm still wearing my robe, but I have a silver-blue floor-length dress hanging on the closet door. I'm almost ready to put it on if he'll give me a few moments to finish.

Living with him hasn't always been easy. I moved because it was practical, and going from distance to broken up to getting back together and moving in isn't something I would advise anyone else to do. But it forced us to learn to communicate. To be completely transparent with each other.

The magic didn't fade with our secrets.

"Can you come zip me, please?" I call out, thinking he's in a different room, but he turns the corner instantly, his gaze assessing me up and down.

"I wanted to be close in case you needed help."

"So you've been standing on the other side of the door, just in case?"

"You are so beautiful." He looks guilty in his new tuxedo, and I've forgotten what I'm doing. He's so handsome. His dimples get me every time.

"Thank you. Now zip me up so we can go." I turn so he has my back as he tortuously raises the zipper, his finger skimming my skin in a way that I swear I feel directly on my clit.

"You ready to cave?" he whispers into my neck. "Stay home with me."

"Let's go, handsome." I step into the sparkly shoes he gave me all those months ago. He'd told me to sell them or give them away and he'd get me a new pair. But I'm reclaiming them. That one night doesn't define our relationship.

He opens the door of his new Land Rover for me and holds my hand as we drive to the other end of the island.

"You seem nervous," I comment. "Everything is going to be great. And even if it's not, it's only one night. We'll figure it out."

He lifts my hand to his lips, kissing the jagged scar I have from the knife wound and surgery. "I know. I have big plans, that's all."

I'm used to his scheming at this point. Now that he's working with Will, he's been loving the challenges, and I never worry he'll cross a line.

At Coastline, he hands his keys to the valet and we pass through the lobby and outside again to the entrance to Arrow's Table. Carina and Orion are waiting by the host stand. I hug Carina who looks stunning in a pink off the shoulder vintage dress.

"I can't believe you're wearing a suit," Ransom says to Orion as they shake hands and embrace quickly.

"Trust me, I wasn't happy to pull this out of storage," he says.

"You even cut your hair," I say. It had gotten so long in the last few months, but it's shorter than I've ever seen it.

Carina leans in close to him and brushes a lock behind his ear. "It'll grow back, and thankfully his sailing skills were not contained in his hair."

They kiss and I squeeze Ransom's hand. I'm no longer jealous of them. I have everything I want.

The host leads us to a round table at the center of the room where Alex, Sienna, Christian, and Bristol sit. Sienna is wearing a gold beaded dress and Bristol is rocking a purple corset top with a long green maxi skirt.

Orion and Ransom immediately drop into a conversation about the weather. It's not boring small talk for them—no, it's the only thing they care about. Ransom bought a paddleboard and thought he would be out on the bay every day, but he didn't take to it the way I'd hoped he would. He doesn't love it the way I do. But he still likes being on the water. He's just taken up windsurfing. So now he and Orion talk about the wind all the time. When they come over, the two guys sit on the dock for hours talking about the water and the wind, while Carina and I sit on the patio talking about anything else.

Alex and Christian have both warmed up to him. Alex accepts that he's around now and even lifted the fake probationary period for the locals' section.

I look around the room to see who is already sitting and if they appear to be enjoying their meals. My parents sit in a booth with Paige and her girlfriend. They wave and give me a thumbs-up. I know they'll love anything I'm a part of, but I feel a weight leave my shoulders, knowing at least a few people like it.

No one from Spare Capital is in attendance. The new point person claimed he couldn't leave London during December for any reason. It never was a passion project for him the way it is for us. As long as we stay on budget, he doesn't bother us.

Ransom and I traveled to London for the first time in September so that I could meet his family. I loved everything about the trip. We packed up his things in his flat there so his sister could move in. He still stays there when he visits each month and I plan to go at least four times a year, but his home is in Florida now.

The meal passes in a blur. I can't believe we're finally here. It's been so long in the making, and over the last few months it seemed like it would never get here. That the fantasy we envisioned would never arrive.

About halfway through our meal, Will stands from the table he's sharing with Alma and her parents. "Thank you all for being here tonight. This place has long been a dream of mine, and the support you've given over the last year means so much to me. I'm so impressed we were able to open on time. That's a testament to the team, more than anything, that staff shake-ups, building code changes, and a hurricane didn't stop them. I have a long list of people to thank, so please be a little patient. Servers have a free round of champagne or sparkling cider for everyone, so hopefully that's enough incentive to tolerate me."

The room chuckles as we accept the drinks.

He continues. "I want to first thank Lisa and Mitchell Foley, for not thinking I was crazy when I approached them about using their lovely hotel as the location for a fine dining restaurant. Chef Norah Grand, of course, for humoring me when I have a new idea that she very politely declines, and for making the best food in the country. My business partner, Ransom West. Arrow's Table would not exist without you. Your hard work, your scheming, your inability to sleep made this place possible. Haley Stewart, for holding everyone's hand the entire time and being the best advocate for the vision. And, honestly for simply existing. If it weren't for you, Ransom wouldn't have given a shit about this place, so thank you. And finally, my heart and soul, Alma. Everything I do is for you." The entire room *awws* at the last statement, while Ransom leans in and kisses my neck. "Thank you all for being here. To Arrow's Table."

We lift our glasses in a toast and echo, "To Arrow's Table."

After our dessert of deconstructed Key lime pie, Ransom takes my hand. "Come, love. Let's walk on the beach."

I stand and follow him. "Really? It's freezing out." Okay, it's in the fifties, but as a born and bred Floridian, it's freezing to me. Ransom removes his jacket and helps me into it. We step outside and it's not quite as bad as I thought it would be. I'm warmed from the champagne we had, and Ransom is holding me close. It's dark out, but the fairy lights on the terrace allow me to see the outlines of the waves coming ashore.

We step onto the sand and I stop to take my shoes off.

"Just leave them," he says when I move to carry them in one hand.

"Someone might steal them," I protest.

He shrugs. "I'll buy you a new pair."

I chuckle because that's probably his goal anyway. I place them on the steps, pick up the hem of my skirt with one hand, and take his with the other as he leads me to the edge of the water.

"Do you think it went well?" he asks.

"Yes. I'll talk with Norah in the morning. If they had any issues in the kitchen, they certainly didn't let it show in the front of house."

"Brilliant. So, overall good night?"

"Yes, great night."

He pulls me in for a kiss and I can't put my finger on it but he's acting weird. "I love you, Haley Stewart."

"I love you too, Ransom West."

"I was thinking, in the new year, we both take some time away from work and go back to the Maldives. We can have a redo of that night." He holds me close, his arm braced across my low back, like we're dancing to the music of the waves. He takes my left hand and holds it against his chest.

"You just started a new job. Is your boss really going to give you leave so soon?" It's half a joke. Will tells Ransom he works too much all the time.

"I'm sure I'll be able to make a case for why I need the time off," he says.

"I'm not opposed. We can sleep in and spend the day on the water." The way his hips press against mine makes me think of a lot of other things we could do. "Depending on how private our villa is, we could spend entire days naked."

He taps the back of my fingers with his. "You bring up a great point. But there is one thing I would like you to wear the whole time."

He lets go of me, except for my hand, and it takes a few seconds for me to realize why he's shrinking.

He holds up a ring from his kneeling position. "Haley, will you marry me?"

I still feel like I'm catching up as he slides a ring onto my finger. "Yes, of course! Yes!"

He stands, kissing me and holding me tight against him. I don't even care about the ring, I just want to be close to him. We'd talked about this, but I thought we'd wait. We have plenty of time.

A cheer rings out from the terrace, and I turn to see a crowd of people watching. "Did they all know?" I ask.

He shakes his head. "No. Just Carina and Orion. And your parents. And I asked Will for his advice."

"I think word got around when we left," I say since at least half the restaurant is outside.

We walk back to the building and are ushered inside to another round of champagne. I lose track of the number of people who hug me and offer their congratulations. It's everything I'd ever want.

"Home?" I ask Ransom when I finally feel like the excitement has died down. I somehow have been reunited with only one of my shoes.

"I got us a room here," he says, leading me out of Arrow's Table and to the far wing of the resort. We take the elevator to the top floor where he opens the door to a suite with his phone. The bed is covered in rose petals and a bottle of champagne is chilling next to it. "Lisa and Mitchell might have also known."

"Well, everyone was very good at keeping your secrets. I had no idea."

He stands behind me, wrapping his arms around me. "As long as you're mine forever."

And then we get our own happily ever after.

sailor's warning

1.5 oz Silver rum
.75 oz Lemon juice
2 oz Pomegranate juice

Add all ingredients to a cocktail shaker and add ice. Shake for about twenty seconds. Strain into a cocktail glass. Toast to making a good impression on your new girlfriend's friends.

acknowledgments

This book took much longer than I had planned to get out into the world. So, first, I want to thank you readers for your patience.

Now, for everyone who held my hand over the last year...

Tere Michaels for walking with me through the ridiculous first draft of this book that looks nothing like the final the day after I had my own cooking injury. My beta readers, Andie James, Bri Castellini, Jennifer Trice, Hayley Fleming, and Adeline D. Wright. You all had one comment in common and you were all right. My editor, Julia Ganis. There were two comments you made that had me jumping up and down because I knew that I had done what I wanted to do. Sorry for having so many opinions about hyphens. My proofreader, Laura Helseth. Thank you for sitting me down and explaining why my opinions about hyphens were wrong. And you know, for letting me cry on your shoulder at a boozy book fair.

The team at Qamber Designs for making this cover just as beautiful as the cover of Rum Sips. And for knowing what to do when I said it gave me an emotion.

My writing groups, The Procrastination of Romantics and the Contemporary Cuties. You all have made my life so much better in so many ways. Thank you for cheering on Ransom and Haley from the beginning. The Spellbound Writers Group and Dani Keen. Thank you for letting me message you when I'm having a meltdown about color. All the Central Florida authors that I know, especially Mary Dublin for designing my beautiful logo, and Sydney Wilder for always checking in on everyone else. The

Wednesday Write-In with Sarah and Bess. You were a constant on some of the hardest days of 2025. I know you'll be there every week of 2026. #teamtea

My friends, Kaely, Sam, Cody, and Brittany. You all always ask about the writing and you've been the biggest cheerleaders and marketing I could hope for.

My sisters, for talking plot relevant rums with me while I was cocktail testing. For sending me bags with my book names and signature on them and nail polish color customized to match to my cover. My parents and in-laws for being supportive even if you have no idea what the books are about.

My therapist, Samantha. For always asking how the writing is going and for asking "what are you whispering in your writing that you should be shouting?" My psychiatrist, Dr. T. I wish I had reached out sooner.

Jessika. For sitting next to me when I wrote the first sentence of what would be my first finished novel. (It's complete crap. No one needs to see it.) We've been friends over half my life now. I still consider introducing myself to you the bravest and most important thing I've ever done. Thank you for always being there.

And finally, of course, my very sexy accountant, Wesley. I'm still not sure why I can't deduct all our groceries. I was writing a chef. You are my best friend and soulmate and I love every minute with you.

also by rebecca v. archer

Standalone

Staged: A Cupid/Psyche Fake Dating Novella

Alma Blake and Will Caron

Wendell Beach Series

Rum Sips and Salty Lips

Carina Webb and Orion Edwards

Red Skies and Golden Lies

Haley Stewart and Ransom West

You can subscribe to her newsletter for bonus content, writing updates, and sneak peeks either at:

https://rebeccavarcher.com/newsletter

Or by scanning the QR code

about the author

Rebecca V. Archer writes contemporary romance about characters who are afraid of their own emotions. She lives in Florida with her soulmate, drinks copious amounts of tea, and is always looking for a new cocktail or food recipe to try.

Check out her website at:

www.rebeccavarcher.com

instagram.com/rebeccavarcher

threads.com/@rebeccavarcher

facebook.com/rebeccavarcher

tiktok.com/@rebeccavarcher

amazon.com/author/rebeccavarcher